The Lie
of the Land

Also by Amanda Craig

Foreign Bodies
A Private Place
A Vicious Circle
In a Dark Wood
Love in Idleness
Hearts and Minds

Novella
The Other Side of You

The Lie
of the Land

AMANDA CRAIG

Little, Brown

LITTLE, BROWN

First published in Great Britain in 2017 by Little, Brown

1 3 5 7 9 10 8 6 4 2

A CIP catalogue record for this book
is available from the British Library.

Hardback ISBN 978-1-4087-0929-0
Trade paperback ISBN 978-1-4087-0930-6

Typeset in Goudy by M Rules
Printed and bound in Great Britain by
Clays Ltd, St Ives plc

Papers used by Little, Brown are from well-managed forests
and other responsible sources.

Little, Brown
An imprint of
Little, Brown Book Group
Carmelite House
50 Victoria Embankment
London EC4Y 0DZ

An Hachette UK Company
www.hachette.co.uk

www.littlebrown.co.uk

To my mother

'It is my belief, Watson, founded upon my experience, that the lowest and vilest alleys in London do not present a more dreadful record of sin than does the smiling and beautiful countryside ... But look at these lonely houses, each in its own fields, filled for the most part with poor ignorant folk who know little of the law. Think of the deeds of hellish cruelty, the hidden wickedness which may go on, year in, year out, in such places, and none the wiser.'

– Conan Doyle, 'The Adventure of the Copper Beeches',
The Adventures of Sherlock Holmes

Like everything else which is not the result of fleeting emotion but the creation of time and will, any marriage, happy or unhappy, is infinitely more interesting than any romance, however passionate.

– W. H. Auden

Contents

1

There is No Money

There is no money, and the Bredins can't afford to divorce.

'Are you sure?'

'Yes.'

'Not a chance?'

'No.'

It's so long since they have spoken to each other, rather than exchanging curt texts on their mobile phones, that talking face to face seems strange.

'God, this is pretty bad, isn't it?' Quentin says. He pours himself a third glass of wine and inspects it. 'I never thought that *divorce* was something I wouldn't be able to afford.'

'In any case, things can't go on like this,' Lottie says. She does not drink. One of them, and it is always she, has to keep a clear head.

The ruin of a marriage is a trivial thing to the persons not involved. Since Quentin's infidelities were discovered, there have been revolutions, earthquakes, hurricanes, acts of terrorism and a worldwide economic crisis, yet as far as the Bredins are concerned, none of these matter.

'I simply don't believe the bloody house won't sell.'

'It will, but not for what we need to buy a home each.'

'What about renting?'

'The only thing that will raise an income is if we rent this house, and move somewhere cheaper. A lot cheaper.'

In the kitchen it is perfectly quiet, though the nearby flyover murmurs lamentations. The trees are dull with dust, unrelieved by rain and swollen with summer sun. Upstairs their daughters are asleep and Lottie's son Xan is locked in his bedroom wearing a onesie and watching a film downloaded via Pirate Bay. On the table is a meal, the first they have shared in many months, cooked by Quentin with ingredients bought by Lottie. Every domestic task is now supposed to be shared. Half of the long beech veneer table from Heal's, the half at which Lottie and the children eat, has been meticulously wiped clean. The other half, at which Quentin sits, glitters with microscopic crumbs that catch the evening light like pulverised jewels.

'You mean moving to the country,' Quentin says.

'Yes.' Lottie looks into the white china bowl before them, where a few last strands of spaghetti swirl vertiginously in their red sauce, as if disappearing down a plughole.

A dozen recriminations rise, and are bitten back. No matter how much each feels violently wounded by the other, they must keep talking.

A gloom lies over the world. Only a short while ago it seemed as if they were all on an endless soaring ride up to heaven. Now, they are plummeting down so low that nobody is sure when the fall will stop. Banks have defaulted, businesses have gone bankrupt and millions have lost their belief in a better future. Everybody is anxious. Some continue to live as they always have done, or possibly even better, but more see their income shrivel and their hopes fade.

Waking with fortitude, living with compromise and sleeping with stress is normal for an architect in Britain. Even during the

2

best of times, Lottie has spent weeks drawing up plans for projects over which clients have then backtracked, changed their minds and cancelled. Experience has taught her that nothing is ever built without compromise, and yet she had expected better of marriage. For just as we expect sweetness from the milk we first drink, so the child born to a happy union is wholly unprepared for disharmony. Lottie had failed to understand what she risked when marrying Quentin; but then waking with optimism, living with laxity and sleeping without self-reproach is normal for a journalist.

What a fool I was, she thinks. Yet he had never been violent, dirty or mean with money; there are plenty of men who are this, and more. In the beginning, Quentin had brought colour, humour and fun into her life, just as she had brought order, calm and seriousness into his. They shared many interests, and were both the children of teachers. Yet the differences between them have made it clear that no reconciliation is possible.

Work has defined Quentin, as a mould does jelly. Without it, he is prone to depression, irritability and loss of libido. He has been adept at sidestepping the bile and smuggery of the Left and the guile and thuggery of the Right; being clever and talented, versatile and ambitious, he has been courted for almost thirty years. Since losing his job, however, it's as if he no longer exists. People he has known since university let their eyes slide past him. His bitterness about the collapse of his career is more than equal to Lottie's over her marriage.

This particular day of crisis had come about through a typical oversight: Quentin had forgotten to renew the parking permit on the family car. He has always taken care of the taxing and servicing of vehicles as a contribution to the smooth running of family life, but having detached himself from it he had failed to take care of the paperwork. Consequently, he had received a parking fine which he neglected to pay, followed by interest which mounted rapidly into hundreds of pounds that he was too angry or impatient to deal with. At dawn this morning, two bullet-headed bailiffs from a debt-collection agency had tricked their way in, and demanded goods to the value of £1000 for the money owed. Lottie, white as wax in her nightdress, had been forced to give them a flat-screen TV; Quentin, his motorbike.

Lottie says, in a low voice, 'I can't believe that somebody could do something like that, in our own home.'

'It's not our home.' Quentin, too, is shaken. 'The bank owns part of it, remember?'

For the first time in their lives, they feel poor, and frightened. Their gaze has always been fixed slightly upwards; if they have been conscious of poverty it has been largely as a source of ugliness. Until this day, it had never occurred to them how swiftly the accumulated privilege of two professional careers could be lost. Each had jumped through the right academic hoops, worked hard, saved, paid taxes and been able to acquire that golden ticket to a better life, a house in London. Everybody in the world wants this, and even though the Bredins' home is in what has been an unfashionable and run-down area, it is now, at almost £1 million, absurdly valuable.

Before the crunch became a downturn, before the downturn became a recession, it was taken for granted that their children would be privately educated, their health insured, their holidays exotic and their minds stimulated by all the intellectual entertainments the capital has to offer. Their five-bedroomed home at the wrong end of Randolph Avenue, the joint total of two incomes and some unacknowledged luck, has added many thousands of pounds to its putative value: if they have been smug, as members of the luckiest generation in British history, then so have many others.

The sensations of acquiring a home are not dissimilar from those elicited by romantic love, not least because the house they bought has been transformed from a shabby rooming house to a place where they were once almost entirely happy. Here they have thrown lively parties, taken deep baths, filled large fridges, and returned from holidays with relief. Stripped, replastered, rewired, repainted and reconfigured, the house has been the third party in a charmed union. When they borrowed an additional £100,000 to give it three new bathrooms, a splendid new kitchen extension, stair carpets, fitted bookshelves and cupboards, it seemed like an entirely rational thing to do. No longer: for both have lost their jobs.

'We *have* to move.'

Despite her best intentions, Lottie's eyes suddenly brim with hot tears. She looks away.

Quentin is filled with weary dislike. The whole disaster is as much her fault as his. For many months after Stella was born Lottie changed from an enthusiastic lover to one who was perpetually exhausted, unwell and rejecting; he had been grateful to be living in an age of computer pornography. In the end, however, he had been a starving man offered a steak sandwich. Most normal men would have cracked in such conditions, but he never meant to hurt his wife.

'It was just sex. They meant nothing,' he had said, aware of the banality of his words.

'Am I *nothing*? Are your children *nothing*?'

Lottie's fury and distress astounded him, for he had always seen her as supremely self-controlled. Yet she became a madwoman, screaming and sobbing, and had even confronted one of his mistresses at the annual summer party of the magazine he then edited – much to the entertainment of his colleagues. Mortified but unrepentant, Quentin fled to a new job in America, and the Bredins separated. For three years they had led separate lives, coming together for brief family Christmases and tense summers, pretending to the girls that it was all temporary. When he returned, jobless, he found that Lottie had neglected to have the locks changed, and promptly moved back in. It has been thoroughly unpleasant, but he refuses to budge.

'I am not going to clear out or live in a hotel just because your pride has been wounded.'

'It's called adultery, Quentin. You promise not to do it when you marry someone, remember?'

She is no longer tearful, but her contempt for him is withering. Someone who automatically ascribes the worst possible motives for everything you do is an experience that even the joy of being with his children again can't obliterate. Yet he has no option but to continue to squat here, sleeping on the sofa in his study and trying to drum up freelance commissions while Lottie pays the mortgage she had taken out in happier times. However, even this has gone wrong now that she, too, is unemployed.

Lottie, looking at him, sees her redundancy as her husband's fault. Had she not been devastated by the collapse of her marriage she would probably have kept her job; as it is, she has lost everything. Her vocation has demanded years of training and testing: to design and build is what she's wanted to do ever since she first laid her hands on a Lego set. (It had been intended for her cousin Justin, who was far more interested in the pink tutu given to his sister.) The loss of her career makes her feel as if she is falling into an abyss. There is no money for their daughters' school fees, and she is racked by anxiety about her son. He has failed to make his offer from Cambridge, and instead of shrugging his shoulders at what is always a lottery, has withdrawn from the other universities in anger and despair. She's desperately afraid that he has taken rejection so much to heart that he'll now go off the tracks altogether. Trying to galvanise him to reapply, trying to keep the household budget under control, looking for new schools for the girls and making the effort of appearing cheerful has been achieved only with antidepressants.

'There must be *some* economies that would help.' Quentin's voice has taken on a note of bewildered complaint. 'Can't you just sack the cleaner?'

Lottie gives a small, weary smile.

'I did, months ago.'

'Ah.' Quentin gulps more wine. 'That explains my shirts. What about the girls' schools?'

'We've been living off the refund of the school deposit.'

'Surely any local primary would be thrilled to have them?'

Lottie winces. She has never been comfortable with this kind of assumption.

'No. They are all oversubscribed.'

Why did I marry her? he asks himself.

It was his first wife's money that, once he'd agreed to a hasty marriage and a hastier divorce, had provided the initial deposit on his flat in Camden during the halcyon of the 1980s. Since then, he'd ridden the property boom, trading onwards and upwards until, at forty, he owned a nice two-bedroomed flat in Islington. So what was it about Lottie that made him forget his instinct for self-preservation? It wasn't beauty: though ten years younger than him, she looks older, these days. In addition, she irritates him more than anyone he has ever known – apart from his father – and the more miserable she looks, the more he dislikes her.

'I just want this to be *over*.'

'Exactly. That sofa-bed in my study seems to have both the rock and the hard place lodged in it.'

'Perhaps it's your conscience,' Lottie says, in a rare flash of wit.

'I am trying to be sensible—' he begins, but it's too late. The rage between them is flaring up, like phosphorus in water.

'If you were *sensible*, we would not be in this predicament. We would, at least, have each other.'

'One must be thankful for small mercies, I suppose.'

Lottie returns to the main subject with an effort.

'This house has to be rented out, and we have to rent another that is cheaper.'

Quentin pours himself another glass.

'We'll both get other jobs.'

'No, we won't,' Lottie says. 'We may *never* get another job. The life we had before is gone. If we're very, very lucky, the property market will rise enough for us to be able to sell this place and have enough for a flat each. But it will take at least a year, and in the meantime we can't continue here.'

Quentin says, grudgingly, 'This house would bring in, what, £4000 a month?'

'Think half that, minus the agent's fees and tax. We'd clear enough to cover the mortgage and rent somewhere else, but probably not quite enough to live off.'

'*Live* off?'

'Yes, Quentin. We have to live on something, even far, far away. We're lucky to have even that option.'

'What about France?'

It's like talking to a child, she thinks. 'No. The euro is too risky. There is, however, Devon.'

Appalled, he stares at her.

'I am *not* going back!'

'I don't see why not. Your parents might like to see more of you.'

'Lottie, you know as well as I that my work depends on my being *here*. Here in London, where everything happens.'

'It is the only solution.'

Quentin feels sick. 'You've no idea what the countryside is like to live in, especially Devon. If you stand still for a minute there, fungus grows between your toes. It rains all the time. They don't like strangers.'

'We wouldn't be complete strangers because of your parents. The girls can go into a nice village primary, and Xan can find work.'

'But neither of us will *ever* get another job there.'

'There's the Internet, and the train from Exeter. You could commute if necessary.'

'Like *you* have any idea how other people live.'

8

Her cheeks flush, but she makes no response.

'I might consider it for just one year.' Quentin pauses. 'But I demand a room of my own.'

Lottie says, 'What about Xan? He can't sleep with the girls, he's a young man now.'

'You're talking four bedrooms, minimum, then.'

'Actually, there is a possibility. A farmhouse, available now.'

Quentin looks at her with deep suspicion.

'You've actually *found* a place?'

'It's near Trelorn, outside a village called Shipcott. I've got it on my laptop, see? Four bedrooms, big kitchen, beautiful views and best of all, amazingly cheap. Your mother says it's lovely.'

'If she says that, it'll be a nightmare.'

He knows what Devon longhouses are like: all built to a pattern for dwarfs with thick skulls, and this looks no exception. It's a long, L-shaped whitewashed cob building, no thatch but roofed with slate, bound to blow off in winter. The kind of thing that fools in the city think is picturesque, but which anyone with experience of country life knows is riddled with rot, rats, bats and beams. The photographs of the inside show lashings of pine and a lavender bathroom suite circa 1972.

'What about the local primary school?'

She clicks on the Ofsted report. 'It's rated Outstanding. It has lots of outdoor space, good teacher-to-pupil ratio, and only about eleven children per year. In London you'd be paying through the nose for that.'

Yes, Quentin thinks, and it'd be worth it, too.

'How much is the rent?'

'Five hundred pounds,' says Lottie.

'A week?'

'A *month*.'

Even Quentin is surprised by this.

'There's got to be something wrong with it.'

'There isn't any central heating; and we would have to sign

9

up for the whole year. We can't afford to be fussy. We just can't,' Lottie says. 'Besides, it's too late.'

'Too late for what?'

'I've found tenants for this place.' Lottie almost laughs at his outraged expression. 'Canadian lawyers are moving in next month. Unless you'd like to return their deposit?'

So it is fixed.

'It'll be fun, you'll see,' Lottie tells the children the next day; 'it'll be an adventure for us all to move to the country.'

Quentin says, 'In the countryside nobody can hear you scream.'

2

Ten Green Bottles

Lottie is sitting outside a café in Highgate, trying to seem normal. Bad as it had been to lose her husband, getting him back is infinitely worse.

Each minute of each hour, she feels maddened by sharing the same air, let alone the same roof. When she first found out about his infidelities she had been so shocked she could barely breathe, but now their arguments, really always the same argument, go round and round like clothes in a tumble dryer. She accuses him of being shallow, promiscuous, irresponsible and a liar. He accuses her of being a sociopath, frigid and the most controlling person on earth.

'All you want is to keep everyone on a leash.'

'What you call a leash is fidelity.'

'It's not my fault I can't be faithful to you.'

Few things are more painful than loathing and despising someone you have once loved and admired. She has been through each stage of misery, from looking for scraps of affirmation that he might still love her, to obscene sexual fantasies about what he must have done with his other women, to hating

11

him so much she wanted to put ground glass in his food, to thinking that they might be able to work it out if he has therapy, to despising herself for having ever been with him in the first place, to thinking that if she had a revenge affair then he might come to his senses. What she wants most is just to stop feeling. She thinks about her marriage almost as much as she thinks about being poor, which is to say, every waking moment. Other than his professed love for their daughters, Quentin has no redeeming qualities – though he accuses her of poisoning the girls' minds against him.

'No, you do that all by yourself whenever you shout at me.'

'Why would I do that? You're the shouter, not me.'

This is one of his most odious techniques: implying that his awful behaviour is all in her mind. Another is to say,

'You have a serious issue about trust.'

Lottie is astounded by how low someone she loved could sink, and how much he can still hurt her. She wants to crawl away into a hole and sleep for a hundred years, but because of the children she has had to summon every reserve of will to find a way forward, even though it means leaving London and almost everyone she has ever known, including her mother.

People who have not been through what she is going through just can't imagine it. She has poured out her miseries to her cousin Justin, who had originally introduced her to Quentin, and to her school-friend Hemani, who through her own lawyer friend Polly Noble had put her in touch with a specialist in divorce. They have listened sympathetically, and suggested seeing a therapist, but she can't even afford that. Her redundancy payment has dwindled to less than £2000, and the most important thing is to minimise the suffering of her children.

Yet Lottie is more English than the English (which is to say, half-German). When her boss sacked her in April he'd said,

'You're a tough cookie, Lottie, and I know you'll survive.'

What he meant was that she could be relied on not to burst

12

into tears or sue him for constructive dismissal. Lottie has the kind of shield-shaped face that always looks calm, but she has so many things to be angry about that she often finds herself humming Ten Green Bottles.

'And if one green bottle,
Should accidentally fall . . .'

In one bottle is her heartbreak over her son. Lottie thinks of all the work she has turned down, the promotions she missed and clients she annoyed, simply to support Xan, her first-born, fatherless and until recently, only child. Gifted, gentle, handsome and hard-working, his conception had been the accident which turned out to be a blessing. Now, he hates her.

'Just fuck off and leave me alone!' he roars whenever she taps on his bedroom door. His hair is one big puffball of neglect; she's terrified he is clinically depressed. His two best friends have both got into the universities of their choice: Hemani's son Bron to UCL to read Medicine, and Dylan to read Philosophy at Oxford. Xan is reapplying nowhere.

'I wouldn't mind so much if Xan were lazy, but he's so bright and he worked so hard,' she told her mother, Marta. 'I keep telling him that Oxbridge doesn't matter, that all Russell Group universities are terrific, but he takes no notice. He's always driven himself too hard and now he's blaming my marriage, or going to a private school, or being mixed-race or just being too boring.'

'I know, but that way, madness lies,' her mother answered. 'Have faith.'

'Faith in what?'

'In your son. You can't rescue him; he must rescue himself.'

Marta, too, has put a lot of time and effort into Xan's upbringing. Lottie had been just twenty-three when she discovered she was six months pregnant. She did not even know the name of her child's father, except that he had been drunk, like herself, at a large party, and overwhelmingly attractive. It was like one of those encounters with a god in Greek myth: he'd appeared, and

13

then he'd disappeared. What made it all the more humiliating was that she was the last person anyone would have expected to become a single mother. Marta had converted the top floor of her house into a small flat, shifted her own workload, and enabled Lottie to complete the crucial second part of her training as an architect. It had been Marta's face, not Lottie's, that Xan had looked for at the end of every school day.

'If he could be off at university, Mutti, the rest would not be so bad.'

'My darling, there's something to be said for disappointment early in life.'

It's all very well for Marta. Her mother has so much self-confidence that sometimes Lottie wonders whether she has colonised her own share of it, much as in some families one member seems to have a disproportionate amount of luck, leaving little left over for the rest. But Marta adores Xan with a fierce, steely love quite unlike Lottie's own, where to love and to worry are inextricably intertwined in her mind: why else should the word 'care' hold its double meaning? Xan now accuses her of being a 'helicopter mother'.

'All I want to do is protect you.'

'But you can't. And in any case, you failed the moment you married Dud.'

In another two bottles are Stella and Rosie, the innocent casualties of their father's selfishness. They are so young they are almost transparent, like tiny snails; she can see every emotion pulsing through them.

'But why don't you love each other any more? Why can't you stop quarrelling?' Stella asks.

'We just can't,' Lottie told them. She longs to be able to say, 'Because your daddy is a selfish, lying philandering bastard,' but must not. She must suffer, like the heroine of a fairy tale, and not say a word. Oh, there are so many fictions – Quentin has almost written a three-volume novel justifying his own actions, and she

14

is so weary of it – that the cause of their mutual loathing is as mysterious as love. Yet whatever they do or don't believe, the emotional damage is likely to be far-reaching: as a consequence of all that has happened, her daughters must leave behind all the tender infant friendships made in London, and adjust to being at Shipcott Primary, where they know nobody.

'I'll never make another friend like Bella, never,' Stella sobbed. 'Why can't I stay here?'

'Because Daddy and I won't be here to look after you, sweetie.'

'Then why can't I stay here without you?'

'Another family is going to pay us to live in our house in London, while we move to a new home in Devon. It's cheaper to live in the country, you see.'

'Is that because nobody wants to live there?'

Rosie doesn't ask pointed questions like these. She wakes, night after night after night, her bed and nightdress sopping with urine, and demands to sleep in Lottie's bed. So at 3 a.m., Lottie has the choice: wake up enough to strip her child, and the bed, or allow her to sleep, restless and reeking, with her.

In the fourth bottle is Lottie's grinding sorrow at having lost her job, and with it any hope of hanging on to a few remaining shreds of self-respect or a viable future. For all its frustrations and complications, architecture is not just a profession but a vocation; and she had loved it.

In the fifth bottle is being forty-two. The cruelty of biology is such that, if she were to find another man, he'd probably be in his seventies, because men never look for a partner who is their own age. It's no consolation to see that Quentin, ten years older than herself, is still a handsome man, whereas the most that can be said for her is that, having put on too much weight during her pregnancies, she can once again fit into the clothes she wore as a student.

'People keep asking if I have cancer,' she remarks to her cousin Justin, when they meet.

'Sweetie, it's called the divorce diet.'

'Just take my advice and don't marry Sebastian. Anyone who marries is insane. Look at your sister, shackled to that toff.'

'Lottie, we want to get married for the same reason you did. We're in love, and we want to have the legal rights we've been denied for centuries.'

Justin and his future husband look so alike they remind her of Tweedledum and Tweedledee; they have a cottage in Stoke Newington, and radiate happiness.

'Darling Justin, I've longed for you to find true love with someone worthy of you, only I don't think it exists.'

'I hate seeing you like this, Lottie. You will find happiness again.'

'People make far too much of happiness. What we ought to be seeking is autonomy. That's the essential thing.'

There is a whole row of green bottles boiling and swirling with venomous mist involving Quentin's girlfriends which she mustn't think about because they are, essentially, blameless. However sordid it is to have an affair with a married person, they are not the ones who made a promise of fidelity. No doubt he had broken their hearts, too, though how can one romantic disappointment measure up to the destruction of a family?

All things considered, Lottie would really prefer to see her mother in private, but Marta insists on a brisk constitutional walk across the Heath every morning with her white terrier.

'Darling!' she says, bestowing a kiss redolent of Revlon. Her glasses match Heidi's bright pink collar, and her thick white hair is immaculately styled. 'Breakfast?'

Lottie shakes her head. Marta orders a double macchiato for herself, a poached egg with toast, and a smoothie.

'How are you?' Lottie asks, to forestall further enquiries.

'I am in mint condition. So, you are upside-downing?'

'Downsizing. Yes,' Lottie says. Her mother had rescued her once before, when she had Xan, but it's out of the question she

16

could do so again. An adult and three children, one now eighteen, could not fit into the two spare rooms of Marta's tall, thin house, not that she's offered.

'Are you really not interested in breakfast? You are too thin.'

'No.'

There are so many things about divorce that you are never told, Lottie thinks, ducking to avoid being seen by someone she'd been at school with. Those who have been lucky in love, like her mother, have a kind of virginal innocence about what a really bad marriage is like.

But then, Marta had been widowed young. Edward Evenlode had been thirty-four when he died of a brain aneurysm after a recital at the Wigmore Hall. He had come from a large, dull upper-class family which mostly confined itself to farming and soldiering. Lottie and Marta were perfectly happy to live without such relations, and even happier when Xan arrived.

Having a baby so young meant that she was largely cut off from the companionship of her peers, but it also meant that she was able to continue living under her mother's roof. They all got on so well, and Marta's respect for her privacy meant she was free to entertain any guests; the occasional flings with men who couldn't handle her son's jealousy persuaded her that she would remain single. Then she met Quentin.

Justin, who worked with him on the *Rambler*, warned her when it was too late.

'He has what the Americans call a zipper problem. Don't fall in love with him.'

Lottie trusted Quentin for the most idiotic reason: when they met for the second time on a dirty train, he had taken off his own coat, opened it, taken hers and folded it so that her coat was wrapped in his, unsullied. She noticed that he was good-looking, well-dressed and, unusually for a British man, did not smell bad; but she was also charmed by the twinkle in his eye, the liveliness of his mind and a warmth she mistook for kindness.

17

Like herself, he was not entirely English, having a Jewish South African mother. He was not intimidated by her intelligence, drawing out a flushed and laughing self that she had forgotten. By chance, they met again, and in the course of a train journey from London to Leeds discussed everything from politics to films to an exhibition they had both enjoyed. He invited her to dinner the following week. She never intended to sleep with him so soon. Even now, with a vividness which makes her flush to the creases of her body, she can still remember how astonishing the sex had been. For the first time she understood why a man might be irresistible.

Quentin also had a son of his own, now grown-up, fathered in South Africa when he was only twenty-one. It was another bond between them, though he, typically, had been paid to marry, then divorce, his child's mother by the mother's family. Which should have warned me, Lottie reflects. Quentin seemed to appreciate Xan, teaching him to ride a bicycle and taking Xan's opinions seriously. Her son, so watchful and suspicious of other men, worshipped him. Quentin had actually asked his permission to marry his mother before he asked Lottie, and Xan had given his solemn consent. It had been a master-stroke.

'Are you sure, Xan, that you are OK if he becomes your stepfather?'

'Mum, he's cool even though he has a silly name. You really like him don't you?'

'Yes, I do,' she said. 'I even like his name. It sounds romantic, not silly.'

Three months after, they were married.

She wondered why more people didn't take this step. To be licensed by society to do all those wicked, secret, thrilling things and for it to be not just legal but expected felt wonderful. Once Quentin sold his flat, they had put down a deposit on the run-down house on the edge of Kilburn where they expected to live for ever. Both their careers took off to new levels, and she got to

18

work on transforming their Victorian semi into a Modernist miracle of light and space. In retrospect, she thinks, they had been nauseatingly pleased with themselves, and each other.

'You are so serious, so good,' he told her. 'You do a proper job.'

'So do you.'

'Oh, journalism is totally ephemeral.'

'But one that's vital to democracy. Architecture – well, if you make a mistake it's there for generations, and people hate you for it.'

She met his parents, liked his mother immediately and his father less so – but that was fine, because Quentin detested him.

'He's a shit, and if he were ten years younger he'd have tried to seduce you,' he said.

Lottie couldn't help laughing at the idea; Hugh Bredin was old and some sort of minor poet. His wife, Naomi, was a potter.

'They seem sweet,' she said.

'I have no interests in common with them, especially not my father,' Quentin insisted.

What did interest Quentin, she came to realise, was money. His friends and ex-girlfriends were always wealthy, some quite staggeringly so; Lottie, however, had not gone to a private school, and money had always been tight. Yet the fluke of London property prices means that her mother's house in Church Row, bought for a thousand pounds after the War, is worth, conservatively, £5 million. One of Lottie's most bitter reflections of late is to wonder whether this was what he had found attractive about her all along: she will never forget the way Quentin's eyes lit up when she first brought him there. He views the London property market as a kind of magical force in his life which has made him, alongside everyone else who bought a home there in the 1980s, rich beyond his wildest dreams. The £20,000 which his first wife's family paid him to disappear had, by the time of his second marriage, grown into £300,000, and now into £500,000, all thanks to property. The thought that he might lose any portion of it when they get divorced gives her savage satisfaction.

Lottie says, 'I hope you'll visit us.'

'At Christmas, I will definitely come, my darling.'

Marta says, gently, 'I can't help you, you know that?'

'Yes,' Lottie says. She has made her own bed and must lie in it, even if the bed in question will be a thin mattress on a wire base rather than the super-king-sized Vi-Spring that must remain behind for the tenants.

'What a shame you did not marry that other man.'

Lottie groans to herself but answers, 'He disappeared.'

'Oh, not Xan's papa, obviously – but, the architect you lived with – what was his name?'

'Martin. Not my type, or I his.'

Martin had been another architect, plump with red hair, a bit like William Morris. They had shared a place in Spitalfields together, when the houses there had still been such slums that students could afford to rent them, and he was just one of a group of friends, though particularly loyal. She had tried to stay in touch, but Quentin had picked a fight with him because his idea of small talk was to discuss metal fatigue in motorway flyovers. Still, when Lottie thinks of all the men she might have married, she remembers something her old friend Hemani had said:

'Why didn't we realise when we were twenty-two that we could have married almost anyone?'

Hemani loathes Quentin, and says she should divorce him immediately: but her friend is an eye surgeon married to the nicest, most civilised kind of American. Lottie sighs, and watches the people at other tables: the young mothers, exhausted but still hopeful; the resting actors; the retired people whose pensions have not yet imploded; the joggers and dog-walkers. All around her are Londoners unaffected by what is being called 'the current economic climate'. They still drive big cars, go on foreign holidays, wear designer clothes and send their children to private schools. They expect to be able to go to the theatre or restaurants or opera, to not clean their homes and to shop at artisan farmers' markets – just as she had done until very recently. It's hard not to hate them.

'This cottage,' Marta is saying. 'It looks charming in the link you sent.'

'Looks, but isn't,' Lottie answers. 'There's no central heating.'

'My darling, all we had when you were born were storage heaters.'

'Yes, and heaven knows what it'll do to Xan's asthma.'

Lottie's mobile buzzes. It's one of the children asking plaintively when she'll be home. Xan is supposed to be babysitting, but he's probably playing *Call of Duty*. I'd like to see a game about the real Call of Duty, Lottie thinks, in which you jump from log to log with a feverish child under one arm and a laptop under the other, a game in which the blood is real and there are no second chances.

'You will be fine, my darling. Many people dream of escaping to the country, to live in peace and quiet.'

'Ha! With my husband around I'll be certain to have neither.'

When Marta takes her leave, Lottie runs all the way home. The hard grey pavements jar her knees. She hates the pollution, the parking fines, the noise, the drunken teenagers riding children's bikes, the rubbish and dried vomit, the overpriced shops selling nothing useful: yet the thought of leaving London is terrifying. Apart from her years at university, this has been her home all her life.

The new house, by contrast, is ludicrously rural. Not only does it have just one bathroom, but there's also a dank little room behind the stair at the back, half-buried in the hillside, with a kind of granite bath on one side. A big iron hook hangs over it from the ceiling.

'What on earth is this for?' Lottie wondered aloud.

'It's where the farm pig would have its throat cut, every year, and be salted,' Quentin said.

'Ugh.'

'Useful as a wine cellar,' said the agent, brightly. 'Or a broom cupboard.'

How bad can it be to live in the country? Boring, but not as boring as being utterly broke in the city, Lottie thinks. Below the garden a big field sloped down, quite steeply, towards a small river, invisible in its wooded valley. On the other side, field, wood and hill rose until the flanks of Dartmoor bulged against a vast, cloud-flecked sky.

'Beautiful isn't it?' the estate agent remarked.

The view is the reason why the house might be bearable, although the tenebrous kitchen has mean, metal-framed windows looking out to a small orchard burdened with large, wasp-flecked apples, a withered vegetable patch, and a rusting clothes airer.

'What a pity there's no window on the gable end, looking down the valley,' Lottie remarked. The large pine dresser was not to her taste either.

'Probably to keep the wind out,' the agent told her.

It was all energy-saving light bulbs, wall-to-wall carpet, brown furniture and thin sagging curtains. It would need every scrap of furnishings she can scrounge out of her own home to make it bearable.

As usual she is organising everything. She's cleaned their own house from top to bottom, arranged with the agent for the tenants to move in the day they leave; she's booked the removal lorry, been in contact with the village school at Shipcott to enrol Stella and Rosie; put down the deposit and signed a rental agreement with their new landlady. It will probably be the longest year of her life, but she has to hope that the rise in the London property market will make it possible to sell for a higher price the following year, and escape.

As Lottie lopes along, her wedding ring falls off her finger, and rolls tinkling along the pavement before falling over onto its side. She's tempted to leave it there, but stops herself. It's gold, and she'll probably end up selling it.

3

One Bungalow Deep in Village Idiots

Lying on his bed, Xan is woken from his stupor by the tread of heavy feet banging up and down. What the fuck? Is it the bailiffs returning again? Then he remembers, groaning. Today is the day he must leave home.

Xan's life is ruined. There's no point in lying to himself that it isn't.

All through secondary school he had been told he was 'Oxbridge material', and he'd been foolish enough to believe it. He'd applied to read English at Cambridge, and when he visited, he fell in love with it. To fall in love with a place can be just as rapturous and all-consuming as to fall in love with a person. As the rows between his mother and stepfather grew increasingly intrusive, all he could think of was how much he wanted out. He'd got the standard offer of two A*s and an A, and had been confident that he'd worked hard enough to make it.

Only when he logged on to discover his results, he found that instead he had got one A* and two As. Nothing would budge Cambridge. He had failed.

It hurt so badly that he thought he'd never recover. People talked about being disappointed in love, but this was far worse. It meant nothing to him that even his stepfather told him that Oxbridge was overrated and that he should take up any one of his other choices: Cambridge was everything. He's withdrawn from the UCAS system, and spends most of the time in his bedroom with giant headphones hugging his ears so that he can't hear people shouting, knocking on his door or calling to ask how he is.

Now he's being moved to the countryside, and it's all Quentin's fault.

He's furious at his own gullibility, as well as his mother's.

'I still love him,' she wept, when he asked why she didn't divorce him immediately. 'You don't suddenly stop loving someone because they've done something awful. It's not like turning off a tap. He's suffering too.'

'Is he?' Xan asked. 'I'm glad.'

At least when Quentin went off to his job in America, they'd had some peace. Life had been, if not happy, then less disturbing. Xan can't believe that Lottie has let him return. Why doesn't she just throw him out? But they all have to go on living together in the country. It's like an awful joke.

His mobile vibrates. 'What?'

'Alexander?'

Xan tries to snap out of his haze.

'Oma. Hi.'

'Darling! How *are* you?'

Xan sighs. Everyone keeps asking him this. He loves his grandmother, who is a crazy German pianist, but OK. If only he and Mum could go back to living with her!

'Surviving.'

'If you get a job, you could go travelling.'

As if, Xan thinks. 'Look, Oma, I must go now.'

Lottie's voice comes up the stairs, 'Xan! We are leaving in ONE HOUR!'

24

When she uses that special shriek, it goes through him like a pneumatic drill.

'Promise me you will stop being so hard on yourself, and do something practical,' Oma says.

'The packers are coming.'

He heaves himself off his bed and opens his window, waving at the tell-tale smell of weed just because he knows it will worry Lottie more. He knows what the countryside is like because ever since Quentin came along they have gone there to spend Boxing Day with Quentin's parents, who live in what Quentin calls The Hovel, or the coldest cottage on Dartmoor.

'It can't be that bad, can it?' said Bron, and Dylan asked, 'Don't millions of people go there on holiday?'

'There is absolutely nothing to do there except watch TV and get pissed. It's basically all tiny villages one bungalow deep in village idiots, and old people waiting to die.'

Neither Bron nor Dylan had ever been into the countryside: why bother? For £30, you could catch a flight to somewhere abroad. Xan has looked at where they're going to live on Google Earth, and the Devon and Cornwall peninsula sticking out into the Atlantic like the deformed trotter of a pig. Nobody in their right mind would want to go there.

'Promise you'll come and visit.'

'It's, like, a long way away,' said Dylan.

'Maybe in summer,' said Bron. It's as much as any of them can manage just to get to Camden Lock by public transport, and Xan knows they never will.

'XAN! XAN! We are LEAVING!'

Lottie has already shouted at him that morning for not closing down his Netflix account.

'Don't you understand, we just can't afford *anything*?'

'It's only £6 a month.'

'You pay for it, then. Get a job.'

25

'How the hell am I going to find a job in the country when I don't know anyone?'

'Oh, I don't know. There must be some farmer or something who'd like an extra pair of hands.'

'Mum, Devon's full of *white people*. They'll probably turn their dogs on me.'

They've seen Home Farm already, so he knows it's even worse than The Hovel. It had taken four hours to drive there, five to get back. There is a tiny village which has *one* shop. Even Exeter, the kind of provincial city where everyone is a screaming toff, is forty-five minutes away along the A30. The house is beyond awful. Its living room has one sofa and two armchairs, upholstered in a sort of brown fake leather like giant turds. There is only terrestrial TV.

'You aren't seriously suggesting we live with this?' he shouted.

'The furniture can be stored, if you wish to bring your own,' said the agent, a bloke who didn't seem to realise that tweed was weird, but Mum said No, that they were letting out their own home.

In the whole place there was only one item which they would ever have considered having at home. An upright piano loomed out of one corner of the living room, showing its teeth like a dog unsure whether it is smiling or snarling.

'A Bösendorfer,' Lottie remarked.

'Is that good?'

'Yes. Not a Steinway, but still good.'

Xan sat down on the stool, and played a few chords.

'Fucked, like everything else in my life.'

To his surprise, Quentin said to the agent,

'We'd expect the piano to be retuned.'

'I'm sure the owners will agree,' the estate agent said, making a note.

'I don't like it,' Stella whispered. 'It's ugly, Mummy.'

'Oh, we'll make it nice, don't worry.' Lottie answered. 'We can put a swing in the tree!'

'Can we get a dog? Or a cat?'

'I'm allergic to cats, remember?' Xan said, indignant.

'But what about all my toys?' Rosie asked.

'Nothing important will be left behind. It'll be fun!'

She talks about it back in London as if they'll all be prancing about like the Von Trapp Family.

There is a tentative knock on his bedroom door.

'WAIT!' he roars.

The screech of duct tape sounds as if his home is being tortured. Xan glares at a poster of Amy Winehouse on his walls, drags his fingers through his corkscrewing hair and sits up just as the door is flung open.

'Ew,' says Stella primly. 'It reeks.'

'I didn't invite you in.'

'Mum says you have to come. Do you have *any* clothes on yet, or are you naked as a newborn babe striding the blast?'

Stella has been at a prep school notorious for super-achievers, she's taught herself French by listening to audiobooks at night, and how on earth is she going to cope at an ordinary primary? Rose won't be a problem, everyone likes her, but Stella has Quentin's quizzical sharpness and Lottie's fierce intelligence in her pale pointed face. Xan can see how tense she is.

'Hug?'

He loves his little sisters, the only good thing to have come out of this clusterfuck. Wrapped in his arms, Stella perks up a little.

'Mum says Rosie and I are going to have a tree house.'

'Great, we can take up full-time residence in it.'

'Dad is going to grow our vegetables. I *quite* like carrots . . .'

They still adore their father. Xan can't believe he was ever as innocent as his little sisters. They see only the unpredictable, warm, charismatic man who makes everything fun. When Quentin wants to charm you it takes a superhuman effort to resist, even when you can *see* what he's up to.

27

Thud, thud, thud. The packers are huge, cheerful Australians who manhandle the boxes downstairs as if they were filled with foam. When the removal lorry roars off, the house seems like a ghost of itself.

'You can all bring just one bag in the car,' Lottie says, ticking off a list. Her face is as pale as paper. 'Xan, have you got your Ventolin on you?'

Xan grunts.

'Well, at least country air will be good for your lungs.'

'You know that I'm hating every minute of this?' he says. 'London is my *home*.'

Mum says, with a sad little laugh, 'I'm sure you'll be back soon.'

The Multipla is stuffed to the ceiling. Mum is driving it, at least until halfway, when Dud will take over. From now on, everything is divided equally. Mum will cook for half the week while Dud washes up, and then they'll swap. Everyone will clean their own rooms, and everyone is responsible for their own laundry. Xan barely knows how to put a wash in a washing machine, he's never used a Dyson.

London is trickling away. Cars, road, supermarkets, churches, houses, cars, road, trees, road, hills, more and more of them, occasionally dotted with sheep or cows. This is all vaguely, drearily familiar. Beside him, Rosie wriggles, and over the unctuous tones of Stephen Fry reading another Harry Potter audiobook he can hear the inevitable complaint about needing the toilet.

'Hang on, sweetheart.'

They pull over at a service station just before Bristol. Xan is left with Quentin, who sips the coffee he has bought for himself.

'Disgusting,' he says. 'Now I know why Socrates preferred death to exile. Still, at least I'm getting a column out of it. The Questing Vole. After—'

'Waugh, I know,' says Xan, bristling. His stepfather's appetite for turning life into journalism has always irritated him.

'It will be,' says Quentin, 'a single Malteser on top of a pile of dung.'

Lottie is returning from the toilets, dragging the two girls along with her and looking unutterably weary. All his life, she's taken care of them by nagging and organising and often it's driven him mad, but maybe it's just how she gets things done. She once told him that every time she looked at a new building, all she could think of was the trouble it must have caused.

'Why?'

'Because everything, down to the last door handle, will have had to be imagined and designed and ordered by someone,' she said. 'Nothing just happens, Xan. Buildings don't grow like trees. You spend weeks and months and years working to get it all right, in every detail, and it never is.'

Maybe this is why Lottie is such a control freak, Xan thinks; she wants perfection and can't have it. Even now, it turns out she's remembered to make sandwiches for everyone so they don't have to be bought from the service station. She tries so hard, he thinks, and nobody ever gives her anything in return.

'Hold on, will you?' he says to his stepfather, and darts off. A supermarket franchise is selling roses for £3. Xan chooses a bunch that is bright yellowy orange, with reddish tips like flames. When Lottie returns, he thrusts them at her.

'For me?' she asks, surprise and pleasure illuminating her face.

'Yes,' he says, and turns away before she can hug him. It's the last of his money.

'Will it be cold and stinky, like Grandpa and Grandma's?' Stella asks.

'Not at all. The landlord is giving us a year's supply of logs to burn,' Lottie says.

Whoever the landlords are, they must be bloody desperate to get Home Farm occupied, Xan thinks. I wonder why.

4

Everything Has to Be So Slow

Self-pity is a trait which Quentin despises, and yet it's hard not to feel that his life has taken a turn for the worse.

What is *wrong* with country people? Why can't they move faster, and get on? As a child here, it seemed normal to have adults sleepwalking through life; as a teenager he had been shielded from rustic torpor by the wild eccentricities of school; and as an adult he had escaped. But on his way to see his parents before catching the train back to London, he is almost bursting out of his skin with impatience.

There's a fashion for calling children Devon, as there used to be for calling them India or Africa, he's written in his column. No wonder. Devon is a foreign country. The only thing you can be absolutely certain of, as in India and Africa, is that you'll live in a state of permanent frustration.

This morning, he has had a particularly nasty row with Xan.

'Why don't you get up off your arse and *do* something?'

'Why should I?'

'You're eighteen. You don't even empty the dishwasher.'

'I've just finished twelve years of fucking education. I'm enti-tled to a fucking rest.'

'No you are not, and how *dare* you swear at me! Who do you think you are?'

'Who do you think *you* are?' Xan retorted. 'Why don't you piss off?'

Actually, that is precisely what Quentin is doing. He will go insane if he has to spend another week at Home Farm. As the temperature drops, it's increasingly infested with mice. The first they'd realised it was when the soap in the basin showed signs of being eaten. Next, a pillowcase emerged from the airing cupboard looking like lace, and Stella spotted a furry grey blur shooting across the kitchen floor. It is he, of course, who has had to buy traps and position them strategically around the house. At night he lies awake listening for another 'clang!' which means there will be a tiny corpse to dispose of before the girls get up. It's really the business of their landlady, Mrs Tore, to sort the problem out, but his main aim is to get through this year with as little contact as possible with yet another local yokel. Quentin goes round dutifully refilling little bowls with poison, which is guzzled down to no effect. This morning, he'd come downstairs to find three mice running round the hearth rug in a circle, like something out of the nursery rhyme. When even *mice* fail to fear you, he thinks, that's when you have problems.

Stuck behind the kind of small turquoise car always described as 'nippy' for mile after mile of narrow, twisting road, he rocks back and forth in his seat in his desperation.

'Come on, you stupid hag, move your arse!'

Eventually, two short, peremptory blasts of his horn announce he is preparing to overtake. Why *should* he be impeded by some cretin sticking to 40 mph through tiny, straggling villages lack-ing any sign of a speed camera? Why *should* he be forced to inhale the weeping smoke from bonfires, the bitter reek like the guilt, sorrow and fear which he refuses to let in. If the car ahead doesn't give over, he'll be late for seeing his parents, which in turn means missing the train to London.

'Get out of my way!'

When she does give over, awkwardly cramming into a shallow lay-by in the hedgerow, he shoots ahead, good temper restored.

'*Viv'il buon vino! Vivan le femmine! Viva le glorie d'umanità!*' he sings along with Don Giovanni on the radio. So how has he come to be married to Charlotte Evenlode, of all women?

As with everything, it was partly a matter of timing. To be a bachelor at twenty is normal, at thirty is sensible, and at forty prudent; but to be single at forty-five smacks of failure. Quentin had never found children interesting until the row of small shoes lined up in the front hall of his friend Ivo Sponge's house became strangely affecting. The next instant, it seemed, he was gazing into the large brown eyes of his future wife, and talking about wanting a family of his own. Biology, it was all biology – or perhaps it was property.

How could he have done this? And yet, how could he neuter himself *just because he's a father?*

Up until Stella was born, she'd been so keen, and after she'd lost all interest. There had been the traumatic C-section, and then Stella never stopped crying. It seemed simpler while Quentin was ejected to sleep in his daughter's room, surrounded by smirking soft toys.

The moment Lottie got Stella to sleep through the night, he was back and everything had been delightful, but a month later she became pregnant with Rosie and the whole business began again. On the whole, Quentin thought, he deserved a medal for not having an affair until Stella was three. He worked in an office surrounded by lovely young women. If you were an editor, adultery was almost part of the job description.

'Sorry, I need to go to this conference in Madrid,' was all he needed to say, and Lottie seemed to find it, if anything, a relief. He'd even told himself that he was doing her a favour: she could have two uninterrupted nights, and he could slake his libido on someone who was actually enthusiastic. Thinking of Tina, his latest girlfriend, made him feel quite hot.

'Slow down,' he tells himself; 'slow down, or you'll miss the turn-off.'

Dartmoor looms over him like a headache and so does the prospect of dropping in on his parents.

To his parents, Devon is not a county so much as a kind of separate, shamanic space. Hugh is obsessed by its wildlife and history, which is all very well in a poet who was actually born in Trelorn, but his mother will come out with ridiculous statements like, 'Do you know, Devon has more cheeses than the whole of France?' She even takes pride in the way that, living in a place of prevailing westerly winds, they usually experience any change in weather a day before London. Most Jews hate the countryside, for perfectly understandable historical reasons, but when they don't they seem to love it more than the English. His mother is one of these. Quentin sighs, and turns off the main road into smaller and smaller lanes that narrow like ageing arteries.

Just as he has to slow down for a herd of alpacas wearing flowery wreaths, his mobile rings. It's Ivo, now not merely his friend and rival but his only regular employer.

'Excellent piece,' says Ivo, briskly.

'Thanks.'

Ivo clears his throat.

'I don't suppose there are many *Chronicle* readers in Devon, are there?'

'Not as far as I can see.'

Ivo sighs. 'Good. Let's keep the identity of the Questing Vole a mystery. More fun.'

Quentin says, 'Actually, I am still a Name—'

But Ivo has already rung off. Quentin hates writing under a pseudonym. To be a columnist is the difference between being a celebrity and a civilian, and he hopes his style is sufficiently distinct for the people who matter to know he's the Vole. Still, it's an easier way of earning a living than many – if only a living were to be made from it.

He has even had to have his hair cut locally, an agricultural shearing that has turned him into a cartoon of himself. Alas, it's not just barbering.

'Daddy, why do you look so sad when you're not smiling?' Stella asked him this morning.

'Do I?'

The thing is, he does feel sad almost all the time. He longs to lose himself, and not only in hot sex with Tina. He wants his life back.

His mobile rings again.

'Hello? Hello?' His father's voice is so loud he almost jumps.

'Fa?'

'Just wondering when we're going to see you.'

'I'm almost there.'

'Fine. I'll get your mother to put the kettle on, then.'

Off the main road, the landscape is so quilted as to resemble a green velvet eiderdown draped over a giant recumbent body. Once inside Devon's Golden Triangle, as estate agents call it, people are visibly wealthier, with fewer bungalows and more pretty cottages, mostly immaculate. The one that belongs to his parents is an anomaly, with patched thatch that flexes around the top windows like bristly eyebrows. Several implements are rusting beneath a cacophony of ceramic wind chimes. Raffles, his parents' blind, malodorous Staffordshire terrier, waddles over, drooling.

'Piss off.'

Quentin rings the familiar iron bell, and lets himself through the unlocked door into a multiplicity of small, dark rooms, crammed with books and his mother's work. To him, these look like glazed mud, but Naomi has built up quite a following, and even exhibits in the craft galleries of Dartington and Tavistock.

'Hello, dear.'

34

His mother is wearing her usual uniform of smock, trousers, wellington boots and a pair of glasses on the end of a long necklace of large lumpy glass beads. Quentin kisses her soft, round, crumpled face. She smells of verbena soap.

'How are you, Ma?' Quentin asks.

'So-so. Tea?'

'Coffee, please,' says Quentin, remembering too late that this will mean Nescafé. 'How is he?'

'Declining,' she says.

His father doesn't rise from the cane chaise longue where he lies all day long, looking down the sloping garden and its fading tapestry of foliage. Quentin says with false enthusiasm,

'Hello, Fa.'

Hugh is shockingly wasted. They'd dropped by after first seeing Home Farm, and he must have lost another stone since then. A mossy jumper bulks out his upper body, but his legs in their worn fawn corduroy are half the size they used to be. He grunts a greeting.

'Still unemployed?'

'I'm self-employed.'

'Ah, freelancing.' Hugh pronounces it with the emphasis on the latter word, as if Quentin were a knight in a tournament. 'Better than nothing.'

'It's not easy, no. The money is terrible.'

'Everything's bad. I keep telling your mother to turn up the heating, but she's penny-pinching as usual.'

Quentin has already noticed that the room is hot to the point of discomfort.

'Have some tea.' Naomi wheels in a tea trolley. It's the kind of thing which he finds most mortifying about his parents, calcified in the 1970s.

Quentin glances surreptitiously at his watch.

'Look at that view,' his father murmurs. 'You know, there isn't a day goes by that I'm not grateful for the beauty of nature.'

35

'It's age,' says his mother. 'Young people are too busy to stop and notice.'

'Grateful to who?' Quentin asks.

'Life, maybe.'

'Ah, life. Personally, I'd like to give life a kick up the arse right now.'

His parents exchange glances.

'It's a shame you can't bring Lottie and the girls again. It'd be good to get everyone together.'

'Lottie will probably have you over for Christmas.'

He has no idea what Lottie plans, of course.

The latest row is over his hiring a woman, Janet, to do his share of the cleaning. Lottie is outraged because he's supposed to be doing penance by cleaning out the toilets himself, but it's worth £100 a month not to do it, and Janet also irons his shirts. She's an odd woman, and Quentin had taken one look at her false teeth, and nearly told her to go away. Then he remembered how much he hated housework and welcomed her with enthusiasm.

'Do come in, and bring your friend too.'

'Dawn's my daughter. She'll be quite happy in the car,' Janet said.

'You've cleaned for other houses in the neighbourhood, I gather?'

'I'm housekeeper for Mrs Tore.'

It was clear he was supposed to be impressed by this. 'Who?'

'Our landlady at Shipcott Manor. Xan,' Lottie said before he could stop her, 'why don't you take a mug of tea out to Dawn in the car. Milk? Sugar?'

'Both.'

'It shouldn't take too long,' Quentin said.

Janet sniffed. 'It's how long is a piece of string with housework, isn't it?'

'Yes, sorry about the smell,' said Lottie. 'There's a stray tom around and it keeps coming in and spraying.'

'I like cats,' Janet said. 'Though my awful Ex couldn't abide them.'

'Well, we don't want to let this one in. My son is allergic.'

They had gone round the house, and he'd almost relished having a new audience to complain to about it.

'Unbelievable. No loft insulation and no central heating. We're going to bloody freeze. If you're coming to us from the village, do you think you could pick up a couple of pints of milk, a loaf of bread and a newspaper on the way? We've got an account with the village shop.'

'Quentin, that really is extravagance.'

'No, it's not. Just because you're on the long trudge to martyrdom doesn't mean I have to be.'

The sound of music came from the next room. An odd expression crossed Janet's face.

'Who's that?'

Lottie said, 'My son. He's at a loose end.'

'Be wanting a job, then.'

'Yes, if he could find one. He might like helping on a farm, if you know of anyone.'

'The pie factory in Trelorn is always looking for people.'

'It sounds like something out of Peter Rabbit.'

She took no notice. 'My Dawn works shifts.'

Quentin could hear the piano was being played remarkably well. Maybe all Xan needed was someone his own age to hang out with, though Janet's blobby daughter would not have been his own first choice. Just then, the girls came running up, carrying something wrapped in a bit of cloth.

'Mummy, Mummy, look what we found!'

Stella held out a small, muddy body.

'It's a dead baby, Mummy. Poor little thing.'

Janet's hand flew to her throat, and she blurted out,

37

'Jesus!'

She looked almost green, and Lottie said sharply,

'Don't be ridiculous, Stella! It's only a doll, for heaven's sakes. Here, sit down Janet, you look as if you're about to faint.'

Janet swallowed.

'It's nothing – I never could abide dolls. My awful Ex kept buying them for Dawn.'

'It's not a doll, it's a baby,' Rosie said obstinately.

Lottie sighed. 'Well, give it a bath or something.'

Quentin's thoughts return to The Hovel. 'Sorry?'

'How are the children getting on in their new school?'

'Too young to know the education that they're missing,' he answers gloomily.

Hugh frowns. 'I heard Shipcott was pretty good. Tiny, but well run.'

'What about the house?'

'Lottie only lets me stay indoors if I chop logs for her.'

'Well you do need it for the wood-burners,' Naomi says. 'I don't imagine chopping logs is easy for a woman.'

'Oh, I don't know. Those axes are weighted so that almost anyone can split a log with one.'

His parents exchange a glance, as if debating whether or not to say something. He knows they will be siding with his wife.

'She's not what you think, you know.' Quentin feels he's entitled to sympathy from his own parents, at least. 'She's got so hard.'

'Ah.' His mother sighs, and looks away. 'Maybe she has reason to be.'

'*Love is not love/ That alters when it alteration finds/ Or bends with the remover to remove.* I've always thought that bollocks, myself,' adds Hugh.

His parents are chalk and cheese, and yet they have somehow stuck it out.

'So what's the secret?' he asks his mother, helping her wash up in the stainless-steel sink. The kitchen is in a lean-to, and astoundingly primitive – one blue Formica surface to chop on, an electric cooker with four hobs, an ancient, rattling fridge whose services are barely needed, and a store cupboard. Yet somehow, from these unpromising surroundings, his mother conjures wonderful meals.

'Of what?'

'Marriage.'

'You have to not look too closely, and never forget your manners.'

Quentin gives an exasperated bark of laughter.

'What's gone wrong with me and Lottie goes far beyond such superficial matters.'

'Why do you think manners are superficial?'

'Woman!' Quentin can hear his father bawling from next door. 'Where are my glasses?'

Naomi walks over and finds them, then returns.

'Anyway, Fa's manners are appalling. You just put up with it.'

She looks at him quizzically.

'Is that what you think? He puts up with me, too.'

'You're a saint, he's a shit and I must get going, or I'll miss the London train,' he says.

His mother comes to the door.

'Don't stay away,' she says softly. 'He isn't going to last another year, you know.'

'I'll come as often as I can,' Quentin lies.

'Good. Bring the girls, too.'

As she kisses him, he can feel her put something in his pocket.

'What's this?'

'Just a little something.'

Surely, they can't afford to spare £100? Guiltily, he thinks of handing it back. But then they don't seem to need much to live on, whereas he does.

'Thanks,' Quentin says, with more warmth.

39

He parks at Exeter St David's next to a rusting black Ford with a sticker announcing in Gothic lettering, THIS CAR IS PROTECTED BY WITCHCRAFT. In a different mood it might have made him laugh, but all he wants is to get back to civilisation.

Outside, a huge speckled cloud of starlings streams out across the sky then gathers in a swirling mass over the sodden fields of the Exe Valley. For a single moment, in which the flock keeps pace with the train, they coagulate into a succession of forms – a dog, a wave, an axe, a giant skull. Quentin can't help but shudder. These are purely random shapes, to which his brain has given a meaning, so why is he filled with foreboding?

5

Sally and Baggage

There's no doubt about it, she's stuck in the ditch.

As Sally's wheels spin uselessly, she wonders how people can be so selfish. That bloody grockle in the Golf who chased her for miles, flashing his lights and making rude gestures so that he could overtake, *must* have known how badly he was behaving. Far from being ashamed, however, he seemed triumphant when he finally forced her into the ditch.

'Poop-poop!' she murmurs. Behind her, the dog whines in sympathy. 'Never mind, Baggage. Whoever he is, he'll learn.'

Sally shakes herself. Road-hogs are a fact of life; perhaps the real thing to wonder at is the number of good people she knows: people who give way when meeting another car in a narrow lane, with a smile and a wave, and who if they find £10 on a pavement, don't think twice about handing it in to the police.

Sally's business, however, is with looking after this small part of the world – which feels vast and varied and teeming with interest – and she's thankful every day of her life to work where she does. Though it's not like this for everyone, granted.

'Come *on*,' she says to herself, and Baggage.

'Talking to yourself is the first sign of madness,' says her mum's voice reprovingly, but Sally believes that it's people who don't talk to themselves who lose all sense of who they are. The funny thing is, the voice she hears in her head or coming out her mouth is Mum's. She jokes to Pete about how she channels Mum, and he rolls his eyes because truth to tell her husband and mother never got on well, even when she was alive. Mum had distrusted Pete for no better reason than the way his own dad had behaved to his mum. That, and being related to the Ball brothers.

'No good ever came out of suchlike,' Mum said.

Still, she'd taken no notice.

'Pick yourself up and brush yourself down,' said Mum's voice, which does have a tendency to speak out during moments of stress.

'Oh, be quiet, do!' Sally answers aloud. But Baggage needs reassuring. She's a sensitive dog, and understands every word Sally says. Why else would she have taken to sleeping on Peter and Sally's bed?

'And you a farmer's daughter!' her sister Tess had said, scandalised. But the truth is, Baggage is as lovely as only a springer spaniel can be, and Sally can refuse her nothing. Her coat of creamy white flecked with rich brown, a magnificent ostrich plume of a tail (Sally refused to have it docked, because to deprive a dog of its tail was in her view as cruel as cutting off a person's tongue), and on her brown face she has a white hourglass with brown specks falling inside it. Her characteristic expression is of heart-melting appeal, especially when a sausage is in the vicinity. How could anyone doubt that Good existed, when they look into a dog's eyes? Even when sorely tried, all Baggage ever does is look sorrowful, with that profound, gentle sadness which smites her conscience far more than anger.

Pete had given her to Sally as a puppy for her fortieth birthday. There have been other dogs, but they were always his, for work, and they both know that a dog is the next best thing to a baby. Baggage's warm, soft, squirming little body, her affection and enthusiasm for everything, but particularly Sally, means Baggage is given a bath every day, and her teeth are brushed with special, chicken-flavoured toothpaste. Her temperament is as lovely as her looks, and ever since she began to accompany Sally on her rounds, families have greeted her with less suspicion and more trust.

'There, there,' Sally says to Baggage, who is whining with almost inaudible anxiety. 'It's only a ditch, my lovely, and not a real prang! Let's ring our twelve o'clock, shall we?'

Unfortunately, this is a mobile black spot. She can't get a signal for several miles on either side of Shipcott, and now she really starts to feel annoyed.

It has already been a trying day. This morning, she's been to check up on Lily Hart, who has already had three children by as many men and lives on a one-acre smallholding in two caravans. She's not one of Sally's usual mums, though her type is familiar, all multiple piercings, blonde dreadlocks and deep Green principles underpinned by the use of her mother's tumble dryer when things get too damp for the washing line. Lily and her kids have a sawdust toilet which, though perfectly clean, means that if you needed a pee you had to stand over two planks in the certain knowledge that disaster lay just below. Sally had done her best not to use it, but the fact is she had ended up on those ruddy planks, feeling most apprehensive and wiping herself with a square of the *Western Morning News*, which she was most unhappy about abusing in this unseemly way.

'Best use for a newspaper,' Lily said, interpreting Sally's expression. 'I never read them, Mum hands them on.'

Lily's parents are incomers who run the White Hart hotel in Trelorn. Lily and her twin had gone to Trelorn Secondary School, and though Daisy had flourished and left home at eighteen, Lily has always been aggressive and suspicious of all authority. Her kids, in consequence, have not been immunised.

'We're all vegetarian, but I make sure my kids take omega-3

fish oils, so I'm not up for a ticking-off,' were her first words to Sally.

'I'm not here to do that,' Sally responded in her mildest tones.

Persuading parents to bring their children to be vaccinated is part of Sally's job, and it's always harder when she comes up against someone who is convinced that homeopathy and alternative medicine will protect better than science.

'I don't trust vaccines. Why should I put something into my kids that might give them autism?'

'You can get autism and measles, you know,' Sally answered, well aware that all her arguments about bad science would be ignored. 'Why not protect them?'

She has to keep hoping that gentle persuasion will bring Lily round to immunisation, but there's no knowing. And now she's running late to see a mum whose new baby is colicky.

Annoyed, Sally revs the engine again, but the whine of her wheels only rises in pitch. The rutted road is full of puddles, and when she looks at the ditch from outside, she knows she'll have to call for help because she'll never get her car out without it. Everything is on a deadline now; there's never enough time to have a proper chat with new mums, it's all form-filling and paperwork. Once, health visiting was about taking care of every vulnerable person within a radius of thirty miles. Cradle-to-grave socialism, but the most important are the babies.

Sam, she thinks; if I can get hold of Sam, he'll have finished his round now. The postie is always helpful and friendly. She'll just have to get to a stronger signal.

Sighing, she gets the dog out and begins to walk.

The lanes are so sunken that at this rate, she'll be walking to Shipcott ... Over the bend in the high hedgerow she can see someone on a tractor. Perfect! Sally waves and calls, but he can't hear or see her, and she's not going to chase him across a ploughed field.

'Heel, Baggage,' she says as the dog forges ahead, tail wagging.

It's a beautiful day now that the rain has rolled east at last; she can hear a pheasant's squeaky cackle. They turn a corner and there it is pecking at something on the road, its bright red cheeks and neat white collar reminding her of the Vicar.

With a yip of excitement, Baggage bounds forwards. Sally starts after her dog; she can't blame it for breaking its training when such easy prey presents itself.

There is a screech of brakes, and Sally rolls herself over her dog, shielding it. A door thuds open, and a woman's voice says,

'I'm so sorry, so sorry, are you hurt?'

Sally picks herself up, and sighs. It's obviously going to be one of those days.

'I'm all right. Just. Baggage?'

Baggage wriggles out of her grasp, and makes it clear she's far more interested in the pheasant.

'Idiot!' says Sally, too shaken to know whether she means the dog or the woman.

'I'm afraid the pheasant's dead,' the woman says. 'I hope it wasn't yours or anything?'

Sally bursts out laughing.

'No. Happens all the time, the poor things. You could take this home and eat it if you hang it upside-down for three days, pluck and roast.'

The woman looks startled, then to Sally's surprise, picks up the small corpse.

'I wouldn't say no to a free meal. Lovely feathers . . . My daughters will enjoy those.'

'We were just walking along the road to get a signal for my mobile. My car's gone into a ditch.'

'You must let me help, then. Could my car pull yours out, do you think?'

Sally looks doubtful.

'I think I'll need a more powerful engine. If I could get to a landline, I can make some calls.'

'Of course! Come back to my house and use mine. It's the least I can do. Are you *sure* you're both all right? I live just down the lane ahead.'

'I'm fine, really. Though if I see the chap who pushed me over, I can tell you, I'll give him a piece of my mind. Some lunatic in a red Golf.'

The woman sighs, and says,

'My husband, Quentin. Sorry again.'

She smiles, and Sally realises that she's deeply unhappy.

'I'm Lottie Bredin.'

'Sally Verity.'

'We're renting a place nearby. Let me drive you there to make amends for bad manners.'

As they go back along the lane, Sally tells her about growing up near Trelorn before training as a midwife in London, and gathers that Lottie is an architect. She doesn't know a soul here apart from her in-laws. Lonely, poor thing, Sally thinks, though the village school is a good start. These people parachute in from other places and expect to fit into a new community, but it just doesn't happen like that.

'So have you not met our local celebrity?' she asks.

'No. Who's that?'

'Gore Tore.'

Lottie slows the car in surprise.

'Really? *That* Tore? I used to love all his records as a teenager, back in the day. He's been going for ever, hasn't he? My goodness, I'd no idea . . . '

'He lives on the other side of the village. Nice chap, though it's mostly his wife and kids you might see about. He's always off doing concerts.' Sally gives her a glance and decides to risk a little gossip. 'All those alimony payments to keep up, they say.'

'How old are the kids?'

'Young. About seven or eight.'

'I wonder whether they're at the village school.'

'Yes, I think so,' says Sally. She knows they are, of course, because Tess is the school's head.

'My elder daughter is finding it a bit hard. She misses London.'

'And you? Do you miss it?'

'I miss my friends and my mother, and working.' Lottie looks out of the window. 'But at the same time, on a fine day this is just . . . I've never lived in the countryside before.'

'The winters can be hard, but the summer makes up for it.'

'I suppose weather matters more here than it does in the city.'

'We do find other things interesting, too,' Sally says dryly. It always amuses her, the way that Londoners think all they ever talk about must be weather and animals, as if country people aren't interested in politics or TV or even books and music. There are quite a lot of things going on, but it's too soon to tell her about those, yet. Or, indeed, why Home Farm will be familiar to anyone local.

Bumping along the drive in Lottie's car, she even spots a scrap of blue and white plastic police tape left tied round a tree. The estate agent must have missed it.

Home Farm looks as if it's been having some care given to it, for there's a wheelbarrow full of brambles blocking the entrance to the house.

Inside, Sally goes into the living room to call her next appointment in Trelorn. She makes another call to Sam. He'll be quicker than the AA.

'Course I'll come my love,' he says at once. 'Don't you worry.'

While Lottie brews them both tea in the kitchen, Sally looks around. She was last in here a long time ago, at the start of her career when Home Farm and the Manor House had belonged to old Sir Jerry, and both of them falling to rack and ruin. It's never been given much TLC, but now there are photographs on the dresser – two pretty little girls, and a handsome young man who looks like Lottie but with dark skin and curly hair.

That would be the mixed-race son she's heard about, though hardly anyone has seen him out and about, yet. Maybe they'll stay, she thinks. Young families are what every village needs to stop it dying.

A tall boy, whom she recognises from the photograph, shambles in, and looks at her with surprise.

'Hi,' he mutters. Sally returns the greeting, as does Baggage. Xan laughs as the springer rolls over and invites him to tickle her tummy.

'This is Sally, Xan. Quentin pushed her car into a ditch.'

The boy rolls his eyes.

'Typical Dud. It's freezing next door because he hasn't brought in any wood, again.'

'Split us some logs and I'll sort you some breakfast,' Lottie says. Over the sizzle of eggs in the pan, Baggage whines softly.

'They never stop eating, do they, at this age?'

'No, though he needs to get out more. He's desperate to get some sort of job, poor boy.'

Sally looks out of the window, at where Xan is standing, legs apart, chopping an upended log with a maul. She shivers, and wonders if that is the axe that ... But it must be a replacement.

'Can he drive?'

'No. In London there was no need. I've got an old bike, though.'

'Jobs, well ... there's always Humbles in Trelorn. Mostly it's Poles, but they also employ locals.'

'Yes, our cleaner, Janet, suggested that too. He could give it a go.'

Xan has come in, carrying a basket full of logs.

'We're talking about a job for you, darling.'

Xan grunts, but Sally, used to the ways of teenagers, says, 'Probably no good to you. It pays only the minimum wage.'

'How much is the minimum wage?' Xan asks; and when Sally

48

tells him he says at once, 'I'm up for it. It's doing my head in just sitting around all day.'

A nice boy, Sally thinks, as Sam finally turns up and drags her Polo out of the ditch; nice family, apart from the dad, and living in that awful house. As she drives away, she wonders what they'll do when they find out.

6

This is England, Too

'When are we going back to England?' Stella demands.

'London isn't England,' Lottie says. 'This is England, too.'

They don't believe her. How can it be true, when there are no streets, shops and lights?

Yet since moving to this place the fraying fabric of her nights has been replaced by profound, velvety slumber. Is it the darkness? The sounds of the city have gone, but the country isn't entirely silent either, for the hills rustle with water and when the wind isn't blowing she can hear the cry of owls. Is it the air, so clean and cold and lively? Whatever the cause, it feels like a miracle. She is sleeping through the night again, and so is Rosie. Even if she still experiences the lurch every morning when she wakes and thinks things are still good, grief feels manageable.

It is not a feeling shared by her family.

'The water tastes nasty,' says Rosie.

'It's full of iron, and look how lovely it's made your hair, sweetheart.'

They don't care: their long blonde tresses are soft anyway.

'There are bugly spiders everywhere, and you know how we hate them.'

'It's a spooky house, Mummy. It makes noises,' Rosie says.

'It's an old house. All old houses creak. It's just stretching a bit as it warms up, like a person.'

At times, though, she too thinks she can see odd things out of the corner of her eye. Quite often, she feels as if there is a presence in the room with her. Could it be haunted? She doesn't believe in ghosts, but to live in the country feels as if a kind of prop to rational existence has been removed. She doesn't mind being without immediate neighbours – after all, in London she never knew hers – but she misses her mother.

'How are you, Mutti?' Lottie asks, once a day.

'My darling, I am in mint condition; how are you?'

'Fine.'

'How are my darling granddaughters?'

Rosie has settled into the village school, a Victorian Gothic building of brick and slate, without difficulty. She is always popular, being the kind of six-year-old child who likes pink and kittens, and has immediately found a new best friend in the local doctor's youngest daughter. Stella is a different matter.

'Country children don't know anything about anything!' is her angry cry. 'They're all stupid, and I'll become stupid too unless you take me home!'

Lottie folded her daughter's tense, angry body in her arms.

'I'm sure that's not true, sweetheart.'

'I'll *never* be happy here.'

'Never is a very long time.'

'You've got pink cheeks, Mummy,' Rosie observed.

'I expect it's blood vessels breaking from the cold,' Stella said.

'Just give it a try. It's not even for a year.'

'A year is a very long time if you are eight.'

Quentin puts it in characteristic fashion:

On the plus side, there are no mini-chavs with tattoos or
future members of IS, but unlike the private system, a sizeable
proportion is disabled. There are kids here who are dyslexic,
autistic, Down's syndrome and so on, and to the school's
credit, they are not excluded for fear of dragging it down the
league tables, but integrated.

We're in the honeymoon period of switching, giddy with
relief at no longer having to sell a kidney in order to educate
them. How we'll feel if half the class can't read by eleven is
another matter.

Like all his columns, this has caused a storm of outrage online, attacking him for hating the disabled, for being a snob and a racist. Lottie can only be grateful that her husband is writing his column under a pseudonym.

'I don't understand why we have to *walk*,' Stella says.

'It's good exercise, and it saves us money. The car is only for when it's raining hard.'

It has all taken a lot longer to balance their books than expected, but even if everyone is sick of apple crumble made with apples from the orchard, they have a roof over their heads and £400 a month left over for food, petrol and utilities. Though very tight, they can just about manage on it. She will get back some tax from the Inland Revenue due to her fall in earnings, and Quentin's freelancing is also yielding some income, even if it is always paid at least two months in arrears. Lottie doesn't want to think about what will happen if the Canadian tenants decide to leave, or if she can't find another job. It's bad enough to be forced to do accounts every week with her husband.

'I just don't understand why everything is so expensive!' Quentin keeps saying.

'It's called the cost of living. I can't feed a family of five on less than £60 a week.'

Lottie knows this because she is good at budgeting. It's a

dismal thing to be proud of, given that Quentin is the one whose meals they all look forward to. He has his mother's gift for being able to throw a few leftovers together and make food that is, as he says smugly, nutritious *and* delicious.

Another ten months of this with him will drive her mad.

She has been applying online to every architectural practice within fifty miles, but there are so many outstanding, prize-winning firms in the South-West that, even with her two decades of experience in commercial building for a top developer, she won't stand a chance.

'Maybe I'll get a job stacking shelves or something,' she says to Marta. 'It's not as if I ever made much before.'

'No, you are a professional, with qualifications. Something will turn up.'

The two-mile trek into the village is punctuated by what become familiar sights: an old grey horse which comes to the gate to nuzzle them for a mint; a view down the valley towards a pair of white wind turbines under the vast, refulgent sky; brown birds and bright berries. As they trudge along, the girls chat to her about their small doings and she answers their questions, which she has rarely had time for before. Perhaps I can teach them myself about some of the things they might be missing at school, she thinks. She encourages them to speak German; they look for mini-beasts, pick autumn leaves and berries to put in jugs at home. It's more enjoyable than she would ever have thought, if also deadly dull.

Her daily walk usually includes a visit to the village shop, a Portakabin crouched in the church car park. The design makes her wince, but just to talk to another adult who doesn't hate her is a relief.

'Home-made?' she asks, pointing to pasties, keeping warm in front of the counter.

'Oh yes. We don't hold with Humbles.'

'It's good that Shipcott still has a shop.'

'It doesn't make a profit,' the woman says, shyly. 'We volunteer, though we all worry about being held up at gunpoint.'

'Do you really?'

'You'd be surprised. There's crime here, my lovely, just like everywhere else. But how else are pensioners without cars going to get their food and money once a week?'

She has never known people like this, with their terrible teeth and terrible clothes and kindness. That's what astonishes her the most: the kindness. In one month, she's had more invitations to drop by for tea than she ever had in eighteen years of mother-hood before. Maybe it's true what people say about Londoners being unfriendly, she thinks, but after experiencing her daughters' private school system, rammed with snotty bitches who ostracised her because she couldn't come to charity coffee mornings, she's relieved.

These women all work, too. There's a nurse who works for Marie Curie, and a farmer's wife who is run off her feet with bed and breakfasts, and two who run a care home for the elderly, and one who is a hairdresser; there are mothers who do all kinds of jobs, not only in Trelorn but as far away as Bristol and Bude. Her new-found popularity is not, however, due to any quality of her own.

'We're so pleased you came, because it means the school won't be closed down,' says one.

'Do two pupils make such a difference?'

'Oh, yes. If the numbers fall too low, they'd all have to be reallocated and this village would die just like so many others.'

'I'm so glad we helped, then.'

That she is unemployed is nothing out of the ordinary, even if any expenditure over £1 has to be justified. Most people here are considerably poorer than those they knew in London, and it's like driving along a road without suspension: you feel every jolt. Yet still her husband insists on having a cleaner.

'I really don't like having Janet around. Why can't you clean up your own mess?'

'It's my money, and I'll do with it as I please.'

That's the maddening thing: she has always earned less than her husband. She says to Marta,

'I spent ten years qualifying to become an architect, and still got paid less for designing buildings than Quentin gets for writing rubbish in a newspaper.'

'Be patient. This too will pass,' her mother says.

'Will it? It doesn't feel like it will ever change. It's always a struggle to be a woman architect, you know. Less than a fifth of us make it through their degree.'

'Can't you set up on your own?'

Lottie gives a bitter laugh. 'With what?'

'You aren't poor,' Marta keeps insisting. 'You have no idea what real poverty is like. Millions of people would envy your situation, not pity you.'

'You're right, I know, I just can't feel it yet.'

The leaves on many trees flush amber, umber and bright gold. The swallows have left, and now the birds flocking together are starlings. Winter is coming, and the cold glare of the energy-saving lights is driving her mad.

'Red lamp shades, red cushions,' she mutters. 'That's what we need, to counteract the sodding green.'

She searches on eBay the moment the first rental payment comes through. It's worth £30 on her credit card, just to make the living room look less miserable.

'It's horrible, no matter what you do,' is Quentin's only response.

'I'm not doing it for you.'

'You're doing it because you're incapable of not controlling things.'

'Well, at least I *try*.'

The odd thing is that the more she does try, the more she feels an odd affection for the place. The furnishings are atrocious, the insulation non-existent, and yet each time she wipes over surfaces, it's like stroking an animal whose rough, matted coat is gradually turning soft and smooth. She likes the cob walls despite the dreary magnolia emulsion of all rental properties. Perhaps I can paint it, she thinks; after all, there will be a tiny bit more to spend next month. The big pleather sofa and armchairs are much less obnoxious when draped in Indian cotton bedspreads, and the energy-saving bulbs are replaced by brighter, warmer halogen ones. The light from the small deep windows is redoubled by putting up a large mirror on the wall opposite, speckled with damp and age but still reflective. A ratty old kilim enlivens the brown carpet. Little by little, as she unpacks, it feels more like home. She finds two plain red interlined curtains, and splits them into four to replace the short, thin ones in the living room.

'You are completely crazy, Lottie. It's not ours. Stop all this obsessing.'

Once, in the early days, Quentin gave her a row of mugs with letters on which, when hung up in order, spelt out: I DO NOT HAVE OCD.

'I bother because, unlike those disgusting drapes, the new curtains will keep out the cold.'

He gives an exasperated sigh.

'Do you still wipe the basins in aeroplane toilets?'

Lottie disdains to answer.

Apart from the pig-slaughtering place below Xan's bedroom, now used to store the vacuum cleaner, mop and buckets, the saddest space in Home Farm is the kitchen. At right angles to the house, it must once have been some kind of small barn, but is badly converted. If only the ceiling had a skylight! If only there was a window at the far end ... To be able to always see how things should be is a particular curse of her profession.

Stella is also miserable. When asked to admire Rosie's friend's pony, she commented on its 'well developed *gluteus maximus*'. Predictably, this led to teasing, and tears.

'They're all potato-heads here! Why can't we go home?'

Lottie says, 'Sweetheart, it's like *The Railway Children*.'

'Is Daddy going to prison?'

If only, Lottie thinks. 'No. We just don't have much money for a bit. When we sell the house in London, each of us will buy a really nice flat, I promise.'

'Can't you and Daddy not divorce?'

'No, I'm sorry darling.'

Stella bursts into tears. Then she shouts,

'This is all YOUR fault, your fault! You are a horrible woman and a bad mother.'

Shocked, Lottie tries not to cry herself. Quentin has never explained to the girls that she's the innocent party in all this because he wants to stay being their hero. She is the drudge, resented by them for doing the dull nagging that responsible parenthood involves.

'Remind me how men came to rule the world?'

'Women have children,' Marta says.

Stella continues to be miserable, and rude, which leads to a call from the head teacher. It's not the first time she's been called in on account of her elder daughter's behaviour, and Lottie braces herself for intrusive questions when she goes to the school office. She has had all kinds of suggestions made about Stella's behaviour in the past, and is prepared to do battle with the usual patronising cow in charge. However, what Miss Anstey says takes her by surprise.

'Stella is a very nice, intelligent child, and it's inevitable that she'll take longer to settle. I expect she's used to doing more activities outside school, isn't she?'

'Well, yes,' says Lottie, cautiously. 'She's musical ... I don't suppose you can recommend a teacher?'

She can't afford one, but asking can do no harm.

'We used to have somebody, but he died. Actually, he lived in your house before you.'

'He did?' Lottie feels a brief quickening. 'That explains the piano. We're glad to have it.'

'Perhaps Stella and Rosie might like to join the choir on Tuesday lunchtimes, then.'

Lottie says she'll think about it. She can see Miss Anstey's shrewd eyes seeing the doubts she isn't expressing.

'It's difficult, adjusting,' she says.

'You might like to be more involved too, Mrs Bredin. We're always looking for volunteers.'

'I could help with reading.'

Miss Anstey nods. 'As long as you don't mind helping boys whose only interest is football, it does make a real difference.'

'Sure,' Lottie says, her heart sinking.

'Good. Your predecessor volunteered too. Nice chap. Such a shame.'

'Why, what happened to him?'

Miss Anstey seems to start. 'I'll be in touch soon.'

Another irritant, literally in Xan's case, is the ginger tom. The creature appeared one day, walking delicately across the grass with a discreet air made more notable by his insanitary habits indoors. They do not feed him, but it's clear that the cat, which Quentin dubs McSquirter, is determined to extract food and admission from them. The Bredins are equally determined not to give any.

'Out, damned cat!' Quentin bellows whenever McSquirter, with a trill, dances up to the door the moment it is left ajar. 'Spread your infernal lusts elsewhere!'

McSquirter's mate, a tabby, is pregnant.

'Can't we have just one tiny kitten when they're born?'

'No, absolutely not.' Lottie seizes a broom. 'Shoo!'

'Don't you like pussies?' Janet asks, pausing. 'Who's a beautiful boy, then?'

Janet never speaks like this to her daughter, who usually sits slumped on the sofa while her mother cleans. Lottie can't but recoil at the glutinous adoration in the other woman's voice.

'My son gets such bad asthma from cats, he could die if one comes in. Keep it out, please.'

'Shame, they're good at keeping mice down. I've heard a few scuttling about.'

'Mice!' Xan laughs, with an edge of hysteria in his voice. 'As if this place weren't bad enough!'

At times, Lottie is tempted to agree. Yet the astonishing thing is, everyone she meets is convinced that life in the country is better than life in the town.

'Aren't you glad to be out of the city?' they ask; and one says, 'From London, are you? I went to London once. Did my head in.'

Xan is the most miserable of them all.

'I'm so BORED and there's NOTHING TO DO,' he says a dozen times a day.

What will become of her daughters here? Will they end up like Janet's Dawn, swaddled in sugar pink and without a trace of animation?

'You know, Mum, there's something odd about Dawn,' Xan says when they are alone.

'In what way?'

'When she first came, do you remember that I played on the piano for a bit?'

'Yes, I heard you. The *Goldberg Aria*.'

'No. That wasn't me you heard, it was her. I was fiddling about, and then she just sat down beside me and played it. Honestly, Mum, it was weird. She's *good*.'

'Maybe she's autistic.'

Xan looks doubtful. 'But why isn't she at school? She's younger than I am.'

'I don't know. Maybe she needs the money. She does seem lonely.'

Nor is Dawn the only one. The wind howls round the roof and down the chimney, devouring logs. It sounds like somebody

59

moaning, or crying, a word she can't quite catch. When she looks in the darkened glass of the windows, she jumps.

'You should come down for a weekend,' she urges Justin and Hemani, but they say, 'When are you back again?' or, 'Perhaps in summer.'

It would be easier if I did live in another country, Lottie thinks.

7

Xan Gets a Job

Getting a job isn't half as hard as people make out, Xan thinks. Keeping going at it, however, is another matter. He wonders if it's the same with marriage.

Lottie and Quentin are making a reasonable job of maintaining civilised relations, at least in front of the girls; with him, they don't pretend. He's shocked by how two people who presumably once felt closer to each other than to anyone else could be so nasty. He takes Lottie's side, of course, because there's no question but that Quentin is in the wrong and has destroyed the family through his actions – and yet, she is so scornful, so harsh, that Xan finds himself wincing.

He doesn't want to hear them quarrelling, and has been finding it harder and harder to wake before afternoon. How, even with Lottie and an alarm clock shrilling in his ears, had he managed to be out of the house by 8 a.m. to get to school? He has no idea, but why should I get up, he thinks, when there's nothing to get up *for*? All he can do in the country is either look at the rain, or else walk for miles until he comes to the village, which has precisely one shop and one pub, then walk back. He doesn't want to read all the classics he told himself he'd power through this year, and he's given up looking on Facebook to see what other people are up to, bitterly hurt that none of his mates have bothered to get in touch.

The only other person his age is Janet's daughter. They have nothing in common, and she has not repeated her astonishing performance on the piano, but he tries to be friendly.

'Have you always, like, lived in Devon?'

'No.'

'Where were you before?'

'London.'

Xan felt a slight quickening of interest. 'Which part?'

'I dunno. We lived with my dad.'

'Oh. Where is he now?'

'He's dead,' she said, and her eyes filled with tears. She has remarkable eyes, navy blue, though it's easy not to notice them. She seems to be getting fatter each week, and although he feels sorry for her he wonders why she doesn't take more care of herself. Still, he's even more of a freak than she is, here.

Occasionally, he has gone into Trelorn with Lottie just for a change of scene, and he can always feel people staring. Once, a little girl came up to him and asked if he were made of chocolate. Her hopeful tone made it impossible to be angry, but both Xan and Lottie had been depressed. The locals don't even know how racist they are.

'Honestly, I'd be better off getting a job in London.'

'How? You don't have any qualifications or experience.'

'I could get work in a bar or something.'

'The only person you could ask to stay with is Oma, and if she hasn't invited you I don't think you can invite yourself,' Lottie said. 'Look: your problem is that you have to get a job to get a job. As soon as you have a bit of experience, you'll be employable.'

'Do you know what they pay someone under twenty-five, Mum? It's not even the minimum wage, it's £5.25 an hour. Why should I do some shit job for shit pay just because I'm stuck in the fucking country with nothing to do?'

'Please stop swearing.'

'I'll swear as much as I fucking well want. You got us into this mess with that tool you married.'

'Xan, we're talking about you, not me. But I did babysitting from the time I was thirteen, and saved up enough from that to travel round Italy by your age. You've never even washed a car.'

'You didn't ask me.'

'Well, I could really do with some help now. Not just with housework, but because I really, really need more money. Winter is here, and just to fill the oil tank for the Rayburn costs £600. I'm trying to find another job, but as of next month, I don't have enough for the weekly shop. That's how poor we are now.'

'All RIGHT! Jesus, there's no need to lay on the fucking guilt.'

Xan expected nothing, but when he slunk into the employment agency they almost bit his hand off to get him to sign up at the food factory. This was, the agency interviewer said, the busiest time of the year because of the run-up to Christmas; they couldn't get enough shift workers. He emerged beaming.

'I do night shifts from 6 p.m. Even though the agency and tax takes a lump of that, I can make £150 a week.'

'Is it a zero-hours contract?'

'They text me to say whether they need me the next day, but that's cool.'

In his old life, he had enjoyed an allowance of £200 a month. It never seemed much – some people at school often got that every week – but now it seems immense.

Lottie, characteristically, seems more worried than pleased at his news.

'I don't like the idea of you cycling there at night in winter. You won't forget your inhaler will you?'

'Mum. Mum. Haven't you noticed, I haven't had an attack for years.'

It's dark when he leaves in the evening, pedalling away on Lottie's old bike, a squashy package of sandwiches in his pocket. She's insisted on him wearing a reflective jacket and a helmet, as well as lights. It annoys him, even if he is a bit startled by the profound darkness of the countryside. Yet all of these things seem to fall away as he pedals along, the chill air slapping him to wakefulness.

Trelorn is the smallest market town on the River Tamar, and in daylight its houses and shops tumble down the banks like dirty sugar cubes. It has always been a liminal place, with its Cornish name and postal code, but counts as part of Devon. Its railway line had vanished in the 1960s, but it has its old Norman church, a secondary school, a library, a doctor's surgery, various supermarkets, banks, charities and pubs, a main square punctuated by a granite monument dedicated to those who died in two world wars, and a run-down hotel, the White Hart, largely patronised by travelling salesmen and the occasional unwary tourist. Even in the height of summer, few visitors wish to stop there for long. Its industrial zone sprawls on one side of the town across what would otherwise have been a pretty little valley; on the other is the road leading to Dartmoor, and an abandoned quarry.

The factory resembles nothing so much as a gigantic corrugated steel shed surrounded by a scribble of razor wire and tarmac. Lit up, with steam fuming out of its chimneys, Humbles looks grim.

Xan wheels his bike over the gritty forecourt. He's arrived half an hour before the start of the night shift. The entrance is through a door to the side of two giant gates, presumably so that lorries can be loaded with produce.

Inside, the noise from the production line is much more than expected. The foreman who shows him what to do is a huge fellow with cheeks and nose stained bright red from broken veins. He shouts,

'Do you speak English?'

'Yes.'

'What?'

'YES!' Xan shouts back, nettled. 'I *am* English!'

The man looks doubtfully at him and says, at the same volume, 'Any ID?'

Xan never thought he would be mistaken for an illegal immigrant, but Lottie has had the foresight to get him to photograph his passport.

'Can you read English?'

'Yes,' Xan says. 'The sign over there says NO TRESPASSERS.'

The man grunts, and tells him to get changed. Xan scrambles to find a white nylon uniform and boots and to put his clothes in a wire locker. Other men are also changing, and there's a general stir when Xan comes in. Having to bundle his mass of squiggly locks into the hairnet is embarrassing: he hasn't noticed, but he's grown an Afro. When Xan emerges, the man bellows,

'Anyone who tries to steal your boots, which they will, I'm not interested. You clock in here with your card, and you clock out the end of your shift or you don't get paid at the end of the week. We text you on the days that we need you, and you don't ever go into areas where people wear red. Understand?'

'Yes. Why not?'

'Cross-CONTAMINATION!' the man roars. 'Anyone who goes from raw to cooked is a biohazard, and gets sacked ON THE SPOT. Understand?'

'Yes,' Xan shouts. The noise will be a constant irritation.

'You get a thirty-minute dinner break after midnight. Toilet breaks every three hours. The managers watch you all the time from the gods.'

'The gods?' Xan asks, bewildered.

'Up there, see?'

The foreman points a chunky pink finger up, where the small figures of people look down on them; it reminds Xan of the Royal Opera House. Unlike its dilapidated exterior, the inside of the factory is dazzlingly white, with fluorescent strip lights making it as bright as daylight. It is clean in the way that a hospital is clean, without germs or joy. The floors are smooth, sealed concrete. A machine sucks the dust out of the ceiling, where gigantic fans spin unceasingly. Three long stainless-steel conveyor belts circle on an endless loop of noise. A dozen moving parts are squealing or shrieking or jiggling as the pies move along the various stages of composition.

'EARPLUGS!'

He can barely hear the words, but fumbles for the foam plugs. They're wholly inadequate, and he soon takes them out because if he doesn't, he can't hear what anyone says. All over the factory, men and women in white overalls, hats and white rubber boots are assembling to take over from the day shift. The overalls are so plastic that they show only the vaguest outline of the person wearing them, and no sweat stains them, though after an hour, everyone is dripping with exertion. He must have seen pictures like this in geography books, or maybe on the TV, but the noise is so much worse than imagined.

'Now, let's see if you can work like a Pole,' roars the foreman. 'I'll put you in with Maddy.'

Maddy is a short, scrawny woman. She gives Xan a brief nod.

'Copy what Maddy does. If you need the toilet, make sure you take all your clothes off before you go, and wash your bloody hands. No smoking, ever. When the alarm goes, you step forward to take this man's place in front of you. At the end of your shift, twelve hours from now, he will take yours. There must be no stopping the flow. Understand?'

Xan's sense of his own personality coalesces into a solid knot of anxiety. This is real, he tells himself. The alarm blares, and he steps forward to tap the shoulder of the man in front of him. The changeover happens so smoothly that he's filled with a sense of triumph. His body, so often a source of anxiety and shame, has not let him down.

Maddy mouths,

'All right?'

'Yes!'

They aren't supposed to talk to each other, but under the tremendous noise of the machinery they do, even if much of it is lip-reading. After ten minutes, Xan feels as if he's been doing it for ever.

Xan has probably eaten a Humble pie many times in his life. Their logo, an image of green hills under blue skies, is such a familiar part of life that nobody notices it, for their produce can be found in supermarkets, cafeterias, service stations, snack bars and canteens across Britain. A uniform golden-brown, Humbles' pies look and smell fine, and are always filling, in that each conveys the sensation of having swallowed a lump of lead which sinks straight to the bottom of the stomach.

At present, they are making meat pies rather than desserts. At one end of the factory, the raw ingredients are peeled, diced, sliced, cubed, seasoned and cooked in vats. It has to be done by hand, for though rumble machines can strip the skin off a potato in seconds, only people can cope with the odd shapes of other vegetables.

'What's the meat?' Xan asks.

Maddy mouths, 'You tell me.'

He wonders whether she's trying to indicate something. It's now past midnight, well after his longer break is due, and he's ravenously hungry. Lottie's sandwiches now seem like a very good idea.

'Are all the pies always the same?' he asks Maddy when the relief workers give them their breaks.

'Yes, apart from when they change filling. Then you get apple with raspberry mixed in. They don't stop the belt you see, it's not worth it, so those pies get thrown away, or sold cheap, from the shop if you like.'

'Do they ever change the recipes?'

67

'Well, they're supposed to be inventing new fillings, like they're supposed to have trainee food technician apprenticeships, but I've been here for years and never tasted any different. They were invented by the first Mrs Humble, a Victorian farmer's wife with seven hungry sons.'

'And were they?'

'This factory only got going in the nineteen fifties.'

'So it's all made up?'

'When the crust is put on, some bluebirds fly down and crimp them,' she says.

The pies are, in a way, a feat of technology. Each requires exactly the same amount of time to have exactly the same-tasting filling squirted into it from a huge vat. What Xan has to do is numbingly simple: he just has to push them into a line as they travel down the conveyor belt to be baked.

What seems easy at first becomes tiring, then worse. Just because it's boring does not mean he can switch off concentration, or the nausea induced by watching continual motion. An hour after his first break, Xan wants to pee, but he has to hold on for another two hours. Once in the toilet, nobody bothers to undress, as they are supposed to, and despite notices on the mirrors, few wash their hands before putting them into plastic gloves.

'How long have you been here?' he asks Maddy.

'Two years. One bloke's been here for twenty, but most only last a few months.'

'I'm not surprised.'

She grins at him. 'You're British, aren't you?'

'Yes.'

'Well, that makes a change. Don't think I've seen you around before, though.'

'My family moved here from London.'

'Where are you living?'

'Shipcott. We're renting.'

'My stars! You're not the ones who've taken that place, are you?'

'What?'

'Home Farm.'

'Oh, yes.'

'Not superstitious then?'

'Um – no.'

He isn't listening, as he eyes the girls nearby. They're the first people his own age he's seen in Devon, apart from Janet's daughter. (There's someone who looks vaguely like Dawn shuffling around with a trolley, but he can't be sure, because so many women here are shapeless.) These are pretty, slim and he suspects Polish, for they have those smooth, wedge-shaped faces, heavily made up. Even in overalls, they are seriously fit.

One of them glances his way. She has pale green eyes, a full mouth and skin as smooth as cream. Xan blushes and pushes his hairnet back.

'Stop fiddling with that, or you'll lose a week's wages,' Maddy says. 'Whole place can be shut down for a hair.'

'How do they know?'

'Spot checks. Keep up!'

Speed isn't Xan's only problem. There's a bloke who has a job walking up and down, some sort of overseer. As Xan stands, his hands occupied, he suddenly feels his buttocks being fondled.

At first Xan thinks that he must have imagined it because his muscles are pinging with pain. But the hands fondle him again, and the worst of it is, Xan can do nothing because his entire attention has to stay on the conveyor belt.

'Hallo darling,' the bloke breathes into his neck.

'Piss off,' Xan mutters, furious.

The hands, which have now moved to the front of his trousers, grip his hips. Xan feels the man's erection grind into his back. Everyone else is carefully not looking his way.

'Hey!' Xan says more loudly. He is terrified. What should he do? He can feel his legs trembling.

69

'Only havin' a laugh, darling, only havin' a laugh,' the man says. His breath, hot and sour, sprays in Xan's ear. Xan catches the foreman's eye, but the man shrugs.

'It's just Rod,' the foreman says.

Xan thinks he might be about to vomit, but then there's a crash. A trolley has collided into his persecutor, spilling trays on the floor, and suddenly people are all around, clearing up the mess, and the conveyor belt stops with a great shrilling of sirens. The foreman shouts at the small, dumpy female who caused it. It *is* Dawn, bobbing her head in apology. The conveyor belt starts again, and his assailant is needed elsewhere. Xan catches a glimpse of him: a lean red-faced man with a turkey-cock nose and ginger eyebrows. What the hell had that been about? Miserably, he meets the gaze of the Polish girl he'd noticed before. She is looking at him, and now she shrugs slightly, as if to say, What a jerk. He nods gratefully.

Maddy says, 'You take care with those girls.'

'Why?'

'Well, a little British baby is what they want, and benefits.'

Xan flushes. 'Really?'

Maddy rolls her eyes.

'You think they can get what we offer in Poland? Course not. I'm not saying they're not good workers, but nobody does this job for long. Free health care, free education, child benefit, who wouldn't jump at it? Plenty of little Polish kids in local schools.'

Xan drags his eyes away from the girl. He doesn't like this kind of talk, which sounds pretty much like racism, but he knows nothing.

'Do you have kids, Maddy?'

'Three. One year, six and seven. Girl, boy, girl.'

'Do you ever get to see them if you work nights?'

'I get home in time to take them to school, sleep for six hours, make their tea, do the housework and come here. My husband does the rest.'

'What does he do?' Xan asks, politely.

'He was a soldier in Afghanistan. Lost his legs.'

'Oh. Oh, I'm sorry.'

'So is he.'

His own arms and legs and head feel hot and heavy. He's not used to any of this. The last two hours are pure torment. He wants to cry, only there isn't enough moisture in his body for tears. Perhaps he'll go on until he himself falls onto the conveyor belt and is carried off to be put in a pie. Suddenly, a hand taps his shoulder. The far end of the factory is open, and crates of pies are being loaded onto lorries for distribution. The shift has ended.

Like weary ghosts, the night workers step back and the day shift steps forward. The machinery continues to squeal and rumble as the workforce shuffles to the changing rooms. He's never been able to understand why adults complain about being tired all the time, but now he understands, it's what work does to you. Your vitality, in exchange for money. All at once, he understands how privileged everyone he has ever known is, in having the education and opportunity to not do what he has just done, and must do again.

Men around him strip off, throw their hairnets, gloves and overalls into a laundry bag. The relief of being out of them is almost pleasurable. Xan still has to cycle back to Home Farm, an uphill journey which now fills him with dread. The Polish girls emerge from their shapeless clothes like butterflies, in tiny brightly coloured vests, jackets and skin-tight jeans. Released, their hair tumbles in luscious waves of chestnut or blonde. The green-eyed girl turns out to be a brunette. He had known she would be, somehow.

She talks, in a low husky voice, and her friends suddenly burst out laughing. If only she spoke English! He wanders nearer, following them out of the factory door. The group stops, and the girl turns, and looks at him enquiringly.

'Hi,' Xan says. She looks at him with a faint smile. Greatly daring, he points to himself and says, 'Xan. Alexander.'

The girl smiles, and says,

'Hello, Alex. I am Katya.'

Perhaps Devon won't be so boring after all.

8

Quentin Unleashed

Quentin's new girlfriend lives on a houseboat, conveniently close to Paddington Station. Their affair has been going on since summer, and at present it feels like a life-saver.

He was walking along the canal one sunny afternoon soon after his return from America when a pretty woman on one of the barges moored in the canal asked him for a light. Her grin was so cheeky that Quentin could not help laughing.

'I don't smoke, I'm afraid.'

'Neither do I.'

Tina took him into her long narrowboat and her wide soft bed that very afternoon, and since then he has stayed with her whenever he comes up.

'O the deep, deep peace of the double bed, after the hurly-burly of the chaise-longue,' he quotes, and Tina, like every woman before her, laughs. She laughs a lot, which is a pleasant change, and he enjoys her languid bohemianism.

'I have a gypsy heart,' she says, though her home is connected to electricity, water, sewerage and broadband, and not really going anywhere. 'I can't afford to rent, let alone buy anywhere, sweetie.'

Sunk below the usual noise of the city, the barge's air of watery impermanence and its central location both suit Quentin very well. So does Tina. With her Roberts radio tuned permanently to Heart FM, her rows of silver rings and her lickerish enthusiasm, she is infinitely preferable to a nagging, angry wife. Unleashed, he wakes with a reliable erection, and a sense that his greying hair has become invisible. How glorious it is to be back in the city!

Yet London is also a torment to him. People who once sent him fawning letters asking for work no longer bother to reply when he now pitches ideas to them. He has discovered the truth of the advice to be kind to those you pass on the way up because you will meet them again on the way down. One email to him began,

Quentin,

When I came to work for you as an intern, I made your coffee, fetched your dry-cleaning, covered your back and even cleaned shit off your shoes. You didn't pay me lunch money let alone a living wage, and never once said thank you. You are the rudest person I have ever worked with. So you will understand why I say now, We have no vacancies of any kind that you might fill.

Others are more diplomatic, but convey the same message. It's like that moment in a game of Snakes and Ladders where, after shooting triumphantly up one ladder after another, you find the board has become hideously alive with long, green and yellow snakes which swallow up your counter no matter how often you roll the dice.

So the upshot of all this bad feeling is that apart from Ivo Sponge, nobody will give him a regular weekly slot. At the *Rambler*, which he edited so successfully, he is billed as a 'contributing editor', something that sounds grand but is a public admission of impotence. Even this is entirely due to his former assistant, Katie, who is now deputy editor of the magazine and living with his grown-up son Ian.

Quentin wishes he and Ian liked each other more, because it would be convenient to have a second crash-pad for his London visits, even if it would mean staying near the dreary East End Academy where his son is now head. They have nothing in common. Ian is a fine young man, as honest, hard-working, conscientious and professional as the best kind of South African, only he has absolutely no sense of humour. Apparently, he is a big success at his school and is spoken of as one of a new breed of teachers transforming inner-city state schools. It is now too late for any kind of relationship, although Naomi and Hugh get on tremendously well.

'Such a *nice* young man,' Naomi said, adding in a tone of offensive wonder, 'and he looks very like you.'

Perhaps if his first marriage had not been so easy to get out of, he'd never have tried again. Other divorced men are full of belated advice which boils down to: never, never, ever marry.

'I'm just the boring man who pays the bills, while she takes herself and the kids off on three foreign holidays a year,' said one former colleague, now completely bald from, it is said, tearing his hair out. 'The bottom line is that all women are mad. They hate us the moment they have a baby and they bitch about us for the rest of their lives. Even if you think there are tax advantages, don't do it. A guy will always be better off not married than married, especially in Britain. Why else does every foreign wife want to live here? So she can get a shitload of alimony.'

'I don't have anything but the house.'

'Then prepare for the Shed of Doom.'

The Shed of Doom is what all erring husbands dread. It is built at the bottom of the garden, supposedly as a study or a spare room, but its true purpose is to be the place where a man is banished, to stare at the house on which he pays the mortgage while his ex-wife enjoys the life he can no longer have.

'You want my advice?' said Mark Crawley, when they met for a drink. 'I should have taken a knife and stuck it in my heart before divorcing. I'm no happier than I was before, I've lost all my money, and I never get to see my daughter unless I threaten my Ex with a court order.'

Quentin pushes this out of his mind. Tina is refreshing, and almost twenty years younger than him.

'I always prefer married men. Especially if they're older,' she says.

Quentin can't help but preen. 'Really? Why is that?'

'They don't want emotional commitment.'

Why can't more women be like this – free-spirited and filthy? His post-marital affairs have until now been laden with expectations. Cecilia, his final fling at the *Rambler*, yapped on about how much better his life would be with her if he left his wife and family; as if that was what he wanted. It was worse in Washington, where there had been no thrill of the chase, just perfectly groomed women circling any unattached male in the manner of raptors. Tina, however, is a sensualist. She believes that the French have got it right with the *cinq à sept*.

'What's the oldest man you've ever had?'

'Seventy-one.'

He snorts with laughter.

'Good God!' Then he pauses, as the ramifications of this sink in. 'Why?'

'Why do you want to know?'

'I'm just curious.'

Tina strokes his leg with her feet. She wears a silver ring shaped like a snake eating its tail on one toe. He finds it both disturbing and arousing.

'He had a big cock, and he was rich.'

'Which mattered most?'

'What do you think?'

She knows he owns a house nearby, and her generation think that anyone with a house anywhere in London must be a millionaire – which, on paper, is true. The whole of Britain is obsessed by property, but none more so than Londoners, for bricks and mortar, no matter how poorly situated or inconveniently located, are the closest thing to magic. When he arrived in London in the mid-1980s, the life-changing tide of credit had been rushing through the market like the Gulf Stream, and it has gone on getting warmer and warmer until the whole city is bubbling and steaming with greed and desperation. Anyone with money from every corrupt country in the world wants to invest it in the one sure thing: not gold, but London property. Even the 1930s semis on the ring-roads are being restored rather than knocked down.

Yet Quentin loved London even when it was dingy, when ordinary people like teachers and nurses had been able to live in nice parts of the city for a modest sum. In fact, looking back, he loved it most of all then. To be a Londoner, Quentin thinks, is to be in a Britain that is more confident, more tolerant, more civilised, more enterprising and more beautiful than the rest of the country. Even when it drives him mad with its traffic jams and pollution, even when it's overrun with tourists and oligarchs, even when he needs to get away for a holiday, he's always happy here. It is, far more than any woman, the love of his life.

All cities have this in common: they are wonderful if you have either youth or money, but horrible if you have neither. Quentin's poverty is now of the kind that dares not use a credit card. Like a stomach that is being forced, inch by painful inch, to shrink, he feels sick with something beyond hunger. Until now, he has never understood quite how much success has added a spring to his step.

'God, I'd give anything to be back for good,' he says.

'Why don't you just sell up?'

'That's the plan, but it takes time.'

When Tina goes to work (she designs lingerie, appropriately), Quentin walks to the West End. He needs to find somewhere to go before a book launch with enough canapés to make up a meal before he has to return on the last train . . . Incredible, to be back doing this kind of thing, as he had thirty years ago! Civilians believe that parties are about enjoying yourself, but they are work, and when fewer and fewer people have staff jobs, attending them is a question of survival. If you don't turn up, people assume you are dead.

He stops off at the Slouch Club, where he hasn't renewed his membership but can brazen his way in. There, he can nurse a cup of coffee indefinitely, and access the Internet for free.

Soho is still pleasingly sleazy, but even here the sterilising effect of money is creeping onwards. Will the whole city become one bland series of franchises? He goes through the revolving door of the club in an unusually pensive mood.

'Hello, are you a member?'

Quentin gives his most saurian stare and says,

'Ivo Sponge.'

Of course she hasn't a clue what Ivo looks like, only that he's on the membership list; and Ivo is probably far too busy and too grand now to come here. Quentin toys with the idea of having lunch on Ivo's tab and charging it to his former protégé, but the idea is too risky. He remembers when, if a staff journalist didn't claim at least £100 a week they were hauled up by the editor and told to get some expenses in, quick. No wonder newspapers have become so dull.

Quentin drops a lump of sugar into his Americano and opens the *Chronicle*'s website on his tablet. His Questing Vole identity has been guessed by those in the know, as all journalistic pseudonyms are, but it enables him to be as rude as he wants.

I have exchanged the reek of burning car exhausts for the smell of silage and sheep shit. I spend most days wrapped up in an old duvet, hiding from village bumpkins trying to persuade me to join them in the Methodist Chapel.

78

Quentin groans. So far, he has written about the hell of living in mud, the aggression of rustic beams, the monotony of food without multiculturalism and the disappointment of trying to grow his own vegetables only to see them eaten by slugs. He's not making any of it up, and it isn't half the story, because the real horror is living with Lottie. The bloggers loathe him.

Stupid townie . . . you think your poor, try living on so-called benefits . . . go back to where you came from, posh git . . . You're idea of the countryside makes me sick . . . What a pointless waste of time. Why don't you snobs write about the way real country people live? . . . More rubbish from Vole. Out here, we know what to do with rodents!

Who *are* these people?

He scrolls down the page, and comes across something unexpected.

Dear Mr. Vole,

You claim that Devon is a place where nothing ever happens apart from incest and morris dancing. Well, I wouldn't be too sure about that. Ask yourself why your rent at Home Farm is so low. They still haven't found his head. Sweet dreams!

Quentin feels a needle of ice slide down the back of his neck. Not only does somebody know who he is, and where he lives but . . .

Impossible! The rent is low because it's winter, when tenants are like hens' teeth, and the house has no central heating. Yet Lottie has mentioned how none of the village children have wanted to come back to play with his daughters. Natural shyness, surely; yet Quentin's fingers are already tapping out the words Devon+murder+Shipcott into Google. Up pops a link to the *Daily Telegraph*:

HEADLESS BODY FOUND NEAR DEVON FARMHOUSE.

Oh, Christ, he thinks.

The body of a decapitated man was found near Shipcott,
Devon, police revealed yesterday.
    Detectives have confirmed that the victim was a man
of around 40–50. A detailed search of the surrounding
countryside is being carried out.
    One of the men who found the corpse said, 'A big black dog
was standing over it, whining, but it ran off when we approached.
    'At first we thought it was an animal, but as we came closer
we could see the body of a man. There was a gaping hole
where the head had been hacked off.'
    Detective Chief Inspector James Drew, who is leading the
hunt, said, 'We don't know exactly how long the body has
been there, but if anyone has seen someone acting suspiciously
or has information relating to the victim or his killer or killers,
we ask them to get in touch with the police.
    'There is no indication of who the victim was but we are
working to identify him. We have people going through the
undergrowth but it is a very large area.'

There is an aerial shot of the River Tamar with white arrows
pointing to Trelorn, and a white building which looks ominously
familiar.

There are comments underneath this, too, from the bloggers.

What a dreadful thing to discover in such a beautiful place . . .
What is happening to this peaceful, civilised country? . . . I
feel sick just thinking about what that poor man must have
suffered . . . Is anybody looking out for the black dog? . . .
Maybe it was the Hound of the Baskervilles.

Nothing about Home Farm, and yet when he clicks on the next
link, from the *Daily Mail*, there it is, and beside it is a two-page

80

spread featuring the face of a rock star so famous that even Quentin knows at once who he is.

GORE TORE IN HEADLESS BODY MYSTERY

A decapitated body has been found in a property belonging to the rock star Gore Tore.

Quentin can feel his jaw drop. Two thoughts collide in his head: his daughters are living in the scene of a murder, and his landlord is an international celebrity. Why has nobody told him? Do his parents know? Though he has never had any interest in rock stars, even Quentin has heard of Gore, not only as he has heard of Mick Jagger and David Bowie but because Tore was once a pupil at his old school, Knotshead. He had been given a scholarship in the early 1960s, and he is now one of the richest people in Britain.

A blizzard of pictures fills his screen. Tore, his ex-model wife Di and their two small sons smile up at him. They are, of course, far more important than the victim. Though creased and almost freeze-dried with age, the star is still handsome, his long dark locks abundant and his teeth ... well, they have to be fake. Much of the first page is taken up with describing how Tore bought Shipcott Manor for £6 million four years ago. Formerly, it had belonged to Sir Gerald Fox, a notorious playboy who died bankrupt, leaving the house in ruins. Since when, Tore has been restoring the house, blah, blah and then the meat of the story:

The murdered man found in West Devon six weeks ago has been revealed as Mr. Oliver Randall. Randall, a piano teacher, lived alone at Home Farm. He was believed to have left the area at some time over the Christmas holiday. Police are following possible leads.

Quentin looks for other links, but it's clear there have been no further discoveries since the discovery of the corpse and their own rental of Home Farm, nine months later.

What a creepy thing. Quentin shivers. At the very least, he hopes the maniac has not left the head on the premises. He saves his search, and clicks off the page. He mustn't mention it to his daughters – or Lottie. His mind wanders morbidly over the property, wondering where the crime was committed. Could it be the back hall, where there is a darker patch in the carpet? Or on the cold spot in the bathroom? (But then, where is there any room without a cold spot?) Why had Randall been killed, and in such a gruesome way? He's never liked the farmhouse, but now he feels positively revolted. If only he could make it the excuse for leaving! But he knows they can't afford to.

So why had his mother recommended it? A case like this would have set the whole county buzzing. She must have known, or she thought he knew and didn't care.

'Would you like another drink, sir?'

The waitress stands over him. Quentin can hardly tear his eyes from the screen, but she is very pretty, so he says,

'Whisky. Make that a double, actually.' When it arrives, he tosses it down, gasps, and says, 'Bring me another. No, wait, better not.'

He's just remembered that he only has £5 to last him till the next day.

9

Up on Dartmoor

As soon as she gets home, Sally exhales. It's as if she has been holding her breath all day long, and though there's a lot of paper-work still to do, the worst part is over. Some days are like that, especially after visiting the Burt family in Trelorn. Joe is trying to cope with a six-month-old baby, two other kids, and he's going mad with post-traumatic stress. But what else can they do? Maddy is never present when Sally calls, or if she is, she's sleeping off her shift. Joe has to do everything. Effectively, he's the mum.

'I can't push her around in a buggy, but our Ella loves doing that,' he says. 'Just as well.'

Joe had many months at Headley Court, learning to adapt, but now he's invalided out he has no support from Social Services apart from what Sally can bring in. He's stopped wearing his artificial legs, and yet he has been told he is fit for work and not entitled to disability benefits. Like all soldiers he refuses to complain, but it's obvious he and his family are not in a good way.

'I can manage,' he says, shifting his wheelchair about this way and that. He still has a soldier's short-cropped hair, a soldier's square jaw and a soldier's patience, but he sleeps downstairs where the children can't hear a soldier's bad dreams.

Devon has been producing soldiers for centuries, huge young men as big as bulls and as strong as oak that she sometimes comes across on training exercises on Dartmoor; and although you couldn't think of a country more different from this one, with its dry dusty plains, the war in Afghanistan seemed to make sense at first, given the suicide bombs. Joe Burt had signed up at seventeen, done well and left for his second tour of duty in Helmand Province last year. He'd returned with both legs gone.

The Army itself has been cut off at the knees. Despite all the promises, despite all the fine speeches made by generals and politicians, men like Joe are forgotten. Sally doesn't think it's a coincidence that, by and large, soldiers come from the country-side where, if something goes wrong, they can be pushed out of sight, and out of mind. If Maddy hadn't had a baby soon after he came back, he'd have had no support. She's from over Yeovil way, and the Burts, unusually, have no immediate family nearby. You need family in the country; not for nothing do she and her two sisters live within five miles of each other. Friends are a wonder-ful thing, but when things go really wrong, only family will pick up the pieces.

Joe won't tell her much, beyond the fact that the Land Rover hit a mine, and flipped over.

'I thought, there's my right leg gone. Then I looked and I thought, my left leg's gone. Then someone got a tourniquet around them, and a line of morphine into me,' he said, adding, 'Bloody marvellous, morphine. Same as heroin, isn't it? And there we are in Afghanistan, trying to stop them growing the stuff.'

'Yes, well . . . it's not safe,' said Sally.

Joe's face set.

'I know. And I know how hard Maddy works trying to keep everything going for us. It's just – she'd be better off if I were dead.'

Sally sighed.

'Dr Viner will prescribe you antidepressants.'

The baby is supposed to be her real patient, not Joe. Men aren't supposed to be frail or ill or depressed, even though they are far higher risks as suicides than women. The Burts have been together since they were fifteen, and despite what people say about young love and early marriage, theirs is strong and true.

'Maddy says she married me for better or for worse, but nobody really knows what the worst means, do they?'

'No, they don't. But when bad stuff happens and someone stands by you, that's real love.'

At Moor Farm she can get away from the world, for Dartmoor is to Devon what Devon is to the mainland. It's a place apart, whose shadowy mounds and deep clefts look like the flanks of some great rough beast, a lion perhaps, especially in the low winter sun. The granite hills that hump themselves into the sky are crowned with boulders said to be the remnants of Stone Age forts, and the people who lived here must have been desperate indeed, for the rain that blows in from the Atlantic is dumped on these hills, so that in winter and spring and summer and autumn the roads can turn to rivers at any moment. It's a place of beauty and terror, where the littleness of man is made manifest.

But it is also home to all kinds of wild creatures, and its rivers and woods, hills and fields are some of the last places in Britain where you can hear a cuckoo or see a wild pony. The Veritys own and look after some of the Dartmoor ponies that wander nearby: they are not wild, as many believe, and Peter has just finished the annual round-up of ponies from the commons. These days, feeding even one small horse is expensive in winter, and they are lucky to have had a good crop of silage.

Sally's house is folded into a valley with a scrubby oak wood shielding its sides. Low and old, its warren of rooms is 'the closest thing to living in a hobbit-hole', as Peter once said, and it looks as if it has grown out of the surrounding landscape, especially

85

now its thatch has grown thick with moss. Its bulgy walls are made of clay, straw, small stones and horsehair, mashed together into cob which badly needs a coat of paint. It has a huge stone fireplace and smells of woodsmoke because on all but the hottest days and nights of summer, there's always a fire burning in the hearth. On the other side of the passage is another room, much bigger, which is used when they have visitors and is otherwise a place for the best china, family photographs, pot plants, and bits of furniture which the animals are not allowed near. Above it are two more bedrooms, for Moor Farm was built to house a family with children – only no children have come.

Sally parks her car in the yard where a stream falls into a duck pond. Facing it are two black steel barns, one for hay and one for the sheep. She doesn't have time to garden, though the walls are fronded with ferns and foxgloves, and on either side of the front door are two granite troughs planted with spring bulbs.

Pete is away with his sheepdog, Jip, but the goose, five red hens and a bantam all rush forwards. She loves this moment.

'Shoo!' she says. 'You wait for your suppers.'

The dog and the cat are curled up together, something people never believe possible until they see it with their own eyes. Of course Baggage will chase other cats, given the chance, but Bouncer is different. They are all one family: husband, wife, dog, cat.

'As good as it gets,' Sally says aloud. 'I'm a lucky woman.'

The Aga chortles to itself. It's the one luxury the Veritys have, though Sally cooks on her Aga, dries laundry on a clothes-airer suspended from the ceiling and has even warmed half-frozen lambs in the bottom oven. They bake better than any other oven invented but some people never take to them, and they tend to be the ones who can't live in the country, poor things.

Sally has lived all her life within ten miles of where she is now apart from when she trained as a midwife in London. She'd enjoyed going to exhibitions and parties, but hadn't enjoyed the noise, the dirt, the way everybody rushed about, and no stars, just the dull red lid of light pollution at night. How can people stand that? She and Peter are both hefted to the land, like their sheep. She's Devon to the bone, and even crossing the Tamar into Cornwall feels funny.

She goes out to the yard at last.

'Here Penny-Penny-Penny!' she calls, and the flock rushes towards her with a gabbling shriek. It's all rescue hens from Holsworthy, russet Rhode Island crosses rehomed from breeders who would otherwise slaughter them at seventeen months because they have started to produce fewer eggs. They arrive like survivors of a concentration camp: bald, half-crippled, crazed by their tiny cages and not even knowing how to get out of the rain. Yet within weeks of receiving proper care, they perk up, grow new feathers and show their inquisitive natures. They never behave quite as a hen should, needing to be herded out every morning into the light and air denied them for half their lives, but the difference is astounding, not least because all have begun laying again.

Sally checks for eggs: only four, which is part of the inevitable falling-off of winter, or perhaps age. How strange it is, she thinks, that hens lay their eggs every day but human females are born with all the eggs they'll ever have in their life, only to lose them one by one.

Her two sisters have eight children between them: Tessa, the eldest, has three grown-up children, and Anne, the youngest, has five, ranging from seventeen to six. So it's not as if the Anstey family is going to die out. But there will be no more Veritys farming this land unless a miracle happens. She's forty, she knows the statistics. Sally chops up some squash, potatoes, tomatoes and onion from her garden and puts it in a pan to roast with a shin of beef. She and Daphne, her sister Tess's husband's sister, swap meat for their freezer, and nobody's ever the wiser.

The door bangs open.

'Heard you had a spot of bother with your car,' Peter calls, taking his boots off in the boot-room.

His face is always ruddy and glowing. He smells of wood and mud, and there's something caught in his unruly grey-brown hair that is probably a leaf. Sally twitches it out, automatically, and reaches out to give him a hug, though these days she can hardly wrap her arms around him. Baggage has got there before her, and is giving him the usual ear-licking treatment reserved for the alpha male in the pack. Dogs: such snobs, she thinks, smiling.

'Some Londoner drove me into a ditch near Shipcott. Such a rude man, never even stopped to check I was all right. I met his wife after, though, poor woman, traumatised by having run over a pheasant, and she helped me.'

Peter chortles.

'She'll have to get used to 'un.'

'They're the ones who've rented Home Farm.'

'Oh, yes?'

Peter always pretends he knows what's going on, but like most men, rarely does.

'Remember what happened there?'

'Do I?'

'Last Christmas?'

Her husband is less interested in gossip, but his eyes sharpen.

'Oh! That place!'

They're both silent a moment, remembering the police going from door to door asking questions.

'Can't say as I'd like to live there myself,' Peter says.

'Well, it can't be left to fall down, even if you're as rich as Tore.'

'No, it can't,' Sally agrees. 'You know what cob is like when the damp gets in.'

'Wonder whether they'll stay.'

'The little girls are at Shipcott Primary.'

'Ah.'

Sally and Peter have known each other for most of their lives: they went to the same primary school – in the next village along from the one where her sister Tess is now head teacher. Peter had been a truculent, stubborn boy, and Sally was his sworn enemy because he was always doing awful things like bringing his slow-worm into school and telling everyone it was a poisonous snake. She would fly into a temper with him for making other children nervous or upset, whereas he said,

'The more you know, the less scary it is. I'm doing people a favour, really.'

That was Pete all over. Had there not been the farm she likes to think that he might have become some kind of scientist, only there hadn't been enough money to send him to agricultural college, even. It was such bad luck: his father had shot himself when Peter turned eighteen, and there was no choice but to take over the farm and try to make a go of it. He hasn't read a book since *The Hobbit*. They watch TV together in the evening; at least, he does while she knits or quilts. But these are the tiring times, and they're both getting on, with no children growing up to take some of the strain. There's no rest from looking after livestock, not really, and then there's the mountains of paperwork for the hated EU when you come in. It's not like raising crops: these are living creatures that need to be fed, watered, kept clean and healthy, and that is every day including Sunday.

'We'll keep going until I run out of strength,' Pete says. 'When I'm too old for farming, I'll sell up.'

Sally agrees, though when push comes to shove she thinks it will break his heart. It's not only the farm and the land, it's the flock. Pete has devoted his life to improving his herd, although few breeds beside Whitefaces and Blackfaces can take a Dartmoor winter. He buys the best rams he can at market, raises the lambs to adulthood, frets over their health, and, Sally teases, would sleep with them, if he could. Yet when the time comes, half the herd has to go off to slaughter.

'It's them or us,' he always says, and she agrees. But they never eat lamb.

More and more farmers have sold up, including the one who used to be their nearest neighbour. That house has been done up to the nines, and is hardly ever used except in high summer, but the land has gone to ruin. There are brambles and thistles growing where once there was turf cropped close as velvet.

'It's always the trouble when people who aren't farmers buy land. It needs looking after, or the heart goes out of it.'

'Still, who knows? People can fall in love with a place, and learn.'

During the last property boom, they had had visits from a couple of estate agents trying to persuade them to sell up. Unmodernised – as they liked to call it, as if the Veritys lived without electricity or plumbing – it would still fetch half a million, because of its views. Pete had roared with laughter, but the agent, a woman with bottle-blonde hair and a string of fat pearls, had gone on and on about the linhay barn, and how easy it would be to convert, being just outside the Dartmoor National Park Area.

'Why on earth would I want to do that?' he asked.

Plenty of farmers had cracked, when offered what seemed like money beyond their wildest dreams. But maybe one of their nephews – or nieces – will be interested in farming, one day. It's too early to tell. Tess and Annie's kids all enjoy visiting, helping with the lambing and running around, though Tess's children are almost grown and gone now. It's not without its difficulties, but when the weather is fine it's the best job in the best place in the world. That's what makes the crime at Home Farm so shocking.

It's almost a year since it happened, and the police have got no further with what the papers called the Headless Corpse Mystery, but there are ever so many things I'd be wondering if I were investigating it, she thinks. Knowing how to use a maul to chop off the head must mean it was someone used to wood-cutting, for instance.

Of course the house had to be re-let. There are too many properties locked up and falling to pieces, and even if the housing crisis is less deep here, they should still be lived in. Tore is a good landlord, unlike old Sir Jerry; he grew up poor himself, and even if he's rich now, he knows the importance of a home. Without people in them to see when the roof leaks or there's a flood, a house can go to rot and ruin in months.

Sally looks out of her window, where the skies have darkened from dark orange to plum to deep violet, like heated copper cooling. The feeling of safety is one she takes for granted. She wonders, though, what she would feel if she were Lottie Bredin, and whether she and her husband are the only ones not to know the hideous crime that happened in their new home, less than a year ago.

10

Cabin Fever

With wild, roaring winds, winter arrives: stripping trees, bleaching grass, boosting bills. Lottie has never been so aware of how little stands between her family and the ferocity of nature as she is now. Lying in bed, she thinks of the story of the Three Little Pigs, and how each represents an advance in building technology – from grass to wood to brick. Home Farm, effectively made from wood, clay and hay, doesn't look strong enough to withstand the assault – yet so far, it does. She finds this slightly surprising.

However, once the rains come, damp is everywhere, bubbling through the paint at the base of all the walls; even some of the skirting looks ominously soft.

'Yes, this is precisely what estate agents mean when they describe a place as "oozing with character". Look at the character, rising up from the floor! The landlord should be paying us to live here, not the other way around,' Quentin says, filthy from digging out the ditch behind the house where the water is pooling. This unpleasant task is one which, to his credit, he has already done once before to stop more damp coming in. Lottie trudges round mopping up puddles with old newspapers and turning on dehumidifiers. Every day, she empties two litres of water from these down the sink.

In the cold and gloom, Lottie feels the loss of London as an ache indistinguishable from the loss of love. It's not the city itself she misses so much as her mother and her friends, the comforting feeling of other people living all around, and a corner shop at the end of the road so that running out of milk isn't a major disaster. Above all she misses her home, with its big windows and high ceilings. It's not only the lack of light that's so depressing. There's a smell which no amount of cleaning seems to budge.

'It could be that something has crawled into a hole and died there,' Janet says.

'Your mouth, maybe,' Quentin mutters, under his breath.

'Yes, a mouse, maybe. If you'd let the cats in, you wouldn't have this problem.'

Lottie sighs and says, 'I'll put down more poison.'

'You should tell Mrs Tore. It's her responsibility, after all.'

Janet's position as the Tores' cleaner and housekeeper has, Lottie sees, given her a status and sense of her own authority she might not otherwise possess. She's not an agreeable person, and her 'Awful Ex' seems to be her main preoccupation, even though she has a new man called Rod whose services she periodically presses on them as a handyman. Lottie was tempted, briefly – there was so much to do, and she hated asking Quentin to do it – but luckily, Sally warned her against Rod Ball. They ran into each other in Trelorn, and when Sally heard she was even thinking of employing him her friendly face changed.

'If you want a word to the wise, I wouldn't.'

'Oh? Do tell me. I know nobody here.'

'Him and his brothers, well, they don't have a good reputation. Who recommended him?'

'Janet, the Tores' housekeeper. Quentin hired her to do a bit of cleaning.'

'Has he?' Sally said.

93

'Why, is something wrong with her too?'

'That's the trouble with incomers. No offence, but you arrive without knowing anything about anyone – who's honest, and a hard worker, and who's been trouble from the day they were born.'

'But Janet is from London too.'

'Yes,' said Sally, without expression.

Lottie feels sorry for Janet, not least because she, too, has been abandoned by the father of her daughter. After Lottie made sympathetic noises about Men, their faithlessness and laziness, Janet would talk to Lottie about her Awful Ex with the kind of relish that most angry women seem almost to revel in.

'When did you divorce?'

'Divorce? The bastard wouldn't marry me. There I was, carrying his child, and he wouldn't do the decent thing.'

'Oh dear,' Lottie said. It was such a common story, and a sad one. 'I had to bring up my son without his father too. Did he help you after?'

'Only when it suited him. He didn't want a baby, but he fell for *her* the minute he clapped eyes.'

The bitterness in her voice was still raw, yet she keeps returning to it like a wasp to meat. Bitter though she feels herself, Lottie can't help feeling that dwelling on her hurt might not be doing Janet any good.

All in all, Lottie really doesn't like having Janet around once a week, especially as she often brings her daughter, who slumps on the sofa and often falls asleep, making Lottie feel guilty for resenting her. She tries to compensate by being friendly instead.

'It's an endless struggle, being a single mum,' Janet said.

'Yes, I know.'

'Then you were lucky to find someone else to take you on,' Janet remarked. (Lottie could not help bridling at this: she hadn't wanted to be 'taken on' by anyone.)

'You're not from round here, are you?' Quentin asked. Lottie can never tell the difference between different kinds of English accent, but Quentin does.

'No, I'm from the Big Smoke, same as you,' Janet answered. 'I was working in a hotel, and one of Mr Tore's staff was there, and asked if I'd like a job. Only bit of real luck that ever happened to me, with a house and a car thrown in.'

'And you don't find it lonely?'

'No.' Janet sniffed. 'Course, the country people keeps themselves to themselves, but what do we care? Dawnie and me both got jobs.'

Ludicrous, Lottie thinks, to be employing her when I'm unemployed myself.

'I hate being poor, Mutti,' she says to her mother.

'Darling, you aren't poor, you're broke,' Marta responds. 'You aren't going to food banks, are you?'

Quentin thinks his contribution is growing vegetables.

'My potatoes are coming on nicely,' he announces, as if these are going to save them. 'We'll be having home-grown sprouts for Christmas lunch.'

She has never felt so irritated by another person in her life. The worst colleague, the sort who picks their nose and downloads pornography during office hours, is less bad than her husband. Every day she has to listen to him, wheedling and cajoling the few contacts he has left for a commission, from book reviews to opinion pieces about current affairs. Sometimes she almost admires him. Whatever else he is, he's not a coward.

'I don't know how you can stand it,' she says, hearing him being turned down again.

'I stand it because I don't take it personally, like a woman,' he answers.

'I'm applying for every job I hear about, but no luck so far.'

'I thought you could set up on your own, as an architect.'

'With what capital? With what clients?'

'This is the most depressing place I've ever lived,' Quentin

95

says, eventually. They look out onto the muddy expanse of grass and a large leafless tree, scratching the sky with its black-tipped nails. 'That ash should be cut down.'

Lottie found it creepy too, but his dislike made her instantly protective.

'It is a shame that there isn't more light in the kitchen. If only the Tores had put a window in the end wall . . . '

They have not yet met their landlords, which rankles somewhat.

'Why bother, for tenants?'

'Well, *I* would, but I'm cursed to live in an age which chooses ugliness.'

Quentin says, 'If it's any consolation, I hate this far more.'

Lottie wills herself not to respond. She's heard of people in their situation who actually build a wall down the middle of each room to avoid seeing each other. Tempting, she thinks.

At least in Devon she can be wretched in private. Once the news of her marriage spread among her acquaintances, everyone wanted to know the details: how she found out about his treachery, how he had reacted, how she had reacted, the details of their rows, what story he had composed to justify his behaviour. It was clear that what caused her agony was to them a source of entertainment, and even enjoyment.

'But how are you *feeling*?' they kept asking, as if she were the victim of a natural disaster or a terrorist attack. The temptation to enjoy the sympathy of strangers was easier to resist, but even Hemani, who had been through a difficult divorce herself, recommended Lottie keep her lips buttoned.

'Don't tell people anything. Keep your dignity.'

Even if Lottie were not inclined to do this anyway, she has to protect Stella and Rosie. For them, she has to not shout, not cry, not express her contempt or blacken Quentin's name further – because he is still their father, and always will be. Yet Xan is just as angry and upset, and in many ways this worries her more.

96

Lottie knows that her husband no longer gives a damn for his stepson, if he ever did, whereas Xan truly loved him and looked up to him. Now, they lock horns like stags every day.

'Fuck off, Dud' is how he always ends rows with Quentin. 'What do *you* know, old man?'

'I just have to keep going,' she tells herself every morning, when the fear and despair rise up. 'Don't look back, and don't look ahead.'

The winter is forecast to be particularly cold, and in January the whole round of tax, insurance, heating oil and so on begins again. Lottie has just £200 of savings left. The £33.70 a week child benefit for Stella and Rosie, which she applied for once she and Quentin both lost their jobs, is now crucial. Quentin contributes £100 a week for his part – but it doesn't seem to occur to him to do more.

The person who does is Xan.

'Mum, I got my first pay packet, and I thought, maybe, would £70 rent be OK?'

'Let me hug you,' she says, and for the briefest moment, he allows this. It's such an unfamiliar feeling now to hold him in her arms – to hold *any* man in her arms – and it gives her a jolt of pleasure. Adolescence has swept over him like a wave, leaving him solid and shining. Somehow, her limp, fair, Anglo-German genes and his African father's have merged to produce a being whose tall, strong, perfectly proportioned body and face is not just a mixture of races but something better than either.

'Is it really enough?'

'Yes – yes,' she says. 'It's fantastic. My redundancy money is gone and – thank you.'

By December, the sun seems to have sunk to a smouldering ember. Frosts turn long grass the colour of old hair, and the east wind whines through all but the thickest hedgerows. At night there are no lights other than stars, and the odd car slowly traversing the flank of a faraway hill. They have nothing to look forward to but cold and dark and quarrelling; and as soon as the girls are at school, it breaks out in earnest.

The depths of nastiness to which two people who once loved each other can sink is not edifying. Each is, by the end of the day, exhausted.

'You have absolutely no idea how much I despise you,' she says to him, after one such round.

'I couldn't care less.'

That's the trouble: in the beginning, everyone is encased in a bubble, like the angelic young lovers in Hieronymus Bosch's *Garden of Earthly Delights*. But inside this bubble are also two animals, lusting, mistrusting, terrified, and equipped with sharp elbows and sharper claws, and eventually the bubble must split into two, or pop. Lottie knows that Quentin must fantasise about her death, just as she fantasises about Quentin suddenly dropping dead. Imagine, she thinks, if instead of paying £500 an hour to a lawyer I could simply become a widow, with the mortgage paid off by life insurance . . . The whole experience is making her feel like a character in the most vulgar kind of soap opera.

So much of the nastiness seems to revolve around money. She isn't earning: Quentin is. She had no deposit to put down on their house: Quentin did. He has profited from his mistake and she has been ground down by it. Over and over, their quarrels seem to be, not about the grand operatic aspects of betrayal but about whose turn it is to pay for petrol. It's the same for Janet with her Awful Ex.

'He wouldn't give us any money to live on.'

'Surely you could have demanded child maintenance from him?'

'No. I didn't want his name on her birth certificate. She's mine. But look—' She fiddles with her mouth and suddenly, horrifyingly, her face falls in like an old woman's.

'That's why I have no teeth,' Janet says. 'I couldn't afford a dentist, so I had all my top teeth out.'

'Oh,' Lottie says, faintly. 'That must have been very painful.'

'It was, but not as bad as what he did.'

'I'm glad you got away, to a better life,' Lottie says.

'She's mine now, all mine, and he's gone to Hell.'

'Was he violent to you?'

'No.' Janet's face closes. 'He was a bastard, though.'

Lottie trudges along the long drive to the road to fetch the girls from school. She passes strange people on her walks, for the countryside is never as empty as it looks. There's a man, a real gypsy with a horse and bender, who camps by the verges sometimes. She always smiles at him, a little nervously because she is after all a woman on her own and he looks odd; he nods but never speaks. There's a farmer who must be local, riding high in his tractor, who often shouts something incomprehensible, but apparently cordial. There are numerous people commuting to and from work, delivering things or removing them: rubbish collections, supermarkets, online orders and then the kind of things that you never see in the city, like livestock and feed and raw materials, all travelling along these narrow little roads with their high hedges and poor surfaces. Sam the postie is the friendliest, though he's also odd – he always wears shorts, and someone at the village school told her he's done time for GBH. All kinds of people live down here, from web designers to white witches. Sally has told her that this part of Devon is 'poorer than Romania', and it's easy to believe.

A veil of light rain hangs in the west, drifting slowly towards her; she hopes she'll get the girls home before it arrives. Being so close to the sea fills the air with radiance; it's never entirely dark outside during the day, though the nights are the blackest imaginable, filled with a silence that is not silence but the creak of boughs and the drip of damp. She is continually astonished by the trees, each of which is beginning to assume a distinct personality even if she doesn't know what they are. Landscaping for her has always been about drawing computer-aided saplings

99

in raised concrete boxes, not the enormous, irregular presences which punctuate hedgerows, lean out of giant stone walls or swarm down valleys. The large black-tipped one close to the house, which Quentin says is an ash, is the most sinister, and when its claws dance against the sky it looks as if it's exulting over something dreadful.

'Settled in at the place, have you? Everything all right?' the other mothers ask.

There are a number of single mothers collecting their kids, even if some have partners. To be married before you have a family is an exception: people here wait until they have children so they can have bridesmaids, if they bother at all. While the women all have jobs in cleaning, catering or caring, the men seem more likely to be unemployed.

'That's why there are so many tattoo parlours,' one remarks.

'Course I wouldn't mind getting married, but only to a man who worked hard,' says another.

'And who took off his dirty boots when he came home,' added a third, and they laugh, as if to say that such a creature would be impossible to find.

Their children seem friendly, healthy and sensible: Lottie remembers how, at Stella's seventh birthday in London, one after another of the little girls who came refused to eat any cake but asked for it in a party bag, 'to eat later'. Already on the verge of anorexia, they had never played games, preferring to have 'make-overs' with their own cosmetics. Stella hadn't liked them either, but she's almost as angry with their new life as Quentin.

'It's so *boring*! There's nothing to *do*. I hate, hate my new school.'

Matters came to a head after two boys marched her over to the goal at break time, and tied her to one post by her long fair plaits before aiming footballs at her. Stella, unsurprisingly, burst into angry tears. The first Lottie learns of it is when summoned by Miss Anstey.

'I tried not to mind, Mummy, but the ball hit me in the face.'

Lottie, trembling with protective rage, glares at the boys, whose shock of blond hair is obviously inherited from their mother.

'You know that we don't find this kind of behaviour acceptable,' says the head.

The boys' mother, a tall and unexpectedly pretty woman in a turquoise raincoat and bright pink wellington boots, bursts out,

'Dexter, Tiger, I'm ashamed of you guys. Say sorry *right now.*'

Lottie notes the Australian accent with surprise.

'Sorry,' the smaller of the two mutters. The elder boy kicks him.

'They can say it, but they won't mean it,' Stella says fiercely.

Miss Anstey says, 'What you must do, Dexter, and you too Tiger, is to write a letter of apology, and give it to Stella tomorrow. One whole page each.'

The boys' faces fall in almost comical dismay.

'If they do give me a letter, I'll tear it up,' Stella says.

'See what I mean, Mum?' says Dexter. 'Even if we write a letter, it won't do no good.'

'It won't do *any* good,' Stella corrects.

'I'll say no good if I want to, snotty,' says the boy.

Stella stamps her foot. 'Stupid, stupid, *stupid!*'

'Oh dear,' Lottie says. She exchanges a glance with the boys' mother, who rolls her eyes.

'My guilt glands are going into overdrive,' the woman says. 'They've got their dad's temper.'

'All the more reason for them to learn to control it,' Miss Anstey remarks.

'It's very wrong to hurt people,' Lottie says. 'But correcting people's grammar *is* very aggravating, Stella.'

'I don't care.'

'Good on you, Stella,' says the boys' mother. 'I'm Di Tore.' She adds, as an apparent afterthought, 'You're our tenants at Home Farm, aren't you?'

Lottie says awkwardly, 'Yes.'

Di Tore and Miss Anstey exchange a wordless communication.

'Listen, why don't you bring your kids to my place for tea?' Di's smile is disarming. 'Go on. I'm dying to talk to a grown-up, and I've never seen a kid yet didn't make up over pizza.'

'I've got my other daughter, too. She's waiting outside.'

'Oh, bring her too,' Di says. 'She's in the same class as Tiger, isn't she?'

'Yeah,' says the younger boy, adding pointedly; '*Rosie*'s OK.'

Lottie hesitates, but despite Stella's angry grimaces she is intrigued; besides, what is there waiting for her at Home Farm but loneliness?

'We walk, and it'll be dark soon.'

'I've got the car,' Di says. 'I'll drive you there and back.'

Lottie agrees, and the tension lessens.

'I don't want to go to Dexter's manky house,' Stella says, as soon as the Tores go off to open up a large Toyota jeep.

'They've got a ginormous TV,' Rosie pipes up. 'Plus an indoor swimming pool.'

'Oh, wow,' says Stella, sarcastically; but Lottie can see her wavering.

In Di's car, it only takes minutes to get to the Tores' drive, which has a Gothic Gingerbread-style gatehouse by its entrance. Lottie has hardly noticed it before.

'That looks like a witch's cottage,' Stella says.

'It's where Janet and her daughter live,' Di says. 'She cleans for you, doesn't she?'

'We don't like her,' Rosie announces.

'Witch,' whispers Dexter, and the children all giggle, as trees swish past.

The road goes over two cattle grids and a stream, then a line of shrubs, and an orchard, and another drive. After a few minutes, a broad curl of gravel reveals a big white house ablaze with light. Lottie stares at its towers, its battlements, its ogee windows and its twisted chimney pots: Shipcott Manor is Strawberry Hill Gothic. The architect in her is thrilled.

'Come in,' Di says, over the bark of a dog. She opens the heavy oak door, which is unlocked. 'Don't be afraid of Bluebell. He's very gentle.'

A lean black hound comes up to them, sniffs, then trots away and lies down by the fire crackling in the hall.

Rosie says, 'May I pat him?'

'Yes,' Di says. 'Now, I'm putting tea in the oven. Maybe you'd like a swim before?'

'They haven't brought costumes,' Lottie says, but Di says,

'We've got dozens for visitors, haven't we boys?'

Dexter and Tiger nod.

Stella says, 'Is there *really* a pool?'

'Yes,' Dexter says. 'With a wave machine.'

'Cool!'

The children dart off. Di leads Lottie past a high-ceilinged drawing room with exquisite white mouldings and a reassuringly vulgar leopard-print carpet, and into the kitchen. Here, banks of gleaming steel machines are interleaved with hand-crafted oak cabinets, all with pointed Gothic doors, and French windows giving onto a wide terrace, landscaped gardens and a view of Dartmoor, dyed by the sunset.

'Spectacular.'

'Yeah, well I told Gore that if I had to live in this country, I needed as much light as possible,' Di says.

'Who's your architect?'

'We got a local guy, Martin Briars?'

'Oh!' Lottie says in surprise. 'I know him. At least, I used to, if it's the same one.'

Di laughs. She is like the many tall vases of white narcissi all around the room, and even prettier than first realised. Lottie has a vague feeling she might once have been a model.

'Are you OK in that house? We didn't really do anything to

it, I'm afraid. Home Farm came with the estate, and we thought it might be useful as a holiday rental, but it's never really been sorted. I don't suppose you are interested in buying it?'

Lottie shrugs apologetically. 'We have to sell our own home in London first.'

Di goes to an enormous corner fridge, and opens it. 'Wine, beer, juice . . . ?'

'Well, maybe just one glass of red.'

'OK! I knew you were a red wine girl. So, what are you actually doing here?'

Lottie shrugs, warily. 'Waiting for the recession to pass.'

'Your husband's that journalist, isn't he? I used to see him on TV.'

Lottie nods, and looks towards the sun. It's sinking so fast that only a streak of gold is left.

'I haven't been this warm since we arrived,' she says, shedding her fleece. (Later, when she goes to the loo, she is shocked by her haggard, unkempt reflection.) 'Why are *you* here?'

'Gordon is a Devon boy, and he thought our kids should be raised here.'

'Do you like it?'

'Yeah, but I do miss the Aussie weather, and Gore is always on tour,' Di says. 'I love this house and that little school is a gem – but the weather here is for ducks.'

'When does it stop raining?'

'July. For about three days.'

The children come in, damp and exuberant, to devour pizza and ice cream then retreat to the other end of the room, where a giant screen descends from its invisible recess in the ceiling. No wonder they don't miss London, Lottie thinks. A gust of wind rattles rain on the thick glass. The dog, which has been lying quietly, raises its head expectantly, and then subsides, sighing.

Di says, 'Bluebell misses Oliver, the guy who used to live in Home Farm.'

'He left his *dog* behind? As well as his piano?'

'He couldn't help it.'

'Why not?' Lottie asks, though she already senses the answer.

'He died.'

'Oh.' Lottie can see a strange expression on Di's face. 'Was it sudden?'

'Very.' She can see Di deciding to tell her something unpleasant. 'He was murdered.'

'*What?*'

They are both whispering, though the children are absorbed in the film.

'Not in the house. But outside.'

Lottie is stunned. A thousand questions rise to her lips.

'Did they find who did it?'

'No.'

'What was done to him?'

'You don't want to know, trust me.'

'No, no I do!'

'Someone cut off his head with an axe. It was horrible. We were in Oz for Christmas, but the papers were all over us because of the connection.'

A burning knot of fear twists itself in Lottie's stomach. It's irrational, and yet she feels, deep down, as if this confirms something she half-sensed.

'Is that why the rent is so low?'

'Well . . . It's not always easy to rent a remote property . . . and I guess a lot of people knew, so I suppose so. Oh,' says Di; 'I shouldn't have told you.'

'No, honestly. I'd rather know. I'd have found out anyway.'

She thinks, Quentin will blame me for this. I found the house.

'Normally, this is one of the safest parts of the UK to live, I promise.'

'And they've found nobody?'

'No, and no head either. Just the axe, which had no finger-prints. Nobody saw anyone arrive or leave, the weather was bad, nobody came by until the postie did.'

There's an uncomfortable silence. Di says,

'We took his dog in. Poor beast. I hope it doesn't affect the way you feel about living there.'

'Even if we were superstitious, we can't afford to give up the lease.'

I mustn't tell the children, and especially not Quentin, she thinks. It'll just be an excuse to leave, and then I'll be completely alone here. She shivers.

'What do you think the reason for it was?'

'A burglary gone wrong? Though nothing was taken, that anyone could tell. He had almost nothing apart from his piano. A lunatic? The whole thing was completely weird. Mind you, the police down here are a joke.'

'I think I should get back, now it's dark.'

Di insists on driving her home, though the girls are reluctant to leave.

'Will your boys be OK on their own here?' Lottie asks.

'Oh, yes. I'll get Janet to pop in.'

'She's all right to look after them, is she?'

Di laughs. 'Well, she's a bit odd, but she's been our housekeeper since the boys were little. She's had a hard life but she looks after the house and dog when we're on holiday, totally reliable.' She gives Lottie a searching look. 'You won't talk to your husband about this, will you? Seeing as he's a journalist.'

'No, of course. Besides, we're hardly together any more.'

'I understand. Thanks for the reassurance.'

'Thanks for the wine, and company.'

'No worries. It's great you've moved in. I hope you'll come again. I think the kids have . . . '

'Buried the hatchet?' They both laugh, and make a face. 'Yes.'

'See you again. It's a long way round by the road, but you can

106

go from ours to yours in about fifteen minutes if you go by the river. It's a lovely walk in summer.'

When they get back, Lottie is glad to see Quentin has (predictably) left all the lights on, and the curtains open. For once, it looks bright and cosy. Surely every old house has had someone die in it? She's no more frightened of a house being haunted than a surgeon is of ghosts.

Yet when the wind howls she can often hear another voice joining in: high, inhuman and full of grief. It's the voice, she is quite sure, of Randall's dog, calling for its dead master.

11

Why Bother?

Xan had always supposed that, sooner or later, he would get a girl-friend, though how this would ever happen mystified him, even before his family left London. Here, it's as if everyone normal in the country has been abducted by aliens, leaving only the very young, the very old, and weirdos like Dawn.

He can't help being interested in Dawn, partly because she's his own age, partly because of her musical gift and partly because, underneath the fat that has overwhelmed her, she is pretty. Her features are delicate and regular, and although her hair is very blonde she has dark brows and lashes. If she still had cheekbones, and no double chin, she'd probably be stunning.

One thing he noticed from the start, when she took off her puffy pink anorak, is that she has thin white lines laddering her forearms. He knows what these mean: at some point, she's been depressed enough to cut herself. He's seen it on other girls, cutting being the new anorexia, but it makes him pity her more. Maybe she was bullied at school – that might explain why she dropped out.

'Are you OK?' he always asks. The reticence they both have about talking in the factory falls away at home.

'I don't know. I'm so tired all the time.'

'Do you have to do night shifts?'

'Yes.' She seems sunk in herself, yet dimly alarmed.

'Maybe go to your doctor.'

'Mum doesn't like doctors. She doesn't believe in them.'

Janet, Xan thinks, is both overprotective and domineering. She talks to Dawn as if she were still a child, and drops her off at the factory after her cleaning for the night shift (though she never offers Xan a lift) and picks her up again in the morning. Surely, Dawn might get a scooter or something instead? He can't help feeling sorry for her. Bundled up in thick sweatshirts and jeans, it's hard to tell just how fat she is, but he can tell her waist and breasts are humongous. Once, he sees Janet giving her a little white pill from a brown plastic bottle in her pocket.

'There you go, my poppet.'

'More,' Dawn said.

'No more. That's the dose.'

When Janet was vacuuming at the other end of the house, the door shut, Xan asked,

'Are you sick?'

'Yes,' Dawn said.

'I'm sorry.'

Dawn turned her blank blue gaze onto him. 'You are kind.'

He looked at her enquiringly, and suddenly she blushed, a colour that swept over her pale face, so that she turned away. Xan had never seen a girl do this before, and felt confused. She couldn't fancy him, could she? He knows he's looking fitter than before, from all the cycling, but poor Dawn ... He'd sooner fancy a seal.

'You helped me when that man was assaulting me.'

'Rod.'

'Do you know him?'

'He's Mum's . . . ' She stopped, and fell silent.

'I thought he might be some kind of weird gay. Not that I've got anything against gays.'

Dawn said nothing. He wondered if this man Rod was round at Janet's a lot. That hot, hungry glare wasn't one he'd like to have fixed on any teenage girl.

He said,

'Do you want to play again?'

'Yes.'

Dawn was always drawn to the piano, and he was consistently surprised by her ability: not only Bach, but Chopin, Ravel, Debussy, pieces he knew were challenging; only she played them far better than he ever did, by heart. She was like some great, waddling bird which, the moment it is on the water, is all power and grace, in its natural element. Yet he noticed something else. As soon as the Dyson stopped, so did she. If Janet came near the living room, she would heave herself off the stool and subside back on the sofa as if she had never left it.

From this, Xan surmised that Dawn was intimidated by her mother, and despite her talent, not supposed to play. He couldn't understand how she could seem so stupid, yet be so musical. It was a mystery which puzzled him, but which he soon forgot.

Within a week of starting at the factory, Katya had taken him back to the tiny house in Trelorn she shared with six other girls, where they had energetic sex on her single bed. Even now, Xan can't believe the calm, smiling manner in which she first placed his trembling hand on one of her breasts. It felt fantastic, and there were two of them.

'You like?'

'Er – yes.'

She put her hand on the zipper of his jeans, laughed, and said,

'You want sex?'

'Yes.'

He followed her upstairs, hardly able to make his knees bend.

Her bedroom is shared with two others, though the room was empty. He could hear her friends giggling in the kitchen below, until someone turned up the radio.

It was nothing like what he'd been led to believe. His generation has grown up with online pornography, largely because their parents were too innocent to realise what could be seen, and so sex felt like the secret his generation had discovered. At eighteen, Xan has seen more weird things involving men and women than his forefathers had probably ever dreamt of. Yet the feel of Katya, the smell of her, the taste, the touch, the movements are all startlingly different. He feels less like a child who has become an adult than an adult who has become a child: delighted, frightened, curious and unable to think about much else.

Since then, he has spent almost every day with her. Katya doesn't seem to mind, and neither do her housemates. The person who does is Lottie.

When he switched on his mobile after the first day together, he saw he'd missed about twenty messages and calls from her.

Irritated, he texted back, 'I'm ALIVE.'

She rang back, instantly.

'Thank God. Where are you?'

'I'm with a friend in Trelorn,' he said, and Katya chose that moment to giggle.

'Oh.' There was a pause, as she digested this. 'Well – take care.'

She's still upset, though, when he returns two days later for a change of clothes and a toothbrush.

'I thought you must be lying dead in a ditch after being knocked off your bike.'

'It's OK, Mum,' Xan says, irritably. 'I'm just, like, having a normal time, with some normal people.'

It isn't normal, though, because Katya could have anyone.

'I like you because you are different,' she said, adding, 'Your skin is different.'

111

Normally, Xan would have been exasperated by this. His skin is his skin, he's comfortable in it, but it's different for Poles, apparently.

'So smooth,' she says, stroking him. 'No hair.'

She is a year older than him; both shrewd and experienced.

'Do you live here always?'

'I should be going to university next year,' he tells her. 'To read English.'

'Can't you read English already?'

She's genuinely puzzled about this, and the more he explains the more doubtful he becomes himself. What is the point of it all, those imaginary people in imaginary situations? Why had they seemed to matter? Surely it was all worthless and fake, whereas to work and be paid is real. His old life, which was supposed to be so privileged and glorious, has already led to humiliation and mortification. A line of Yeats comes back to him, '*Poetry exists in a valley of its own making/It alters nothing.*' So, why bother?

Why bother with the whole stupid conventional future? He's never had a choice about what he should do, just done what he was told, and yet university isn't the only thing in life. What's the point of more education? Cycling between the factory and Home Farm, he feels a kind of thrill in his new fitness, and the ability to earn money with the labour of his body. All the people he'd grown up with live almost entirely in and on their intellectual capabilities, seeing manual labour as something unpleasant and unrewarding, so much so that his mother is the only person he knows who can even use a screwdriver. He absorbed their attitude, and now he's seen it isn't the only way to live. Had he gone straight to uni, or had a gap year, he'd still be the same flabby, unformed boy he was a year ago, trundling along the safe paths laid out by education and expectations, whereas now . . .

As Christmas approaches, they have to work harder than ever. Xan has never realised before that the Two For One offers in supermarkets, known as BOGOFs, are not in fact caused by the manufacturer deciding to take a hit. They are produced by making people like himself work twice as fast, and by cutting the prices which farmers receive. It's cripplingly hard to keep up the pace, even though some, like Maddy, are desperate enough to do back-to-back shifts. Every week, she seems to have aged another decade.

'If I don't do this, how on earth am I going to give the kids a decent Christmas?' she says to Xan.

When he finds out what she's buying for her three young children – the latest gadget that will be broken in days – he's horrified, especially as she has debts to pay off already. How can someone with so little money do this? But he knows that if he were ever to comment on it, Maddy would take deep offence; and in any case, he might be wrong.

They are all exhausted. Such is the frenzy that different pies get mixed up on the conveyor belt, and then fights break out. There are a couple of Romanians who are just crazy, and they'll throw pies at each other or anyone who annoys them. Xan can't help flinching – for a hot pie, straight from the oven, is not a thing you want smashed in your face, but a cold one is also a sticky, slimy mess. But this side of Christmas, nobody gets sacked. All that happens is that Dawn has to shuffle round and clean it up.

'She used to be the prettiest girl, you know,' Maddy remarks, following his gaze. 'Clever, too.'

'What happened?'

'Who knows? She and her mum keep themselves to themselves.'

'Don't they have any friends?'

'Not really, unless you count Rod.' Maddy jerks her head at the man, and Xan grimaces. Rod's wandering hands have slackened off as far as he's concerned, but he remains loathsome, a sex pest who nobody dares to denounce. 'Janet either doesn't know or doesn't mind his reputation.'

'Why is he interested in her?'

It's a rude question, but he's curious.

'With most I'd say sex, but with her it's probably the housekeeping job at Tore Towers. There's plenty as would have liked that, what with the salary and the cottage and the car. You ask me, he's got his eye on that. Unless it's Dawn. He likes them young, apparently.'

Sometimes, when he's joking with Katya, Xan sees Dawn looking at them. He almost wonders whether he's overestimated her ability, but his Oma stuffed him with music almost the moment he was born, and he knows that Dawn played the tiny drop of pure gold that is the *Goldberg Aria* quite brilliantly. Dawn has got the special touch, the grasp of silence between the notes, that is the difference between a born musician and one who has nothing more than proficiency.

Why does she stare at him? Her face is like that on the moon, so sketchy that she seems to be losing her eyebrows.

'Why do people care about who works for the Tores?'

'Aren't you interested in him?'

'Um, not really,' Xan confesses. 'I know he's a sort of genius, but . . .'

'I expect you're into garage or whatever it is now, but Tore – well, he's one of us, only he's an international celebrity, too. There's always paparazzi hovering around, trying to bribe people to tell them stories about orgies and drugs. Even though he's pushing seventy.'

Maddy sniffs, either from disapproval or because she has the bug that is going round.

More and more of the workers at Humbles are falling sick. They complain of fever, sore throats, streaming noses, but Christmas means they still come into the factory, and sneeze or cough over the food going past. Xan can almost see the mucus flying into the meals. He's never thought about who actually made this stuff, but this factory, and others like it, is where almost all instant meals in England are prepared.

'Well, what else are you to do with the bits of meat and veg nobody will buy?' Maddy points out. 'If shoppers learnt to cook, Humbles would be out of business, only who has the time to peel the bad bits? Not me. By the time I get home I'm like every other woman, too bloody knackered. So I get out my ready meal, and I don't have to do anything but heat and eat.'

'Even with snot in it?'

The bosses would be furious if they knew how often, and how deliberately, Health and Safety rules are breached. However, for the workers there is no pride or sense of responsibility, only the fear of losing a trickle of income so small that their wages are all topped up by benefits. Cheating is rife. The tracking documents, called hasps, are always falsified, because to fill them in honestly would mean nobody met their targets. They are a part of the machine, and the machine doesn't care if somebody gets food poisoning somewhere far away.

Xan soon finds he doesn't care either. Humbles is the only big employer in Trelorn, and it's built almost entirely on shoddiness.

'They wanted to call them Cornish pasties, but they couldn't, not being Cornish,' Maddy told him. 'Devon pasties have to have the crimp on top, not to one side. Anyway, pies have made Humbles a fortune. People like the idea of Devon, see, they think it means the goodness of nature, not people scraping a living.'

Her laugh turns into a cough.

Such is the ill-feeling among many workers that some deliberately put things in, like nail-parings or actual nails, to cause trouble. This happens especially when the immigrants, who have been promised full-time work, discover that they are only given part-time.

'If I get only four shifts a week, is no worth it, I cannot save enough,' Katya says angrily. She was recruited six months before Xan, and not being able to earn every day is a nightmare for all of them. However, the immigrants, too, have no bargaining power.

115

They can only save out of their wages because they're prepared to live in what would be slum conditions if they weren't so scrupulously clean.

'British people, they don't want to work hard like Polish peoples,' she says. 'If they do, why so few do this work?'

Xan has lost over a stone as a result of his own labours, and whenever he feels tired, he has only to think of his stepfather to be powered by rage again. He's proud of giving half his earnings to Lottie, and keeping the other half to spend or save for travelling or (if he gets around to applying again) university. He has felt miserable about Cambridge, but Maddy tells him things about her own life that make him feel ashamed of ever feeling sorry for himself, though she treats it as completely normal. If it weren't for her earnings, they'd be at the food bank, like half of the town.

'Are you all right?' Xan asks one night. She looks more and more like a wet hen, her pale face lined.

'Not really,' she shouts back.

'Has something happened?'

'The health visitor thinks my baby isn't putting on enough weight.'

'Oh. Won't she eat?'

'She keeps sicking up.'

It sounds disgusting, but then most things to do with babies are. One of the things Xan likes best about Katya's place is that it's always crammed with adults, all talking and drinking vodka after a night shift. The men have pale, broad faces and small dark eyes; they can look like angry scones until, suddenly, they smile. They turn their hand to anything: building, joinery, plumbing, electrics, decorating, mechanics. Some are only a year or two older than himself, but beside them, Xan feels like an ignorant child. Most seem to be employed by an especially big Pole called Arek, who is some kind of master-builder; when he enters, everyone falls respectfully silent.

116

'He has good business,' Katya tells Xan, when he asks about Arek. 'Also, a wife and kids in Poland.'

She says it as if she is giving him important information.

'That must be hard.'

'Yes. They see each other once a year when we go home, for Christmas.'

'Why don't his children come here?'

'The schools in Poland are better. Here, there is no discipline.'

It's true that the Poles have an almost military sense of how to behave. The tiny, shabby house in Trelorn, though always crammed with shoes in its narrow hall, smells of bleach. Every evening they cook, and three times a week they bake bread, a dark heavy substance that is plaited or twisted into something that tastes completely wonderful.

'Why me?' he asks, eventually.

'I see you nice English boy, and I think – I like him.'

Xan can't help flushing with delight.

'Really?'

Katya gazes at him with her slanting eyes. 'You are not like the others.'

Xan doesn't want to think about the others, though he knows there must have been at least one.

'Well, I'm very glad you like me,' he says, shyly. 'I like you too.'

'I am a good Catholic girl,' she says giggling; and it's true in that she and the others go to the small Catholic church every Sunday to take Mass, like all the Poles. Afterwards, they sit around the tiny kitchen table, drinking beer and eating the rich, spicy food that is always freshly made.

'One day, you Polish will be the ones employing us, I expect,' he tells Katya.

'Maybe,' she says, wryly. 'In one hundred years. There is no work there.'

When Xan returns to Home Farm, he's startled by how different it all is. There are books on the shelves, framed pictures

117

on the walls, Le Creuset pots, newspapers, shabby clothes, and an attitude of self-conscious, mildly apologetic irony and entitlement. How has he never seen this before?

'Katya is amazing. She's had to struggle for everything.'

'Do you think Oma didn't, after the war?'

'Yes, only that was different, surely.'

'I don't somehow think your Polish friends had to eat rats and hide from Russian rapists,' Lottie answers dryly.

'I don't think the Poles had it easy either, Mum. And then they had to live under communism.'

Quentin calls him 'cunt-struck'.

'Just *look* at his expression,' he says, on the rare occasion when they are eating together and he sees Xan staring into space. 'Like a duck in a thunderstorm.'

'What does a duck in a thunderstorm look like, Daddy?' Stella enquires.

'Like your brother.'

'Oh, shut up!' Lottie says fiercely. 'Just because Xan is—'

'*Pas devant les enfants.*'

'*Pourquoi pas?*' Stella demands. Xan groans aloud. '*Nous avons déjà vu les érotomanes sur l'ordinateur*, haven't we Rosie?'

'Stella!' Lottie says, appalled. 'Have you been teaching yourself French?'

'She downloaded it ages ago.'

'You'd be lucky to find anything on broadband this slow,' says Quentin.

Home Farm has other problems. The scurrying under the floorboards has become bolder, and now they've all seen mice scuttling under furniture.

'We've got to get rid of them before my mother and your parents come for Christmas,' Lottie says.

'Oh, must they?'

'Yes. They are your parents.'

'Why must I?' Quentin launches into his familiar rant.

'Marta's living all on her own up in a vast six-bedroomed house in Hampstead worth millions while we're slumming it here.'

'It's her home. You can't ask her to sell up just so we can have a better life.'

'That's the problem with the property market in this country,' Quentin says. 'If it weren't for old ladies rattling round enormous houses, there'd be no housing crisis.'

'We like Oma, don't we, Xan?'

'Yes,' says Xan, yawning, and glaring at his stepfather.

I must send my UCAS form off, he thinks, hazily, but that life of study and lectures is increasingly remote to him. Whenever he starts to think of his future Katya's image interrupts it.

'You like this? You like it?' she whispers, and he murmurs over and over, 'Yes.'

'Xan? Xan,' his mother says patiently. He wakes up with a start.

'Xan, Oma is coming to spend Christmas with us, and I would like you to be awake for her.'

'I could stay at Katya's.'

'No, I'm sorry, Xan, that won't do. Family is family, I want you to be here. She's coming down to see you as much as anyone.'

Xan sighs, and agrees. He does love Oma, even though he resents any time away from Katya.

Christmas decorations are going up everywhere, and Mum has gone into her usual annual frenzy.

'But Lottie, do you know what a Nordstrom *costs*?' Quentin interjects.

'Oh God!' Lottie clutches her head in her hands. 'We *must* have a tree.'

Christmas with his family is a big deal. No matter how cynical Xan feels he has become, he can't suppress a little throb of joy when he sees the familiar decorations. He'd been wondering whether Mum had remembered to pack them, but of course she has. There are the fragile bubbles of red, green, gold and blue, the carved wooden angels, the twisted glass icicles, the pressed

119

tin snowflakes, the glittering silver pears, the tiny birds with real feathers, the gilded Venetian glass sweets which will be mixed with real foil-wrapped chocolates. Right at the top of the tree goes a smiling gold sun, because it is the return of light and life, rather than the Christian ceremony, which they celebrate. Every year, they are put away as things that are no longer remarkable, and every year they are unwrapped as rediscovered treasures, saturated in nostalgia.

'I've been making your presents at school.'

'So have I,' says Rosie,

'Only mine's better.'

'Thank you darlings.'

'I intend to spend the whole of the festive season in an alcoholic stupor.'

'It can't be as bad as last Christmas,' Xan says to his stepfather.

'Why not?'

'Last Christmas was when you came back.'

12

Quentin's Hellish Hols

Adultery, like misery, loves company.

Quentin stays in London as long as he can, the excuse being that he must attend as many Christmas parties as possible, for professional reasons. In reality, as Lottie and he know perfectly well, it's about escape. He hates Home Farm, hates the mice and mud, the darkness shivering with stars, the loneliness. He hates being middle-aged, hurtling towards decrepitude, and the only thing that had cheered him up was having affairs. Why can't Lottie understand that? He never wanted this hideous, unending warfare, he doesn't want to lose his daughters or his home, but ever since he turned fifty some kind of chemical reaction has been going on inside him for which he really isn't responsible. He still can't really understand why she is taking it all so personally.

'It's just sex,' he's tried saying. 'It's not love.'

But like most women, she can't distinguish between the two. Women, especially ones like his wife, are so binary, so black and white, either/or. Lottie can't see that people are messy, that they blunder around making the wrong choices or even no choices.

She thinks happiness is a question of choice, rather than luck. Being punished by provincial life makes it no better, not unless his wife thinks he should shag sheep instead.

Yet whenever he returns to London, it feels like revisiting the scene of a catastrophe.

He's been to a handful of Christmas parties, but especially the *Chronicle*'s. This is held every year in one of the great Pall Mall clubs. Passing between its flaming torches is like being returned to life as it should be, crammed with interesting, clever, stylish people all talking, laughing and drinking twice as fast as civilians. The *Chronicle* has always thrown the best do – it's one reason why it gets away with paying its contributors so little – and under Ivo's editorship it is even more lavish than before, with champagne and canapés, instead of the usual white wine and crisps. People dress up for it, look forward to it, and of course attempt to crash it, but Quentin's stiff thick white card means he is still a player. He deposits his raincoat in the cloakroom, rubbing shoulders immediately with half a dozen acquaintances, and seizes a glass filled with what tastes like almost neat gin. The sound of a good newspaper party is a kind of roaring tinkle, as if a dozen chandeliers are scattering rainbows of merriment, and when he hears it he almost snorts in his eagerness to get into the room.

At the top of the wide marble stairs, sleek and affable, is Ivo Sponge, now disgustingly rich and well-suited. Without his influence and encouragement, Ivo would never even have gone into journalism, yet now his former protégé is one of the leading lights of his generation. He hesitates, for there is no knowing what success will do to anyone. Ivo, however, beams at Quentin.

'Hello old chap!'

'You look well,' says Quentin – meaning, fat. Ivo answers,

'It's just like what Schopenhauer said: "Getting married is like being asked to put one's arm in a sack full of snakes and being expected to extract an eel." Luckily, I got the eel.'

Ivo's wife is beautiful, wealthy, and for some mysterious reason adores him as much as he does her. Consequently, Ivo's nature has expanded almost as much as his waistline. That is the single most irritating feature of seeing your friends succeed, Quentin thinks: they can afford to be kind. They get nicer, and more popular, while you spend your remaining energy trying not to be bitter. Inside, he sees many old faces but an alarming number of new ones. Who *are* all these people? Were he still employed, he would be besieged by the many single women shimmering round the room in their glittering black cocktail dresses, but news of his troubles has spread far and wide.

Many actually turn their back on him, to his anger and surprise.

What started out as an exciting re-entry to his old life rapidly becomes an exercise in mortification. Despite the encouragement of other serial shaggers (who are ominously keen for him to 'live your life', i.e., join them in the Shed of Doom), most former colleagues avoid him. Even people he thought he liked, and who liked him, steer clear. It isn't only professional: some of them had liked Lottie, and taken her side, the women especially. Women do tend to gang up against an errant husband, whether from genuine sympathy or because they don't want another unattached female on the circuit he can never tell; and as journalism has become worse-paid, so it is dominated by the opposite sex. He can feel that they don't want to acknowledge his presence, avoiding eye-contact or moving quietly away when he tries to approach – presumably in case he asks them for work. He chats, or rather shouts, to the few whose faces he remembers even if he can't recall most of their names, but he can see that they don't really want to waste any time on him. Why should they, after all? Few people return favours in professional life, particularly if you are no longer powerful.

A few feet away, he can see Cecilia, his former mistress. She was once in love with him, and he had very nearly left Lottie for her, but now, looking at her, he feels not a flicker. She's very pretty, but, he thinks, more like a lapdog than a woman; it's clear she now hates him for not loving her in return. Is he to blame for this? No, a part of him responds, but he certainly is to blame for seducing her when he was married, and she a vulnerable intern.

The gin makes his head spin, and he feels unpleasantly hot. The walls, hung with luxuriant crimson damask, look as if they're on fire. Other men shout about their own dire experiences in the family courts, and how broken these have left them. The noise is so loud that they can bellow out the most gruesome details in complete confidence that nobody else will understand a word. On blasts of stress-soured breath, Quentin hears about their grand passion, their hopeless boredom, their betrayal.

'You only get one life, so why stay with a person you don't love?'

The person who bellows this in his face is a plum-faced drunk. Quentin can't remember his name, but he's so hideous that it's hard to believe any woman would touch him, or that if one did, he'd ever want to let her go.

Worst of all is when Mimi lurches over.

'What *happened* to you?' she keeps saying, almost in tears. 'You're like Aslan on the slab.'

Quentin feels sick. Mimi was once like a lovely flower, and his editorial assistant. A nice woman, clever, funny – and she probably wasted the best years of her life by being with him. Mimi will probably never find a husband now, never have a family, both of which she longs for, because she wasted that crucial window of time between twenty-nine and thirty-five, pining after him. He manages to get away, furious with her, furious with himself. Circulate, circulate, that was the rule. Civilians who hated hacks never understood that they were not (as a rule) vicious or unkind, simply pragmatic. Everything was work. You drank not to get drunk or because you were thirsty but because it gave you an excuse to move on to the next bit of gossip; and in this world, gossip is the only currency that matters. Most of it is about adultery and affairs. Who is sleeping with whom, who is no longer sleeping with whom, who has taken out an injunction and why, these are (to the sharp-witted) far more important than party politics or news stories.

He finds himself talking to a man who seems to know a great deal about his career.

Soothed by being recognised, he says at last, 'I'm sorry, you are—?'

'You don't recognise me, do you?' the man says. 'I'm your agent.'

Half a lifetime ago, Quentin dashed off a couple of non-fiction books; one, featuring interviews with famous people, had done quite well. His agent for this had been a thin young man with a thick head of hair. Now, he is portly and bald as an egg.

'Of course I do,' he lies.

'So, how is life in the Wild West? Any interesting people your way?'

Nettled, Quentin finds himself talking about Gore Tore, implying that they are not only neighbours but bosom friends; bragging being the first rule of journalism.

'Really? The most famous rock star in the world, and you land up on his doorstep,' says his agent in some excitement. 'This is splendid, Quentin! You know Tore's never given an interview? The last of the greats ... just think of all the stories there. I could get you serious money for a biography.'

Quentin can't think of anything more demeaning.

'I'm not a music journalist. I have a Name. I'm not a bloody ghostwriter.'

'Doesn't matter. Think about it. This could be your big comeback.'

The idea that a rock star's biography could count as such depresses him. It's no good telling himself that everyone else is also staring down the same twin barrels of redundancy and penury: they live in London, not exile. His Questing Vole column has already been cut twice, from 1000 words to 800 and now to 650, with his fee reduced accordingly. Like everyone, he's working twice as hard for half the money, but there are limits.

The next day, after a somewhat bilious night on Tina's barge, Quentin goes shopping. Now that he has to buy his own gifts, it's almost worth having a wife just to do Christmas. All around him other haggard, near-hysterical men are also completing their desperate contributions to Mammon and Guilt just before the shops close. He can afford presents only because he has vented his spleen about the festivities for a tabloid which actually pays properly in return for putting his prose through the mangle of its house style, a sacrifice he now has to accept. He buys half a dozen sparkling things from Accessorize for the girls, some Top Man vouchers for Xan, books for his parents, and knows he must buy Lottie something, too. This quest is the most daunting, as she has such impossibly high aesthetic standards. Eventually, after tramping the length of Regent Street, he spots beeswax candles for £5 a pair. He knows at once she will like them, and suddenly a bristling knot of anxiety loosens in his gut.

Maybe, he thinks, I can get through this after all.

At Paddington Station, people are surging forwards and sideways at every announcement. The biannual exodus from London is in full swing, and a brass band breaks into the theme tune from *The Dambusters*.

'Dear God, no,' he mutters, but the fools actually get applause. Once, this place with its soaring glass ceilings and elegant white ironwork showed him the silhouettes of domes and spires. Now, he must turn his back on it and return to the Land that Style Forgot.

Whenever he sees someone in a tunic, jerkin and furry boots, he knows where they're heading. What *is* it about the West Country that turns minds to mush? There are those who arrive in suits and change into wetsuits in the train toilet, ready for

126

surfing; there are commuters getting noisily drunk, and families joining relations instead of staying sensibly apart. There are large and small dogs, children, workers, holidaymakers all crammed into Second Class, while First Class stays practically empty. It's so crowded that he can't get a seat until the train is past Reading. Beside him, a middle-aged couple chat to each other in a way that would be nauseating if it were at all self-conscious.

'Only two more hours,' the man says. 'Do you think the hellebores are out?'

'Not yet, but the winter jasmine might be.'

They even look similar, like dogs and their owners. Have they always been faithful? Have they never had scorching rows, or are they simply afraid of being alone?

The train rattles and squeaks its way towards the setting sun. He looks out at stiff yellow sticks of willow and the frizz of frosted fields, their puddles blinded by ice. Every hawthorn is twisted into arthritic knots, the incarnation of age and misery. Mile after mile, and he's returning to a house which has been the scene of a murder.

A little hope returns when he thinks of the last. To hell with ghosting rock stars' autobiographies! Failing the discovery of a cancerous lump in his body, investigating a murder is just the thing for his column. *They still haven't found his head . . .* Disgusting, and quite what he would expect from such a location.

By now, Quentin has trawled through every website to find out more about the case. He's read the inquest report from the *Western Morning News*. Oliver Randall, forty-seven, had grown up in Buckinghamshire, gone to the Royal College of Music, and emerged as a professional musician and composer. His parents were dead; he had been an only child. There's a small biography of him online, and some signs of success, composing for a couple of one-off TV shows and the score for a film that had won a prize at the Sundance Film Festival. Was this how he had been able to afford to rent Home Farm? He'd moved to Devon seven years

127

before, working as a part-time music teacher at Trelorn Secondary School. He'd been a popular teacher, expected to continue once the proposed change to Academy School status had happened.

From the school gates, he has learned that three current pupils at Shipcott Primary had also been taught piano by Randall. All the mothers spoke highly of him.

'Did he come to your house for lessons, or did your kids go to him?' Quentin asked.

'Oh, we came to him. It was easy, with him living so close to the village – and he had that lovely piano,' said the wife of the local GP. She had a pleasant face, albeit of the kind Quentin never remembers. 'I wish I could have learnt from him myself.'

'Was he a good teacher?'

'Yes, he was, poor soul. He was always gentle, never lost his temper – you know, like some teachers do,' said the farmer's wife whose daughter was Rosie's particular friend.

She blushed, faintly. Attractive, then, Quentin thought.

'Did you stay with your daughter during lessons?'

'Yes.' The farmer's wife knew exactly what his question meant, like all parents. 'Of course, he was vetted by the police, but there was no point leaving her just to come back again. I spent many an afternoon in Home Farm.'

'Seems a big house for a man on his own. Did he have a girlfriend?'

'I don't know. There's certainly plenty would have been interested.'

'I got the impression he was divorced,' another mother said.

The GP's wife said, 'I always felt there'd been some tragedy in his life.'

'I think there was some woman who stayed with him, some-times.'

'Really? Why?'

The farmer's wife frowned. 'I'd wait for my Lisa in the room next door, and sometimes I'd use the loo. It had a medicine

128

cabinet on the wall, and inside there were, you know, sanitary products. No man would have those if he didn't have a woman visiting. But I never saw her.'

Definitely interesting, Quentin thought. There had been no mention of this in the newspapers. He wondered whether the police even knew.

'Did he teach any adults?'

Di Tore, they agreed, had been a pupil. Quentin raised an eyebrow, and the women giggled.

'Don't think it didn't cross a lot of minds,' said one. 'She's such a beauty.'

'I don't think she has eyes for anyone but Gore. You think, how can it be when he's twice her age, but when you see them together, well . . .'

'She's kept Oliver's dog, though.'

'You ask me, Di Tore just has a kind heart. He loved that lurcher. So awful to think it might know who killed him. It wouldn't leave his body.'

The dog, he thinks, as the train jiggles and squeaks its way through the darkness by the River Exe. Had it been with Randall when he was attacked? Would it have defended its master? Had it known the attacker? Had it been let out afterwards? His daughters say it's called Blackberry. No, Bluebell. The police have found nothing, but that is insignificant. Quentin has a poor opinion of the police. Solving a crime has been helped enormously by forensics, but basically, you just have to keep asking questions. The trick is to ask the right ones. He remembers this from his early days as an investigative reporter. So what, or who, have the police not asked?

How did Randall get in a position in which his head could have been cut off is one question. After all, it wouldn't be as if you'd kneel down as if for an executioner. Had Randall been drugged or knocked out first? If the latter, it might explain not only why he'd been decapitated but that the head had gone missing. Forensics could find out all kinds of things from a blow. If he'd been drugged, then it must have been by someone he knew, and the police were keeping that quiet. Really, though, what a strange and gruesome way of killing someone.

He trudges over to the distant station car park where he leaves his car. A text pings into his mobile: Marta caught an earlier, faster train, then a taxi, so he does not at least have to give her a lift. Such is his relief that the sight of Dartmoor undulating past the A30 fails to fill him with the usual sense of dread. The night sky is flocculent with clouds, and a moon is racing up to herd them. For a moment, thinking of log fires, he almost feels excitement.

Back at Home Farm, he immediately walks into a bauble hanging from a beam.

'Happy Christmas Daddy!' Rosie cries.

'Why don't I just give you *my* balls to spray too, while you're about it?' he shouts, clutching an eye. 'Fuck, fuck, fuck.'

'Daddy, don't *swear*. We couldn't wait any longer to start decorating.'

'We've cut loads and loads of ivy. If you get the straight bits growing up trees they're best.'

Marta, Lottie and the girls have indeed been busy. There's a smell of cloves, oranges and woodsmoke. For a moment, despite his smarting eye, he feels a rush of strong emotion. All through parenthood the boredom, anxiety and horror have been cross-hatched by a sense of wonder at his daughters' beauty, and watching their delicate fingers unhook the remaining decorations floods him with this sensation. He can't remember when, in his own past, Christmas stopped being magical, but the moment Stella was born, it had returned in all its force. It won't last: one day they'll lose it, just as he had done himself. Yet while it remains, he can't bear to reject that feeling that all might be well in the best of possible worlds.

'Drink?' he says to Marta.

'Oh, I'll just have whatever is open,' she says, as always.

'I'm offering because nothing *is* open.'

'I've brought you a bottle of Riesling.'

Quentin draws himself up, appalled. 'That is the ONE wine no drinker touches.'

'Please, Quentin,' Lottie says, in a martyred tone.

To venture into the wilderness Marta has donned tweed trousers, a cerise cashmere twinset, pearls, and a brilliant pink silk scarf that matches her dog's collar. Her thick white hair is immaculately styled, and her feet shod in lace-up leather brogues as shiny as conkers.

'Are you warm enough?' Lottie asks.

'Darling, I am in mint condition, but perhaps, more wood on the fire? Aha, the piano. How did a Bösendorfer come to this place?'

'It belonged to the previous tenant. I'm giving the girls lessons.'

'*Well* . . .' She tries an experimental chord or two, and says, 'Fortunately, not too out of tune. You know, this can be almost as good as a Steinway?'

Marta, with an expression of rapturous concentration, begins to ripple out some chords. Quentin longs to laugh, but if it keeps the old bat occupied he's not complaining.

Lottie turns to him. 'You're just in time to collect the turkey from Trelorn.'

'But we *always* have goose,' Quentin says.

'Too expensive. My mother finds turkey easier to digest, anyway.'

At least he can retreat to his room. He goes upstairs to discover Marta is already in occupation, her suitcase unpacked and reeking of *Je Reviens*.

'Where am *I* supposed to sleep?' Quentin asks, returning in a fury.

Marta gives him an old-fashioned look. 'With your wife.'

'I'll ask Xan to sleep on the sofa, then,' he says.

'I don't think so, he's too tall. No, if anyone sleeps on the sofa, it will be you,' Marta retorts.

'Christ, I only moved to the country to escape that.'

Trelorn is heaving with cars. He's never seen so many vehicles or people; he even glimpses Janet and her daughter emerging from Asda. What a lumpen pair they are, he thinks. Their supermarket trolley is piled high with cat food, nappies, vodka, crisps, tinned ham and plastic bottles of some kind of fizzy drink. Is this what they're having for Christmas?

His mobile rings. It's Lottie on the landline.

'I think you should fetch Xan. He's done a day-shift which ends now. It may start snowing, and he shouldn't have to cycle back in the dark if you have the car.'

Lottie rings off before he can protest.

Quentin hasn't thought too much about what Xan's job involves, but when he sees his stepson emerge from the factory gates, wheeling his bicycle in the shredding white snow, there's something forlorn about him.

He flashes his headlights, hooting, and Xan looks up, puzzled.

'Get in.'

'Fuck off, Dud,' Xan says. He's wearing a black woollen hat that bulges out at the back. Quentin takes a deep breath to control his temper.

'It's freezing, and I can drive you back.'

Xan is too tired to argue. Quentin gets out, folds the back seat down, and puts the bike in.

'Interesting headgear,' he says. 'Makes you look as if you're growing a brain tumour.'

'That's why I like it.'

Quentin smiles. 'How's the girlfriend situation?'

'Butt out,' Xan snaps. Then he sighs. 'Katya has gone home for a month. Christmas is a big deal for Poles.'

'Ah. We're in the same boat, then,' Quentin says.

'Don't kid yourself, *Dud*. I'm not like you, I'm a—'

'One-man Taliban,' Quentin finishes. 'I know.'

Back in the house, the Rayburn is out. Disaster. They ring the estate agent, the landlord, the emergency number for repairs: everyone is away or not answering.

'Is there no other cooking source?' Marta asks, and Lottie shakes her head.

'There's the microwave, but otherwise only the top of the wood-burner. We can't roast anything. Oh, Mutti, I *am* so sorry! You've come all this way and I can't even give you Christmas dinner.'

'Nonsense,' Marta says briskly. 'Quentin, you must prostrate yourself on your tummy, which I see is getting far too big, and fix it.'

'But I don't know a thing about Rayburns.'

Marta fixes him with a look. 'Are you a man or a mouse? *You will do it.* Meanwhile, we prepare a meal. We had far worse than this in Berlin.'

When Lottie's mother invokes her post-war childhood, there is no arguing with her. For the next hour, Quentin lies prone on the cold quarry tiles, inhaling the dust as he fiddles with plugs and oil feeds. Marta turns up the radio. A boy's voice rings out with glassy purity:

Once in Royal David's city
Stood a lowly cattle shed . . .

Tell me about it, Quentin thinks. The wood-burner next door is cracking like a whip, and Lottie is in her element: Christmas is a control freak's heaven.

She hadn't bargained with sharing her bed for the night, however. They have whispered arguments about this.

'Why didn't you *think* before inviting your mother?'

'I somehow thought that as there are four bedrooms we'd be able to put up six people.'

'The girls can't sleep double up, you know how restless they get, and Marta certainly can't be moved.'

133

In Quentin's view, the girls would probably be fine sleeping top to toe, but of course the children must come first. He finds himself thinking, *she used to be such* fun *before she had them.* He has a brief memory of Lottie laughing, dazzling as a fish jumping out of a deep pool. How much easier it would be if she were dead, he thinks. No division of the assets, no more rows, just freedom. No, he doesn't really think that. He's just so weary of the fighting . . .

'Well, Xan can't sleep with me.'

'No, that'd be altogether too much like Hamlet. Jesus, Lottie! Am I going to have to go back to my parents' and sleep at The Hovel?'

'Why not? You're driving over to fetch them for Boxing Day and you've slept there before.'

Despair clutches at him. He wants to be here on Christmas Eve, with his daughters, not his aged, dying father.

'I am prepared to sleep in your bed, if you are prepared to have me.'

Lottie glares at him. 'Dream on.'

Eventually a meal is made, with microwaved baked potatoes finished on the embers and stuffed with grated cheese. The children sit huddled together under a blanket on the sofa with their plates balanced on their laps, watching *It's a Wonderful Life*.

'Do you believe in angels, Daddy?'

'If only I could get one to make the Rayburn work, I would.'

'Dexter and Tiger have an Aga. Why don't we have an Aga?'

'Because we're poor, and they're rich.'

'You can do it, Daddy,' says Rosie. He smiles at her, then looks down at an odd flicker of movement.

Beside his mother-in-law's immaculately shod feet is a large rat. It must have crawled out to die from the poison he'd put down. Beside him, Lottie tenses, too. The terrier, fortunately, is fast asleep.

'Mutti, there's a rat – a ratty old pile of sheet music that I found in the piano stool, maybe we can all sing some carols round the piano before we go to bed?'

Xan raises an eyebrow at this, but Marta nods and says,

'Of course, my darling.'

He offers her his hand to aid her rise in a show of gallantry, which she accepts without looking down. Once at the piano, she loses all interest in anything but making music. The girls follow her, skipping, and even Xan comes too.

Quentin and Lottie exchange a single glance, then he seizes a sheet of newspaper and she a plastic bag. The rat is definitely dead. Its yellow teeth show slightly in a grimace, and its little paws look weirdly human. The long, hairy, greasy-looking tail flops down. He can see the nausea in Lottie's face, and takes the bag from her at once, deftly rolling up the limp lump. How many more are there? Clearly, the poison is working; now he must go round to check it's nowhere that Marta's wretched dog can find it.

'What will you do with it?' Lottie murmurs.

'Take it to the bin outside.'

He puts on his wellingtons.

'Just getting more logs for the fire,' he says, not that anyone pays any attention.

The air is sharp with woodsmoke. Frost gleams in the garden, its thin crust crunching underfoot. At the end of the garden, the line-up of overgrown ash trees scratch their black nibs against the sky. All this stuff I have in my head from a country child-hood, he thinks; I can name every tree and plant I see, and who gives a damn?

He trudges to the bin shed. The tomcat and his pregnant wife are snuggled up there together for warmth in some old hay bales, their eyes reflecting in his torchlight. He looks at the little feline family, guiltily.

'No room at the ruddy inn, moggies.'

Still, they are probably happier than the human beings at

Home Farm. He pours them some kibble from a bag, and fresh water.

'Turkey tomorrow,' he promises. Absurd, to be talking to cats because he can't talk to his family!

The voices of Marta, Lottie, Xan and the children come to him through the curtained windows.

Stille Nacht, heilige Nacht,
Alles schläft; einsam wacht
Nur das traute hochheilige Paar.

His eyes stinging, he re-enters, stamping his feet, then lowers himself back onto the cold kitchen floor and lights another match for the Rayburn. Lottie stands over him.

There's a long pause.

'Thank you for not letting my mother see it,' she says, stiffly.

'That's all right.'

It's the first nice thing she's said to him for years.

'Quentin?'

'Mmm?'

'I was thinking . . . you've given up your bed so . . . if you like, you could share mine.'

Quentin jerks his head up, and bangs it on the Rayburn door. '*What?*'

It's lucky she has no sense of humour.

'Unless you'd rather not.'

'Well, I—'

But at that moment, there is a faint tingling sound, and the Rayburn catches.

13

The Deep Midwinter

By now, Lottie is so knackered from writing a hundred Christmas cards, battling through shops to buy special food, peeling vegetables, wrapping oddly shaped presents, searching for the Christmas decorations she carefully packed six months ago in London, putting up fairy lights, taking down fairy lights, replacing several bulbs on the fairy lights, cutting boughs of holly and ivy, making a wreath for the door and another wreath for the table, sewing angel costumes for the girls, forcing hyacinths and making up the bed for her mother in Quentin's room that she is not sure whether she is drunk on gin or exhaustion. Ever since she was told about the murder, she has been sleeping with a poker by her bed, just in case, so sharing a bed for the night with her husband is the least of her worries.

The Rayburn roars into life. Within seconds, heat and normality are creeping back into the room.

'Of course.'

Her mother is right: he is thickening at the waist, and his ears are getting that tufty look of a middle-aged man infrequently acquainted with a barber. Yet he's still handsome. Had he not been, maybe he wouldn't have been ruined.

Few handsome men, she reflects, have the moral fibre to withstand their own good looks. They are accustomed to getting away with all kinds of bad behaviour, and Quentin still has the kind of profile that makes her understand why barbarians liked smashing the noses off Greek statues.

He is not, in fairness, all bad. He isn't a spendthrift or wholly irresponsible. He might one day choose to be better, to be kinder, to be less faithless and philandering, if he could only realise that it *was* a choice. Like most of his tribe, he will never restrain himself from saying or writing something cruel if it's funny, whereas to Lottie, malice is the lowest form of wit. If only I had not idealised him, she thinks. If only I'd known then that there's a window of two years when a man will do anything you want. I got him to give up smoking; he could have given up spite. Though what I should have said to him is that, if he ever strayed, I'd leave. But it never even crossed my mind, back then.

Much of this has flooded over her on seeing Marta again. They know each other too well for words, and by the merest flick of her eyebrow, Marta dismisses country life.

'After Christmas, you and the girls are coming back to London with me for a week. This is my present to you. I have tickets to see *The Marriage of Figaro*, and I am taking the girls to see *The Nutcracker*.'

'How generous, Mutti.'

Lottie is cheered to think of a holiday in the city, even if it feels like an odd reversal. To see her closest friends and some culture will fill the festive void and have the added benefit of annoying Quentin enormously. Meanwhile, there is Christmas to be got through. She sets her alarm clock to start the turkey at 6 a.m., and the girls bounce into her bedroom to read 'The Night before Christmas', followed, shyly, by Xan, who is far too old for this but likes the tradition.

'Let's open the curtains in case we see Santa,' says Rosie. Stella does so, then cries,

'Mummy, look! It's snowed!'

The whole landscape is lit up, silver and black, with the tors of Dartmoor thrusting up against a dazzling spray of stars.

'This is, like, *real* winter isn't it?' Xan says. 'I mean, you could freeze to death.'

'Exciting, isn't it?'

'My darling, how can you possibly find it so?' Marta enquires.

'It's just . . . It makes the house feel cosy.'

Rosie says, 'We've got a proper fireplace for Father Christmas, now.'

'He still has to squeeze through the wood-burner, though,' the practical Stella responds.

She's happier at school, especially since the girls played angels in the Nativity play; at their old primary school, they had only ever been sheep. The village production contained several surprising features, including a real lamb to offer Jesus, donated for the day by Sally.

'I wish you could have seen it,' Lottie told her mother. 'It was adorable.'

'And *what*,' asked Marta with a shudder, 'did they do about the droppings?'

The Nativity play had been performed in the village church. There are dozens like it all over the county, smelling of damp and bats and (very faintly) incense. Shipcott's square Norman tower and Victorian stained glass are almost apologetic in their modesty. The thick hassocks have been tapestried by the hands of generations, including the new one, for the children learn subjects like needlework and bee-keeping, as well as the National Curriculum. Quentin was appalled at this ('It's merry peasants, I thought this kind of crap had been left to progressive schools like mine') but the church, like the school and the shop, is what is keeping the village alive.

The play was charming. Every child had been given a speaking part, and the script had some incomprehensible local jokes which made parents rock with laughter. The biggest surprise was that the piano was played, and the choir directed, by Dexter and Tiger's father.

'I can't believe I'm seeing this,' Quentin murmured. 'Isn't he usually ripping the heads off gerbils or something?'

'Oh no! Our Gore isn't like that at all,' said a villager.

'He offered to stand in as a replacement for poor Mr Randall,' said another.

'Gave £1 million to Trelorn School for a music centre last year. They wanted a gym, but he said—' the first woman giggled and whispered, 'He couldn't see the point of gym unless it enabled boys to give themselves . . .'

Snorts of ribald laughter rose from the pews, and Lottie scowled at Quentin, hoping that he wouldn't describe it all in his column. He didn't have a good view of the rock star; nobody did, for Gore sat behind a pillar so that only the kids could see him. Lottie wondered whether this was a precaution against amateur paparazzi: she knew from Di how much the rock star hated being photographed unawares.

'He loves performing, but he's a private person.'

So their landlord remained a figure of mystery, though everyone knew when he was at home because of the 4x4s with tinted windows which swept along the lanes, conveying session musicians, personal trainers, a manager, a PA and more to Shipcott Manor. Once, Lottie would have thought that absurd: but Tore is not just an individual performer, he is a business upon whom many others depend for their livelihood. He has a recording studio in one of the old stables, and though it's kept locked, she's looked in one of the windows and seen not only an array of guitars and keyboards but a long bank of knobs and buttons which are part of a high-tech sound and recording system.

'I didn't realise my landlord was from these parts,' she said to

Sally, who had turned up to support her nieces and nephews in the play.

'Gore was born here. Changed his surname, because who'd buy a record by Gordon Smith? His mum was housekeeper to old Sir Jerry, lived in the gatehouse with her son.'

'Our mother used to visit him, being a nurse before me,' said Anne. Lottie had by now worked out that the GP's wife was Sally's other sister, alongside the head teacher, Tess Anstey. 'She was a handsome woman, Ruby Smith, people said she was more than a housekeeper if you get my meaning – and it was filthy dirty in most rooms. But it was such a huge old place it would have been far too much for one woman, especially given the condition it was in. Sir Jerry was a terrible old tearaway, spent all his money on wine, women and song, never married and died bankrupt. Gore, though, he could play any instrument and sing like an angel. You know he was at Shipcott Primary, too?'

'No!' said Lottie.

'He was the weirdest, skinniest boy according to our mum, though even then, girls fell for him like ninepins. Ruby died before he had any success, and when Sir Jerry died the whole place fell to rack and ruin. It was just rotting away, until Gore popped up and bought it. Spent millions restoring it, as you've probably seen.'

Of course, Lottie thought, the village tom-toms must have informed her. She and Di have become friends in the speeded-up way of parents with young children. They are chalk and cheese, but Di is good fun, and the only person whom Lottie has found so far who gets excited about design; while their kids are friends, it works.

'I'm glad it was saved. It's a beautiful example of English Gothic. Though Home Farm has turned out to be a bit odder than we expected too.'

Lottie saw relief in Sally's eyes.

'I didn't know whether you knew.'

'Di Tore told me. It was a bit of a shock.'

Sally said at once,

'We've never had a murder. Most people don't even bother locking their doors at night.'

'It sounds completely horrible.'

'It was. My sister Tess had to identify the body. He'd worked here, you see, and she – well, she's got a strong stomach, but it still gave her a turn.'

They had to stop whispering, because of the service and more carols, but when there was another chance Lottie murmured,

'Where was he *actually* killed?'

This is the question she had been longing to ask.

'Somewhere near the woodshed, I heard.'

'*Something nasty in the woodshed . . .*' Lottie quoted, wryly. But Sally hadn't read *Cold Comfort Farm*, clearly. She was relieved it wasn't in the house, as Di had said.

'The killer used the maul, I've heard.'

'What's a maul?'

'A kind of axe. It chops through anything.'

Lottie shivered. She'd seen Quentin and Xan split logs for the wood-burner with a single blow, and had been impressed. It had come with the house: presumably, not the same one.

'Does anyone have any idea why he was killed?'

'It wasn't robbery – that's what the inquest said. His wallet was left on him, and nothing in the house had been disturbed as far as anyone could tell.'

'So either it was a lunatic, or he disturbed an intruder. Neither of those makes me feel safer.'

'There's hardly a home in twenty miles around that hasn't been upset by it. From what I hear, the Tores couldn't let that house for love nor money.'

'Do they need the money?'

'I doubt it. He's one of the richest men in Britain. But he's a shrewd businessman. He's got planning permission for a new

142

scheme on the edge of town, affordable housing, and it's on the edge of his estate. He could have just sold the land but he's developing it himself, with the council. Six hundred new homes for £200,000 apiece, and he'll take half the profit. But my guess is where your farmhouse is concerned, he just wanted it lived in.'

'I'd love to see *your* farm,' Lottie said impulsively. 'I've never seen a real, working farm.'

'You're welcome any time I'm home. If you want to bring the girls, lambing time is best.'

'Is the lamb in the play yours?'

Sally laughed. 'That's just the product of our ram getting out too soon and covering a couple of ewes before we could stop him, randy old thing. Any lambs you see this side of March are usually mistakes, as it's too cold.'

All this goes through her head on Christmas Eve. The previous tenant must have bathed in this bath, and slept in my bed, she thinks. Poor Oliver Randall, what brought a killer to his door?

The snow outside still falls, it's freezing. My hair smells of onion, she thinks, and washes it quickly before she has time to consider how uncomfortable drying it in an icy bedroom will be. The mauve bathroom walls make it seem even icier, somehow. As soon as I'm over Christmas, she thinks, I'll repaint it. It's too vile to be endured.

When she emerges from the bathroom, Quentin is there, wearing a grim expression and the striped pyjamas that make him look like a 1920s convict.

'I hope your offer still stands.'

It's on the tip of Lottie's tongue to retort that it doesn't. She says stiffly,

'Yes.'

'Your bedroom is bloody freezing. You need an electric fan.'

'The last time I looked the oil tank is only a quarter full.'

143

Quentin looks startled, then embarrassed. 'I've just paid for the oil tank to be refilled after Boxing Day.'

'I can't pay you back my half.'

Quentin is silent for a moment. 'Think of it as my Christmas present.'

'To yourself,' she says. 'One moment.'

He watches while she takes a fresh towel, wraps it in a long, tight sausage, and positions this in the exact middle of the mattress.

'That's—' Quentin gives a snort.

She says, fiercely, 'You keep to that side, or you're out.'

'Fine. The marital Maginot Line will not be crossed.'

They both open their books. Lottie is too angry with herself to concentrate. This man has given grief to her children, broken her heart, ruined their future and made her poor. He never apologises.

I thought you were the best of men, and instead you are the worst, she told him. Trust is like a bowl, the easiest thing in the world to break, yet once broken its shards are sharp as knives and virtually indestructible. You could perhaps find bits of her marriage in a thousand years, just as archaeologists do pottery.

She switches off her light with a snap, and he does the same. The room is plunged into total darkness.

Lottie lies there, tensely, and then Quentin murmurs,

'*Westron wynde, when wilt thou blow,*
The small raine down can raine . . . '

She remembers the poem, and continues it silently,

'*Christ, if my love were in my arms,*
And I in my bed again.'

Tears stream down her face silently. That needy, warm-blooded mammalian heart is more treacherous than any snake's. Pig, she thinks fiercely. Stupid, adulterous, selfish *pig*.

Then it comes to her that he, too, is miserable, frightened, lonely and cold.

'Good night, Quentin.'

'Good night, Lottie.' There is a long pause. 'And thank you.'

In sleep, people can run frantically away from each other or lie as if thunderstruck. They can kick obstacles out of the way, roll together, roll away, embrace and fight. None of this will be recollected. In the longest hours of winter, sleep claims Home Farm. Even Marta, who usually rises several times a night to relieve her ancient bladder, enjoys an uninterrupted night. The flies clinging to the memory of summer; the mice dreaming of cats; the cats dreaming of mice; the little birds turning to ice inside hedgerows all slumber on.

At dawn, there's an insistent tapping on the window. They sit up, puzzled, and Quentin draws the curtain. There, on the slate ledge, is a robin. Its bright orange breast is fluffed up against the cold, its spindly legs look no bigger than threads. It taps again.

'Oh!' Lottie exclaims in delight, and Quentin opens the window. The robin swoops in on a knife of cold to perch on the frame of the wardrobe. It chirps again. They both laugh.

'This is my gardening robin.'

'It must be desperate to be so tame.'

'Or hungry.'

Lottie says, in a panic, 'My goodness, the turkey! It'll be *raw*.'

'I put it into the oven an hour ago while you were sleeping.'

'Thanks.'

They exchange glances, slightly puzzled by how polite they are able to be. But why shouldn't good manners come into marriage? Lottie thinks. We say please and thank you to everyone else in our lives, just somehow not to each other.

A moment later, the girls bounce in to open their stockings. They're at the age when, like the Mayans, they value chocolate more than gold. The traditional trinkets and treats are discovered with glee. Only then is the robin noticed.

'Oh!' Rosie whispers.

'Is he *real*?'

'Yes.'

The girls become very still, thrilled. Eventually, the robin flies whirringly downstairs to the kitchen, where it eats a number of breadcrumbs with a bold yet inquisitive air. Then it fluffs its feathers up, and settles in on the Christmas tree to roost. Guiltily, Lottie puts on her thickest socks and jumper, and fills up the bird feeders outside. She has bought some fat balls and peanuts; the poor things that have survived the night attack these ravenously. The feeders will be emptied by nightfall.

Quentin is chopping and frying. He loves cooking as she never will, and seeing him relaxed like this makes her less stiff towards him.

'I'll do the potatoes, and the sprouts,' she says.

There is comfort in following the pattern ordained by habit, the BBC and family tradition. Xan wakes at noon, and shortly after this, Quentin's parents arrive in their ancient red Ford, parking as close as possible to the front door. Naomi supports her husband, who is so frail he can hardly walk. She's still bright and strong; like Marta, she has an active life and many friends and interests. The two women like each other, sharing a keen interest in their grandchildren.

'Ian sends his love,' her mother-in-law says. 'The champagne is from him.'

'Thanks,' Quentin says. His indifference to his grown-up son is yet another thing that irks Lottie. She'd like her daughters to get to know their half-brother; his exclusion is rude, and wrong. Naomi, she discovered not so long ago, has been communicating with Ian ever since childhood, and says he's lovely, but she's barely met her stepson because Quentin finds him boring.

After everyone is gathered, the children are allowed to open their gifts in a frenzy of delight. Then the adults follow.

'Oh darling, this is lovely!' Lottie exclaims, stroking her new cashmere scarf. Its exquisite softness, and pure green dye must have cost Xan a good deal more than the stipulated maximum of £10. He's gruff about how he can afford it now he's working; I must talk with Marta about university, Lottie thinks. She goes to the kitchen with Naomi to make the final preparations for the lunch. The table, with its red cloth and centrepiece of holly and ivy berries surrounding tea-lights in tumblers, looks lovely.

'So, are you happy here?' Naomi asks, once the pots are bubbling.

'Apart from the circumstances, fine,' Quentin says, coming in.

Lottie turns away, and rests her forehead on the cold glass of a window. There's no point being nice to her husband, because the moment she tries he's vile again.

'Are you OK?' Xan asks.

'Not really.'

Suddenly, unexpectedly, he puts his arms around her and gives her a quick hug.

'We'll be fine, Mum. We love you, even if Dud doesn't.'

'I know – I know. Thanks.'

If only, Lottie thinks, that was enough for me.

14

Swim, or Drown

Left alone with Quentin after Christmas, Xan is apprehensive. They've not spent any time together for years, and Xan's rage at his stepfather is even higher because of Quentin's behaviour to his own parents.

Xan is fond of Hugh and Naomi. Naomi has always been kind and warm, as well as a fantastic cook and potter: he still has some of the quirky little animals she made for him as a child – toads, pigs and fish, the glazed clay grooved or scaled – they might have been twee but are collected as art. He can remember what Hugh was like only a few years ago, how vigorous and keen to engage in discussions about books and ideas, encouraging him to read not only English literature but European, American, African, Russian and Indian. He never dismissed what Xan said, drawing out his ideas, praising them, reformulating them and asking him questions. Some years later, Xan realised that his stepfather's father had been a brilliant teacher, as well as a poet.

They loved many authors in common, and it did not matter that Xan was encountering them for the first time, and Hugh for the last. 'Inside a great novel, or poem, or play,' he told Xan, 'there is no time, only a place of joy where readers may meet and embrace each other. To share a love of reading is to share the best love of all, because although there is no democracy of taste, there is one of feeling.'

The Bredins' cottage was effectively insulated by its floor-to-ceiling shelves of books; their cat-litter tray was lined with copies of the *TLS* (which justified the cost of subscriptions because it occasionally published Hugh's poems). Toppling towers of the *Spectator*, the *New Statesman*, the *London Review of Books* and the *Rambler* were piled by the loo – whether as emergency literature or emergency toilet paper was never entirely clear – and all kinds of things from a wobbly table to a door which tended to swing open were kept functioning by wedges of paperbacks. It was eccentric, and almost heroically filthy, but also a place of enchantment. Xan loved staying up by the fire, talking to Hugh until long after midnight, when his family visited.

'I wish Quentin liked books as much as you do,' he said.

'My son doesn't read,' Hugh told him. 'That is, he reads about history, but history is just a higher form of journalism. People like him think facts are the truth.'

'Why aren't they?'

'Because, dear Xan, facts are not synonymous with truth.'

'Is that why you don't get on?' Xan asked.

'Partly,' said Hugh. 'He certainly doesn't see the point of me.'

Quentin's contemptuous behaviour to his father was almost painful to see. Even with Hugh visibly waning, it was Xan or Lottie or the long-suffering Naomi who checked that the old man was warm enough, who brought him tea or helped him to the toilet. At lunch, Hugh sat in a chair piled with cushions, and even then could only manage a couple of mouthfuls of mashed potatoes and gravy, accompanied by several stiff gin and tonics which, as it was Christmas Day, Naomi allowed him. He went back to lie on the sofa again afterwards, supported by Xan.

'Bet the girls are all chasing you, hey?'

'I do have a girlfriend. She's Polish.'

'Is she? Good people the Poles. Fought with us in the war, when they weren't helping Nazis murder Jews. Thanks, dear boy. I hope you meet my other grandson, Ian.'

Xan was touched at being called this.

'I'd like that.'

'Good views here. Reminds me of our cottage, when we first moved in.'

Xan came and sat by him. Despite his relationship with Katya, he felt lonely and deeply hurt by his friends' neglect. Neither Bron nor Dylan had bothered to message him since he moved down; they hadn't even sent him texts on Christmas Day.

'Read any good books lately?' Hugh whispered. It was an old joke between them.

'I'm not reading now I'm working in the pie factory,' Xan said.

'Ah. Not even Orwell?'

Xan knew that he was being teased, but winced.

'I have read *Animal Farm*.'

'Try *Down and Out*. Much better.'

Quentin's father shut his eyes.

Xan feels a compassion that is so close to revulsion that there is hardly a difference between them. Hugh is already like a ghost of himself, yet how can such a huge personality vanish? Both he and Naomi are worried and sad about Mum and Dud, he knows. Hugh calls his son a bloody fool.

'Would he listen if you said anything?'

'No. Besides, it'd be a case of, Do as I say, not what I've done.'

The hypocrisy of the whole situation between his mother and Quentin is what gets to Xan most – the pretence that things are normal, when they're not. He was shocked to find out that they had slept in the same bed for two nights. Stella asked him if they were 'sexing' again, but he hopes not. His mother isn't that stupid.

'So – boys together, then,' Quentin says, when Lottie and the girls leave with Marta.

'I wouldn't call either of us *boys*.'

It gives Xan a stab of satisfaction to see Quentin wince. He hates being reminded that he's an old man. Presumably he's staying behind over the New Year because nobody in London will put up with him; Xan, though also invited to stay with Oma, is determined to earn as much as he can at the factory. Deprived of the immigrant shift workers, Humbles are actually paying overtime to their remaining workers – which is to say, an extra 50p an hour. No wonder Maddy and the other Devonians say that next election, they'll vote UKIP, because nobody else cares. Xan has always despised anti-immigrant feelings, but out here he can, reluctantly, see that it might be different. Going in to work is weird, because he recognises almost nobody apart from Dawn, drifting about with her mop and trolley. She's fatter than ever, her stomach sticking out even under the overalls. Xan gives her a smile.

'Hi Dawn,' he says. 'How are you?'

She bobs her head.

'You should come round and play the piano again. You haven't been for a while.'

'I can't.'

What does she do during daylight hours, when not pushing a mop in the factory? The desolation of her life strikes him.

'I'm sorry,' he says. For a moment her face seems to swim up out of the fat that has overwhelmed it, like a diver coming to surface.

'I wish—'

'Can I help you?' he asks, on impulse.

She hesitates, then shakes her head, turns away and shuffles off. Xan sighs. Katya has noticed Dawn staring at him, and remarked on it with startling unkindness ('She is like pig, why do the English get so fat?'), and yet there's something about her. Such a waste, he thinks, remembering her playing.

151

He has spent two days in Custard, which is a steel vat the size of a jacuzzi, filled with a slowly swirling yellow gloop, kept just above freezing. New batches of egg powder, water, milk and some kind of thickening agent must be made up and poured in every ten minutes to replace what is piped out to fill the sweet pies. It's a particularly unpleasant job, even if it's less boring than pushing pies into lines.

The bloke who works with him is chattier than normal, and like Maddy, local. He once had his own shopfitting business in Trelorn, until the recession finished it off. Two years away from being able to claim his pension, and Humbles is the only work he can get. Custard Man (Xan never learns his name) is both too old and too intelligent for the work, and has hurt his back pouring water into the vat, but he can't stop.

'I'd never do it if I had any choice, but if I don't work, I don't eat. They keep putting the pension age up and up, and haven't a clue what it's like to do physical labour when you're over sixty. I never used to be a socialist until I worked here, but I am now,' he said. 'If I thought Labour still cared about workers, I'd vote for them, but no politician gives a damn, do they?'

Often, Xan has felt sunk in a dream. It's becoming increasingly hard to think of any life beyond the factory. At midnight in the canteen, he caught sight of Dawn again. Her face was waxy yellow.

'Are you all right?' he asked.

'I'm cold,' she said.

It's warm in the canteen, and Xan wondered what to say next.

'You're pretty good at playing the piano.'

Her face brightened for a moment.

'My hands remember.'

'Especially the Aria from Bach's *Goldberg Variations*,' he prompted.

'I liked those.'

It sounds as if she's talking about something that happened a hundred years ago.

'Who taught you?'

She didn't answer, but just as the bell went for them to return, she seized his wrist, her cold fingers making him shiver.

'What is it?'

'Help me,' she muttered. She pressed something into his hand. It was a tissue with some brownish red spots on it.

'What's wrong?'

'Look at my blood.'

'What? Are you bleeding?'

Dawn started to speak, then slumped to the ground.

There was a moment of shock, then a general hum of concern as others rushed forward.

'Should we call a doctor?'

'Anyone have a number for her mum?'

One of the managers came down, and made her sit with her head between her knees. It was strange to find them caring enough about one of the workers to do so; but they weren't bastards, just stuck in the same system. Dawn recovered, though she seemed to be in pain, and left before the end of her shift.

'She shouldn't be working here at all,' Maddy muttered. 'She should be at school.'

'Why isn't she?'

'They must need the money.'

Dawn has not returned to work for almost a week, being off sick, Janet said. Cycling to and from the factory, Xan wonders what she meant. What did she mean, *Help me*? Help her how? He has kept the tissue in the plastic bag that held his sandwiches. It wasn't used, but neatly folded.

'Why don't we go to the pub?' Quentin asks. It's New Year's Eve, and the TV is full of shrieking celebrities in sequins pretending to get in a party mood.

'All right. I'm bored enough for anything.'

'The Shipcott Arms isn't bad.'

'I'll only come out with you if we go to town.'

153

Rain and mud spatter the windscreen as they drive to Trelorn, the humped hills of Dartmoor discernible as deeper areas of darkness against the night. The lodge lights at the Tores' gates shine through the drizzle with a dim, greenish tinge, like corpse-lights. Dawn must be in there, ill and with nobody but Janet for company. Xan shivers.

'What a climate, eh? Straight off the Atlantic,' Quentin says.

Trelorn, a sodden mound of greyish render and scaly slate, looks utterly deserted, the multicoloured lights strung up along the main street swaying and blinking.

'You know, in Italy or France, a small town this size would have cafés and a restaurant in a square,' Quentin says. 'People would be walking around in fashionable clothes, and there would be flowers, and entertainment, and *life*.'

'An Internet café would be good,' Xan agrees. 'I wonder why there isn't one.'

'They're all sitting at home watching pirated DVDs over a single can of strong lager from Morrisons.' Quentin jerks his head at an off-licence which is boarded up. 'Madness! This part of the country has the best meat, the best fish and the best ice cream, yet finding a decent place to eat is like looking for gold.'

'Maybe you should start one yourself.'

'What, and live down here? I'd sooner scoop my eyes out with spoons.'

They go into a pub. Every head is white, and every head turns to stare at them. Nobody speaks. Xan and his stepfather sit by the sullen fire, sipping warm beer and munching Twiglets to occasional bursts of laughter from the wall-mounted TV.

'I used to be on that,' Quentin mutters.

'Sorry?'

'The show.'

'Oh. It's crap.'

'Yes, it's become worse since I left it.'

There seems no point in staying, so they move on to the bar of

Trelorn's only hotel, the White Hart. It has Union Jacks dripping from twin poles on the front and a big plastic stag crouching over the front door as if too exhausted to run anywhere else. Inside, the lobby smells of gravy.

Quentin orders them a double whisky and soda each, then slumps into a chair by the fire.

'Well, if the next year is like this one, we're fucked,' he says.

'Cheers,' Xan says. Quentin drains his glass, then looks round.

'Why is it that people never seem to understand that you should never, ever, put lighting in the middle of the ceiling? Are they *trying* to make everyone who sits here look like death?'

Quentin is definitely on the way to getting drunk, because after pronouncing this loudly, he gets up and switches off the offending light. Nobody seems to object. Deprived of its noonday glare, with lamps on at the side, the room does look a little more inviting.

'Hello Xan,' says a middle-aged woman he vaguely recognises. 'I'm Sally Verity, remember me?'

'Oh, um, yes,' he says.

'Pete and I thought we'd see the New Year in somewhere.' Sally smiles at the burly, red-faced man beside her, sipping a whisky and looking uncomfortable. 'And this is your stepfather I think?'

'Oh, yes. Haven't you met?'

'Only in passing,' Sally says dryly.

Quentin, ignoring her, marches over and turns off the drizzle of pop music coming out of the concealed speakers.

'Utter and absolute shit. You know, every morning I wake up and think, the best years of my life have gone,' Quentin says. He looks at Xan, intently. 'You *need* to get out of here. Are you going to go to university?'

Embarrassed this is being said in public, Xan mutters, 'The deadline is the middle of January.'

'So you've missed reapplying for Oxbridge.'

Xan shrugs. 'I'm rejecting them, not the other way about.'

'Don't you realise, it's up to you? You're an adult now, and nobody will help you unless you help yourself. Have you done a new Personal Statement?' Quentin asks. 'I expect you won't listen, but if you do, write about working in a factory.'

'Why should they care? All they're interested in are my grades, and I fucked them up.'

'What have you learnt from it?'

'I've learnt that I'm a spoilt dick-head.'

Quentin sighs.

'Do you think university is just about passing exams?'

'Well, wasn't yours?'

'No,' says his stepfather. 'In my day, it was about learning to *think*, and that's something I use every day of my professional life.'

'University will just land me with giant debts.'

'Really? Americans are quite used to paying almost twice as much for their education, and they do that because they know that graduates have a better life.'

Xan feels tears of anger and shame rise to his eyes.

'There's no point in my going to uni, because the only place I want to go to doesn't want me. I'm a failure.'

'There's nothing the matter with you, Xan, other than a sense of entitlement.'

'That's so rich, coming from you of all people.'

To distract himself from his growing wish to punch Quentin on the nose, Xan walks over to the other side of the room. Another bloody piano. Maybe they breed with each other at night. He sits, and thumps out a couple of angry chords.

'Go ahead,' says Sally, kindly, and Xan, after a couple of experimental ripples, plunges in.

A long time ago, he was told by his Oma that jazz was inspired by the rhythm of the trains carrying slaves escaping from the Deep South in America to the North and freedom. Whether this was true or not, he didn't know, but he learnt to play it

156

as a bear lays down fat for the long winter months. The heart-stopping beat, the chords of pain, joy and forgiveness, an entirely new kind of music forged out of suffering and courage. His rage at Quentin, his frustration at being here, his uncertainties about the future, his amazement at Katya, the monotony of his job, the longing to escape, his loneliness all flow down his arms and out onto the keyboard.

When Xan stops, he's aware that Sally and her husband are smiling. A couple of other people he hadn't noticed in the room clap.

'Can you play another?' someone asks.

'Er – sure,' Xan says. His brain is pleasantly fuzzy with the whisky, and his fingers kick out 'Ain't Misbehavin'', 'Boogie Woogie Stomp', 'Handful of Keys' and 'I'm Goin' to Sit Right Down and Write Myself a Letter'. The guests listen as if they've never heard these before: maybe they haven't. More and more people come from out-side – it's as if the music is somehow reeling them in from the cold and dark of the dying year to buy drinks, and talk, and smile and clap, and buy more drinks, including some for Xan. He can see Quentin and Sally deep in conversation, the last thing he'd have expected, and Peter is talking to someone else, but they're also lis-tening. As he plays, something in him steadies.

Long before, everything about playing the piano came easily, until inevitably he hit the first of many plateaus. The notes that had entered so easily through his eyes and into his fingers turned to clots of wriggling tadpoles that swam through the bars on the page.

It was a terrible feeling, one mistake cleared up only to be replaced by the next. He couldn't breathe. His fingers felt like sausages, until he'd thrown up his hands in a rage and exclaimed,

'I can't. It's too hard.'

Marta had said, sternly,

'You are climbing a stair, and to rise up it to the next level will take everything you can summon. But you *will* go up it, and then

157

you will wonder why you found it so difficult, until the next step, and then the next. Do not be afraid! Do not listen to the voice that tells you, I can't, only to the one that tells you, I can. Life is struggle. Everyone who lives now, or has ever lived, is plunged into despair over and over like a swimmer falling into the raging sea, and must swim, or drown. To swim, all you need do for now is to learn to play this little piece of music, this beautiful little piece. Believe you can do it, and you will.'

Later, Xan called Oma's speeches of this kind 'matronising', a different concept from patronising, being more benign, if no less annoying. Yet she was right. The tadpoles untangled (until the next time and the next) and now he can play for pleasure.

An invisible warmth spreads and relaxes in the room. He plays riffs on the Beatles, which they especially like, and then some begin to sing. One woman who has multiple piercings in her ears introduces herself as Lily Hart, the hotelier's daughter. She stands there with a baby on her hip and two more kids playing on the floor, and belts out 'Here Comes the Sun' with one of those singing voices that encourage other people to sing better. Even Quentin has joined in.

At midnight, he stops so that they can all wish each other Happy New Year. By now, the room is actually crowded, and everyone is smiling and friendly.

'Best night we've had here in ages,' one says. 'Simon, you should do this more often.'

'It wasn't my idea, it just happened, thanks to this young chap.'

Quentin says, 'Time we got back home, Xan.'

'Are you local?' one of the tweedy men asks, in mild surprise.

'We live at Shipcott. My son is staying with us until he goes to university.'

Xan is startled to hear himself referred to in this way by Quentin; then he thinks, He probably wants to make it clear I'm not his boyfriend.

'Ah.' The tweedy man pauses. 'I wonder . . . What's your name?'

'Alexander Bredin. But people call me Xan.'

'Well, Xan, maybe you'd be interested in coming in and playing again. Saturday evenings.'

'How much?' Quentin asks, before Xan can open his mouth.

'Say . . . twenty pounds for two hours.'

Quentin snorts. *'Ten pounds an hour?'*

'I'll take it,' Xan says, glowering at him.

'This is my mobile number,' the man says, giving him a card. 'Simon Hart. Call me.'

Xan takes it, and when they go out into the dark, Quentin says,

'Do you still think there's no point in anything?'

'Maybe not,' Xan says, and this time, when they go out into the New Year, he makes up his mind to try again.

15

A Far Better Place

Christmas is always a sad time of year for Sally, because as a health visitor without children of her own, she's often out covering for those with families. Her workload has almost doubled since mid-December, and this year is going to be a cold winter.

Peter, rising in the dark to check the water troughs for the livestock, has to break the ice not just with a hammer but a blowtorch. In a bad winter, the springs freeze altogether and pregnant ewes can die of thirst. Sally's hens have stopped laying, and hardly poke their beaks out of the chicken shed. Bouncer curls up by the fire, and refuses to budge. But Peter has to go out every day, without fail, to look after the herd. The snow, which brings joy to ordinary people, is what they are most afraid of. A light sprinkling is one thing, but when more falls on Dartmoor, men and beasts can die.

'What a way to make a living!' she says, stamping her feet to get some feeling back into them. Together, they have rounded up the flock from the higher field, brought them lower down to safety and left them some precious bales of hay.

'Well done, m'dear.'

'Well done yourself.'

A man as kind and honest as Peter is a rare being, even before she adds in the fact that he has a shower every night and has most of his teeth. Of course they can get cross with each other on a bad day. He isn't interested in many of the things with which she fills her life: music, for instance, and reading, not to mention knitting and quilting and cooking and gardening; for him, it's the herd or the land or tinkering with machinery. He doesn't need company, whereas she enjoys the company of others, and her friendships, mostly female, are almost as important as her relationship with her sisters. Some people don't get on with their siblings, but Sally, Tessa and Anne are not like this. Though they are all married, their husbands will never mean as much to them as each other.

'Sisters for ever!' they'd say to each other as children, and so they are.

At times, she suspects that it might be a relief to Peter that they do not have children.

'I love you and only you,' he said to her, when they were still trying and hoping. 'It doesn't matter to me. I don't need anyone else.'

It isn't the money, or the time. He can't understand that a heart can expand to accommodate and embrace all kinds of love. Sally has often come across mothers who are fearful they will not love a second or a third child as much as the first, and yet they do because love, though it feels so unique in each instance, is not a finite thing, but is reborn with each new person.

Sally has so much love to give that, were it not for her work, she feels she might burst with it. It's always been this way. She looks maternal, with her billowy breasts and round face framed by its soft hazel curls, and she feels maternal, but her dreams of actually ever having a child are ever more remote now she's middle-aged. All she's ever wanted is to be a mother, and the sorrow of this is such that sometimes, when alone, she finds herself crying. Of course, she does have Baggage, and her lovely nieces and nephews, and the hens she's rescued – but none fills the place for her very own. Sometimes she almost feels she will go mad with it.

What is so frustrating is that, according to the tests, there's no reason for it. They have sex every few days, mostly the roll-on, roll-off kind which is more about affection and comfort than pleasure. She and Peter are in their early forties, it could still happen, but she knows the statistics. There's no explanation why she hasn't become pregnant. They'd been to have fertility tests in hospital, and they'd told each other the same thing: nothing wrong, just luck.

'What about IVF?' Sally suggested.

'I don't believe half those doctors know what they're on about,' he said. 'I'd sooner trust a vet. Let's leave Nature to take her course, m'dear.'

'Yes,' Sally answered, with a cheerfulness she didn't feel. 'It's bound to happen.'

She always accommodates Pete, because one of the few pieces of advice for a happy marriage her own mother had ever given the three of them was never to deny your husband, even if you don't feel like it. He's totally devoted to her, and she doesn't want to upset him. Yet still she can't conceive.

Sally would happily have adopted, but Peter is definitely not keen on this.

'I can't believe people are very different from animals, and any animal I take on I want to know exactly what its parentage is,' he says. 'What kind of people would give their child up, anyway?'

As far as he's concerned the farm can pass to Sally's own flesh and blood if they want it, as if that were the main issue. Anne has even said to Sally that if the problem is Peter, she can see nothing wrong with a sperm donor.

'He needn't know. After all, you're the one who wants a family,' she said. Anne is almost terrifyingly practical, but Sally can't, not when there's a chance of having Peter's child. Trust and honesty must lie at the heart of a good marriage, or what is the point?

Though having a child does take a lot out of anyone.

Lying in bed later that night, unable to sleep while Peter and Baggage snore in counterpoint, Sally remembers her latest case, when she had arrived at a straggle of isolated houses to see a new mum she hadn't met before. The roads were bad, and the air had taken on the peculiar ringing silence of deep midwinter. When she pulled up outside the new mum's house, the creak of her brakes seemed to echo.

There had been no response to her first ring. All the curtains were drawn, and the house had a look at once forlorn and chaotic. A washing line jagged with ice sagged in the front garden.

'Hello, um, Julie?' Sally called, after ringing the bell and flapping on the letterbox. 'Hello? It's your HV, Sally. Are you awake?'

More silence, and then the baby cried, a sound that rang out like an alarm bell. Sally is used to every pitch of cry from a newborn, and what she could hear made her prickle. There was a note in it that in an adult would be called despair. Of course, this is the kind of thing that health visitors never talk about, except perhaps to each other, but when you've worked with babies all your life you know at once when they are in real distress.

Sally gave up on the bell, and started thumping. The need to protect a child is so strong that she'll break a door down if necessary.

Suddenly, there was movement behind the wavy glass panel, as if someone were rising up from underwater. Then a woman, presumably Julie, heavy-eyed and barefoot, appeared with a bundle in her arms. Under her pink towelling dressing gown Sally could see the swollen breasts juddering with every motion.

'Here, you take him, and keep him,' she said, thrusting the bundle away from her, violently. Sally took the baby, automatically wrapping it more tightly, and looked at its mother. They

163

hadn't met before the birth, but she was another one of those poor deluded souls who'd moved to the country thinking it would be a better place to raise a family.

'How are you feeling, then?' she asked, as if everything were normal.

The woman, tense as a vibrating string, gave a sudden gasp and ran out into the snowy front garden. There she stood, wringing her hands, while rooks flapped and cawed in the skeletal trees and the thin ribbon of empty road spooled before her. For a moment Sally believed she was going to run out into it and keep on running.

'Julie,' Sally called, her heart thudding. 'You haven't even got slippers on, and you'll catch a cold.'

Julie wasn't crying, but she was moaning,

'Shit, shit, shit, shit, *shit*! I can't do this.'

'Julie, you and your baby need to stay warm indoors.'

'Keep it away from me!'

Sally fished out her mobile with one hand, trying to call the crisis team, but they were in a mobile black spot. Very gently, she asked if she could use the landline. Julie paced up and down.

'Yes, yes, do what you want, just take it away. It's destroying everything.'

That's the thing about babies that nobody tells you before, and that everyone tells you after: they send most women crazy. Even the ones who get an easy baby can lose themselves for weeks, months, years. The physical and mental exhaustion of it, the absence of rest, the responsibility, on top of childbirth is too much, and that's without the crippling expense because you need two salaries now. No wonder the birth rate plummets as soon as women get contraception. Yet even then, standing in the chaos of Julie's breakdown, Sally craved a baby so strongly that she felt her arms might float off for want of the weight of one.

'I don't want it, I'm no good at this,' Julie moaned.

'Don't worry, help is coming,' Sally said, with all the calm she could muster.

She thinks of some of the cases her mother, a health visitor before her, had told her about. She'd been retired by then, and dying of cancer, and maybe the drugs for the pain made her less discreet than she should have been; but there was one case she was haunted by, of a young woman who killed herself after having had a baby.

'There she was, hanging in her father's kitchen. Such a bright, lovely girl, only not as careful as she should have been.'

'Why is it always the woman's responsibility? Why not the man's?'

'Oh, I agree. But the father of her child never bothered to take that kind of precaution.'

It was Gore Tore, of course.

'What happened to the baby?'

'Somebody adopted it, I think. But if that poor girl had had better support, she probably would be with us still.'

'Who was she? Anyone we know?'

'You didn't know her, but her dad was a GP in Trelorn. He never got over it either.'

'Was she under age?'

'No! No, he was never like that, I believe, even though plenty of young girls threw themselves at him. So I couldn't blame Tore, or not too much, though I've never forgotten it. I was the one who found her, you see. She knew she was due for a home visit, she'd wrapped her child up ever so carefully first.'

Sally's mother's generation had called it the baby blues, somewhat dismissively. Sally knew that, on the contrary, it could be life-threatening to both mother and child.

'There, there, sweetheart, you're going to be fine,' she murmured to the sobbing baby, putting her little finger inside its mouth. It sucked furiously, which let her use her other hand to make the call for immediate support. Rapidly, she checked all the usual things while waiting for the backup. The nappy was bone-dry. There was no fever. She found a clean bottle and filled

165

it with cooled boiled water from the kettle, and mixed in some formula, but after a couple of sucks, it was refused and the cries began again. Even putting the baby over her knee failed to bring up any wind. She knew that the screams were loud, but for the mother a kind of torture, because parents are uniquely attuned to their own child's cries.

'I can't cope, I can't cope,' Julie kept saying. Her eyes seemed as though they'd start out of their sockets.

The baby screamed again, a piercing needle of sound, and this time it was clear what the problem was. His upper gums were bright red, and swollen in one place.

'Poor little mite,' Sally murmured, fishing around in her bag. She washed her hands again, then put a dab of clear gel on the gum. The screams changed to roars, then stopped abruptly. The child drooled and smacked his lips, before falling silent.

'He's dead, isn't he?' the mother said.

'No, just teething. He's fine.' Sally showed her the baby, now calm, and then put the bottle in his mouth. It was drained inside three minutes, the baby gave a huge burp and instantly fell asleep. 'Nothing is wrong with your baby, but you might want to talk to a GP about your own health.'

Very gently, she had kept the woman company, and when the GP arrived, she took herself discreetly to the bathroom. She wasn't supposed to touch anything, but she saw the piles of dirty laundry, and a load sitting in the machine, wet. If it was left there, it would smell rank, so she opened the door very quietly and hung it up, then put in a new load to run. At least the dad wouldn't have to cope with it, on top of the rest, when he got home.

She'd been that upset, she and Peter had gone out for a drink on New Year's Eve. It wasn't what they normally did, but she'd persuaded him to come out to the White Hart, and there she'd finally met Lottie's husband Quentin.

What a piece of work that man was ... though she knew he wasn't to be trusted, either as a man or a journalist, she'd

166

found herself telling him all about Tore's baby and the suicide. It was old, old news, and why she'd brought it up she couldn't say except that he had the knack of making you want to tell him things, just to prevent boredom from crossing his face. Poor Lottie, she thought. Somehow, her own work has given her a kind of X-ray moral vision over the years in which she knows whether somebody is a good or bad person – Sally is convinced of this – and Lottie, she has no doubt, is one of the former. But Quentin, well, even if he hadn't driven her into a ditch, he's what therapists call a narcissist, and what she calls selfish. Lottie deserves better.

Sally tucks herself deeper into the duvet. Outside, Jip is barking at something – a rat, or a shadow probably. He gets like that sometimes, now he's old. When they'd got him, ten years ago, Sally had been thirty, already older than the woman with PND.

'Is your partner helping you?'

'He's driving his lorry, mostly.'

'Where is he now?'

Julie burst out, with passionate anger,

'It's different for him, he's not chained to it like me. I can't stand it, the worry, the noise, it just goes on and on and on.'

Sally had been upset both for the mother and her baby. Children don't suit everyone, but how do you know in advance? If you were rich you could let other people do some of the heavy lifting – or most of it – which might be why the rich have as many kids as the very poor. Tore is said to have fifteen, or is it sixteen, all by various women and most unmarried.

Driving back past the entrance of Shipcott Manor, she turned her head. She always does this, perhaps in hope of glimpsing the mysterious Tore; but the person she saw was Rod Ball, whose foxy face and insatiable appetite for women keeps all the HVs busy. Sally stiffened in her seat, and pulled over, watching him in her rear mirror. What was he doing there, and how had he got in? Every bad thing that happened in the area seemed to be down to

167

the three Ball brothers, only they never got caught. They'd been interviewed by the police after the murder, but not only had they all given each other alibis but they had witnesses for the day.

But then Janet appeared, and the couple exchanged a long kiss. She wondered if the Tores knew that he was sleeping with their housekeeper . . . I wouldn't be leaving any valuables around if I were in their shoes, Sally thinks, back in her own bed that night. Something else is nagging on the edge of her consciousness, only she's too tired to remember.

She sighs and turns over. They'll be lambing soon. It's an endless cycle, rearing the new stock, replacing the old, being screwed by the supermarkets to sell at lower and lower prices. Many dairy farmers give up when milk costs less than bottled water; there's no point. Everyone wants cheap food, even if it's organic, and people in cities never think that to have bread, milk, meat and fruit, someone has had to go out and work every day of the year, hard, back-breaking labour, and they also need money for electricity and fuel and winter feed. No wonder those who are willing to farm are getting older and older. Peter, under fifty, counts as a young farmer; the farm that was sold to the hippies had gone because their neighbour, like Pete's father, shot himself.

'What else was he going to do, when things are this bad?' Peter said bitterly. 'You know there's talk of turning what remains of dairy farming into factory farming, with cows spending their entire lives indoors, eating computer-controlled feed rather than grass?'

'I'm sure people wouldn't stand for it,' Sally remarked. 'A landscape doesn't look right, does it, without animals. Besides, what else is pasture good for?'

She has always feared Peter would give way to depression. She hadn't realised how needy he is until they were married, and sometimes it makes her feel as if she's his mother as well as his wife, the mother he'd lost as a child, whom his father had never bothered to value. Or maybe the knowledge that he'd hit his wife

168

as well as his son meant the risk was too much for any woman to take on. He'd been related to the Balls, and her own parents had been worried about her marrying into such a family, even though Pete had never done a violent or dishonest thing in his life.

'Drat the dog!' Sally says, as Jip continues to bark. She stumbles up, knowing Peter won't stir, then puts on her fleece dressing gown and, at the utility room door, her boots.

Outside, the cobbles in the yard are rimed with frost.

'What's wrong, boy?' she says softly to Jip, who whines. He's chained up, and after a moment's hesitation, she releases him.

Off he goes like a rocket, towards the hen house. Sally hurries after, torch in hand. When she gets there, she sees the door has not been properly shut – in the race to rescue the sheep, she'd forgotten to bolt it, though she'd taken away the hens' ramp to the rafter where they roost. When she looks up, she thinks at first that they may have escaped the fox, for they are all still huddled there in a line, along the main beam. But then she sees Jip, snuffling around the floor like a mad thing.

The fox has not just taken a couple of hens. It has jumped along the row of all her flock, her poor rescued hens, and bitten off their legs. Sally stares, her gorge rising and her skin crawling.

The shed is awash with blood, and the smell of blood.

16

Lottie Resurgens

Lottie and the girls re-enter London like people stumbling into sunlight. The South-East is lighter, brighter and drier than the West: no wonder most people in Britain want to live here, she thinks.

'It's so lovely to be back.'

'It's my present to you, *Liebchen*,' Marta says. 'I'm only sorry dear Xan can't come too.'

'I'm sure he'll be up soon,' Lottie answers, though if she's entirely honest she is glad to have a break from him, too.

'Dearest Lottie,' her cousin said the moment she called to say she was returning for a week; 'You must, MUST come to dinner with us immediately. I can't bear to think of you being stuck in the mud with that awful man.'

'You could always come to us in Devon.'

'We might descend, but you know they'd practically run us out with pitchforks,' said Justin. 'I grew up in the sticks, I know what country people are. They have photographs of the Queen everywhere, and *not* in irony.'

Lottie laughed, but when the train glides into Paddington she is overwhelmed. The graceful white wrought ironwork above the station platform looks like the outlines of gigantic flowers, leaves, hearts. It's all so familiar, yet oddly alien. The busyness, the lights, the colour, the shops, the traffic, the sirens and the crowds almost stun her with their profligate revelry. This is life, this is youth, this is energy and success, she thinks: but is it still home?

'Mummy, why isn't there grass?' Stella asks.

'It makes it easier and cleaner for lots of people to get around,' Lottie answers. The girls are in wellington boots, of course. They all, she realises, look faintly grubby.

'Poor trees,' Rosie says. 'They live in cages.'

It *is* strange to see trees growing out of concrete and tarmac, surrounded by steel bars to protect them from people rather than weather. They look through the taxi windows, as it carries them towards Hampstead. The rancid air ('What's the nasty smell, Mummy?' Rosie keeps asking) is unpleasant, but, Lottie tells herself, it's the smell of a great metropolis. She's never noticed it until now.

Stella says doubtfully, 'London's not clean, is it, Mummy?'

'Ach, pollution,' Marta croaks. 'Heidi has a bath every day to keep her fur white.'

The dog, who sits primly on a copy of the *Times* between them, makes Lottie suddenly self-conscious of her unkempt appearance. The girls need new clothes, haircuts, shoes . . . and so does she. Above all, she must get them to the dentist. The idea of getting Devon teeth is frightful.

The minicab drives past the end of the road that leads to her old house. She is relieved to feel no pang of nostalgia. Think of the rental money, she keeps telling herself. We couldn't afford to go on living here.

'Home!' Marta says with satisfaction as they turn off Hampstead High Street into a thin, elegant terrace of old brick, with a church at the end. 'Civilisation!'

To Lottie, her mother's home has become, after the initial rush of sentiment, annoying. Church Row is far too big for one person and Marta will not modernise anything. Its bathrooms are unheated, its lighting atrocious, and its cupboards bulge with musical scores left by her father. Lottie can barely remember him. Such memories as she has are mostly of him singing, 'Me, me, me, me, me.'

To Marta, it's still as if Edward Evenlode has just walked out. She will never move, not least because it represents the quintessence of Englishness, and safety to her as a refugee from post-War Berlin. To be asset-rich and cash-poor is not unusual these days, but for Lottie it's hard not to feel slightly cross at her mother rattling around in a six-million-pound house, pleading poverty.

'I put you in your old rooms, darlings,' Marta says. 'I knew you'd need it again one day.'

Back in the familiar flat, she misses Xan with terrible pangs. I must do something, Lottie thinks. He can't stay sunk in despair, and neither can she. The energy of London fizzes in her veins like a sugar rush.

'I've got to make a plan for Xan.'

Justin says, 'If you nag him, you'll only make it worse.'

They have met for coffee in Camden Town; the ease of this is a little intoxicating, because all she had to do to get there was catch the 24 bus. Even in six months, London and Londoners have altered: shoes have become more pointed, orange has become fashionable, and all kinds of films she's never heard of are being advertised on buses.

'But what can I do?'

'Darling, you are a wonderful mother, but he can't be a Mummy's boy for ever. He has to live his own life and make his own choices.'

Her cousin is Xan's godfather, and especially dear to her and she to him. They had befriended each other as teenagers, when

172

Lottie had pretended to be her cousin's 'beard'. Justin's wedding will be in the summer, and she is determined to come up for it.

'Do you think I'm mad for insisting on fidelity?' she asks.

'No. It's an ideal state, but like all ideals, hard to achieve.'

'Not for me.'

'Maybe you've never been tempted.'

'I'm too fastidious, I think.'

'I think ugliness, like beauty, is in the eye of the beholder,' says Justin.

It's wonderful to be having conversations like these, not least because Lottie can remember that, very recently, she had been in so much pain that the noise of London had been indistinguishable from the grinding roar of misery and self-hatred in her head. Yet she is not as happy as she thought she would be. Not only is it difficult to sleep again, but she is shocked by the way those two nights of sharing a bed have disturbed her. Despite everything she knows and hates about him, he is still attractive to her even if she, clearly, is not to him.

Perhaps we can find a long-term modus vivendi, she thinks; after all, Quentin adores their children. They could still have long, interesting conversations. They could, in a broken sort of way, be friends. But then some memory strikes her like a shard of broken trust, and the pain and fury throb again. She hates this feeling, but it's a kind of addiction, because hatred makes her feel alive.

When she goes for a walk on Hampstead Heath with Hemani, it's also less enjoyable than she hoped. It's so full of *people*, unlike Dartmoor. Her friend is tired, having come through her own family celebrations of both Diwali and Christmas.

'Do you think you're going to be able to come back to London?'

'I don't know. The Devon place is not ideal, but—'

'I remember when we rented somewhere in Cornwall one summer. It rained every day.'

Lottie sighs. 'I just wish I weren't stuck there with Quentin.'

'So will you divorce him?' Hemani asks, abruptly.

Lottie can remember urging her friend to leave her own husband, many years ago. He was one of those apparently civilised men who believed he was justified in not only controlling but hitting his wife. When she saw the bruises – always made in places which wouldn't normally be exposed, so the idea that he couldn't control his anger was self-evidently untrue – Lottie had been appalled. It was very difficult for her friend to take such a step. But Hemani had only been twenty-seven at the time, and young enough to meet someone else.

'It's complicated,' she says at last. 'There's still the money issue.'

Hemani snorts. 'You can and will find a buyer for your house. Never forget the money! But otherwise, why delay? Do you think he will ever change?'

'I'm not sure. He doesn't understand that other people are real, I think. Though he does love the girls, and he does love his mother. So maybe it's just me.'

'No!' Hemani says fiercely. 'Men who have behaved badly always want to put the blame onto their wives. They think it's our fault for not being young any more.'

'You're right about Quentin not wanting to admit he's at fault. Sometimes I almost feel sorry for him. I mean, if he'd had a one-night stand or a *coup de foudre* for someone else, I'd have gone mad with jealousy, but sort of understood. As it is, I just feel part of a sordid midlife crisis.'

'You can't let him treat you like this, that's what you said to me.'

'Quentin thinks we can carry on as we were.'

'But what do *you* want? Why do his opinions matter at all?'

'I don't know. You're right, they shouldn't. He actually said to me at one point that he wanted to feel the cage door could be left open for him to fly in and out. I told him I didn't see marriage as a cage. I thought we'd be mated for life, like those swans.'

Hemani says, watching the pair gliding across the waters of

the Hampstead Ponds below, 'A biologist once told me that their fidelity is due to a diet of weed; they just don't have the energy to go off with other swans. Nut-eaters, on the other hand, are enthusiastic adulterers.'

'If I had the energy for adultery, I'm not sure I'd bother. I'd learn Italian or something instead.'

'So there's nobody else?'

'What's the point? All sex does is mess you up. I just feel an idiot for ever having been taken in by him.'

It's good to unburden herself to an old friend, but when Lottie returns from her walk she finds herself bursting into tears the moment she enters her mother's house.

'Sorry. Sorry.'

'What has upset you?'

'I just don't know what to do any more. Everything is so *difficult.*'

Marta looks at her with sympathy, but also sternness.

'My darling, you aren't homeless, or hungry. You are living in a charmingly rustic part of the world. Your children are at a good school. You are not ill. So why do you cry?'

'I know, I do know. It's just that ... ' Lottie says the one thing she knows her mother will grasp. 'Xan is working in *a pie factory.*'

'Has he reapplied?'

'I'm not even sure he can see the point of further education, now.' A silence stretches out between them: the great unmentionable fear of middle-class life, that a person can be downwardly mobile, rather than upwardly, is in both their minds. She adds, 'I don't feel safe in the house, either. It was bad enough having the bailiffs in London, but now I sleep with a poker by my bed. The previous tenant was murdered.'

Marta raises an eyebrow. 'Unpleasant. Who?'

'Oh, some poor man called Oliver Randall. It's his piano you played on – why, what's the matter?'

Marta says, 'I knew him.' Lottie stares, her tears drying. 'He was a pupil of mine, many years before I retired. I often wondered what became of him.'

Lottie asks, 'Why?'

'He was a most talented musician – a composer as well as a pianist – but he disappeared. How did he come to be in Shipcott?'

'I know nothing about him, beyond his renting from Gore Tore.'

To Lottie's surprise, her mother nods.

'He, also, was a pupil of mine. From a much earlier vintage.'

Lottie laughs incredulously. 'But Tore's a *rock* star!'

'*All* the good ones are classically trained at the Royal Academy or the Guildhall,' Marta says haughtily, 'though few are as generous as Elton John. You know, even the Beatles were choirboys? They would never admit it, because they wished to seem of the people, but their inner ear was trained by the baroque.'

This is so unexpected that Lottie doesn't know how to absorb it.

'How strange, Mutti, that we should have rented that particular house, though.'

'It has a Bösendorfer – of course you would take it.'

Lottie tries hard not to laugh. 'We took it because the rent was so low, not because of the piano.'

'Similar people are drawn to the same houses. Mention my name to Gordon.'

'Oh, his wife and I are quite friendly already.'

'I thought you said you had found no friends there?'

'Well, I do have a couple, sort of. It's just … There's a gulf between being able to choose friends, as you can in London, and having them chosen by circumstance.'

It's hard to leave her mother, but when she and the girls board the train at Paddington for the return journey she's surprised at how keenly she enjoys the landscape rolling past. Lustrous in the low winter sun, the white chalk horse on the hill, the spinneys speckled with starlings, a man walking down a leafless lane all seem like Eric Ravilious paintings. She doesn't know whether she looks forward to being back at Home Farm or not. In the weeks before Christmas, the valley had echoed to the sounds of deep male moaning which terrified her so much that the first time she heard it she had run out to Quentin and said,

'Someone's in dreadful trouble outside, can you hear?'

He listened, then said,

'It's just deer.'

'Surely not! It's a man's voice calling for help.'

'It's male, yes,' he said, supercilious as always. 'Just not human; and what it's after is sex.'

Still she was unconvinced. They were being haunted by something, and one night she was so convinced that she sprang out of bed and ripped back the curtains. Nothing; and then, just as she was about to curse her nerves, something did move.

Around the gable end of the house stepped a large animal, a stag with its improbably wide, tall crown of branching antlers held high. She had never seen such a creature, and its size and magnificence astonished her. No wonder she could hear the noise of hoofs, given the weight of what it carried ... To grow those each year, just to get a mate, must be so exhausting, she thought.

They have found a table seat, and the girls are colouring in pictures with brand-new felt-tips from Marta. She has been generous to them all, buying her granddaughters new shoes and warm, pretty dresses from Gap. She has even taken Lottie to the Clinique counter at Selfridges.

'Darling, do not turn into one of those middle-aged women who never wear make-up! It is so terribly depressing for everybody to see. Nature is not on our side, and nobody admires those over thirty who believe a naked face is better. You *need* this.'

'I'm past caring, Mutti.'

'Believe me, you are a spring chicken. Do these things, not for your husband, but for yourself.'

It's doubtful Quentin will even notice. But her mother is right: a little make-up does help her feel less colourless and depressed.

'Lottie?'

She looks up, and there, of all people, is Martin, with whom long ago she once shared the house in Spitalfields. He looms over her, grinning and holding a paper bag from the café.

'What are you doing here?'

He has changed, she notes. The red-gold beard is now neatly trimmed, and his jacket is fashionable. He looks like a better-groomed William Morris, confident and contented.

'I live in the country now.'

'Let me guess,' exclaims Lottie mischievously. 'Hobbit holes?'

'Not exactly, but almost, yes.'

Martin blushes. She remembers that Di Tore had mentioned him as her architect for restoring Shipcott Manor. No wonder he looks prosperous.

'So – you're busy?'

'Yes. People are still building, despite everything.'

His eyes look at her with enquiry. Lottie says in a rush of frankness,

'I've been jobless for a year. It's dire.'

'Bad luck.' Martin pauses. 'And Quentin?'

'Well—' She grimaces and indicates her daughters with her eyes. 'You?'

'We divorced seven years ago.' He grins. 'I set up a practice in Devon and things are OK. Better than OK, really.'

How strange it is that Beardy Martin, as Quentin calls him, has become a success, while she, working for one of the big firms, should not be.

'Lucky you. We're renting a place near Trelorn and trying to sell our home in London.'

'Trelorn? That's very close to me. Look – why don't you bring your portfolio over?' Martin says. 'I might be able to put some work your way.'

178

'Really? That's very kind.'

Especially, she thinks, after how my pig of a husband behaved to you. He gives her his card – another sign of how much he's changed, Lottie thinks – and she sends him her mobile number and email. The ping as it arrives makes them both laugh.

'See you,' Martin says, and lurches off.

It's as if the life she has left behind, with its web of connections, has not abandoned her after all. She stares after him. He knows who he is now, she thinks, and it suits him. Memory prompts her to another thought: there had been a time when he had knelt before her, like a Victorian suitor, in an unspoken plea, and she had as silently discouraged him. But in those days, Lottie thinks, I was in my twenties, and I could, as Hemani said, have had almost anyone if only I'd known it.

The train goes through one long tunnel, then another, and emerges to run alongside waterlogged meadows. Here, too, there are swans. As Lottie watches, two begin to beat their wings with gigantic, ponderous slowness, their large webbed feet almost waddling across the water until, in a rush that lifts them, improbably, up and up into the thickening air, with long necks outstretched they fly together into the sunset.

17

Anything is Better Than Nothing

For week after week of the New Year, the wind, cold and mud and rain seem relentless. The only time Quentin feels a normal temperature is when he has a bath, but then getting dressed and undressed in a bathroom without radiators is an ordeal all by itself. He remembers some grande dame he once met who said, when descanting on the joys of rural life, 'In the country, you know, one need only change one's knickers every week.' No wonder, he thinks.

He splits logs every day, wheeling in barrowloads to feed the wood-burner, but even when he gets this burning strongly, he feels listless and weak. It takes some time to realise that this sensation is not entirely physical. The confidence that once drove him on is flickering and fading just when he needs it most. No matter how hard he tries, he simply can't believe in himself any more. Again and again he wills the landline or his mobile to ring with a call from a commissioning editor, but it won't.

Even the robin that keeps him company when digging seems to have decided he isn't worth bothering with. Doggedly, he heaves dead leaves onto the compost bin at the end of the garden, mixing it with ashes from the wood-burner, vegetable peelings, shredded newspaper and anything that will rot down. He is, he admits to himself, slightly obsessed by composting these days – another cliché of country life.

Without the girls, he has to admit he is lonely. Exhausting though it is to be a parent, Stella and Rosie never fail to amuse and without them the bleakness of his new life is intolerable. Though he can't afford it, he stomps out every evening to go to the pub in Shipcott, a mile away. Tiny and smoky, it has a log fire and a bar and serves a limited menu of home-made food and (blessedly) hand-cut chips instead of the vile frozen kind. There's a darts board, which draws in custom, and best of all no bloody music. Quentin has always loved pubs, but it's not the beer so much as the atmosphere of the true pub which he likes: the informality, the freedom to talk or be silent, the absence of feminine fripperies and the presence of masculine simplicity. In addition to beer, the Shipcott Arms also does a decent house red.

'Not bad,' he says aloud.

There's only one other customer there, a thin, raggedy old man wearing a hat, with a black dog at his feet. A tramp? Quentin sees the man looking at him, and on impulse raises his glass.

'What'll you have?'

Surprised, the tramp considers. The publican stops polishing his glasses, opens his mouth, then carries on.

'Same as you. Thanks.'

His voice is low, with a faint Devon burr to it, and his grin very white. A Traveller, maybe, Quentin thinks, but they get chatting about this and that, and he finds him surprisingly bright and sharp. The tramp asks if he'd like a game of darts, which they both enjoy, and then have another round of drinks. This time, to his surprise, the tramp pays. After that, Quentin looks out for the tramp and is always pleased to see him.

'What do you do here, mostly?' Quentin asks him once.

181

'Plant trees,' said the man. 'Or cut them down. You?'

'At the moment, gardening.'

Quentin needs the company. There is a critical number of enemies that a person can make before their career self-destructs. He very much fears this to be the case with himself. His dread of permanent exile is the worst thing. It isn't just the money, it's the stimulation and companionship of his former colleagues, for if journalism is now one of the professions most despised after banking and politics, with its fair share of rogues, cowards and liars, it also attracts the bravest, brightest and least boring of every generation.

I have failed at everything, he thinks: career, marriage, fatherhood.

'If I could go back in time, I would,' he blurted out to his mother on one of his visits. Even though she is exhausted by looking after Hugh, she will at least listen, unlike anyone else in his life. 'It wasn't perfect, but there were happy times, and I didn't realise it.'

'People never do,' she said. 'But you need to start looking forward, not back.'

'I know – I know – I know.'

Each day, he can feel himself slipping deeper into the place from which there is no return, and part of his despair is that Lottie ascribes a deliberate malice to his every action which, as far as he is concerned, is not there. He has said some nasty things (as has she) but he is no more in control over his actions and emotions than anyone else: yet she thinks he must be. *Everything* is his fault, including electrical cut-outs in a thunderstorm. She doesn't realise that, stuck in this dismal place, he is exerting every ounce of willpower just to remember who and what he is.

'All men are only half-good you know,' he had said to her. 'Our mothers try to civilise us, but we need another woman to do the rest.'

'Why should it be up to us to do that? Why can't you do it for yourselves?'

'I don't know.'

However, the miserable truth is that he can't become that better person. He lacks both the will and the ability. It's just like when he had graduated, stuffed as full of what he'd learnt as a goose intended for *foie gras*: only to find that in the rest of the world, nobody cared. All he had to fall back on was his energy and his wits. They had served him well, and in due course he had obtained everything most people desire – a home, a wife, a family, a career which seemed to surge upwards as powerfully as a leaping salmon. Then it was all useless again.

But it isn't only my fault, he reminds himself. *She* rejected *me* first.

'Oh why are you so *stupid?*' had been a phrase she had said so many times that it no longer wounded. Lottie has clearly forgotten how often she had turned on him, snarling at his domestic incompetence at everything, from changing a nappy to hanging up laundry. And then there was the complete loss of interest in him after each baby, which for all he knew at the time might have gone on for ever. A horrifying number of his male friends have, he's discovered, turned out to be in completely sexless marriages. They share a home and a bed but absolutely nothing physical, because their wives or partners have made it clear that they are out of bounds, for ever.

Why should anyone put up with that? You might as well be buried alive.

Quentin pushes his spade down savagely. He has dug over and planted a good deal of the vegetable garden at Home Farm now, and something about the mindless exertion this involves, the bending and stretching and careful extraction of weeds, absorbs some of his frustration and improves his digestion. (The girls no longer flinch when he breathes on them.) He had found an old-fashioned spade in the woodshed, the kind whose blade is

183

shaped like the point of a stylised heart, and a fork. Their steel slices through the soil, and the more he works it, the easier it becomes. It's less boring than he thought it would be, thanks to a warm spell. Spikes of wild daffodil on the bank beyond thicken into bud. A wall glitters with snowdrops, and galaxies of yellow celandines.

The ground is riddled with life. Every forkful uncovers the plump ends of worms, frantic to burrow away from the light.

How many finger their way blindly through existence? Everyone is wriggling through the darkness, until dragged up into the glare of the light. Quentin stabs deeper into the ground. The hot pull on his arms and legs and stomach will ache later on, but it is the only way he can keep guilt, grief, anger and fear at bay. Sometimes he finds himself sobbing as he uproots another clump of buttercups. If he lives here much longer he really will lose his mind.

The compost bins at the bottom of the garden are what he visits every day. Presumably, they were installed by Randall, who it is also clear had looked after the garden in his time. Each mound steams with energy, and each has been invaded by glossy weeds: bramble, ivy, primrose, periwinkle. It looks like a bit of William Morris wallpaper, complete with a thrush hopping about.

He plunges his spade in deep. At once a jarring feeling goes up his arms as it strikes something large. A stone? He works his spade around it, carefully, trying to lever it out. It feels less heavy than the usual lump of granite, and the compost grips as if reluctant to release its treasure. Eventually, it comes out with a loud squelching sound, a round, brown object. An old football? Oddly heavy, with some straggling growth half attached, it comes with a reek that turns his stomach.

Sometimes, just before an accident, you know that something dreadful is about to happen, unstoppably. Quentin picks the round thing up, vaguely glad to be wearing gardening gloves, and sees what he's holding.

It is a severed head.

For a few moments, he sees things he wishes he hadn't: the eyes pitted into sockets, the empty hole for a nose, black lips that curl away from grinning teeth. A long worm threads itself in and out of the jaws. He knows at once whose head this is, and he also knows that he must bury it again with all possible speed. He doesn't care if he's breaking the law. What good would alerting the police to its presence do to anyone – least of all the head's owner, Oliver Randall?

Though some scraps of leathery skin remain, it's more skull than head. Some kind of beard is attached to the lower jaw, and then he's emptying the contents of his stomach into the compost, retching and heaving to one side as the head lands, with a soft thud, in the clods of leaves, grass cuttings and ash. If Lottie or the girls, or the police find out then the house and garden will be overrun with photographers, journalists, gawkers – there'll be no end to it.

The hole he's made is three feet deep, but he makes it deeper yet. The sense of urgency is almost overwhelming. Even though nobody is in the house, he keeps his back to it, turning every now and again to check that no one has come, then returning to his task in a frenzy. He feels as guilty as if he'd murdered the former tenant himself.

Poor sod, Quentin thinks, and the wave of disgust that follows his nausea is not something he's proud of either. To cut off a human head ... the place where thought and feeling, personality and reason were contained – to render it lifeless. He'd never thought before how cruel and vile an act it was, for it looks as if it wasn't a clean sweep, the way you imagine it would be with a guillotine. Somebody had hacked at it ... How could it have been missed before? The police must have searched the scene of the crime pretty thoroughly, but somehow they had. Perhaps the other smells in the compost had misled the dogs, or perhaps they had not looked hard enough.

Was the hole deep enough to escape the attentions of vermin? He has no idea. Six feet is the traditional depth, but he stops at five, as far as he can tell, the sweat drying cold on his shaking body as he piles fresh compost over it.

Who had buried it like this? Had it been dragged here by a fox or badger, or had somebody placed it there? The latter, he thinks. It must have been the murderer. But why not bury the whole body in that case? It was such a crazy thing to do, crazier, even, than a beheading.

Now is not the time to be public-spirited. None of his family knows what he does about Home Farm, but he can just imagine what that knowledge will do to his daughters, his vulnerable, innocent daughters whom he has already hurt so badly. That he himself will be haunted by it, he has no doubt, but it would be worse for Stella and Rosie.

Any parent, if offered the choice between being woken relentlessly every night by terrified small children, and breaking the law, will choose the latter.

For the first time he feels real fear about where they have chosen to live. Chopping off someone's head suggested hatred of a kind he can't begin to imagine. Yet there was a horrid logic to dismemberment, because it made the crime harder to detect. Maybe the rest of the body was going to be cut up and dispersed – he's heard of cases like that. No matter, he isn't going to think about it.

'I dread to think what will happen to Stella and Rosie if they stay down here,' he tells his mother. 'They're far too bright for a village school.'

'You worry too much about their future,' his mother tells him.

'I want the best for my daughters.'

'I wouldn't be so sure that what you want, and what they need, are one and the same.'

The more he plods around in between deadlines, the more

he broods on Randall. Why would he have been attacked during the one period of the year when normal life went into hibernation? Did that make it more or less likely to be someone who knew him? More likely, Quentin thinks, given how many people go away at Christmas. Besides, who would bother to come down the long lane to Home Farm unless they knew a particular person would be at the other end of it? You'd have to know the area well to come off the B-road, and how many people do that?

Every time he gets out the maul to split logs, he thinks of it, the heavy blade coming down on the frail human neck, the hot fountain of blood. Whoever attacked Randall must have been drenched. Though what better place to get away with murder than darkest Devon, where anything could be burnt or buried?

'Oh, yes, dreadful business,' said Sam the postman when Quentin mentioned it.

'Didn't you find the body?'

'I did, unfortunately.' Sam, normally so ruddy and cheery, looked quite pale at the memory. 'I thought it was a funny bit of a tree at first. Then I saw, and I couldn't get away fast enough.'

'We still get the odd bit of mail for him, catalogues for women's clothes. Did he have a girlfriend?'

'Never saw one.'

'Maybe he was a cross-dresser.'

Sam laughed. 'You never know with people, do you?'

'I suppose not.'

No wonder he has become a regular at the Shipcott Arms. The publican, a magnificently moustachioed man called Mike, has confided his own story, pleased to find a new audience for it. Ten years ago, he'd had a partner who inherited a cottage near Bideford, 'little better than a ruin'. Mike, being handy, had restored it over the years with his own money, with the intention that he, she and their two kids should live there one day. Room by room, the cottage was made good: replastered, replumbed, rewired, redecorated. He'd laboured over every window and fitting.

'It was the sweetest place you ever saw by the time I finished,' he said. 'I put my heart and soul into it, even planted a red rose over the front door. It was my dream home.'

Then, one day, he had returned to find all his possessions in plastic bags and the locks changed. There was a general murmur of sympathy at this point. His partner had met another man online, and Mike was left with nothing.

'If we'd been married, I'd have got half the house, but I didn't think of it,' he said. 'You always believe, don't you, a marriage is for women, but it isn't so. I have no rights whatsoever. She got the lot, I have no home to call my own, and I can't even see my kids.'

All the men shook their heads, agreeing that it was cruel and unjust. Only Quentin wondered why, if his kids meant so much to him, he hadn't thought to marry their mother.

The one good thing that has come out of his own marriage is the children. They are, despite the occasional tantrums and fights, continually surprising and surprisingly delightful. He never minds cooking for them, or reading to them, or getting them to and from school, and this is strange because even though he'd tried to be kind to Xan, he had never really cared for children before they came along. It dawns on him that love is like genius: not, as he has always been led to believe, a matter of inspiration but of perspiration.

He would never have guessed that he would be happier lying in bed with his daughters than with any woman. They are reading *A Hundred and One Dalmatians*.

'I do like Pongo,' says Rosie. 'He's just like you, Daddy.'

'Missus is just as brave, though,' says Stella. 'She's not as strong as Pongo, but she still risks her life for the puppies.'

'Every parent would do that,' Quentin says.

'Would you, Daddy?'

'Yes, of course.'

Downstairs, something cracks like a pistol shot, and they all jump. Quentin's mind leaps to possibilities, each worse than the last, before realising it's a log in the wood-burner.

'There are a lot of spooky noises in this house, Daddy.'

'Yes, but they're natural noises,' he says, as if he too had not for a moment been paralysed by fright.

Does Lottie know about the murder? Sometimes he thinks she must do, and sometimes he thinks she can't. He certainly isn't going to tell her. What would be the point? Still: lightning doesn't strike twice, and in the pub the consensus is that it must have been gypsies.

'They're always at the bottom of everything bad,' said one old-timer. 'Whenever they come near, stuff gets nicked.'

'Better not let Mr Tore hear you say that,' said Mike. 'You know his ma was a pikey?'

'Ah. But she gave up being a Traveller when she met her boss, didn't she?'

'Some say she was given that job and the gatekeeper's cottage because Tore's his child.'

'Didn't Tore get some girl pregnant round here himself?' Quentin asked.

'Ah, yes, that's a sad story,' said the old-timer. 'Anyway, he won't hear a word against gypsies. He lets them camp on his land when they pass by – the real Travellers, that is.'

'Gypsies may be thieves, but they're not killers,' said a heavily tattooed man everyone called Jeff. He lived in a hidden house that was said to have been dug out of a hill, worked installing solar panels and had a voice so deep that nobody would dare tangle with him. 'They're a much-misunderstood people, if you ask me. Besides, the police interviewed every gypsy for miles around, didn't find a thing.'

'Hell's Angels, then?'

Jeff snorted. 'They're only interested in their bikes. If Randall

189

had been into drugs, I'd say it might have been a deal gone wrong.'

'Behind this lies a bitter mind,' said the publican. 'I bet you there's a woman involved.'

'No, it's a lunatic or an Islamic fundamentalist. Either way, not from round here.'

That was the main thing.

One night, the wind blows three slates off the kitchen roof, which leaks copiously. The Tores send round a handyman to fix a sheet of plastic over the hole until the weather improves.

'I'm going to ask the Tores if we can have a Velux window put there instead.'

'But what's the point, Lottie? It isn't our house.'

'We're still *living* here for another seven months. I can't stand being in the dark. It won't need planning permission, and it'd bring lots of daylight in where we need it most.'

'What possible difference can it make to this shithole?'

Quentin writes,

The English have made such a fetish of country life that they believe it to be the Heaven to which all good Englishmen and women should aspire, where the sun always shines, and your vegetable patch isn't devastated by rabbits. At least one can eat rabbits. If things get much worse, I may be trying fricassee of slug . . .

Spring arrives in spurts and streaks, as if something is leaking. It feels like recovering from a long illness, and in fact no sooner does winter retreat than he goes down with flu.

'Don't expect any sympathy,' Lottie says.

'I'm *really* nod well.'

'Take paracetamol, and drink lots of tea.'

The worst of it is, she's landed a job working with Beardy Martin in Trelorn. There's some big building project he's involved

190

in, and Lottie's been hired on a salary of £35,000 a year – a respectable income here. He can't help being stung by envy, and she is even more impatient with his shortcomings.

'If you miss taking the rubbish to the B-road on Monday morning because you're too lazy to walk the girls to school, you can drive it to the town dump,' she snaps.

Lottie can't look after the girls, so the full brunt of childcare falls, for the first time ever, onto his shoulders.

'Shit!' he exclaims, wiping his hand after touching a gatepost.

'No, frogspawn,' Stella says.

'Maybe if you kiss it, it'll turn into a handsome prince,' Rosie says.

Of course, the solution is to take them to his mother's. Naomi is always delighted to see her grandchildren.

'They're like pigs in mud,' he says, watching them through The Hovel's window.

'I long for it to warm up enough for me to go outside,' murmurs Hugh.

Every week, Quentin's father fades, and Quentin can hardly bear to witness it, not least because he knows that he himself will probably look just like Hugh in thirty years' time.

'It'll be warm soon,' he says awkwardly, though they are all aware that for Hugh, summer may never come. A disabled toilet has been installed next door: a grim reminder that from now on there can be no improvement in health and strength. There is a hospital bed in the living room, close to the hearth, and everything stinks of smoke as if kippered.

'Can you really keep him with you until the end?' he asks quietly, when they are alone.

'I wouldn't dream of anything else,' Naomi says.

She would probably offer the Grim Reaper a cup of tea, he thinks. His father's cancer has spread, but Hugh carries on as if the whole thing is a temporary inconvenience from which he'll recover.

'How can I help?'

'I wouldn't mind more firewood,' she says.

'I'll fetch some now.'

'Thanks, Quent. It's not so easy to chop logs with arthritis.'

Who will do this for me one day? Quentin wonders. The question is absurd: he won't be living in a rotting cottage on the edge of Dartmoor. But seeing how dependent Hugh is on Naomi is disconcerting. *He got away with it*, Quentin thinks . . . although Quentin's sister, who now lives in New Zealand, still won't talk to her father.

Hugh pokes at the fire. This has become his great hobby. The open hearth renders the heat almost indiscernible, except when Hugh throws on another firelighter, making it flare up with bright, evil-smelling flames.

'*Rage, rage against the dying of the light*,' he murmurs.

His father had written just two memorable poems in among a great many that are not. 'That's all that were allotted to me,' he said once.

Those two poems, 'Silage' and 'Barn Owl', frequently anthologised, have kept his reputation going – such as it is. They are on the National Curriculum (earning him about £100 a year in royalties) and Trelorn has become quite proud of him, apparently. It must help that Hugh *looked* like a poet, or used to. Quentin had grown up seeing girls at school telling his mother that she should make way for their grand passion. She would be very kind to them, and after a while, they went away, though the fellow teachers he seduced did not. Of course, his adventures were small beer compared with, say, Gore Tore's, but they still mortified his family.

'I'll use the bellows, Fa.'

'No need. Ah, that's better,' Hugh says with satisfaction, while smoke billows out and makes them all cough.

Lunch is excellent, as always. How his mother manages to summon up such meals from a lean-to kitchen whose ancient, lopsided shelves are cluttered with rusting tins, plastic cartons and dusty herbs is a mystery. Surreptitiously, Quentin scrubs the hand-thrown mugs in which coffee will be served. I am almost as bad as Lottie, he thinks.

'Let me make coffee,' he offers, as Stella and Rosie dash outside again; but Naomi refuses.

'Stubborn as a mule,' his father says, once she retreats to the kitchen. 'Any news on the London house?'

'Still rented out. We're waiting until late spring before trying to sell again.'

'I used to think that I could never live anywhere but the Big Smoke,' Hugh remarks. 'I still miss it, only the city I remember doesn't exist now.'

'It changes, like anything that's alive,' Quentin says.

'How could anything be more alive than what's all around us?' Naomi asks, bringing coffee. 'Just look at those lambs skipping about.'

'Charming, but if only every field had a twenty-four-hour corner shop in it.'

'We get a couple of lambs for the freezer in return for the grazing,' Naomi says. 'That's enough for me.'

Quentin grins sardonically. His mother always goes on about living the Good Life, but her family owns one of the best vineyards in the Cape, as well as quite a few other things. He never even knew what she renounced until he went out to South Africa after graduation, and found his relations. The houses, the cars, the jewels, the staff, and above all the money that would have come his way had she been able to accept living with apartheid were the cause of some bitterness. He admires her for her principles in rejecting that life, and yet – how he wishes she hadn't made him pay, too.

'He's a town mouse, not a country one,' Hugh remarks.

'I'm just glad you're living so close,' his mother says.

Quentin sighs. All of his life, Hugh has loomed in the

193

background like Zeus, fulminating, fornicating, fantastically irritating, and yet—

'I'm glad, too.' He pauses. 'Of course, I was very surprised to find you'd forgotten to mention that the previous tenant at Home Farm was the victim of an axe murderer.'

Naomi looks puzzled. 'You're not superstitious, surely?'

'No. But you might at least have told me.'

'I didn't think it would matter to you.'

'How did you hear it was up for rent?'

'Oh, I know Di Tore,' Naomi says, to his surprise. 'She's bought a couple of my pieces, and I've taught pottery at Shipcott Primary.'

'So you actually know Gore Tore . . . ?'

'Oh, not him! He's always touring, when he's not rolling naked in the morning dew.'

Quentin barks with surprised laughter. 'Truly?'

'No, of course not. You never could tell when I was joking! But mostly, he's never around. In fact there were some rumours that the poor man who was murdered was—'

'Yes?'

Naomi's voice suddenly sounds more South African than it usually does.

'Quentin, I do hope you're not going to upset everybody. That column in the *Chronicle* is you, isn't it?'

'The Questing Vole,' says Hugh.

'Er – yes, the Vole, *c'est moi*.' He waits for applause, then continues sulkily, 'I need the work. Of course, it's different for Lottie. She's found a new job.'

'I heard. Her training shouldn't go to waste,' Naomi says.

Hugh says irritably, 'Bloody architects. They should be lined up and shot for what their buildings have done.'

How had his parents survived each other for over fifty years? He loves his mother, but can see how ridiculous she is. Hugh is worse. He had been so embarrassed by them at Xan's age that

194

he thought he'd die if anyone he knew even saw, let alone spoke to them. Yet the strange thing was that other people seemed to accept them.

'You should see what my own parents are like,' said one of his few friends who had ever set foot in The Hovel. 'I used to long to be taken away by social services.'

When Quentin visited his friend in turn, his parents seemed perfectly fine. Quentin said this, but his friend at first professed not to believe him, thinking he was being polite, and then became quite angry.

'Can't you see they're completely raving?' he demanded.

'No. I'd swap them for mine any day.'

'You wouldn't if you knew what they were really like.'

Almost everyone you get to know turns out to be bonkers, Quentin thinks, it's just that most people don't know that, say, your father bites off his own toenails or your mother keeps twenty-year-old cheese in the fridge. Maybe he himself will seem just as loony to his own daughters one day.

Yet children, too, are insane. He listens to Stella and Rosie talking to the doll they dug up in the garden, which they have decided is one of Sleeping Beauty's children. Thank God, he thinks, they'd found only a doll and not the severed head. He's still gripped by anxiety each time he remembers it.

'You know Janet is Malevola,' Stella says.

'You should feel sorry for Janet, not make her a wicked witch,' Quentin says. 'She's just a poor woman who earns her living cleaning.'

When he gets back from his parents', he's surprised to see Lottie digging deep trenches around the back of the house.

'What on *earth* are you doing?'

Lottie looks up, briefly. 'I'm laying a damp-proofing course.'

'How can you *possibly* do that? You aren't a builder.'

'Quentin,' Lottie says, in exasperation, 'I've often told you that I'd make more money as a builder, but that doesn't mean I don't know how to do what builders do. I'm laying down a French drain.'

'A French what?'

'It'll take away some of the damp, maybe most of it, because it's basically just groundwater running down the hill. The slots in the top of the pipe let the water in, and then the pipe channels it away into the ditch.'

'Are you sure?'

Smearing mud over her cheek Lottie says, 'No, I'm doing this for entertainment in my limited free time. But anything is better than nothing.'

'Just stay away from my compost heap,' Quentin says. 'You're not to touch it, d'you hear?'

'As if I'd want to,' Lottie replies.

'How should I know what you want and don't want? You don't talk to me, you pay no attention to me, you are completely wrapped up in your own bloody world—'

'Pot, kettle.'

'At least you could appreciate the efforts I'm making!'

Lottie leans on her fork, and begins to laugh, tears streaming down her face.

'Oh Quentin, you're wasted on us!'

18

Xan Among the Poles

Now that his body has adapted to the night shifts and the mind-numbing nature of Humbles, the real irritation for Xan is that they won't give him enough regular work. He waits for the agency texts telling him he's needed, always anxious that Home Farm's wavering mobile reception has let him down. The problem is that if he does more than a certain number of hours he's entitled to employee benefits, so the management ensure he can never earn more than £120 a week. This is why few local people want to work for them, rather than stay on benefits.

'With one hand they give, with the other they take back,' Katya says.

The Poles not only earn all their income from Humbles, but also rent their cramped and shoddy homes from them. It's better than the caravans where farm workers live, however. They all know that farming is the worst work of all, for who would stand, hour after hour, in freezing mud with a pair of scissors to be paid 5p a bunch, or digging up potatoes? That work goes to the Romanians and Lithuanians, labourers who must pay for their own uniforms out of the earnings they may or may not receive, and who dream of getting a job at Humbles.

Everything to do with food seems to be built on a pyramid of exploitation and unhappiness. Katya and her friends accept it and Xan admires the way they manage to distil a kind of happiness from their disappointments and sorrows, much as they do alcohol from fruit and potatoes.

'UK is better than Poland for work, you understand,' Katya says. 'We love our country, we love our people, but to make business – impossible. We do not want your benefits, we want to work.'

Xan has grown up among people who never discuss money; it's the big secret which even husbands and wives keep from each other. The Poles, however, have no qualms about showing their intense interest in earning and saving, and the banks on Trelorn's square all advertise their existence with signs in Polish. The immigrants' willingness to not only work for the minimum wage but save from it is both impressive and depressing.

'They say we take jobs and homes from English peoples, but how many will live this way?' Katya demands. She treats Xan as an oracle on all things native, but he knows even less than she. 'How many, Xan?'

'Not many, I suppose,' he says. He thinks of the cramped hall, heaving with the shoes they take off so as not to bring dirt into the rest of the house. The only communal space is the tiny kitchen. Yet even this has been made a home, painted with bright stencils and pots of herbs in the window.

'Polish peoples work ver, ver hard.'

'I know you do,' Xan says. He's heard this so often it's a bit like a catechism, and what they don't grasp is that once the Poles returned from their Christmas break, the wages paid to everyone were adjusted back down again.

'There aren't enough affordable homes for anyone to rent or buy,' Lottie tells him. 'That's why the extension to the town we're building is really needed.'

'But won't it be bought up as second homes or something?'

'That won't be allowed. Tore has gone into partnership with the council – he owns the land, so he's not going to lose money on it – but he really does have a vision.'

'I thought he was supposed to be a wicked old rocker.'

'Maybe he was, once. But I think that he wants to leave a legacy. People can change, Xan.'

'Can they?'

'I believe people can become better versions of themselves, under the right circumstances.'

Xan thinks of his stepfather and says,

'From what I've seen, people don't change much. The ones who are tools in primary school are still tools now. People are as they are, Mum, they just get better at hiding it.'

'Yet there are more good people than bad. We're not running around killing each other all the time.'

'Not in this country, no, but this country isn't the rest of the world, is it?'

Sometimes, Xan thinks that this must be the reason why his biological father has never tried to get in touch. He has told himself long, complicated stories about how his real dad must have gone back to whatever part of Africa he came from, and died there. Maybe he was a hero, or maybe he is a villain. Often, he's studied his reflection and tried to disentangle the parts of himself that are not Lottie, to see where in that vast continent he might have come from. He's looked at pictures of actors online, and maybe he's half Nigerian or Ghanaian ... definitely West African rather than, say, Somali. If only his mother had talked more to his father! It seems extraordinary to him that Lottie, so careful and anxious, should ever have done such a thing as have a one-night stand with a man she didn't know. But maybe that's why she is as she is, now. Or maybe – and this is what he hates to consider – she was raped.

'Did you have lots of boyfriends before my dad?'

'No, not at all. He wasn't a boyfriend, Xan, just someone I – well, it was all unintended.'

She doesn't seem to sense how desperately he longs to know who his father was, and he can't tell her because it will sound like reproach. Even if there's no stigma about being the child of a single parent any more, and even if he has never, until he left London, experienced racism, he still feels it as a hole through which his confidence leaks.

Before his mother's marriage, Xan never had anyone but Lottie and Marta as family. (His godfather, Justin, didn't really count.) He'd only become aware of the absence of a father when Stella was born, looking like such a mixture of Lottie and Quentin. Even as a tiny child, he could spot his stepfather's big toes on her, his mother's knees, his grandmother's fingers, his dead grandfather's eyelids. Heredity is such a fascinating puzzle, and although he is pretty sure that his love of music comes from Lottie's side, he wants to know if his ability to jump is his father's, or his asthma, or his poor grasp of maths . . .

'Is smooth, your skin. Like wood.'

'You know, in this country people don't say things like that.'

'Why?'

'It's not polite.'

'In my country, no white person ever touch a black person, or even see one.'

'Why not?'

'Everybody is white. But I am not like the others, so much,' she says shrugging, although her only visible difference is that she has a lot of piercings in one earlobe. Still, he isn't complaining.

In North London, where girls are as sharp as knives and almost as dangerous, he had felt doomed to obscurity and rejection. He wasn't black enough, or Jewish, or the son of somebody famous, or at a cool school; he didn't do drugs or play in a band or even travel to exotic countries. He was just a bit of a nerd, mildly popular but definitely not the kind who'd expect to pull a girl like

Katya. Polish men are larger, tougher, more pale and more male than he, with their giant sausage-fed muscles, clipped heads and practical expertise at any kind of job. Yet she likes him. He hopes it doesn't piss the others off. Most are pleasant, but he can feel that they think of him as a boy, not a man. One, Arek, continues to be pointedly hostile.

Arek is bloody enormous – well over two metres – and heavily muscled. Beside him, Devonians look like dwarfs. He'd arrived at Katya's house radiating fury, and although Xan doesn't understand a word of Polish he'd gathered Arek didn't like him being there. Eventually, the giant had said,

'This girl, Katya – she is from my town, you understand?'

'Yes,' Xan said, not understanding at all.

'You are bad to her, I—'

Arek made a chopping motion onto his left hand, and Xan saw the wedding ring there. He wondered why Arek was so protective.

'Sure. Don't worry.'

Maybe it's some weird Catholic thing, though Katya is a lot more experienced than himself. Xan has tried being friendly, in a polite way: it turns out that Arek works with Lottie and Martin on the housing development, and is, according to his mother, a tireless builder who can turn his hand to anything. It doesn't seem to matter. Arek is fine with the other Poles, but when Xan says hello to him in the kitchen, he just grunts, or glares.

'What's bugging him?' he asked Katya, but she only shrugged.

'Bed mood,' she said. 'Always, bed mood.'

The builder's name is often on the girls' lips, though Xan hasn't a clue what they're talking about. He can tell it makes Katya angry, even contemptuous, for she tosses her tawny hair, and her green eyes gleam like ice. Xan hopes she's criticising the Pole, and that he'll go away. He's so enormous that when he sits in the kitchen, he fills the whole room. Luckily, Arek comes less often after the first month.

201

Lottie never visits either – in fact, Xan has been careful not to tell her Katya's address – but she's always around in town these days. The development is in its first stage, and there are still thousands of tiny decisions to be made, as well as progressing with designs for the second stage of housing which she and Martin are designing.

'*That* is your mother?' Katya says in astonishment, when Xan points her out from across the street.

'Yes.'

'She is important lady,' Katya says, and she seems to look at Xan with new respect.

Xan shrugs. To him, his mother is this irritating middle-aged person whom he loves but has come to see as a loser.

On the other hand, even if a housing development isn't like some fuck-off office block along the Thames, it's still interesting: Xan hasn't grown up with an architect without realising that. For one thing, it isn't the usual row of bungalows plonked down in a country cul-de-sac, but terraced housing arranged around a series of lanes and courtyards, which he can see will look both modern and as if they have been there for a hundred years. It has quirks and corners and dormer windows; each house will be rendered and painted different colours. Of course, she hasn't designed the first lot; it's the work of the man Dud calls Beardy. Years of man-alerts tell Xan that Beardy has a massive crush on his mother of which Lottie, typically, is completely unaware. However, the development is coming with a new extension to the secondary school, a new community centre and a library; and all these, Lottie is designing.

'It's a beacon of hope for us, that's what it is,' Maddy says. 'There's nowhere for mothers and babies to go, apart from the church, which is bloody freezing. We need a bigger school. There are three generations of families who've grown up in Trelorn who can't get their kids school places, any more than you can get an appointment with the doctor. You want to know why we want to leave Europe? That's why.'

Lottie talks with some passion about how neglected this part of the country is.

'They don't understand that the government hates the West Country, poor sods.'

'You sound as if you care about them,' Xan says to his mother.

'You don't have to be born in a place to care about it, and love it, just things like the sky ... Architects are always stealing sky, you know. Only here, it's so big that you couldn't begin to do that.'

'So how much longer are we staying?'

'I've stopped asking. I just have to take each day as it comes, and thank God we have a roof over our heads. Besides, Hugh isn't likely to live many more months.'

'As if Quentin cares about his father!'

'Oh, I think he'll find that he does, you know,' Lottie says.

'He can't be nice to him even when he's practically dead.'

'I'm not making any excuses for how he behaves to Hugh. But he sees a different side to what you do. We all see different things about people. You never know everything about someone, not even me.'

Xan can't help resenting this. Now he's got a job and a girl-friend, he sometimes – just for an instant – sees things from Quentin's point of view. (When Lottie was going into some faff about nothing the other day, he'd caught Dud's eye and they'd exchanged one of those looks that said, silently, *Women!*)

Much as Xan dislikes his stepfather, he does have his uses. On New Year's Day, he helped Xan write his Personal Statement again. Xan had been all for sending the old one off, but Quentin was having none of it.

'You need to think about this again. You're a year older than you were, and this doesn't do you justice.'

'I know never to say I'm passionate about anything.'

'However, *this* can be better phrased, and why aren't you mentioning what you're reading now?'

'I'm too tired, I do a fucking job.'

'If you swear, we'll get nowhere. You want to read English Literature. So do thousands of others. How should you distinguish yourself from them? What have you *read* that isn't on the curriculum?'

So they had battled on, and it had taken a whole day, a whole day in which (as he was often informed) his stepfather should have been doing his tax returns. Of course they both knew that Quentin, as a professional writer, could toss off the right words in five minutes. Xan sweated through it, line by line, trying not to lose heart. It was so easy to slide into the same old misery and sense of inadequacy. Little by little, however, it occurred to him that the thing he really loved had nothing to do with architecture. What he loved was no more and no less than his subject. It simply didn't matter where he studied it. He's applied to the same universities as before, except that this time he's put UCL down too. He'd never thought of applying to university in London when he lived there, but now it seemed obvious.

Even then, Quentin was standing over him saying,

'Come on, what are you waiting for?'

'I don't know whether I'm doing the right thing.'

'Well, you'll never find out if you don't press that button, will you?'

Off it went, and now he feels more hopeful about his future.

Work, and getting to Trelorn and back, is less bad now that the year is turning. To emerge from the factory into the dripping dawn, to see the grey skies flush gold with the advancing sun, and to hear the birds that have somehow survived the winter rustling, squeaking, cheeping, trilling, gurgling, chuckling, cooing and finally singing up and down the hillsides, is what he loves best about the countryside, perhaps not surprisingly, given that he's been led to it by Hugh. Poor old man ... Xan has gone over to see him when Lottie took the girls over

204

for a visit, partly to tell him that he's trying again. Hugh had been asleep.

'Write him a note,' Naomi suggested. 'I know he'll be sorry to miss you.'

Xan did so, awkwardly, because he had become unaccustomed to holding a pen.

I like the look of UCL, and that's where I've applied, he wrote. *It's always interesting talking to you about books, and I hope we can do so soon.*

It sounded lame, but maybe Hugh would understand that he was trying to thank him. He knows, without asking, that his stepfather's father has had his own battles with depression and failure, that he's felt overlooked and undervalued. Even if he's on the National Curriculum, he's a minor poet – though to Xan, several of his poems are as good as, say, Ted Hughes's.

'It's so much a matter of luck, and being in the right place at the right time. The only thing that matters is the work, in the end. You don't know, when you write something, who will read it,' Hugh told him. 'All art is a defiance of death.'

Humbles, on the other hand, is the opposite. The immense labour of producing food still astonishes him. The long wait for seeds to sprout, fruit to swell, herds to mature, can only be partially improved by machinery, fleeces, fertilisers, because at the end of that process there still have to be human beings picking and processing it, and these will never ever be paid properly. Then the business of making meals is another convulsion of effort and will. Fresh or frozen, the potatoes, carrots, turnips, butter, meat, fruit pour in one end of the factory to be cooked, and out the other. It's a relentless embrace of death.

'What did you think it would be?' Maddy asks. 'Lambs skipping to the slaughterhouse?'

'Er – no,' Xan answers. He glares at Dawn, shuffling past with her trolley. Each day, she seems more withdrawn.

'Poor kid,' Maddy says.

'What's wrong with her?'

'Her mum's boyfriend, if you ask me. You've met Rod, haven't you?'

'Yes. Gross.'

Now that he's with Katya, the man who had assaulted him while he was working has moved on to easier targets. There are new Eastern Europeans who have come over to replace those who have moved on, and when Rod is around he always assaults them – as long as they're young. If Dawn is having to live with him, her life must be pretty grim, Xan thinks.

When Xan thinks of all the advantages he'd taken for granted, he feels ashamed. Maddy doesn't have any GCSEs, and although she can read, write and add up, she is likely to spend the rest of her life working at the factory, while her health and strength last. She's honest, kind, hard-working, bright and sharp; only she hated school and school, according to Maddy, hated her.

'All I could think about was how much I wanted to leave home and marry Joe. Only, what would've been the harm in getting some qualifications? It wasn't as if we had to do it right away. Maybe then my Joe wouldn't have joined the Army, and lost his legs.'

'I'm so sorry, Maddy.'

'Sorry for what? I'm fine.'

I have to get out of this, he thinks. I can get out, thanks to my education – but she doesn't even know how trapped she is. Then it occurs to him that she probably does, and that this, too, is part of her dignity.

A letter and a parcel are waiting for him when he gets back to Home Farm. The parcel is addressed by Naomi but contains a note in Hugh's wavering hand.

'You might like this. H'

Inside is a slim paperback of poems.

Mark but this flea, and mark in this,
How little that which thou deniest me is;
It sucked me first, and now sucks thee,
And in this flea our two bloods mingled be . . .

The other invites him to come for a written examination, and an interview, at University College London.

19

Lambing Time

Sally's days shrink to blood, shit, milk and sheep. In March, she can be up half the night delivering lambs with Peter. There are just the two of them, and five hundred and seven sheep in labour this year. She takes her holiday now, and it isn't one.

The frosty days have passed. Outside, the spring winds are blowing from the south-west again, and small birds are tossing from branch to branch under a sky as blue and cream as a Cornish plate. The duck-shaped weathervane on top of the old farmhouse creaks and spins, as if trying to fly off and join them. Any gate or door left open slams violently against its post, and the cats skitter across the yard like kittens, chasing their own shadows in the sharp sunlight.

The pens shuffle with ewes, their thick, matted winter coats standing up around their long pale faces like ruffs, so that they look like a gathering of women in an old painting. All winter they've carried their lambs under their felted fleeces, through the cold dark months of snow and mud. Now, it's time to drop their burdens.

Though the barn is quite full, each needs enough space to

be alone; for birth, like death, is always a private experience, even for an animal. Sheep, like all herd creatures, do their best to behave as one, yet even they are solitary as they lamb. How fearful this nakedness is, and how absolute! Sally has talked to women in labour when she worked as a midwife, trying to make a bridge between the place where they must suffer and struggle, and that of ordinary unthinking life. She's talked about it with her sister Anne, who sees it at the other end.

'It's like staring at the sun,' Anne said. 'If you did think about dying, you'd go mad.'

There are different kinds of aloneness. She has been married for almost half her life, now, and though she loves her husband Sally can't imagine what she'd feel like without her sisters and friends. She thinks of the women who fall for bad men like Rod Ball: how much of it is out of sheer loneliness? There are plenty of her sex who feel that unless they have a man in their life, any man, they are somehow not valid. If only they'd have more self-respect! Or at least better judgement. The best and nicest women have been brought low by this, including her eldest sister Tess. She pretended everything in her marriage was perfect, until one day when her husband hit her so badly he broke her arm. She had just enough sense of self-preservation to take her children and run back to their mum.

She's remarried, long since, and has made a success of her life as a teacher; her children are grown up, she seems calm and happy. But even Tess would never have stooped as low as Rod.

He has such a bad reputation, though it never puts women off. None of his ex-partners will tell the police or social services, and the little gang of men who go out drinking with him won't tell either. To them he's a daredevil, a bit of a lad, famous for setting fire to a hated speed camera on the A30, for vandalising one of the noisy windmills that a farmer (unable to resist the £60,000 grant for putting one up) had ruined a prominent hill with, and various other stunts. He is a real charmer when he wants to be.

209

'He fixes his attention on you like you're the only person there,' said one of his girlfriends. 'How many men ever do that? They'd rather talk about their cars than the colour of your eyes.'

If Rod were a multimillionaire living in Shipcott Manor, would she feel the same about him? Probably: but then Tore, unlike Rod, has always taken care of his children, legitimate and illegitimate. It didn't stop the women getting hurt, but it did mean the kids suffered less – perhaps.

It seems so unjust that this kind of man was allowed to get away with treating women like dirt, while poor Oliver Randall lived all alone. A year on, his tragedy is passing into story: the headless pianist might one day become a local legend, to join the many others. It would be different if Randall had had family here, or even friends, but he'd been one of the many solitary types who gravitate towards the country . . . and life, in any case, always moves on.

Six lambs are being born every hour, mostly twins, emerging tongue first, followed by the feet and long dark-knuckled legs. Several times, however, Sally or Peter must reach in with their bare hands and feel up to their own elbows for a lamb that has got stuck or needs turning.

'I can't manage this breech,' Peter pants.

Sally dreads events like these. Inside, the ewe is like a volcano. Her contractions are so strong that Sally's hand is gripped excruciatingly hard. She yells.

'Ow-ow, my hand!'

'Try, m'dear,' he says, and grips her shoulder. They both know what will happen if the lamb dies inside its mother.

Sweating, Sally just manages to hook her other fingers under its leg. It's a long, delicate business and her bruised hand is in agony, but when it's over and she wipes herself clear of slime she's relieved to see that it's not broken.

'Well done!' Peter pats her.

A butterfly coming out of its cocoon is no less miraculous than

210

the limp, bedraggled body of a lamb becoming the animal that skips and gambols like a baby cloud. Some farmers hate sheep. They call them 'vermin', and treat them as nothing more than meat on legs. Yet sheep know the difference between a friendly face and an angry one, and when Peter walks into their field they all come to him for sheep-nuts. They trust him now.

Within a day, the new lambs will race about, answering their mothers' calls in high, milky voices that sound very like the parent-and-child drop-in mornings Sally helps to run in a shabby, run-down room off the main square. It contains three crates of old toys, a few tattered books and old magazines, a sink and a kettle.

'I know it's all supposed to get better once the community centre is finished, but I can't help wishing they'd just give us more money instead,' one of the mums who comes said.

Sally is hearing of parents who are denying themselves food so that their children won't go hungry. If you lose your job, you can't pay your rent, and once you lose your home you probably can't get benefits because there's no way of contacting you even if a new job does come along. The poorest mums turn up with soggy nappies, in order to cadge a free one from the stock.

Devon looks prosperous, with its houses rising up the rolling hills like flecks of cream rising to the surface, its pastures pocked with cattle and sheep, and its long golden beaches. On days when it's not sheeting with rain from the Atlantic, you can see why it's one of the top tourist destinations in Britain. But you can't live just on tourism, Sally thinks. For Trelorn to stay alive, it has to support real people doing real jobs, like Peter. A music academy won't be half as useful as an agricultural college, and if Tore's housing development helps anybody, it won't be those on the lowest incomes. It's a rich man's fantasy, not real country life like this, Sally thinks.

Still the lambs keep coming, wave after wave of them, day after day. They try to stagger the insemination for this reason, and some ewes can give birth in their field without difficulty – as long as the crows and foxes are kept off. Most, however, are safest in the barn.

'Oh shit.'

Peter is quietly frantic. A lamb has died inside its mother. Somehow, its legs must be unfolded, then pulled out while the ewe stands trembling, unable to push, with blood leaking out in thick, viscous drops.

Slowly, carefully, he puts his hand up inside her and ties a piece of string around the dead lamb's back leg, which is pointing out of the ewe's cervix. It's a finicky job, and at last the ewe moans, a deep, sorrowful sound that seems to come from the earth itself.

'Easy does it,' he murmurs.

To their horror, the two back legs that emerge are detached from the rest of the body. The lamb is not only dead, but rotting away inside its mother. It takes the better part of half an hour to remove the pieces, and they're all distressed by the end. Without a lamb to suckle the ewe's uterus can't retract, but the look of misery on the ewe's face is entirely clear.

'It's not your fault, you poor thing,' Sally says.

They know what to do. Peter gets out his knife and skins what he can from the corpse. It's a grim, bloody job and he's so tired, yet this ewe must be given another ewe's lamb, covered in the smell of the dead lamb's slimy skin so that she'll suckle it. Only then will the creature be given a reason to live – alongside a mighty shot of antibiotics. He is so gentle with the flock, as gentle as he'd be with their own children.

By sundown the next day, the battle is over. The substitute lamb is suckling strongly at its foster mother's teat, with the desperation of all young things to live. The pens are full of little families which need a bit of extra help, but most of the flock are out grazing, at least during the day.

'I wasn't sure we'd be in a fit state to have visitors,' Sally says on Sunday, kissing her sisters and Anne's children.

212

Sally's nephews and nieces love doing things like bottle-feeding the orphaned lambs with artificial milk, and are disappointed if there isn't at least one to pet while their mother and aunts share a cup of tea together. This time, they've brought two friends.

'Oh, he's so *sweet!*' one exclaims.

'Look, Rosie, this is how you feed it,' Anne's eldest daughter says, with a trace of bossiness. Anne catches Sally's eye, and laughs.

'I can't think who she reminds me of.'

'Me neither,' Sally says. They are all bossy, all three of them, and know it. 'Whose are these?'

'Incomers to Shipcott, living at Home Farm.'

'Oh, yes, I know the mum.'

'Isn't she the one involved with the housing development?'

'That's right. Turns out she and Martin are old friends from London.'

'Oh?' Tess says, with a wealth of enquiry.

'Who knows?' Anne answers softly, though Rosie's well out of earshot.

'The husband's none too popular.'

'I'm not surprised!'

'Whingeing on in his newspaper about being forced to live in one of the most beautiful places in the whole country.'

Anne doesn't usually let her guard down; she's very conscious that, like Sally and Tess, she is privy to all kinds of information about the families she encounters. Quentin Bredin must have really annoyed her for her to let off steam in this way.

'The mum is lovely,' Sally says. 'She's even coming to our book group.'

'Yes, of course. Shame a local family couldn't have taken it, though.'

'But his dad is Hugh the poet, born in Trelorn,' Anne says. 'So he's not an incomer, really. I've been over there quite a bit.'

They know what this means: Anne is a Marie Curie nurse.

'I still wouldn't like to live in that house. Ever since that poor chap got murdered . . . '

'I know. It haunts me, too. The most gentle, harmless person you can imagine, killed in that horrible way.' Anne pauses. 'The Bredins have been asking questions about him, or at least the man has. I wonder if there's anything he can discover.'

'The police didn't find anything, did they?' Tess asks.

'I think they thought at one point there might be some connection to the Tores.'

'There were those rumours about Randall and Di Tore.'

'I don't believe them. You've only got to see the Tores together to know they're devoted.'

'Though he's twice her age, isn't he?'

'Since when did that matter to a rock star? Admit it, if he looked our way, we'd probably be unable to resist.'

'Annie! I'm shocked!' says Sally.

Tess says, 'I just wish they could find out who did it, so we can all sleep easy in our beds.'

'But surely whoever did it has moved on?'

'Who knows?' Annie adds, 'He must have been escaping from something, mustn't he? Why else do incomers come here?'

Sally's nieces enter, with Lottie's daughter holding the lamb in her arms.

'He doesn't want any more milk,' she announces.

'That's all right. You put him down now, and let him stretch his legs.'

Reluctantly, the little girl relinquishes the lamb which is growing stronger and more playful by the day, and they all go outside again. Everything thrills the children, from the lambs to their neighbours' horses.

'I wish I could have a pony,' Rosie says, catching sight of their neighbours' horses. 'Oh, look, it's hurt itself!'

Sally, who has come with her, looks and sees. A hind leg

has been cut; the mare is limping slightly, and when she looks closer—

'Come away, my dear,' she says. 'I think I need to call the vet.'

Those bloody Balls brothers, she thinks: I bet it's them. They're the ones who go lamping, and this would be just another bit of cruel fun.

When she gets back to her house, it's not just the vet whom she calls, but the police.

20

Work, Not Love

The skies are still marbled with cold, but the energy of spring is prodigious. A million shades of green unfurl overnight: black-green, yellow-green, red-green, white-green, bronze-green, silver-green, green-green, speckled and spotted, dashed and dotted across the landscape. Birds bustle in branches, trilling like alarm clocks. The grass explodes with miniature suns. Impossible for Lottie not to feel cheered by it all.

To be earning again means that Quentin can no longer push her around. Work, not love, is the one salvation: had she ever been tempted to abandon her career, she is now rewarded for never doing so. Those days of crawling into an office half-dead from broken nights, of struggling to keep going on nothing but coffee and adrenalin, of endless self-doubt that she was doing two things badly instead of one thing well, are justified. She is financially independent.

Martin's practice is a marked contrast to the kind of outfit she once worked for. Not everyone in the town likes him, but as far as she can tell, most respect what he is trying to do, even if there are the inevitable mutterings about how the development

216

will change the character of Trelorn. The extension is his biggest project yet, but he's worked a miracle by persuading the council to give it permission in under two years. It helps, presumably, that the chief investor is Tore.

'We used to talk about what would revive the town when I was working on his house. We both love this part of the world, and so we'd talk about what was wrong and how much investment was needed, how something could be built that's attractive and only for local people, not rich incomers,' Martin said. 'It grew out of that. He's an idealist, you know, and he still wants to change the world.'

'I thought he was a wild man who only cared about sex and drugs.'

'He's nothing like that really. The public want rock stars to be mad and bad when really they're just nerdy musicians.'

Whatever the truth, the project is a big one. It will take over a decade to complete, providing over 100 new jobs. Quentin, of course, calls it Toytown.

'You're only building for people who can take out mortgages. It's paternalistic, nostalgic crap,' he says.

Maybe, though, she is just not the kind of person who is good at sharing life with another person. She knows she is irritating, but he either doesn't know or doesn't care.

'Quentin says everything is my fault.'

'Why?'

'Oh, because I'm "too posh to be a mammal". But he's the one who is complaining about the mud and so on, not me.'

'You really like it there?'

'Yes, I do, despite the murder in the woodshed.'

Her mother snorts. 'If you really like it, why not stay?'

'Oh, do stay!' Di Tore says. Back from Australia, and despite what seem like frequent shopping trips to Paris and New York, she has resumed the playdates and visits, dropping enough gossip about the people she knows to fill a dozen tabloids. 'We need

217

you here. It's different for Gordon, when he's not touring he just wants to relax here without other people, though he only has to click his fingers and about fifty assistants appear.'

'So you think that the new academy will be good enough?'

'Worth a try, I reckon. Just think, you could be designing your kids' future school!'

The build has started and now the foundations have been dug and concrete poured, work is going apace. It must help, she thinks, that Martin can actually make things himself: he's respected locally as a joiner, rather than as an architect. His team are all men, local twenty-year-olds whom even the Army would hesitate to take on.

'But can you trust them?' Lottie asks. 'One dropped a prescription for methadone.'

'You know what they say: ex-junkies turn to booze, religion or hard work. It's just a question of spotting which are the ones to choose work.'

She soon sees the truth of this. However hard the Poles labour, the ex-junkies stay longer, toiling under klieg lamps, in sheeting rain and freezing cold.

'If they do overtime, they'll be able to do more than live with their mothers and drive a beat-up van,' Martin says. 'The young men here are almost unemployable because most have no skills or qualifications. If they don't inherit a farm, all they do is work out, or take drugs.'

'Where do they find drugs in the countryside?'

'Half the weed in Britain comes from the West Country.' Martin's square teeth glint at her surprise. 'Without it, many more farmers would be going bankrupt, you see . . .'

Every conversation with him becomes a kind of lecture. His heart is in the right place, but she wonders whether this is one of the reasons why his marriage went wrong.

They are having a last mug of tea in the Portakabin by the site. The road winding up out of town goes right past it, and even

218

now is quite busy. She enjoys seeing not only cars and lorries but tractors and horses go past.

'You know I've never done a build like this?'

'Don't worry,' Martin says, 'Really: you are overqualified. It's great to have you on board. You should really be coming in as my partner.'

'I don't have the money,' she says.

'Well, one day maybe . . . '

He blushes fierily, and her heart sinks.

'It's always the same,' she tells her mother, later. 'The bores fall in love with me, and I fall in love with the bastards. What a pain feelings are! But he's my boss, and it's awkward, because I do like him.'

'My darling, he seems kind, and that is always the most important thing,' her mother says. 'Not whether he is charming, or amusing, or rich.'

'Quentin isn't any of those things either.'

'You thought differently, at one time.'

'I was mad. Love makes you mad. Now, I'm sane.'

It gives her some satisfaction to see that it is Quentin who now collects Stella and Rosie in the afternoons, supervises their homework and makes their tea. They don't even discuss this: she is the one going out to an office, and she is earning twice what he does at last. His ideas of parenting, however, are very different from hers. She is shocked to find he has been giving them cookery lessons.

'Stop! They'll lose a finger if that blade slips,' Lottie says, horrified. His chef's knives are lethal.

Quentin ignores her. 'Bruise the garlic clove, toss in the oil, then take it out of the pan when it turns yellow. Nothing tastes nastier than burnt garlic.'

Lottie always burns the garlic because she gets bored. Anyway, Quentin may be a better cook than she is, but he's absolutely rotten at washing up.

The trouble is, the more her frayed nerves are repaired, the more she remembers what it had felt like to make love with him. I may never have sex in my life again, she thinks. She wishes it wasn't such a depressing thought.

This landscape with its mud and cold and winds and great, creaking trees fills her with a different kind of passion, inhuman yet bracing. A line keeps repeating itself in her head: *Nature never did betray the heart that loved her.* She doesn't know who said it, but it feels true.

When she had first come here, feeling like a pioneer woman alighting in the uncharted wild with her caravans drawn up in a circle, it had been very different. Both the landscape and the house had been the incarnation of her desperation. Now, familiarity is breeding content. She likes the casement windows set in the deep, thick walls, and the window seats that look down the valley. She has ceased to mourn her large modern kitchen with its granite worktops and shiny steel fittings. The Rayburn with its puttering murmurs is a warm, genial presence, and even the old brown furniture, with its speckled mirrors and sprinklings of woodworm, is more friendly than the smart veneered things from Heals which she had prized in London. Bit by bit, this dank, drab place is becoming a home. In the evening when the wood-burner is lit, with the new cushions, curtains and lampshades, it actually looks cosy. She has repainted the living room (red) and bathroom (blue) and the entrance (yellow).

'I don't see why you're wasting your time on a rented property,' Quentin says.

'Because I am living here, and it's what I do. I don't care what you think.'

'So, how is it going with Beardy?'

'His practice does interesting work.'

'He's the sort of person who makes me want to eat a barn owl.'

Lottie says, 'He's successful, which is more than can be said of you.'

'I am successful too.'

'Yes: nobody will give you a job. Anyway, the beams look good, painted white.'

The biggest transformation, however, is in the kitchen.

When the last dead rat had been found, it was located behind the pine dresser. She had been obliged to ask Quentin for help to move it away from the gable end, but the reward was unexpected: a big old window was revealed, facing south-west. Light pours in and, stripped of the ivy on the outside, it has given the kitchen the best view of all.

'How odd that it was blocked up before,' Xan said.

'Isn't it?' Lottie answered. 'Maybe it was to stop the wind.'

'Amazing! And it was here all the time?' asked Di Tore, dropping by.

'Yes. Did you not see it on the plans?'

Di frowns. 'I think I didn't look.'

Naturally, for the 1000 acres of the Shipcott estate contain many other broken-down farmhouses and cottages, some of which will be restored and incorporated into the Trelorn development. Lottie can't begin to imagine how much it will all cost, because Tore's wealth is so enormous that there is no point in imagining it. Her relationship is with Di, and it's a liking without envy. Would they have become friends in London? Probably not; here, however, they are just mothers who get on. Di makes Lottie laugh with her rude Aussie jokes; though discreet about Gore, she's clearly fond of him.

'It makes a difference that I've got money of my own. We aren't married, even if people call me Mrs Tore. He's a great dad, I adore him, but he knows that I can leave him if he misbehaves. I don't want to know what he gets up to on tour, but I don't think he has the same drive to climb every C-cup now he's pushing seventy.'

'It would never work for me,' Lottie says.

'Yeah, you're a romantic.'

'I think children are, too.'

'That's true enough. Tiger and Dexter would like us to be married. Maybe one day.'

Di is still sorting out Shipcott Manor, and Lottie suspects that it absorbs a lot of the energy that would otherwise make her discontented. She clearly loves making a home, and the house, despite its overhaul, is still not finished. She has a man from the village to help with the garden, but no interior decorator. Sometimes she brings samples of fabric round for Lottie to help her choose.

'You should have seen the state it was in! The old man who lived here before was living in one room, the kitchen, and it was *hopping with fleas*. But Gordon, bless him, gets such a kick out of rescuing it – you know, his mum worked there?'

'Someone did tell me, yes. That must be very satisfying for him.'

'It is. He's said to me that of all the things he's ever owned, it's the one thing that makes him feel rich – apart from his first Fender Strat.'

'So how come Oliver Randall wound up living in Home Farm?'

'Oh, they were friendly from way back. He used to work as a session musician with Gordon, years ago.'

Lottie, who never listens to pop music if she can possibly help it, nods politely.

'I was just wondering how Randall could afford to rent this place.'

Lottie knows she is probing, but Di seems so open that she has to ask.

'Easy. He didn't pay any rent! Gordon wanted to help him, he needed to get away from London. He taught the boys piano, and me too sometimes.'

'Why did he need to get away?'

'Maybe he liked the quiet.'

Lottie has a feeling that Di isn't telling her everything. Maybe

Randall had been in love with her: she's so beautiful that it's entirely possible. Lottie enjoys it as she might an exquisite painting, but a man might feel differently.

'Was he attractive?'

'Olly? Well, not really. He was like this timid animal hiding behind his beard, very gentle and sensitive.' She turns away, sniffing. 'Such a horrible, senseless murder. Nobody deserves that.'

'It must have been dreadful. Were you . . . friends?'

Di gives her a shrewd look, and her tears vanish. 'We were, but not in that sense.'

Lottie feels uncomfortable. 'Sorry. I don't tell tales, by the way.'

'Not even to your husband?'

'Especially not to him, as we're getting divorced. I'm just intrigued, living in that house. Wouldn't you be?'

Di relaxes. 'Well, there really isn't anything to tell. We were all upset, Gordon more than anyone. He felt responsible, even if he wasn't.'

Lottie wonders whether Gore had ever been given cause to be jealous. Yet if he had, she can't see why he'd bother to have him murdered. It's obvious to her that Di hadn't been in love with their tenant.

'You know, my mother actually taught them both at the Royal Academy?'

'No! How weird.' Instantly, Di cheers up. 'So it's, like, karma you found this place?'

'Yes. But, as she herself said, similar people often seem to end up in the same houses.'

'I'll tell Gordon. You still haven't met, have you?' Di sighs. 'You will. He comes and goes.'

'Did Oliver have a wife or girlfriend?'

'I never heard of one, no. I don't think he was gay, either. I think he liked to be alone but was quite lonely.'

Yes, Lottie thinks, Home Farm had been the house of a lonely man. Yet there had been the doll her daughters found, a make

223

that she knows from her own daughters only came on the market a decade ago, and mail-order catalogues for women's clothing. It was strange, though there were rational explanations for both: the doll could have been left by a young pupil, and it was all too easy to get junk mail. She's noticed, wryly, that despite her fall in income, she's been pursued by the usual catalogues of middle-class life, especially since she has started to shop again, not for herself but for Xan.

To her immense relief, he has received four new offers.

'I didn't even know you'd reapplied,' she said, when he told her the news.

'Dud helped me draft a new Personal Statement at the last moment.'

'Oh.'

Lottie was not sure how to take this.

'Which do you think you'll choose?'

'I like Bristol. Or UCL, if they give me an offer. Will we go back to London?'

'It shouldn't matter to you, because wherever you go you'll be *in a city* again. That's what you want, isn't it?'

'Yes.'

But whether it is what she herself wants is becoming another question entirely.

—

21

This Animal Life

Quentin's father won't admit he is dying. There is no hair on his head, his skin hangs off his skeleton like a fine fabric, his pain is barely muffled by drugs, and yet Hugh is convinced it is just another illness from which he'll recover. Maybe everyone has this delusion, Quentin thinks, or maybe his father is being bloody-minded to the last.

'I just want the antibiotics to kick in,' Hugh keeps saying plaintively.

'Yes, darling,' Naomi says.

'Then everything will be back to normal.'

Is it Hugh's appetite for life, or his deceitfulness, which makes him deny the truth?

Everyone lives at the centre of their own existence, with other lives circling around them as planets do the sun. How can it be otherwise, without a lifelong effort of will? Yet even to understand that other people have their own thoughts and feelings, that they have their own version of the truth, and their own tender self-regard just like your own, is to make a step away from solipsism. Quentin can't despise his father without seeing how

225

like him he has become. He loathes this in himself because his life's work has been to not be like Hugh. He thought he had succeeded, in London. Yet here he is, trapped.

His mother is very different, and he wonders whether it is because women seem biologically programmed to be more altruistic. Which is rubbish: there are quite as many dreadful women as there are men, and gender is no guarantee of virtue. Naomi is of the generation whose watchword is always, 'Least said, soonest mended.' She'll never complain, or talk about what she suffered with Hugh. However, Quentin has always known that he could pick up the phone to his mother at any time of day or night to ask for help or sympathy, and he'll get it. Even if she is disappointed in him, she will never stop loving him: but since he can never begin to repay her bounty, there's no point in trying. Before his marriage, he never remembered to ring her on her birthday, let alone send a card or present, and after it he took it for granted that this would be his wife's job. Yet he loves Naomi. However much she irritates him, however much he wishes she didn't accept things with an equanimity which in anyone else would be a mark of stupidity, he will always care about her. If there is any good in him, it comes from her patience and compassion.

It's a different matter with his father.

When he was a child, Hugh had been the great man whose occasional appearances and enthusiasms were treated like natural disasters or bounties. Quentin and his sister were impressed from their earliest days that their play must be quiet and unobtrusive, that meals must be punctual and well-behaved, that holidays were not for their own enjoyment but their father's. Naomi's devotion and conviction in her husband's genius made this seem entirely natural. That had been during Hugh's heyday, when he had been one of a group of impoverished but increasingly well-known poets of his generation, spoken of in the same breath as Hughes and Larkin. Yet his talent, unlike theirs, had not continued to bear him aloft but had plunged him into poverty and obscurity.

They had so little money that Quentin has dim, childish memories of actually being hungry. When the offer of the teaching jobs at Knotshead had come along, Hugh had accepted it. For a poet to teach English at a famous progressive public school was no shame, and given that the deal included free education for his children and subsidised accommodation for his family, it would have been crazy not to.

Naturally, it was a poisoned chalice. Knotshead was awash with the children of those whose liberal politics sat comfortably with exorbitant school fees, rampant snobbery and sexual misdemeanour. Hugh was admired; though irascible, he taught with knowledge and passion. Unfortunately, the latter tended to be reciprocated by the more impressionable. Though not so foolish as to sleep with his pupils while they were under-age and at school, once they left, it was different.

'They are so pretty, how could any man resist?' he said.

Even in the 1970s, that shoddy decade of licentious squalor, it was appalling behaviour. Quentin can't think back to his adolescence without a great boil of rage swelling inside him. Hugh behaved abominably to his wife, his children, his colleagues and his pupils; and far from feeling shame, had sneered at his children for protesting.

'What does a pair of virgins know?' he said. 'Piss off, and mind your own business.'

You bastard, Quentin thinks. I was a teenage boy, I was trying to defend my mother, I didn't need crushing.

Yet Quentin has also spent his life craving his father's approval. Even now, when he wipes Hugh's withered arse, a part of him is waiting for praise which never comes.

His father despises him. Hugh has always seen journalism as the lowest form of writing, and although each time Quentin bought himself a new suit or went on holiday abroad, he mentally thumbed his nose at Hugh, thinking, Fool, this is what I can afford and you can't, he can never rid himself of the wish that his father would acknowledge his own writings. Did Hugh really think that Dickens, Orwell, Virginia Woolf and Evelyn Waugh were slumming when they wrote for newspapers and magazines? Poetry kept you poor and obscure and living in a damp cottage with tiny dirty windows; why not admit that journalism demanded inspiration and talent? Yet these days, nobody remembers a word of anything Quentin has ever written, whereas poems of Hugh's have somehow endured. One, 'Moss', even seems to mock him:

Yes, the rolling stone gathers no moss but
Neither is it cast . . .

What will replace that looming, baleful sense of presence? Increasingly, he realises that simply by existing, Hugh has shielded him from infinite darkness.

His father had said to him, in one of their rows,

'I'll come back to haunt you like Hamlet's father.'

'If you do, I'll still tell you to fuck off,' Quentin shouted.

The Hovel is the place he dreads going to, yet every day he steels himself to enter it. Is it out of love for his mother or duty to his father? He doesn't know. He's furious with his sister for not coming back from New Zealand to help, but she isn't there and he is.

Hugh, his face the colour of batter, is lying where he always seems to lie, eyes half-closed.

'Fa?'

His father ignores him.

'Bastards, crooks and schemers,' he says, to *The World at One*. 'We've had the best of times, and you're going to have the worst.'

The thought seems to give him some satisfaction.

Naomi says, 'Money isn't the only thing in life is it? The sun still rises, the birds still sing . . . '

Quentin murmurs, 'I don't think birdsong is going to be much good to people in Greece, Ma.'

'Don't bother! She never has the slightest idea about politics.'

Quentin takes the rubbish out, separating kitchen scraps from the rest. The bins keep being chewed by rats, desperate to get at the rotting food. His mother recycles everything in the belief that just one piece of plastic will end up choking hundreds of seabirds, but if it means a few less gulls, so what? It's a nauseating job. Unlike Lottie, who swans off to Trelorn every day, he has to squeeze work into the interstices of domestic life. He has, effectively, become a woman.

He hoses the bins, then straightens up. A clump of narcissus releases its sweet scent in the sun, as if in compensation. For a moment, pleasure fills his senses. To live this animal life might almost be enough. Only, it's not.

'I'm looking forward to my first crop of tomatoes,' he says, re-entering.

'I always did think you'd inherit my green fingers, one day.'

'It's just housework, out of doors.'

'Yes, but it's the out-of-doors bit that matters.'

Increasingly, Quentin can't help wondering whether his wife is sleeping with Beardy. Impossible, surely, but something has changed. Lottie is looking different, or maybe her mouth, and her eyes. He had told her once that she was not unattractive. He was ashamed of it immediately afterwards, because it was a double negative. Now he's ashamed of his meanness.

Quentin gets down on his hands and knees to pull up the worst of the weeds, and the act of physical abasement makes him fearful. Right ahead is the stump of an ash tree that his father had cut down decades ago when they first bought The Hovel. Every year, it shoots and suckers before breaking into feathery bronze leaves that are, briefly, beautiful, and it strikes him that whatever existed between himself and Lottie has also been chopped down, suddenly and brutally. Yet feelings, like trees, do not necessarily die; rather, their roots may quicken into not one but many new trees, all growing confusedly in a thicket that must be chopped again and again to keep it under control.

Money and marriage, he thinks. Who isn't obsessed by it, especially in middle age when you face both forward and back, seeing all your past mistakes and how, inexorably, they have led to future disasters. If only we *were* animals, unable to see what is coming.

'Are you sure you shouldn't get Fa to a hospital?' Quentin asked. Exhaustion had crumpled and recrumpled Naomi's face like a piece of blotched paper.

'He wants to be here, at home.'

'Then at least ask for more nursing.'

Naomi shook her head slightly. 'Our doctor's wife is a Marie Curie nurse, and she comes to help with the nights. Anne's lovely, but she can't come every day.'

At times, he goes into the bathroom just to make faces at himself in the mirror. He hates all this, quite violently, and yet he can't walk away. Is it compassion or a dreadful curiosity, like that which still has him trying to find out why Oliver Randall was killed?

Not that he's made any progress there. The people he's probed just clam up.

'Oh yes, you're a journalist aren't you?' they say. 'No comment, thank you.'

Tore is connected to the murder, somehow, he's quite sure – but Randall was too obscure to matter to anyone. Quentin has checked, and he hadn't even left a will. Or maybe, like Hugh, he didn't believe he would ever die.

Hugh lies on the cane chaise longue all day, when not shuffling off to the toilet, and then water sprays everywhere and Naomi has to come and clean everything up. Even then, he shouts at her.

Quentin says, not bothering to lower his voice, 'How can you put up with his vile temper?'

'It's like vinegar around a pickle,' Naomi says. 'It preserves him.'

230

All her best efforts to tempt her husband to eat go untasted after the first trembling bite.

'Don't be a fool, woman!' he snarls. 'It only goes in one end and out the other.'

He hates Hugh, but when Quentin thinks how his own daughters might turn against him in turn, he feels a small cold hand close round his heart. Like Xan, they now call him 'Dud'.

'You shouldn't call me that.'

'Why not? It's funny,' Stella said, giggling.

When Quentin had first committed adultery, on the desk of his office, his assistant Mimi had even asked him, 'Are you sure you want to do this?' What had made him answer, 'Yes' was an increasing urgency which felt like lust but which was the fear of his own mortality. Even if, like all men, he'd had idle fantasies about doing what he did (not to Mimi specifically, just to any woman he worked with), he hadn't really intended to go through with it until, suddenly, he was given the opportunity. For all of three minutes, it had felt terrific. But this feeling, he has come to realise, was bought at the expense of his daughters' childhood. Stella and Rosie will never believe in perfect love. They will hate him, just as he hates Hugh, as a cheat, a liar and a failure.

To see how you are seen by another person, without love or charity, is almost always unendurable. There was a time when he couldn't bear not being with Lottie and another when it seemed that the least thing she did was intolerable. Now that she is remote, she has changed again, and he wants her with a griping, costive dog-in-the-manger jealousy, because if she is sleeping with Martin it's an insult. But how long would *that* last? If the heart, like the eye, is continually in the process of dilating and contracting, how can any one person be certain about another? Or, for that matter, themselves?

'Lottie?'

'Yes?'

'I wondered whether you need help with that.'

'No, thanks.'

Her voice is not unfriendly, he thinks, rather than friendly.

Everyone seems to find him superfluous. Quentin's column is constantly attacked as trivial and pointless by the bloggers who leave poisonous comments on the online version of the *Chronicle*; he reads them just in case the anonymous person who told him about the murder posts again. Of course what he's writing is silly: he's supposed to be entertaining, but rage is the default setting. *Why are you being paid for this rubbish?* is the general consensus. Every time he files more copy he is aware that he is working in a dying profession.

'Your column has been getting a bit too gloomy, of late,' Ivo tells him.

'My father is terminally ill with cancer.'

'Bad luck. Maybe you can do a piece for us about it.'

Ivo doesn't mean to be heartless; he just thinks like an editor.

He has such vivid memories of Hugh as a huge, roaring man, overflowing with vitality and aggression: how can all that have ebbed away?

'Oh, you're here again,' Hugh says.

'Yes, Fa,' Quentin answers. He takes his father's long, thin hand in his own, and holds it, willing it to become warmer. 'Can I get you another blanket? Or a hot-water bottle?'

'It won't make much difference.'

The walls of the cottage are sweating like cheese, but Hugh is always cold. Outside, spring is pouring light over the land, and little green flames run up branches.

'It should be warm enough to go outside soon,' Quentin says.

'Is it?' Hugh looks, his eyes cloudy. 'I can't see.'

Quentin experiences another terrible lurch of understanding. There aren't going to be months or weeks left, now: just days and maybe hours.

'My feet are cold.'

'Let me massage them.'

He's surprised to hear himself offer this, and equally surprised when Hugh grunts an acceptance. Quentin takes off his father's bedsocks, and is repulsed at the thick, cracked, yellow nails. They look more like claws than human feet. Very gently, he rubs the skin with Vaseline, and Hugh whimpers.

'Don't do it like that,' Naomi exclaims sharply.

Hugh says, 'Stop fussing over me, woman.'

Later, Quentin asks her,

'Why do you put up with him?'

'I don't want him turning into one of those old men who die alone, like at Shipcott Manor.'

'Did he? Die alone, I mean?'

'Yes. Never married, and after all the wild parties he wound up starving to death in one room in that big house.'

'That bad?'

'Yes. I'm afraid he deserved what he got. His housekeeper, well, she died before him. Worn out, poor woman.'

'And people say Sir Gerald was Tore's father. Was he?'

'Oh, I think so. Gordon looks the spit of him sometimes. I think that's partly why he's married so many times; he didn't want to be like his father. But his mother was a brave woman. She wouldn't let him be adopted, which in those days was what women who were pregnant and unmarried were supposed to do, and brought him up in the gatehouse.'

'It's where our cleaner Janet lives now, you know.'

'Yes, and I'm sure it doesn't leak now! The Tores have done an amazing job restoring that place, and it's so good it's a real home again. A house is nothing without children. You know, Ian and Katie are going to make us great-grandparents?'

'Er, no.' The news that he will be a grandfather soon is not exactly welcome. 'Have you seen them?'

'Yes. I think they made the journey specially to see Hugh, though they stayed at the White Hart. Ian really is a delightful

233

person, and so is Katie. They're a lovely couple. I think they're going to get married, though they haven't said yet.'

Quentin shrugs. He feels almost jealous of his own son. Nothing seems to bother Naomi. When he'd asked if the water she drank was from the mains, she'd answered,

'No, it's from the well. It's perfectly clean, you know – newts live there.'

He repeats this to his father, and the two of them laugh together, for the first time in years. Then Hugh stops, and Quentin sees the terror in his eyes.

Hugh says, 'She used to be so beautiful, you know. Your mother.'

'I know,' he answered, though he feels angry at the way Hugh implies she is at fault for getting old, as if it isn't the case with everyone alive. At least his father has had his mother nurse him in his old age. Meanwhile, he himself has nobody.

The affair with Tina has fizzled out quite abruptly. He arrived unannounced at her houseboat, and discovered another man in her bedroom wearing only a short purple terry towelling dressing gown, a gold medallion, and socks. This is Roger, a name that has cropped up with increasing frequency since Christmas.

'Sorry,' Tina said, without a trace of compunction; 'but you wouldn't take a hint.'

Quentin left without a word. It was nothing, after all: just sex and somewhere to stay when he came up to London. What horrified him most was that his replacement was so *old*. He keeps being shocked at parties by how haggard, fat, wrinkled and bald his contemporaries have become, and yet it's just the effect of having been away in America; presumably they think the same of him. He returned to Devon as soon as his ticket allowed, and sat in his car in the cindery Exeter car park, the harsh, tingling sound of the tracks vibrating in his ears like eldritch laughter.

Hugh drifts off to sleep, and Quentin, sunk in gloom, sits for a while. The Bredins' Staffie snores loudly on his patchwork cushion in front of the fire, stinking; Naomi is having it put down next week, as it has dementia. He's surrounded by the old and dying. Sometimes he thinks that all the energy of his ambition has its source in the desperation his parents' home, and country life, evokes in him.

Next door, Naomi is singing along with Ladysmith. She still loves South Africa; every August, when the agapanthus bloom, she's sad.

'She wouldn't give up,' Hugh says, suddenly.

'Wouldn't give up what?'

'Us.' Hugh closes his eyes for a moment. 'Ask Lottie to forgive you.'

It takes a moment to realise what his father is saying, and then Quentin feels pure rage. The old hypocrite! Don't do as I do, do as I say.

'Fa, it's not possible to do that.'

'Marriage is . . . work.'

'Even if I wanted to, Lottie wouldn't.'

Many years ago, Hugh had written a poem called 'Ground Elder', about the way you can never eradicate mistakes. It had been one of his better efforts, though like too much of his writing it depended on botanising.

'Ch . . . ch . . .'

What is Hugh trying to say? Or was he snoring?

'I think he needs to rest, now,' Naomi says. She fluffs up the pillows around Hugh's head.

'What about you?'

'Anne will be here soon. She's going to set up a new driver for painkillers.'

Quentin shudders. Pills and intravenous tubes are as common as meals. It feels as if Hugh's cancer has devoured all their lives.

'You're very brave, Ma.'

'Just practical.'

At that moment, a soft voice calls,

'Halloo? All right if I come in?'

A woman with cropped hair enters. She looks vaguely familiar.

'Oh, Anne, hello. This is my son.'

'We've met before.'

'Have we?'

Quentin's mobile rings. It's Lottie.

'I need you to get back at once.'

'Why? What's the matter? Is it the girls?'

Lottie says, 'I have to leave. My mother has had an accident.'

22

Born Lucky

Xan and his mother are driving to London. It's very different from when he made the reverse journey in the car nine months ago. His spots have gone, he has some money in his bank account, and he has a girlfriend.

The biggest change, however, is that he now has offers from five choices of university.

Even when he was summoned to UCL he told nobody other than his stepfather.

'Um. If you're going to see Hugh and Naomi, is there a chance I might get a lift to Exeter?'

'Why?'

'I've got an interview in London. Don't tell Mum.'

'Of course not.'

'I'll probably fail.'

Quentin didn't tell him off, but said, 'Hope for the best, prepare for the worst.'

The whole day had been weird. Back in academia, but also back in London. The paper he was asked to write was practical criticism, and it was a hideous effort to get his brain working again. But one of the passages was Donne's 'The Flea', which he had just read in Hugh's copy, and thought about. He spent so long agonising that he'd only written three pages, but they were, he thought, three good pages, about marriage, parasitism and the unexpected. After many months of stupefaction and idleness, he can think again.

The teenage brain, Bron had told him, sheds many of its connections as a tree sheds twigs in order to grow to maturity. Xan was alarmed by this, fearing loss of something essential and alive. Now he understands that he needs this shedding. It's not about getting a degree or doing the right conventional thing by his education and parenting. University is what he wants and needs to become his true self, from which nothing can be taken.

As Quentin predicted, his interviewers were interested in his experience of working in a factory. They discussed *Down and Out in Paris and London*, and having recently read it at Hugh's suggestion, he managed to remember enough not to sound completely at sea. He even managed to make his interviewers laugh. All the same, when the offer arrived, he was astonished.

'It's the best university in the country,' Lottie said.

'You're just saying that to make me feel better.'

'No. Look it up. The people who went to the Bartlett, like Martin, were far better taught than I, and they worked far harder.'

Xan rolled his eyes.

'Why didn't you say so before?'

'Because it didn't cross my mind to suggest that you apply there when we were in London.'

Despite her anxiety over Oma, Lottie does seem a lot happier. Is it just the work, or Martin? He wouldn't blame her, even if Beardy strikes him as a bit wet. It'd make her feel less bad about his philandering stepfather, and be one in the eye for him too.

At times, Xan almost feels sorry for Quentin. You can become addicted to bad feelings, as to any other stimulant, and he wouldn't have got his offer without Quentin's insistence and assistance.

'I hope I've made the right decision,' he tells Lottie. 'About my offer, I mean.'

She keeps her eyes on the road.

'Xan, I can't tell you what to do. There are no certainties in life. You thought that if you worked hard and got the marks, you were going to sail into Cambridge. I thought that if I worked hard and loved my husband and family, I was going to live happily ever after.'

'But *my* expectations were formed by the system of education.'

Lottie laughs.

'And mine were formed by middle-class morality and fairy tales. What a surprise that they turn out not to be true! Maybe nobody gets what they believe should be theirs, but just getting a bit of it is worthwhile. Just a bit is more than most ever get.'

He can't suppress a throb of joy at his new prospects. What Katya's reaction will be when he tells her he'll be going away is another matter. They have never discussed any kind of a future together, only that she wants to stay in England.

'You don't want to go back to Poland?'

'Why would I go back? Here, I have opportunity. Especially if I have a baby.'

She returned Xan's appalled gaze. Katya let the silence grow between them, then grinned.

'Is OK. A joke.' She dug him in the ribs. 'Alex, I do not want kids, not yet.'

She understood about going back to look after his grandmother, and even approved of it ('Is what Polish peoples do'), though Humbles had not. Even on a zero-hours contract, without any fixed hours, he was supposed to live in fear of losing the miserable wage they paid.

'There may not be an opening when you return,' he was warned.

'I am allowed to take unpaid time off to look after a dependent,' Xan said. He'd checked; it was true, but they still made up their own rules. Well, sod you, he thought. Even if he'd given half his earnings to his mother, he still has £600 saved up, and he loves his Oma. No way is he going to stay away from her when she needs him.

It had been harder to leave his regular Saturday gig at the White Hart, right when the tourist season was getting going, but that job will at least be waiting for him. The regulars in the bar seem to like him, even if they do call him 'a nice young black chap', and don't quite believe he's English. Xan has learnt that breaking into Happy Birthday pays dividends, and asking couples in the restaurant if they have any special requests does too – even if he has to improvise a lot. There is an appetite for live music, and a number of enthusiastic bands around which play at pubs and local festivals, plus a good church choir in town. Tore isn't the only professional musician tucked away nearby, either. If Trelorn does get a music academy, Xan thinks, there will be no shortage of people wanting to learn (or even teach) an instrument.

All things considered, he is feeling pretty chilled about returning to London for a bit.

Lottie, though, is losing it.

'Marta should never be living in that house on her own.'

'Mum, it's only a broken leg!'

'A broken leg isn't a simple matter when you're elderly.'

She's driving like a lunatic. Oma has never struck anyone as frail, quite the contrary, but how much of this is her force of character? It's awful to think of her being vulnerable.

'I knew she shouldn't have that crazy dog, but she wouldn't listen.'

'She's not going to die from it, is she?'

Lottie says, 'Death is like a pane of glass. When you're young, you don't see it there; that's why people your age toss their lives away and try dangerous things, because you can't imagine that you will ever bump up against it. But now, I see the glass, and my mother's breath is on it . . . She could die if she stays in hospital, they are terrible places now.'

'Please, don't get so *German*, Mum. We'll be there soon, and she'll be perfectly well looked after.'

He rings Marta's mobile.

'Oma? It's me.'

'What are you doing?' Lottie cries, almost swerving into a caravan. 'She's in *hospital*, she—'

His grandmother's voice comes into his ear, like a cricket chirping.

'Darling, I am in mint condition.'

'How bad is it?'

'Pah! Not so bad. I am in a ward with crazy people and the nurses spend all day talking to each other. I am anxious only for my Heidi.'

'Give her my love,' Lottie says tensely. 'Tell her to GET A PRIVATE ROOM.'

Xan does this, and Marta says,

'Oh, not to worry darling, I am fine. Drive carefully. We do not need any more members of this family in hospital.'

Xan conveys this to his mother; she slows down, fractionally. But soon the traffic thickens, and the Multipla is forced into a succession of crawling lanes anyway.

'Are you going to see anyone in London?' she asks.

'I don't know. Maybe.'

Now that he has his offers, he's been able to look up mates on Facebook, and forgive them for not having been in touch. It's strange to see the ones who took a proper gap year putting up posts from Thailand and Brazil. Their photographs of themselves in stubby striped hats and baggy shorts, stoned or draped round the necks of strangers, are absurd.

Trelorn has been transformed by sunshine. Every house seems to fluff itself up in drier weather, like a bird, and the walls that were once a bedraggled grey are now white, cream and yellow. The Bed and Breakfast signs have an air of plausibility. People look brighter in the trickle of tourism: as his family have discovered, £50 a month extra is the difference between surviving and living. The turning point in the year has been reached.

'It's always the same with seasonal work, work till you drop all summer then try to keep body and soul together all winter,' Maddy told Xan. Astoundingly, she has a job cleaning somebody's holiday cottage, on top of her factory work. 'As long as we don't get another July and August like the last one.'

'Or the one before,' said one of her friends.

'And the one before that!'

They cackled under their filmy caps.

In London, a sunny day is a bonus, but in the country it is critical. Without a decent summer, holidaymakers get an EasyJet flight to the Mediterranean, rather than staying at home.

Whenever the sun shines in England, it's the most beautiful country in the world, Xan thinks. The landscape is luminous, as if every blade of grass were lit from within. The skies are a deep, lustrous blue, and for miles around, larks evaporate into the skies on a thin sizzle of song. There are foxgloves in tall spires of speckled pink, and bluebells, and daisies as big as moons sprouting so fast you can almost see them grow. The earth and air pulse with energy, the birds seem drunk with joy.

Even Home Farm feels different. Light streams in from the new kitchen windows, and all the rooms have been filled with colour. It's strikingly different from their London home.

'What happened to the tasteful taupes?'

'Mud colours aren't smart when you bring a ton of the real thing in on your boots,' Stella said.

Xan can't help loving his sister for saying things like that. (When asked by the Vicar whom she would most like to meet in Heaven, Stella answered, 'Darwin.') Somehow, her precocity has become just another eccentricity, no more remarkable than any other. She's still teaching herself French at night, and reads more than anyone in the school, but nobody is unkind to her about it, any more than they are to the kids with Asperger's or specs, and so she has become less weird. She and Rosie spend most days galloping through the sloping field below Home Farm and pretending to eat fresh grass.

'Couldn't we just have the *tiniest* pony, like from Dartmoor?' Rosie pleaded.

'Those ponies still need feeding, I'm afraid.'

'You did *promise* us a pet, and all we've got so far is McSquirter, and he's no fun because of Xan,' Stella reminded her parents.

'Sorry,' Xan said.

'We'd rather have you than a kitten, but we'd like to have a kitten too,' Rosie remarked.

They're the right age for country life. They don't want to go drinking, dancing, clubbing and having sex. Now that the afternoons last a long time, they can walk themselves home from school.

'I really don't like them wandering around on their own.'

'Oh for heaven's sake!' Quentin said. 'You can't keep a child in cotton wool.'

Even Xan thinks his mother's anxiety is unnecessary. He's seen enough of Lottie's former colleagues to know that somehow, architects always look as if they inhabit a slightly different plane of experience to the rest of humanity – more structured, less cluttered and so on, which inevitably raises your levels of anxiety rather than decreases them, because *people* weren't more structured and less cluttered, were they?

The girls seem almost to have forgotten London, apart from it being where Oma lives. Even Stella seems to have made friends, especially with the local doctor's daughter. The Viners are another pair of refugees from London; Josh, the GP, turns out to know some of Mum's old crew, and his mother is one of Oma's best friends.

243

'Small world, isn't it?' Lottie said when they discovered this.

The web that connects so many adults still amazes Xan. It had taken him much of his childhood to understand how it under-lies his parents' life and how much they take it for granted. If they didn't all go to the same schools and universities, they met through the myriad ways in which people have always connected even before the Internet. Does everybody ultimately know every-body else? If that were so, then he could find his father, assuming he is still alive. But without a name, how could he go about it?

Yet somebody must have known it, because otherwise, how would he have turned up at a party full of graduates? He'd tried asking his mother where it had been, thinking that would be a start.

'It was somewhere in the East End,' she said. 'I can't even remember the street.'

Could she really not remember, or was she lying? Lottie is a truthful person, but she is odd about some things, especially sex. All women are weird, really, and not just about spiders.

He remembers Dawn's odd words. *Look at my blood.* What did she mean? Did she mean that she thought he couldn't see it when she was bleeding? Or maybe her mum doesn't believe in doctors, like some of the other weird people he's come across, like Lily Hart, who thinks the government is plotting against the people. Xan thinks of the way Janet brushes out her daughter's long, fine blonde hair sometimes before leaving, as if she were a doll.

'There we are my pretty,' Janet says. 'My little girl.'

Only Dawn isn't a little girl, she's a teenager. He thinks again of the ladder of thin white scars he's seen on her forearm, and wishes he knew what to do.

'Mum, if someone asked you to look at their blood, what would you think they were saying?'

'I'd think they were asking me to get it analysed. Why?'

'Oh, just something somebody said to me. How much longer?' Xan asks.

'Three hours.'

On and on they go, past the giant striding statue of a man, swamped by a hideous housing development, past Bristol's wide, gleaming estuary, past fields where horses graze, and apple orchards, and signs to stately homes and other cities. Gradually, the great numinous clouds with their shining strangeness fall away. The sky and the land become brighter, flatter, more mundane. They stop at a service station, where there's a confluence of tall thin people who are quite clearly from London, and their opposites, scoffing down pies that are all too familiar. Don't touch them! Xan wants to say, but Humbles pies still smell pretty good when warmed up. Xan remembers the last time they were in a service station like this, and how Quentin hadn't bought coffee for anyone but himself.

'Are you OK to go on?'

'Yes, of course.'

She shoots off up the motorway.

'Slow down, Mum.'

'I don't like to think of her waiting,' she mutters. 'If she needs a blood transfusion, I'm a match.'

It makes him think, once again, about Dawn. *Look at my blood . . .* Perhaps she hadn't meant what he thought, but during that long drive, he thinks of the one person who might help him to have those dried drops he has kept in his pocket examined.

23

The Recording Angel for West Devon

Wheeling a shrilling trolley round the supermarket, Sally sometimes feels a fool for nodding and smiling at other customers. To
them she's just an odd woman they don't see, or, if they do, perhaps associate with unwelcome authority. Even so, *she* recognises
them. It gives her a good feeling to see the babies grow up, and
even having children of their own – though those who haven't
turned out so well sadden her, because she usually knows why.

'I feel like the Recording Angel for West Devon, sometimes.
I know which children have broken homes, and which are disabled, and all kinds of things which hardly anyone else does. Even
with child protection coming out of our ears, there's so little we
can really do to avert the bad stuff,' she tells Peter. He grunts;
nobody had helped him during his own childhood.

'You only know what parents choose to show you,' he said,
once. 'All kinds of bad things can go on in a family that social
services never see.'

Maybe that's why he finds it difficult to make friends, she
thinks. All their friends are really hers, because she loves company and chatting and getting involved. Of course, she had been

blessed with a happy, sociable, supportive family, while he, well, Peter doesn't expect anyone else to like him. Few would guess that his face is red from shyness as much as harsh weather.

'If I hadn't married you, I don't know what I'd have done,' he told her once. 'Probably blown my brains out.'

'No, you'd have found someone else. There isn't just one person in the whole world for someone, my dear.'

'Ah, but there is for me.'

When she thinks of her husband, Sally always feels a mixture of tenderness and sorrow. He is like the great rock on which their home is built, solid and strong, brave in ways that only she knows. She has known him for ever, even before they were married, she can see the little boy he once was and the old man he will become. Yet without a baby, she will feel forever incomplete, as if some vital spring of hope and happiness is choked off.

Of course, Baggage helps – who could look at her beautiful brown eyes and ostrich-plume tail, her creamy chest breaking into waves and her rich brown ears, and not adore her, even if the melting look she gives is inspired by the prospect of a sausage, rather than devotion? A dog is almost as good as a child, and its love more than most humans deserved. In the end, though, you want your own species. Sally has stopped talking about it, because Pete gets angry and upset, but she wishes now she'd insisted on IVF.

I should have not made that vow about obedience, she thinks. Many women didn't, these days, feeling it to be old-fashioned, but when she got married she'd actually liked the idea. Now, twenty years later, she has come to think differently. She knows, for instance, that the person she was at twenty-two has gone on developing, whereas he has just stopped. He won't read, as she does, he doesn't listen to Radio 4, and he barely watches the News because by 10 p.m. they are both in bed and dropping off. Of course, that isn't the only kind of intelligence that matters. If civilisation came to an end, it'd be Peter and people like him who'd be the most valued members because of their skills. However, that is not the world in which they live, and no matter how ardently Sally longs to admire him in every respect, she knows that she should never have ceded her own authority over herself.

Sally's trolley squeals past the food bank in Trelorn. She wants to donate to it, Pete doesn't.

'They should get off their arses and work,' he said.

'You know there's been more unemployment since the dairy closed.'

'So why are we using Romanians and Poles, then?'

'Because they're young and single and don't mind sharing three to a room for a few months,' Sally answered. 'They aren't *families.*'

Pete simply can't imagine what it's like. That's the problem. Unless you've seen poverty, and smelt it, and touched it, you can't imagine the dreariness and hopelessness.

She gives as much fresh food away as she can spare.

'I just happened to be passing by,' she'll say, dropping in on someone she knows to be frail, or in need. She brings fresh eggs or home-made jam, or, in summer, some tomatoes or courgettes or runner beans.

'You're an angel, that's what you are,' Mrs Drew told her, and although Sally has been called plenty of nastier names in her life, she does like to think that she and Sam the postie form a kind of unofficial watch, simply because their jobs involve daily visits to lonely people.

Sam is an odd one. He'd come down from Yorkshire, having left behind the house he'd bought as a young welder, and given it to his ex-wife and two daughters. 'There was no point in asking her to sell up so I could start again. Neither of us had the money, and she was the one who had to bring up the kids. It wasn't her fault or mine; we just married too young.'

He's a small, wiry man who lives in a camper-van on a bit

of land he rents from a farmer near Shipcott. Though it can't be comfortable for him doing without electricity or running water, he always stands his round in the pub, and cuts poor old Jim's grass and hedge for free because his neighbour is dying of emphysema and has no family to help him. There are so many elderly people who have retired to their dream cottage in Devon when strong and healthy in their sixties who end up like that, Sally thinks, widowed and alone. But Sam drops in on everyone around Trelorn several times a week with the post, which is why he'd been the one to find poor Oliver Randall.

It had been an awful experience. The police questioned him twice, and had taken a DNA sample. For a while, even people who'd known Sam for years believed he must have done it. But nothing, as far as the police could tell, had been taken. He had a wallet with £300 in it, left on his bedroom table. So the matter was dropped, but Sam told Sally he still hated coming down the lane to Home Farm.

'I'm still afraid I'll see his body, lying there with no head on. You can't believe how shocking it was. He wasn't the type to hurt a fly.'

'I only heard him at the Nativity play.'

'Well I'm no musician, but I heard him playing sometimes. The sounds he could make! Take your heart out of your body.'

Sally had only glimpsed Randall once or twice a year, usually walking along the verge to or from the village, always with his dog, the same dog Di Tore has taken in. Would it have attacked somebody for assaulting its master? She doesn't know much about lurchers, but even Baggage had snarled one time when Sally had been shouted at by a mum. Maybe the dog had been locked up, or maybe it had been afraid – or maybe it had known the killer. Impossible to say.

'It's frightening to think how such a thing can happen here,' she agreed.

Sam's kindly face was twisted with worry. 'I keep wondering,

249

Was it anyone I know? Could I even have passed them in my van? But he was dead and cold when I found him.'

'It must have been something to do with people he'd known in London,' Sally said, comfortingly.

'I hope so. Nobody can rest easy if there's some lunatic wandering around, can they?'

A country murder is always supposed to be vaguely comical, only it's not, especially if you live in a place where people have grown together over centuries like the roots of a grove of trees. In fact, it's far worse than a murder in a city, which is the kind of place you expect bad things to happen, what with people being crammed in like battery hens. If you're exposed to nature and weather, you have to look after your neighbour, because one day your neighbour will look after you. Country homes are cluttered because you never know what's going to be needed, from old tyres to baler twine. Everyone keeps torches, jump-leads and First Aid kits because if you don't need them, someone else is bound to.

These days, however, it's far too easy to never see any of your neighbours at all. You don't need to post a letter, and if you don't have children at school or go to church or go down the pub, or volunteer, it's easy to be isolated. Oliver Randall had a dog, which helped, and he took pupils, but like Sam he'd lived alone down a long lane, and nobody really knows what goes on in such places. Maybe he'd been a secret Satanist. Maybe he'd been a dogger. Or maybe he was just one of the many people living in the country who enjoyed their own company best, and some lunatic had found him.

It didn't stop Sally herself from feeling uneasy. However loyal she is to country life, she knows as well as anyone that some villages are awash with heroin addicts: and then the burglaries begin. Ever since the murder, people had started locking doors again. The parents of children at Shipcott still felt funny about letting their kids stay with the Bredins for a sleepover, according to Lottie. Even Lottie has admitted to moments of unease, especially at night. She seems lonely, despite her family and her new job.

Perhaps this is why she has formed a friendship with Lottie Bredin, who is as tall and tense as she herself is round and relaxed. At any rate, they enjoy talking. She has joined Sally's book group, an honour of which she is perhaps not quite as conscious as she might be, and in two months has gone from being someone the other members were slightly anxious about to being genuinely welcome. They have understood, in the way of observant countrywomen, that although Lottie is thin and clever, she is very unhappy.

'As who wouldn't be, married to that arrogant pillock,' said one, after she'd gone.

Lottie talks to people, unlike her boss, who wafts about smiling into his beard in the smug manner of architects spending other people's money.

There are so many odd bods around who don't make the effort. The worst are the hippies, who expect to be made welcome just because they've decided to bestow themselves on a community, knowing nothing whatever about it, and spouting all kinds of nonsense about ecology. They insulate their lofts with organic wool, then have a nasty shock when the moths get in. But so many are fleeing west, it seems. Painters, folk singers, cabinetmakers, children's authors, eco-warriors, yurt-dwellers, yoghurt-makers, yoga teachers, communards, cheesemongers, chefs, mindfulness therapists, you name it, they are all here. As long as they work or, better still, create employment, they have to be a good thing, even if some are the hated bankers buying up country estates in order to have shooting parties and the like: rather that than houses in the Caribbean, Sally thinks. But what is needed above all is youth. Trelorn, like so many places, has to have families staying for more than low property prices.

Meanwhile, Lottie's daughters have become friends with her nieces, and often come up to the farm with them.

'It's so lovely to see this,' Lottie said, sitting in Sally's garden. 'I'd never have believed a cat and a dog could be friends like yours are. It's like something out of a fairy tale.'

'Oh, problems don't go away just because they're in a beautiful place. Still, a different place can make you see problems differently, can't it?'

'I've put our house on the market again,' she said. 'Quentin can't bear the country, though. Every day away from the city is a wasted one, as far as he's concerned.'

'I'd be very pleased if you do stay, and so will a number of people.'

'That's nice to know.'

Yet there's something about Home Farm that worries Sally. It ought to be lovely, especially with all the clever things her friend has done to the inside, only every time Sally pops in and drives down that long sloping lane, it's as if everything from the big beech tree halfway down to the hammering woodpeckers is warning her. She's never normally afraid of anything – you can't live up on Dartmoor and be fearful – yet seeing that house gleaming like a shard of bone, her heart begins to thump.

Sally passes the food-bank appeal again, and suddenly turns round to drop in some tinned tomatoes, condensed milk and soup. So what if Peter doesn't want to give food away: it's her money she's spending, isn't it? He can grump and groan all he likes.

'Come on, Baggage!'

The springer has encountered a terrier, and the two dogs circle each other ecstatically, twisting their leads around their owners like maypole dancers. Sally disentangles her, apologetically, and looks up.

'Morning,' she says, seeing Lily Hart holding on to the terrier's lead while dragging two small kids and a squalling baby strapped

252

to her middle. All of them are wearing brightly coloured knitted hats that could only have come from Totnes. She smiles at Lily, who glowers at her.

'I've just been delivering some veg boxes to Mum and Dad at the hotel.'

She looks at Sally as if to challenge her, and Sally knows perfectly well it's because she still hasn't got her kids to have an MMR jab. Sometimes she feels like taking certain mums by the scruff of their necks and shaking them, they're so obstinate.

'It must be nice for your parents to be able to put "home-grown" on the menu,' Sally says, encouragingly.

'Dad thinks his mission in life is to educate the public about wine, not food,' Lily answers.

If that's the case, then Simon Hart has been his own best pupil, Sally thinks. The White Hart has a dining room with a spectacular view of the Tamar, but most of the windows are obscured by rows of empty bottles.

'I'm sure their customers appreciate both,' she says. Poppy Hart is a good cook, and it's thanks to her that the hotel bar and restaurant has any clientele. What on earth had she ever seen in an old stick like Simon? But then, how often did one look at a couple, and wonder this? Maybe they thought it of Peter and herself. Or, most likely, didn't think at all because the truth was, most people were too busy thinking only of themselves.

Peter emerges from the shop, blinking and looking mildly bewildered. Towns have this effect on him; even though Sally had made sure he shaved, brushed his hair and put on a clean check shirt, he looks like a faded version of himself away from his flock and his fields. She smiles and waves, and his face suddenly relaxes.

'Let me take those bags, m' dear,' he says.

Sally relinquishes the bags, gratefully.

'I gave some tins to the charity, Pete. I hope that's all right,' Sally says.

'Yes, of course.'

Why do I need to ask him? Sally thinks. Her sister Anne has said to her, quite often, that she's too deferential to her husband, but then she chose an educated man, whereas Peter hadn't even been able to go away to agricultural college. He would have got a full grant for college and all, but for Pete's father turning his gun on himself. Nobody missed him: he'd beaten his wife, and they all knew it.

Men! Sally thinks. Almost all the trouble in the world comes from them, their aggression and lust and pride. She trots along beside her husband. When Oliver Randall's killer is found, she has no doubt it'll be a man.

24

The Siren Call

Back in London, Lottie barely pauses to park outside her mother's house before rushing to the hospital with Xan, dragging him along by the hand as if he were eight, not eighteen.

'Wait, Mum, slow down,' he says. 'We haven't even had lunch.'

'You can get a sandwich later,' she tells him.

His resistance is maddening; he wants to listen to the siren call of money spilling out from Hampstead High Street, goggling like a tourist. She's heard it herself, that call, only love makes her deaf to it. The people and traffic are infuriating obstacles to getting through to her mother, whose frailty and mortality have suddenly become horribly urgent.

Marta has always been there, either in person or at the other end of a telephone: fierce, funny, maddening, feminine and above all intelligent. By the time most people are just getting up Marta has filleted the newspaper, listened to the *Today* programme, done the crossword and performed Pilates; she reads all the best books, sees the best plays and recitals, beats everybody at Scrabble and is a popular figure in the cosmopolitan circles she moves in. Yet Quentin loathes her.

'Your tendency to micromanage comes entirely from her.'

'No, it's mine, because that's the only way I can feel more secure,' Lottie answered.

'You see life as a dreary board game which you must always win, whereas I see it as a rope, made up of thousands of tiny filaments twisted together,' Quentin said. 'You can't predict which one will be important.'

'If I didn't micromanage, as you call it, you'd have no toilet paper. Isn't that important?'

When Marta dies, Lottie thinks, I may have nobody left to talk to, and nobody who actually really cares about me or knows me as a person. It's not entirely true, but at this moment it feels as if she is on the edge of disaster. Because of Xan, it has always been the two of them, not exactly contra mundum but unfailingly loyal to each other. Marta and she had formed a perfect little unit, which when she fell in love with Quentin had been disrupted.

But that is the trouble with lust, Lottie thinks. It reminds you that your body has a life of its own. One thing her departure from London has taught her is that her disappointment and fury towards her husband is at least partly composed of self-disgust. Even now, she can't bear to think of the trust she had given him, and worse, how much she had made herself vulnerable to him when he was the most critical man in the world. To *not* think of it requires huge amounts of mental energy – but at least she now has some reserves of this.

London is still steeped in pain. Flecks of her past flick through her memory as she hurries down Haverstock Hill. Here is the Chinese restaurant where she has sat with a handful of perfectly pleasant men whose embraces she neither sought nor desired, and here is the crêpe stall where she'd hung out with other girls after school, pretending to be cool. Here is the plump scarlet post-box where she'd posted off so many applications in pre-computer days. Down there is the road to the Heath where she'd walked with Xan as a boy. Here is where there used to be a hardware shop, now in its latest reincarnation as a bookshop. There is the road where a boy she'd been hopelessly in love with lived, and here is the enormous Methodist chapel at the top of Pond Street outside which Justin's sister – once so close she was often mistaken for Lottie's own – revealed herself to be a Brexit-voter. The hospital looms over it all. It's where she'd been born, and had given birth to each of her children; where, in fact, she'd expected to die. Only now she isn't so sure.

This city, so enormous, so familiar, so endlessly self-renewing, no longer feels like home. It looks the same, but in the way of a building whose façade has been retained while the building behind has been gutted. It's like her marriage, not real any more. Of course, Hampstead Village has been going this way for a long time, only Lottie has been so used to seeing her mother's neighbours that she hadn't noticed when the Jewish faces faded away, along with the people who couldn't afford designer clothes or new cars. But now the whole city is becoming like this, sterilised by money. When did it become necessary to look like a model, or to sprawl on the pavement in yet another café sipping a mochaccino? The enormous cars, the latest iPhones, the banks of flowers flown in from Africa, the sheen of superiority that encases London like an impenetrable bubble – what connection did these have with the cosiness and shabbiness, the high ideals and low heels of her youth?

As ever, the hospital is crowded, as if all those whom age, poverty and infirmity had rendered incapable of surviving the metropolis have been flung through its doors to be patched up or discarded. Lottie shoves £20 into her son's hand and says,

'Get yourself something to eat, and some fruit and *The Times* for Oma. I'll text you the ward number, OK?'

When she is given directions, it's to the top of the hospital, not the humbler lower levels. Not for the first time, Lottie feels mildly exasperated by the way her mother has always gone on

257

about how terribly poor she is, while being, effectively, a multimillionaire. Don't go there, she thinks. After all, her own predicament is due to a national crisis and a bad marriage; Marta deserves whatever money she has saved, and her wealth is like so many Londoners', wrapped up in having bought a house. If she has health insurance, good luck to her. That she and Quentin can no longer afford it, any more than they can afford private education, is something that she has to accept.

Standing in the shiny steel cubicle, she can feel London crackling through her like electricity, addictive and alarming at the same time. Why is it impossible to be in this city for more than an hour without feeling the invisible worms of stress writhing and crawling under her scalp all over again? For a moment, the relentless, soaring sensation is accompanied by the urge to scream; but then the lift slows, and comes to a halt.

The heavy ward doors give way to a calm cleanliness tinged with the aroma of freshly cooked food.

'Sole meunière, with a goat's cheese tartlet and apple crumble to follow,' her mother says, with satisfaction. 'It's better than a hotel, and *look* at the view.'

'How are you feeling?'

'Darling, I am in mint condition.'

On the contrary, Marta is shockingly different in a hospital gown and without make-up. Even her white hair appears to have fallen, like whipped cream which has collapsed. She looks not only old but elderly. Lottie takes her hand.

'Are you in pain, Mutti?'

'I have pills.'

'How did it happen?'

Marta sighs. 'Heidi tripped me up as I was coming downstairs.'

'Ah. Yes, she's nearly done that to me, too.'

Lottie thinks to herself that Heidi is almost a different species to dogs like Bluebell and Baggage. How long will it take for Marta's leg to mend? Weeks and weeks, no doubt, and there are

258

bound to be complications, given her age, and the need for physiotherapy. Xan enters with grapes, a newspaper and an awkward
look.

'Oma?'

'Dearest boy,' she says, brightening. 'Come and give me a kiss.
Ach, you haven't shaved.'

'I'm here to stop you getting too comfortable.'

Lottie can't help feeling proud of her son, whose wide grin
and coppery curls are like an infusion of energy and life in the
room.

'What can we do to help?' she says.

'My neighbour has Heidi, but it's not a satisfactory situation as
she has cats, and they will keep running away. If you could bring
her home and take the poor doggie for walks . . . '

'Yes, fine. What else? I'll set up a regular Ocado delivery, if you
give me your credit card.'

Marta has always resisted this; though impressively good
at the Internet, she doesn't trust online shopping. She says,
unexpectedly,

'Good idea. How long can you stay, darling?'

Lottie thinks about the difficulties of even parking a car outside her mother's house. Marta probably has no visitors' permits,
so she will have to order these, or find a meter. So much that is
stressful about London life seems to be connected to driving. She
looks through the slats of the hospital blind, at the packed postal
districts swarming with people and machines. If I stay here, she
thinks, I'll go crackers.

'Not more than a week. I'm in the middle of a project, and I
don't want to leave the girls with Quentin for too long. Maybe
you could come to stay again too—'

'No, my darling, the house is not big enough, is it?'

'Not really, no,' Lottie agrees, relieved. 'But if you stay in
London, you are also going to need someone to be with you
when you get out, Marta.'

'I worry most about losing my strength in my arms and hands, you know,' Marta says, squeezing some kind of putty with one hand while the other twitches with inaudible trills and semi-quavers. 'But I am to have physiotherapy. It will take six weeks, the doctor says.'

'I'll stay,' Xan says. 'I don't mind. I can walk the dog and do shopping and stuff.'

Marta brightens. 'Are you sure? You do have a job, after all.'

'Yeah, but I'm not in a fixed contract, you know?'

So the affair with Katya isn't serious, Lottie thinks, relieved.

'You are a good, sweet boy, and have made your Oma very happy.'

She does what she can to make Marta comfortable during the week she stays. In truth, the house in Church Row is in a bad way, cracked, dingy, and despite Marta's cleaner, dirty.

'It's not that nice any more, really, is it?' Xan says, looking at the double drawing room. Even its fine Georgian sash windows on the first floor can't conceal that everything is faded, discoloured and worn. There's a big brownish stain on the ceiling where there has clearly been a leak, and the chintz curtains are torn, both in their lining and their fabric. 'I have such good memories of this place, but it's all kind of broken down.'

'A house needs love and attention and energy, just like any other relationship,' Lottie says.

'It's too big for just her, isn't it?'

'I know. But this is where she's been for fifty years. I don't think she's going anywhere.'

All the same, Lottie does make some attempt at sorting through Marta's cupboards. There are piles and piles of greyish, balding towels which must date back from her parents' wedding, which, greatly daring, she puts into a recycling bin, and shelves of ancient browning paperbacks whose glue has long since given up, stacked two-deep in the bookshelves which, after judicious inspection, she dumps as paper. A cupboard yields up four vacuum cleaners, none of which function, a defunct fridge and an electric kettle which, when plugged in, promptly blows a fuse.

'She has this mania about never throwing anything away, even if it's no longer useful.'

'She can't have looked at any of these for years. They have so much dust on them.'

'Careful! I don't want the dust bringing on an asthma attack.'

'Stop worrying, Mum. I'll be fine.'

Of course, she thinks: you don't feel under scrutiny here. In London, being black or mixed-race is completely normal, like voting Labour. It's the one thing she really dislikes about country life.

He helps pile the car high with rubbish to take to the recycling centre.

'D'you think Oma might be getting dementia?'

'Not a bit of it.'

No, the real problem is that her mother is living in a large house that she simply can't afford to keep going . . . Only Marta will never leave Hampstead. She looks for smaller period properties nearby. There's a tiny terraced cottage, fully modernised, up on sale for a mere £2.5 million. Imagine, Lottie thinks, how much easier Marta's life would be with £1 million to spend on herself, and a home which is actually warm and comfortable . . . It's the kind of daydream which can only lead to resentment on one side and regret on the other.

'She won't move until it's too late,' Justin tells her. 'It's the same with my mother. They hang on and on and then downsize to a single room in a nursing home.'

Lottie has visited her own house, to check on some minor repairs that the tenants requested. It's strange to realise that she no longer feels the strong emotions she had once had for it. She'd put energy into her home that she had not, really, put into her marriage.

261

In fact, her former home has been the scene of so much unhappiness that she is really profoundly relieved to be getting rid of it.

'We just love it here,' the Canadian lawyers say.

'I'm so pleased,' Lottie answers. She doesn't mind the ghastly retro tins they have put into the kitchen, or the tasteless prints. The deep taproot of feelings she'd once had about this property has been hacked off, even if those for Quentin still make her wince. (But if she's patient, these too will die, she tells herself.) She can see its faults and its advantages, and maybe if they moved back in she would stop noticing the ugly tower block opposite, and the incessant noise.

Quentin is being more annoying than ever about the sale.

'What if only half the house were sold? It's going to go on rising in value.'

'No, and I don't care. It's over £1.2 million, and that's enough. We'll each get £450,000. And Quentin, with my half I'm going to buy Home Farm.'

The silence between them builds and disperses, like clouds outside pushed this way and that in the unresting winds. He doesn't need to say how much he hates the idea. It's painful having this kind of consciousness of another person, even if you no longer care what they feel. Thank God he doesn't know about the murder, she thinks: he'd make that into a reason for not continuing there.

'You have to come back.'

Lottie clenched her fists. It almost sounded as if he is missing her, but she knows it's just the inconvenience.

'I don't like being away from the girls, or work. Xan is staying behind for a bit.'

'It's grim at my parents', you've no idea.'

He floods her with his own misery just because she happens to be the person who is around, like a mirror. It's so typically selfish. She thinks how different Martin had been when she'd rung to apologise about having to cancel the client meeting.

'Don't worry, Lottie, I can cover the Trelorn build this week, though I'd like to have you back. You've had so many good new ideas. Everyone is impressed. I'm so sorry about your mother. It must be dreadful for both of you.'

The generosity of this touched her.

'My mother has broken her leg. It's bad, but not life-threatening.'

There was a pause, then he said,

'But you're back at the end of the week, yes?'

'Yes.'

'Good.' He cleared his throat. 'You aren't thinking of moving back, then?'

'I'd miss Devon,' she said. 'I even miss the rain.'

'I know, me too.'

The trouble is that these conversations are freighted with too much, after what had happened.

One evening, just before she received the call about her mother's accident, she and Martin had been working later than usual in the Portakabin office. It was dark, wet and windy, and the feeling of being in a warm, dry place was particularly comforting, especially as Martin, like herself, enjoyed having Radio 3 on in the background while working. The pools of light from their computers and work lamps made the outside world disappear.

They were drawing the next stage of the development, the one on which Lottie would have far more influence. It was, as always, demanding. This stage included the community building, and at present Martin's designs looked ominously like those for King Theoden's hall in *The Lord of the Rings*. He wanted it to be built entirely out of oak, whereas she could see how steel could play an important part, particularly now its price was falling.

'I do love the Arts and Crafts principles,' he said.

'So do I, but we can still use modern techniques,' she answered. It's the first disagreement they've had, but each is too sensitive to the other to clash. Instead, they slowly worked through the possibilities. Quentin accuses architects of being egoists, insensitive

263

to anything but their own vision, but it isn't like that, she thinks. You have to believe in your ideas, but nobody can get far without a mixture of resilience and adaptability. Martin, like herself, has the hunger for a really good project, and to get it passed they'll bury any differences without rancour.

This is, she thinks now, partly the product of maturity. It's like any profession: in the beginning, nobody is your friend, it's feast or famine, and you have to be ruthless in the pursuit of commissions. Everyone seems to be a rival: it is only later that you realise how stupid and base this was. Hardly anyone, in any art or craft, cares about it as another artist or craftswoman does, and therefore it follows that you have far more in common with those who make and create than you do with everyone else. These days, all she cares about is that an architect, rather than a computer, is involved in any design. They each know they will not be famous, or rich, and this is not the dream. The dream of the true architect is to build, just as it is for painters to paint and writers to write and actors to act, and the enemies are those who want nothing to happen, to change.

'I always thought you were the one who'd win prizes,' he'd told her. 'Like Zaha Hadid.'

'So did I, but look where I wound up – having my entries for competitions ripped off by the Chinese, and suffocating in someone else's big machine,' Lottie answered. 'You've done far more.'

Of course it was disappointing not to get that kind of recognition, but plenty of architects won prizes for buildings that were hated by those who had to use them, and that was surely worse. The Trelorn project won't draw attention to itself with flashy innovations or unusual shapes; it will merely be useful and graceful, sound and well made. It will *make sense*. It might even be loved.

Lottie was making the card and paper models for it. This was crucial because it gave the council and the public a proper idea of what the development would look like, and she was better at it than Martin.

'We are going to keep the trees on the site, aren't we?'

'Yes, of course. Well, the oaks and beech. Not the ash. I was thinking of suggesting native cherry for the street planting.'

'Do you know, until a couple of months ago I had no idea what the difference was between *any* tree?'

'Shocking. That's what comes of growing up in a city.'

Eventually, it was time to stop. They both stretched, rubbing their eyes and switching off most of the lights when somehow, Lottie was never quite sure how, she found herself being energetically kissed by Martin. It was not an agreeable experience, but she was too startled to know what to do as his tongue, surrounded by what felt like wiry fur, probed her teeth. A car swept round the bend and they were caught in its headlights. She sprang away, trying not to wipe her mouth.

Martin, almost as shocked as she, apologised in a stammering voice.

'I'm so sorry – so sorry, Lottie. I don't know what came over me.'

She knew perfectly well what it was, but also knew that if she made it any more embarrassing than it was already she could no longer work with him. He had felt her recoil: he was a sensitive man and a kind one, who had acted on a moment's impulse and half a lifetime of attraction. She couldn't be angry, so she said,

'It's nothing to do with you. I'm just – I can't cope with anything else, you see.'

She didn't want to hurt his feelings, but neither could she let him think it could be repeated. It was, in any case, true.

Though to be scrupulously honest, it did give her a small degree of satisfaction to know that at least one man still found her attractive.

25

A *Thousand Years as a Sheep*

Quentin has still not talked to his landlady: frustrating on a number of levels, not least because Di Tore and Lottie have apparently become friends in the blink of an eye. How do women manage it? He has glimpsed Di (and of course Googled her too) on several occasions, but remains outside the charmed circle.

In any marriage it's often the case that one partner is preferred over the other, but it's a shock to Quentin to find himself relegated to second-best. He has always been the sociable one, the person asked to parties – not Lottie. The great benefit of journalism is the access it gives to interesting people; and such is the beguiling nature of fame that he, like many another, had mistaken the smiles and charm of the rich and powerful for genuine relationships. The fact that what they were acknowledging was conditional on his employment is one bitter lesson; but that Lottie should have become in demand after detaching herself from him is another.

He can see her blooming in confidence with each new friendship, and it adds to his despair. He had taken it for granted that she always would be quietly supportive of his own success rather than take centre stage. Yet she has, and he is envious. In London, it had been his friends whom they had mostly seen, as hers tended to be dull and he had made no effort to conceal his boredom. He hadn't thought twice about this, or how isolating it must have been for her.

Out here, though, nobody is interested in the latest gossip, or the intricacies of party politics. It's all small stuff, and so deeply agricultural that the one time he had taken the family to see *Far from the Madding Crowd* (driving all the way to Okehampton for this belated treat), the reaction to the hero and heroine's climactic kiss had been muted, but—

'I do hope he won't forget about his *horse*,' said a large woman in his row, anxiously, to general agreement. There was a sigh of relief when, at the last moment, Gabriel Oak did not.

People here are so rooted in one place, through generations, that they might as well be trees. They hate London, the EU, politicians, newspapers – effectively, everything he's interested in.

Lottie, however, has taken to this dreary place with ghastly enthusiasm. It must be the menopause, he thinks. Nothing else can explain it.

'I like people with a moral compass,' she says. 'Don't you understand? I *like* it here.'

'It's all bollocks, Lottie. What you're seeing isn't a moral compass, it's poverty. If you're rich, morals don't apply.'

'What a stupid thing to believe! People all over the world have the same ideas about how to live a good life, Quentin. Do you think Tore was happy when he was squandering his millions on drugs and yachts and women? Of course not. It's only now that he's learnt to give it away that he's found some peace.'

'There's nothing more tiresome than a rock star who has his own charity.'

'How about someone who sits around moaning?'

Whenever it's his night to babysit, she's off: yoga, choir-singing, fund-raising for charity – it never stops. But whom does *he* see? Apart from the peculiar tramp he occasionally bumps into in the pub, there's nobody. He has no colleagues, or friends. Everyone in the country is bunkered down, and it's like a retread of the unforgotten boredom of his teens, only those had been so awful they had powered his ambition to escape. Quentin, once he's read himself into a stupor over a bottle of wine, goes to bed after watching some newscaster with shoulder pads and bad hair reporting on a small conflagration in a seaside town. It was always a small conflagration, and the reporter would ask people what they thought of it.

As the stench of dung fills my nostrils, I recall the Chinese proverb, 'Better one day as a tiger than a thousand years as a sheep,' Quentin writes, then crosses out *the stench of.* His column is now only 500 words, which means he spends two days working at it, because whatever editors believe it's far harder to write a short piece than a long one.

Finding out more about the murder is all he has to occupy him, but he's made no progress. The crime remains unsolved. Randall stares back at him from the short Wikipedia entry on screen. The photograph shows a striking face: long, with fine straight brows over very dark, narrow eyes, thick inky locks flowing past his ears, a big nose and sallow skin. He's smiling, with what looks like real warmth. It's a face that, above all, looks kind to the point of being simple-minded. Despite the Wikipedia stub listing his handful of credits for TV shows and the Oscar-nominated film, nobody he can trace seems to have known him. Like most men over forty, he had no social media profile. (What an idiot, Quentin thinks to himself: in the modern world, it's like not having an email address.) Yet Gore Tore must have known him. Despite the gap between their ages, they'd both gone to the Royal College of Music, albeit twenty years apart.

'That *has* to be the connection,' Quentin mutters.

He hasn't listened to much pop music since Elvis Costello –

but he is, increasingly, interested in Gore Tore. How many of his songs had he heard during school discos? Dozens, for Tore had been the archetypal voice of anarchy before, during and after his adolescence, a music that seemed like pure emotion, guaranteed to make people dance with the same uninhibited frenzy that Tore did. Quentin remembers losing all self-consciousness to 'Let's Go!', a perennial favourite which always makes people dance. He is a real musician as well as a star, his riffs and experiments with melody something that induces millions of middle-aged people to tearful nostalgia and even a sense of awe. Tore himself is famous for the way he was able to inflame both men and women with – is it lust or joy or adrenalin? He has the androgynous beauty which, contrary to expectations, lasts, and even now he is striking – plastered in make-up, his hair dyed, his image always morphing into something unexpected. He probably looks quite different without all the trappings.

He's also a man of some mystery, like all the greatest rock stars. Tore has never given a print interview, and has only done one on TV – for the defunct *Snap, Crackle, Pop!* in 1975, viewable on YouTube. Quentin watches this. Though obviously stoned, Tore seems intelligent, witty and articulate, with barely a trace of Devon in his voice. His private life, according to the tabloids, has been a mess. His first marriage produced one son, killed in an accident. Some of his ex-lovers had died from overdoses, others from suicide; he's been divorced four times. (Quentin feels a wince of sympathy.) Yet he's paid for the education and maintenance of every child proven to be his, and given away large chunks of his immense fortune to all kinds of causes and charities.

Against his better judgement, Quentin is intrigued. He thinks of what his agent said about a biography. He loathes the idea of ghosting a book ... but it might not be as stupid an idea as he thought. Yet nothing will happen if he doesn't make it so, and introduce himself to Tore as a neighbour. He needs to make his lie to his agent come true: something he'd been accustomed to doing as a young journalist, but which now fills him with weariness and discomfort.

Stella tinkles away at the piano next door.

'Is that new?'

'Mummy's teaching me.'

'Really,' Quentin says. He's checking his emails. The broadband is maddeningly slow, and the only way to improve it is to sit right beside the router. 'Mozart?'

'It's Bach, Daddy,' Stella says, with the surprise and sorrow that the musical always display towards the ignorant.

She plays her short piece.

'Lovely, darling. Reminds me of a cigar advertisement.'

'Dawn's much better than me.'

As Janet comes in with the Dyson, Stella slides off the piano stool.

'I can't think with that noise,' she says reproachfully.

'Urgh,' Janet says. 'Give me a good pop song any day. Classical gives me the willies. Besides, what's the point? There's no money in it.'

Apart from cats, the only thing to interest Janet is money, and she will insist on telling them about some discount at Lidl as if Quentin could give a fig. She seems honest, though, and it's worth £100 a month to not do his half of the cleaning, even if she will bring her lump of a daughter round.

Dawn is always slumped somewhere like a white whale. It's annoying, but Quentin can't quite bring himself to ask that she be left behind. She looks so miserable, he thinks.

'How do you find the school in Trelorn?' he asks, trying to make conversation.

There is a long pause. He wonders whether she's understood. Then,

'I don't go there any more,' Dawn says.

Quentin says, 'But you're how old? Seventeen? You'd have a much better future if you stayed in education.'

'Can't.'

'Oh.'

Quentin wishes he'd asked more, because the next day he visits Trelorn Secondary School, both to check it out if Lottie insists on staying and to talk to the teachers about Oliver Randall. The school – the usual concrete egg box from the 1970s – is the epitome of all he fears for his daughters in the state system.

'I'm writing a piece about Oliver Randall,' he says.

'Who?'

'He taught here until last year.'

It's clear from the woman's blank expression that she has no idea who he means.

'He was a musician,' he explains, as if speaking to a child. He thinks it best not to mention the murder.

'Never heard of him.'

'Is he a pop star?' asks one, brightening.

'No.'

'Was he on the staff or freelance?'

'I don't know.'

'The school mostly has freelance instrument teachers, though that'll change when we become a music academy.'

Quentin, exasperated, asks, 'Who would know what pupils he taught?'

There is a general clucking over this, and then one says,

'I think one of them was that blonde girl. Pretty little thing. What was she called? Dina? Diana?'

'Dana?'

'Lovely voice. Played the piano too. Dawn.'

'You mean, the girl who lives in the gatehouse of Shipcott Manor?'

'Yes. That's her.'

It's hard to believe it's the same person, but then maybe they have a different concept of what a pretty girl looks like. If so, he thinks, Di Tore must know more. It's as good an excuse as any.

Lottie has left Di's mobile number on a pad. He invites himself to Shipcott Manor for tea.

'I know my girls get on with your boys, and we're all missing Lottie,' he says, shamelessly.

No sooner has he uttered this lie than he knows it's the truth. Even if she will irritate him all over again on her return, his wife's absence is more than an inconvenience. When she's there, it's like seeing someone close-up, their smallest blemishes magnified. At a distance, he can remember how before everything went wrong, and over supper, or in the car, in restaurants or on walks, he and Lottie would talk.

Of course, absence is preferable to all the shouting and weeping that has gone on subsequently. He had put all the feelings of guilt and shame into boxes, and never thought that one day the boxes themselves might start to leak and bulge. Nor had he thought that one day he might be served up a portion of what he had inflicted on her.

No, that had come a few weeks ago when, returning from his parents' home, he had seen, suspended in a cube of bright light, the vision of Lottie kissing Martin. It was only a glimpse, but quite unmistakable. The shock had made him go ice-cold.

Gripping the wheel, he felt quite numb. So, it was as he suspected. She is no better than he. He could deal with that. Then he drove off the road into a ditch.

It was the surprise that made him react like this, just the surprise. So Quentin kept telling himself. Drenched in sweat that turned instantly sour, he turned off the engine, sat there, shaking, then put his car into reverse, got out of the ditch and drove home very slowly. His mind was working perfectly, but he noted with dismay that his reactions were slower than they should be, as if he were drunk.

Of course she would find someone else – she's an attractive woman, and nine years younger than him. Martin may be the best solution to his own dilemma, only he doesn't feel this at all.

What he feels is that he'd like to punch that gingery idiot in the face, but he can't, because the choices which he has dismissed so airily as insignificant are now lacerating him with their steel claws and iron beaks. He would not have believed how much jealousy could make him suffer, how it has skewered his stomach to his bowels, and turned every night into a fiery pit in which he has no rest. Why should it matter? Surely he has wanted to be free of his wife just as she wants to be free of him?

But however often he has lied to others, he can't lie to himself. His quick bright mind can't outrun the lumbering needs of his body, which moans its miseries to his inner ear. Oh shut up, he tells it, angrily; but it won't. No wonder Lottie had wept and writhed: this is what he had inflicted on her, and now it appears she has done it back.

There is no aphrodisiac like that of rejection. Now, memory floods him: her eyes, her lips, her breasts, her hips, the hot wet suck of her flesh to his flesh, and how at times he felt he might die of bliss. It had been like nothing else, and he'd been afraid of being in some way subsumed as if all his own vigour would be lost if he didn't have a second, secret, life to preserve it. Only it is this second life that has destroyed him.

Making the girls' breakfast, he stopped and groaned aloud.

'What's the matter, Daddy?' Stella asked. She was still nervous; unlike Rosie and like her mother, her default setting was anxiety.

'I'm such a bad man. I'm an awful man.'

Rosie put her arms around him.

'No you aren't. You're the bestest daddy in the world.'

'Yes,' Stella said, patting him as if he were a dog who might turn dangerous. 'We love you, Daddy.'

They are so sweet; it almost sets his teeth on edge. Once they grow older they too will turn on him, seeing him for what he is. He smiled at them, when what he wanted to do was cry. But wasn't that the constant condition of parenthood? You're always pretending to be braver than you are, bolder than you are,

273

brighter and more knowledgeable, and they believe you, until they don't.

The sound of a car coming down the drive jerks Quentin into blowing his nose. He hurries out, his tears drying in the heat of embarrassment.

'Hello there! Any parcels for me?'

It's Sam, looking less absurd in his long shorts now that the weather is warm.

'Yes, a couple. Buy a lot online do you?'

'Oh no, these are books for review.'

'You must be a great reader,' Sam says.

Quentin, embarrassed, says,

'It's work, actually.'

Sam makes a move towards his red van, and Quentin adds hurriedly,

'Did the man who lived here before get many deliveries?'

Sam stops, scratches his head and says, 'Not as I recall.'

'Did you ever talk?'

'Not really.' Sam's voice makes this a long-drawn-out sound. 'I just delivered the mail, like, as I do to you. Poor chap.'

'It must have been a bad shock for you,' Quentin says, with the simulacrum of sympathy that he'd always found effective in interviews.

'I still dream about it sometimes. A body without a head, well, it's not natural, is it? We'd never have recognised him from the papers, though.'

'Why not?'

Sam grimaces.

'He didn't have all that hair! Randall had a big beard, and not a hair on his head. His own mother wouldn't have recognised him.'

'He was bald?'

'Oh no. He shaved it off. You could see it growing back from time to time. I've wondered, after the murder, you know ...'

274

'What?'

Sam's ruddy face flushes deeper red. 'Well, if he could have been in hiding, maybe.'

'This would be a good place to hide,' Quentin agrees. 'But who was he hiding from?'

'Plenty of people minding their own business round here,' Sam says, pointedly.

His own mother wouldn't have recognised him . . . Quentin has seen how men who lose their hair become unrecognisable, and a beard would indeed add to that. But what if the person he was hiding from wasn't back in London, but here? Whom had he known, apart from the Tores?

Well, he thinks: I can ask them.

Quentin piles the car high with malodorous rubbish which, in Lottie's absence, he's forgotten to put out on the verge for collection. The tinkling smash of bottles as he posts them into the giant bins is positively festive, for even a visit to the Trelorn dump is a treat.

This done, he wanders round the town, trying to think what to bring Di Tore, a person who has everything. He goes into a couple of charity shops, spotlessly clean and infinitely beige. There is simply nothing to buy in this place. No posh bakeries, not even a florist.

It appals him, the absence of enterprise. On Saturday afternoons, just when most working people most need to shop, businesses all close. It's the same with cafés and pubs, as if everyone must only want to eat between 12 and 2 or 7 and 10 p.m. Then they complain about the absence of trade. The local estate agent's window is full of shops for sale or rent which, in any thriving town, would be worth hundreds of thousands of pounds, but which instead are soaped blank.

Quentin steps back, scrutinising an empty off-licence to let. The building is on the corner of the square, with big windows on either side. Probably freezing cold in winter . . . but how difficult

275

could it be to fill its shelves with home-made macaroons and baguettes? How hard can it be to have an Internet café? Then he looks at the stolid, solid people plodding past, at the pensioners tottering along with sticks. These people will cluster round places offering stodgy cream teas, but never move into the twenty-first century, being stuck in the 1970s. His passing fantasy shrivels.

'If only Devon could have proper high-speed broadband, it'd make a world of difference.'

'Something will turn up, Quent,' his mother says.

'Ma, nothing *ever* turns up unless you are in London.'

'So will you be going back?'

'Probably. By the way, I've been wondering whether you or Fa ever came across the previous tenant of Home Farm.'

Naomi's lined face is inscrutable.

'Once or twice. He seemed a very nice man.'

'Was he nice to anyone in particular?'

'I know he gave lessons to one or two whose parents couldn't or wouldn't pay.'

'What kind of parent wouldn't pay?'

'Oh, you'd be surprised. Some hate their kids having the brains or talent they don't. And no, I'm not going to name names.'

'Any idea why he came to Devon?'

'I think he was in love. He had that look. He was very happy, for a while.'

'With whom?'

His mother exhales. 'Don't bother about it, Quent. I'm too tired.'

Dying takes so much out of everyone's life. Hugh hardly eats or drinks; just getting a little sweet tea or thin soup into his father's mouth is the most that can be managed. Sometimes he seems to be awake, but the periods between lucidity seem ever shorter, and the opiates delivered through the cannula stronger. Quentin has become used to removing and replacing incontinence pads with a competence that slightly surprises him, rolling his father onto one

276

side and back as the nurse has shown him, and sponging his limbs clean before patting them dry. To his great surprise, he finds that the hatred he has nourished for so long for his father has vanished. This poor stick draped in skin was once a man. Almost nothing remains but pity and the inevitable disaster.

His other most practical task is to ensure that the fire must never die out. He feels it as a kind of religious duty. Naomi shuffles about in the kitchen, making endless pots of chicken soup. It's the smell of his childhood; only later had he realised it to be the smell of all Jewish homes.

'Come out for a drive,' he says. 'The change of scene will do you good.'

'I don't dare,' she says. 'He might need me.'

It's endlessly frustrating, but Quentin does his best, watching his father's face as he sleeps or chatting to his mother as she potters slowly around doing chores she won't let the nurse help her with. She is small and bent and old, too, but he's surprised to see a large mound of clay kept soft under damp cloths in her studio when he passes it.

'Who is this?' Quentin asks.

'Your father,' Naomi answers, turning the cloth back. 'I was just letting my fingers remember.'

'You remember him so clearly?'

'Who is it, really, who loves a person for what they are?'

'Yes, Lottie used to be like that with me. I was her project.'

'Although I loved Hugh for himself, even with his faults.'

'Lottie can't tolerate my spots of commonness.'

'Is that what you think? I think what she can't tolerate is your lack of guilt.'

'My lack of guilt!' Quentin almost howls. 'I'm nothing *but* guilt these days.'

Quentin returns to Shipcott and its manor, pressing a button at the gatehouse and looking into the security camera. Janet must be out, because the voice that answers is distinctly Australian.

'Hi there.'

'I'm Stella and Rosie's dad.'

'Come right in.'

The electronic gates swing open. The drive is long and pleasantly shaded by an abundant wood, bumping over a lively little stream.

Quentin had been expecting the usual brick or granite manor house, so the white, lace-like arches come as a surprise. To one side is an enormous and very ancient magnolia tree, shaped like a lyre. He parks, walks up the stone steps and pulls the iron handle to the side of the large oak door. A bell yelps within – or is it a dog? To think that his wife and children have been coming here all this time ... he's envious, and slightly appalled by his own temerity at inviting himself over.

Barefoot, Di Tore opens the front door.

'Hi. You must be Stella and Rosie's dad.'

'Botticelli's Venus by way of Bondi Beach,' says Quentin. 'Hello!'

'Brisbane,' she corrects, and he knows he's annoyed her. 'The kids are in the garden.'

'Thanks so much for collecting them,' Quentin says. She's no longer young, but has the *noli me tangere* air of authentic beauty. 'Sorry if I'm late. It's difficult being on time, given the situation with my father.'

Her face clears.

'Yes, I'm sorry to hear about that. I hope your mum is OK. Come in.'

He follows her through the hall to an enormous, light-filled room. It's fan-vaulted with delicate white plasterwork branching out like fantastical trees. The view is superb, but Quentin prefers to watch his hostess, and the arse inside her jeans like two perfectly boiled eggs rubbing gently against each other. She is so much a part of the wealth that bought this house that she is, curiously, sexless. It's a relief to realise this.

'It's very good of you to take the girls home for tea.'

They can see their children playing in the garden below.

'As you can see, they get along fine.'

'I'm very grateful,' he says. 'They've settled in well.'

'Great.' Di smiles brightly. 'No bad vibes, I hope? I take it Lottie told you about its past.'

Interesting, Quentin thinks: so Lottie knows about the murder, and didn't mention it.

'No, though I am curious about Oliver Randall. What can you tell me?'

'You know, I think the best person to answer that isn't me.'

A figure rose from the long sofa by the window. It's the tramp from the pub, Quentin thinks, astonished. Then, as if the light has changed, the molecules of the man before him rearrange themselves. The ripped jeans aren't rags. The long dark hair is a product of artifice, the lean frame of the gym, and the deep lines are those of a man who has had everything money, fame and talent can buy.

'Hi.'

'You – *you're* Gore Tore?'

'I owe you a drink, mate.'

279

26

A Pinnacle of Existence

Xan thinks of London as a form of radiation. You can't live here and not be changed. To survive its pressure, its energy, heat, light and power, you must adapt – run faster, find wings, stretch eyes and grow a thicker skin. Above all, you must be young.

It's been so long since he's lived in a population where most of the faces he sees are unlined, with hair that isn't white or grey, that for the first week it doesn't quite feel real. Where are the fat people, the ones in awful clothes, the ones bent over with age and infirmity? He never noticed their existence before he moved to the country, and now he isn't sure whether London has simply abolished the poor, or whether they are afraid to come out. Having chafed at the slowness of country life for months, he is now slightly bewildered at those running or skateboarding or just walking very fast. To be able to go out of his grandmother's house and find himself buying a pint of milk in three minutes seems miraculous.

When he looks around the streets of London he understands, dimly, that he is living in some kind of pinnacle of existence, a great pyramid of labour, ingenuity, law and effort whose base is so remote as to be almost out of sight. These wide streets with their carefully pruned trees and washed pavements, these towers sparkling with brilliant lights, these shops bursting with perfect produce, this rich ferment of commerce and creativity – it is a wonder of the world. Who here knows or cares about the places from which its prizes are drawn? If the countryside exists in popular imagination, it's as a place of recreation, in which food is produced in Elysian fields of buttercups from happy hens and immortal herds. Xan has been to the so-called farmers' markets in which the middle classes sell artisan meats and hand-made goats' cheese to each other from within state school playgrounds, in the belief that this is a more authentic shopping experience. It had been mildly entertaining then, but now he thinks that if people could see the inside of Humbles, or a slaughterhouse, or a field in freezing weather, they might not be so complacent.

And yet . . . Even when he's lying in bed, he can feel the pressure of all those other people sharpening him to a kind of peak of himself. I have been half-asleep, he thinks. Sometimes, at night, he leans out of his old bedroom window just to listen to the murmuring roar of the capital which seems as much a part of him as his heartbeat.

Of course, this isn't just being a Londoner, it's Marta living on a different plane. Xan wonders how much she spends a month on culture; he suspects that it's as much as his family's entire supermarket shop.

'I wish to give these things to you,' she says when he thanks her for yet another theatre ticket, or delicious foreign food. 'You are my beautiful grandson, and you need it. No, don't look embarrassed; you are beautiful because nothing has happened to you yet.'

'I feel as if quite a lot has happened to me, Oma, actually.'

She shakes her head.

'Darling! You are still just out of the egg.'

'There are all kinds of things we have now that your generation didn't.'

'Really?' She puts her head on one side enquiringly. 'Like war?'

'Well, no, but . . . we have the Internet.'

She laughs, and whips out an earpiece from her iPod and
thrusts it towards Xan, who listens for a few minutes. 'Sublime.'

'Don't you ever feel Bach is a bit remote, Oma?'

'Notatall!' Marta's accent always emerges when she feels
strongly. 'Bach is always asking a question, you see,' she says.

'What's that, Oma?'

'Whether we are loved. He had absolutely no doubt that we
are, by God.'

She's never been like other people's grandmothers. One of the
first things she'd asked him to do for her in hospital was to paint
her toenails with brilliant scarlet nail polish.

'Darling, it keeps the nails nice, and I do not want to be one
of those old ladies with hoofs. Ah, listen to this! How can you
listen and not believe in God?'

'Do you believe in God, Oma?'

'Only when I listen to Bach.'

Xan thinks of Dawn, and when she had sat down without
saying a word and played the first of the *Goldberg Variations*. It
still haunts him. Without her playing, would he even have noticed
her? He's grown up thinking of himself as anti-prejudice, anti-
racist, anti-sexist, anti-homophobic: only it's one thing to define
yourself as against something, and quite another to embrace what
you are *for*.

In the brief minutes when she had played perhaps the most
exquisite short piece of music for the keyboard ever written,
Dawn had looked quite different. The *Goldberg Aria* looks
simple, the merest handful of notes, but it is not, and somehow
she had caught the way the *Aria* seems to float on a golden thread
between earth and heaven. How was it possible?

'Oma, can someone very stupid play music really well?'

His grandmother raises her eyebrows.

'One can learn to play mechanically, as far too many Japanese and Chinese do—'

'Yes, like Uchida and Lang Lang . . . ' Xan says ironically.

She sniffs, as he knew she would. Marta is old school: black tie, no showbiz, preferably Russian or Canadian.

'Could you, Oma?'

'There is muscle memory. If someone has learned a piece, their body can remember it even if the brain has forgotten. There are cases of people with Alzheimer's whose memory has gone, but who can still play.'

'Even a piece like the *Goldberg Aria*?'

'Yes, certainly.'

'I wonder why somebody's body would remember that particular piece, though.'

'Perhaps if they needed it very badly, they might. It reminds us that joy is more powerful than sorrow.'

Marta has experienced things she never speaks of, but which they all somehow know about. She had been a child during the invasion of Berlin.

'Seriously Oma, you need to think about moving. Your dog could have broken your neck.'

'Heidi could have broken it in a flat, too.'

Marta is always stubborn. It's another thing she has in common with Lottie, and although Xan admires his mother for having principles, he also wishes hers weren't quite so rigid. Of course hurt feelings matter, and when he thinks of what Quentin has done, especially to his mother, he wants to punch him. But do hurt feelings matter so much that they're worth splitting up a family for? Do a few months of infidelity count for more than a long marriage? Do they matter more than his sisters?

It probably doesn't help that Marta makes no secret that she loathes her son-in-law.

'The *Dummkopf*' is what she calls him, meaning 'blockhead'.

283

Quentin is vain, pretentious and a snob, but there is also another aspect to him of which Xan is, reluctantly, aware. He has been a good stepfather. He's been generous with money. He's encouraged independence. He's taken the time and trouble to teach him skills like riding a bicycle, shaving and tying a school tie. He was the one to give Xan a proper mobile, even when being sworn at. Xan loves his mother a lot, but he also knows she doesn't understand why organising Smarties on a birthday cake according to their place on the spectrum isn't actually necessary.

'Mum, stop it. Just stop it,' he's pleaded, so many times.

Maybe, though, it's a female thing: for Katya is also bossy. In the beginning, her 'do this to me, do that' had been useful, as well as sexy. He'd admired the Poles' energy and enterprise. Yet the other side of this is a private contempt for British people.

'Not like Polish peoples,' is a refrain he hears, uttered with a mixture of regret and satisfaction. 'English peoples so dirty. You can't even cook.'

'Why shouldn't people buy meals? Once upon a time women were expected to churn their own butter. Nobody wants to go back to that, do they?' Xan has retorted, but Katya would only shrug.

'You waste your money.'

'What about wasting time which could be better used by, I don't know, *reading*?'

'But what is the use of that?' Katya asked, in amazement; and that was the moment when he knew he did not and could not love her.

Sometimes, Xan wonders whether he is a thorn in his mother's flesh to remind her that she *has* flesh. Not so Marta. Often when Xan returns from walking Heidi on the Heath, he opens the door to the rumble of male laughter from elderly men for whom seats at Covent Garden Opera House and a lifetime subscription to the *New Statesman* are as much a part of life as bifocals. They may be ancient, and as wrinkled as lizards, but they are actually flirting with her and she with them.

He hopes Marta has had lovers after his grandfather died. It's dreary to think that she might only have devoted her life to J. S. Bach.

'Did you ever want to get married again?'

'I like independence more.'

Whether she can still be independent is the worry. It's a battle for her to get in and out of the bathroom. She refuses his help. To her, discussing medical problems is simply a bore.

'Let us talk of more interesting things. Has your brain woken up yet?'

'I think so. Though I need a break, Oma, after being in an exam factory for years.'

'The modern world is very cruel. In Africa, you would have killed a lion at thirteen.'

'I wish I'd known what my father was good at. I don't even know what part of Africa he came from.'

'He was Nigerian.'

'How do you know? Mum never saw him again.'

'No,' Marta says. 'But I did.'

Astounded, Xan stares. All these years, and his grandmother has known.

'He came here? So what happened? Why didn't they meet?'

'I thought it best not,' Marta says calmly.

Xan knows that both his mother and his grandmother are over-controlling, but this is beyond anything.

'Oma, *why*?'

'She went through a bad time after you were born, much as she did with your sisters. She did not need this extra thing.'

'He was *my father*,' Xan says. 'Not a thing.'

The enormity of what Marta has kept concealed astonishes him.

'Would it have made a difference if he'd been white?'

'No. I'm sorry, my darling.'

How can she not have known that he wanted to have a father? Nigerian, he thinks, and it's as if the shadow he has never quite seen becomes solid at his heels. A thousand questions rise in his throat, and it's his old enemy asthma, squeezing like a boa constrictor. It's what he always dreads, and strong emotion is a trigger as bad as cats. There is an inhaler in his spongebag, at the top of the house, but Marta won't be able to get it in time, and neither will he. Why hadn't he got one in his pocket? His fingers turn cold, but he keeps breathing out, praying for it to loosen. Gradually, the spasm passes. Marta hasn't even realised what he's just been through, for she says,

'I have his name, if you want it. I promised to give it to you.'

Xan says, as evenly as possible,

'So he knows I exist?'

'Yes. That was why he came.'

'How? I mean, he and Mum only got together that one time.'

'They must have had at least one acquaintance in common, to meet at a party. And ... well, people talk. She had returned to live with me, and as a musician, I am not difficult to find.'

'Is he in London now? Was he a student too? What did he study?'

'I have no idea. He asked if he could see you.' Oma sighs. 'I did what I thought best.'

'What was his name?'

'Julius Okigbo. I have it written down somewhere, but I didn't forget.'

Xan seizes this straw. Julius Okigbo, he says to himself. I can find you, if you are to be found. Then a new thought strikes him.

'Did you tell him my name, Oma?'

'Yes, I did.'

Everyone can be found on the Internet, now – and his father has not tried. Xan is on Facebook, and probably has a dozen tags to his name. Perhaps he doesn't want to, Xan thinks. Perhaps he's dead. Perhaps he's changed his mind. He must have another family by now. There are so many reasons.

Or he might just be waiting for Xan himself to get in touch. Oma can be pretty scary at times, and walking up to her front door and announcing yourself as the bloke who knocked up her daughter must have taken some balls.

However, the main thing was that he had tried, perhaps not very hard, but he had left his name. Maybe he thought Lottie was some kind of weirdo, rather than acting totally out of character, being pissed for once. (And what kind of man took advantage of that, by the way?)

He wants to get back to Devon, and talk to his mother. She ought to know what he knows, at least. Marta's leg isn't mended, but she is well enough for him to leave. The sad, anxious look he had seen peering out when she was in hospital has gone. She is back, a little more frail but herself.

'I hope you will not hate me for keeping this under my head.'

'No, Oma, I could never hate you. You didn't know how much it's been eating me up, wanting to know. I think it might help Lottie, too.'

'In that case, I have made an error of judgement. I apologise, most sincerely.'

Marta bows her head, and he kisses her, lightly.

'Hey,' he says. 'Don't worry. Maybe he's a total tool, and not meeting him before now will turn out to be a good idea.'

He stretches. Now that the wheezing has passed, his body seethes with the need for movement.

'Would you like some tea, Oma?'

'Go out, my darling. You have better things to do in the evening than stay in with an old woman.'

'I wouldn't mind seeing a couple of friends,' Xan admits, though really it's Bron he wants to see. They'd met up soon after Xan had been to see his grandmother, and he gave him the tissue with the blood on it. Will he have found anything in Dawn's

287

blood, or will he have forgotten in the end-of-year exams? When Xan calls, however, it's a good time.

'Hey, how're you doing?'

Bron sounds exactly as he always does. He hasn't bothered to call or email during all the months of Xan's exile, that's the way he is. They could probably not have any contact for years, yet pick up where they left off. It's very reassuring, although recently, Xan has begun to wonder why he hasn't heard from Katya, either, which kind of bugs him. Aren't they supposed to be in a relationship? Is she waiting for him to call or message her? He hadn't liked to bother her when she went away to Poland over Christmas, but they'd exchanged a few texts at least. This time, nothing.

He catches the 24 bus into Camden, then the 29. It's strange to think that in just a few months he himself may be living here again. He suddenly feels enormously excited. The centre is still strange to him: all he really knows of it is North London, where he's lived and gone to school. The UCL campus lies over the centre in an invisible web which he can see, like the wizarding world of Harry Potter, but others can't. There's the British Library, and the British Museum, and in fact you could live your entire life in this city and never know more than a fraction of it.

'Did you get a chance to look at the blood sample I gave you?'

'Not yet.' Bron sees the expression on Xan's face and adds, 'It would help if it were a proper sample in a tube, you know. It's probably bacterially contaminated.'

'It was all I could have.'

'The thing is, it's not easy to get anything tested in a lab. I can't do that as a medical student in my first year. Blood tests are strictly regulated, and besides, you need to know what you're looking *for*.'

Xan swallows his disappointment.

'I don't know what it is, but something isn't right. This girl, Dawn, apparently she used to be really bright, and now she's dropped out of school and is a sort of blob.'

'You know what it sounds like to me? Weed.'

Xan shakes his head. 'No. It's more like somebody isn't there. I know what people are like when they're high, and she's not. What could make someone change very drastically in one year?'

He can see Bron thinking.

'It could be anaemia, or the beginnings of MS, or hepatitis, or Vitamin B deficiency or hypothyroidism or cancer. Any other symptoms? What colour is her skin?'

Xan thinks. 'Yellowish.'

'So, probably not anaemia then. How does she move?'

'Like an old woman. She's hardly able to walk at times.'

'It definitely sounds as if she should see a doctor. Are you sure she isn't?'

'She's totally under her mother's thumb, and . . . I don't think she can get anywhere if Janet doesn't drive her there. She lives out in the countryside, like us. I've never seen her use a mobile. I think she's completely cut off, apart from when she's at the factory, where nobody ever talks to her.'

Xan has not even known he has thought all this, but now that he has, his disquiet rises. He adds, 'And she *asked* me to help her.'

'Why you?'

'I don't know.'

'Maybe she fancies you.'

Xan feels himself flush.

'I don't think so. I think she's afraid of something, or someone. But I do think that if it's possible to test her blood, you should.'

'You're asking someone to risk quite a lot. She's how old?'

'My age, I think. No, a bit younger. I think she's seventeen.'

'So too old to contact the Child Protection Agency,' Bron says.

'You think it's serious, then?'

289

'It could be. You can contact the police anonymously, if you are really worried.'

'But what could I say? I've never seen any bruises or anything. Although—' Xan hesitates a moment. 'I saw a lot of thin white lines, scars, up her arms—'

'Lots of teenagers self-harm. Still, not a good sign I agree.'

'I know you can't make a diagnosis without seeing someone, even if you were qualified.'

Bron says, 'Is she hot, this girl?'

'Not at all. The opposite. She looks awful, to be honest, no eyebrows. All blotchy, and puffy, and her voice is hoarse.'

He can see that Bron has an idea, but won't say. He has become very serious about being a medic in a way which perhaps is a surprise even to himself.

'I'll tell you what I'll do,' Bron says. 'I'll find a way to get that sample tested. But I also think you could just try asking her mother if something is wrong. She may think you're being nosy, which you are, but it's always possible she hasn't realised her daughter might be ill.'

Maybe the simplest thing is to do that. Even if Xan instinctively dislikes Janet, she is Dawn's mother and might take her to a doctor herself. Then he can stop worrying.

Unless Janet herself is what her daughter is afraid of.

27

The Business of Being a Woman

Sally is inspecting a sheep's arse, a broad, lumpy clump of brown wool heavily hung with dark pellets of dung. The pungent smell makes her stomach turn; but it's got to be clipped, alongside hundreds of others, now the warm weather is here.

'Sometimes I think the whole animal kingdom should go around in nappies,' she says to Peter. He snorts, obligingly.

But this is the thing about a marriage: you make the same jokes over and over, and they are the regular beat to which you step. Even if she's heard Pete's stories about the goose which fell in love with a bucket or the woman who followed her satnav down their narrow lane thinking she was in Hampshire a dozen times, she still laughs. Her own mother used to say, A marriage isn't about being happy ever after, it's about kindness and forgiving. The trouble is that you only realise this after the event, when love becomes a glow not a blaze. She and Pete had thought themselves very wise and mature, and it's true that compared with some of the other twenty-two-year-olds they knew, they were; you can't experience death or see birth without some understanding of how mysterious every single human being is to every other.

Had it been that which had made her so keen, or was it because Pete had just inherited his father's farm, and to be mistress of her own home was what she wanted above all? He was a catch, Peter Verity, and she had caught him without even trying, at just the point when, having moved back to her parents', she thought she'd go mad if she stayed a minute longer. All of that must have come into it, but the real reason was that during her absence he'd changed from a scowling, round-faced boy into a big, tall, well-knit man. She'd seen him walking through a field one day, graceful and self-contained as an animal; and that was it.

Unlike herself, Pete had been a virgin. They've never discussed it but she's not heard of him ever having a girlfriend before she returned from her training in London. There had been a succession of boyfriends for her, one of them an anaesthetist at the same hospital she worked at. That's how her sister Anne had met Josh, his younger brother. Tom Viner is married now himself, with a wife and three children ... She looks at the sheep and thinks, would I have been happier with that life, or this?

Recently, she's felt more and more restive as well as depressed. Partly it's getting to know Lottie Bredin, and being able to talk to another woman who is bright and switched on. Sally is used, for instance, to reading the national newspapers. She doesn't think it makes her better or cleverer than anyone else, but the news and ideas and opinions in there are just *different*. Pete can't understand it.

'Why do you bother with that stuff? You aren't going to run off to Totnes are you?'

It's always been a joke between them, that town. Most Devonians who do real jobs find Totnes hilarious. Yet recently she'd had a dream in which she was drifting down a long, steep street going down to a river, crammed with little shops all painted different colours, with wind chimes and rainbow flags fluttering, and she suddenly felt happy. Really *happy*. And it was Totnes.

'I was thinking it might be interesting to go there one day. You know, just to see what it's like.'

He was quite upset at the idea. As long as her interests keep her at home it's fine; but if she does anything outside it, he gets grumpy. She had loved singing in the choir, for instance, and had spent six of the happiest months of her life learning the alto part of many hymns. Pete never said anything to forbid her, just got silent and sullen until she worked out what the matter was, and dropped it.

'I don't like you being away from home,' he said.

'It's only for a couple of hours a week.'

'I keep worrying something bad has happened to you.'

He wants them to be like Gabriel Oak and Bathsheba in the film, looking up and there she'd be, which is all very nice except that you need to look up and see other people too, sometimes. Of course, he's the person she *most* wants to see, but when Pete gets out of bed before her every morning what she feels most is an intense feeling of relief. At last, she has some space to herself, mental and physical. Yet she knows how lucky she is to be married to such a good kind man.

She thinks again of that story her mother told her, about the doctor's daughter who'd hanged herself because Tore wasn't in love with her. If only she'd loved her child instead of its father! More and more women are single mums these days, because they don't want a husband, or at least not the kind they might plausibly get.

Men fail us, Sally thinks, because they mostly won't or can't communicate. It's their greatest failing as a sex. Of course, Pete would help anyone who asked, but taking an interest in people's lives, being sympathetic to their problems, talking things over, putting people in touch or doing a good turn, and above all really saying what they feel – this is what she craves. Pete won't talk

293

to anyone he doesn't already know, and on the rare occasions when he does have a chat, he will come away without having discovered a single interesting thing about them, such as the state of their health, the number and ages of their children, whether their business is going well or badly this year and what they think about *Strictly* and, basically, how they are feeling about life in general. Sally is forever astonished and exasperated by this.

'But I couldn't ask about that kind of thing!' he exclaims when she tells him off for his lack of information. 'It wouldn't be polite.'

'No, it's not polite not to be interested,' Sally says. 'What is everybody's favourite subject? Themselves. Not the weather. Not the football. Not cars. You don't have to talk about yourself, but you have to be interested in *them*.'

'But why should I pretend to be when I'm not?'

Of course, she asks questions as part of her job, and often they are intimate ones. Most people never ask each other if their bowels are functioning, or whether they have resumed inter-course and whether it was painful, but Sally does, in order to fill in her forms and make sure all is as it should be. That's her job. However, among men it's as if incuriosity is a badge of honour, with the result that they all go stumbling blindly around in a fog of unknowing, and proud of it too. How did men discover anything, ever, when they won't ask? If all the detectives in the Devon and Cornwall constabulary were women, Sally thinks, I bet we'd have an answer to why Oliver Randall was murdered.

'Now where did I put my glasses?' Pete mutters, as if echoing her thoughts.

'Breast pocket,' she says without looking up, and he sighs with relief. His eyesight is going, whereas hers is still the same as it ever was. She doesn't feel old. But that's the thing, you grow old without noticing. Inside, she's still the young woman she was when she came back to Trelorn to work as a community mid-wife; shiny with the stuff she'd bought in places like Top Shop which in those days even Plymouth didn't have. Pete had asked her out to the cinema. They'd seen *The Shawshank Redemption*, and afterwards they'd spent the rest of the evening kissing under the willows, beside his battered Land Rover in the car park, with the river carrying the night along on its dark waters. She'd wanted him so badly that when he pushed against her she gasped and shuddered like a fish out of water, and he'd thought she was sneezing, bless him. She's never forgotten it, that moment when everything seemed to rush together and resolve itself. That's what matters, though he would even have forgotten her birthday if she hadn't marked it in capital letters on the Devon Life calendar for him.

'That's just like my husband,' her girlfriends would exclaim, when they saw it.

Forgetful or not, she's glad of his presence at night. Sally has been feeling uneasy ever since she'd seen her neighbours' mare with wounds on its legs. The police, when they eventually turned up, took photographs but could find no clue. It's not the first time horses have been attacked; some people blame paganists, though this is rubbish – pagans being keen to worship nature rather than harm it. Others say it's Satanists. She puts it down to sheer nastiness but can't but wonder whether there is more than one lunatic wandering about. Normally, the only things you have to worry about in the countryside are weather or wind farms, not people, not unless they were incomers.

Lottie is now officially that. News has gone round that she's sold her house in London and is buying Home Farm from the Tores.

'So, you're not worried by its past?' Sally asks her.

Lottie pauses, and Sally wonders whether she's been too inquisitive.

'Not really, no. I expect most old houses have had something bad happen in them at some point. It just seems like a good time to move. Loads of families with young children are leaving London; it's too expensive for ordinary people to stay. Besides, the

Trelorn project is the most wonderful opportunity. I never thought I'd switch to domestic architecture, but it feels like being given a second life.'

Lottie's face is animated, though when Sally catches a glimpse of Quentin in Trelorn, he looks drawn and miserable. Her sister says it won't be long for Hugh Bredin.

'Poor Naomi has battled so hard to keep him out of hospital, and now she needs a knee replacement because of lifting him,' Anne remarked. 'Never a word of thanks for it, neither. The way he talks to her, sometimes, it fair makes my blood boil.'

Of course, Anne wouldn't dream of discussing a patient like this with anyone else, any more than Tess would discuss a pupil or a parent, but it's different with sisters. They have no secrets. If I were to die first, she thinks, Pete would go back to being all alone, for ever. He may not talk much, but he still does talk, even if it's only to her.

'One day, maybe, they'll be able to grow meat in laboratories,' Pete says. They are out in the field together, the day's work done. 'No more cruelty then; but I don't think it'd be a better world.'

'Why not, Pete?' she asks. 'If you could grow meat in laboratories, wouldn't that be better than sending lambs to be slaughtered?'

'Just think about it. The land that's pasture now would all get ploughed up for crops, or built on for housing and factories. No, the truth is that our world lives because of death.'

'I wouldn't mind, if there could just be less flies.'

Every year, flies lay their eggs in the sheep's flesh, the maggots chew their way out, and the whole rump becomes a seething mass of agony unless protected by insecticide at just the right moment. The flies will crawl everywhere, and the first you know about it is when the ewe tries to bite its arse off because the pain is so awful it is driven to eat itself alive. Sheep suffer endlessly: lice, flies and ticks will not quite kill them, but leave the animal looking like a moth-eaten hank of wool on twigs. Those like the hippies along the road fill the Veritys with fury because they think pesticides are evil, and so, inevitably, their herd gets infected. It's almost as bad as not looking after your children. Pete's dad had never taken him to a doctor or dentist as a child; he'd had nothing, not even polio drops, until Sally had marched him into Dr Drew's surgery. Dear old Doc Drew had spent almost an hour with him, going over his medical history, and given him all the jabs he'd missed pretty much on the spot.

'No flies, no swallows, my dear.'

The return of one particular family which always nests in the corner under the eaves is an annual delight. The thought of the swallows making that tremendous journey to and from North Africa twice a year, just to end up in their particular patch, makes them feel honoured, and even more so once each new family is hatched. Sally can hear their high, excited shrieks as they shoot, like bow and arrow in one body, chasing each other across the sky.

'That's it, isn't it?' Pete says. 'Done.'

Released, the sheep gleam on the green slopes like pearls on velvet. Behind them, the scraggy, twisted oak, hawthorn and ash are billowing with fresh leaf. Dartmoor is a vast tapestry of hills and rock, wood and water, the velvety cropped turf pricked with the yellow flowers of gorse and threaded with silvery trickles of tiny streams glinting in the evening sun. There's a cuckoo calling in a valley down below.

To be a good mother is a goal that many women now pursue as in other times they pursued the ideal of being a good wife or a virtuous woman, but sheep manage it. All the HVs laughed at the magazine interviews with Di Tore in which she extolled the way she was bringing up Tiger and Dexter in their country idyll, when it's common knowledge they spend most of the time in front of the TV eating crisps, just like other kids given half the chance. Of course, most mums don't look as good as Di Tore, but it was amusing, especially when you knew that the organic veg

297

garden that always featured in magazine photographs had been planted by professional gardeners the week before. Nor are most mums as confident, either.

'Just trust your instincts,' Sally keeps telling her charges; but what if your instincts urge you to pick up a child that won't stop crying and smash its skull against the nearest wall?

Janet's Dawn, for instance: what has happened to her? She'd been such a bright girl, singing away in the choir like a skylark, real talent there, and always getting top marks in school.

'That one, she'll go to university if she keeps on, you mark my words,' Tess would say. She'd always had an interest in her, even though Dawn's mum had given her the brush-off.

'We prefer to keep ourselves to ourselves, thank you,' she'd actually said. As if her sister was some kind of busybody. Tess was that upset when she heard Dawn had dropped out of secondary school, she'd gone round to talk to her, hoping that (as Dawn's former head teacher) she'd be listened to.

'It was one of the oddest visits I've made,' she told Sally. 'Treated me as if I were something the cat brought in – and she has a stuffed cat on the sofa.'

'Are you sure it wasn't just sleeping?'

'No. I touched it. Gave me the creeps.'

'And Dawn wouldn't go back?'

'No. Imagine, the waste. Janet told me it was her daughter's decision. Not that I could get to see her. She's working night shifts at Humbles and her mum picks her up and drops her off.'

Oh, Sally thought, wouldn't I like to get hold of politicians who think that the Maintenance Allowance is a waste! But there must have been some encouragement on Janet's side, because Dawn had been one of the ones to have piano lessons with poor Oliver Randall. Sally had seen her turning off down the lane to Home Farm of an afternoon. Such a pity . . .

Eventually, Sally falls into sleep. When she wakes, her concern remains. She's reminded of it again when, at the end of a long day at the clinic, she encounters Janet's car on the road back from town. It narrows at several points so that one driver has to give way to another, something everyone has to do a dozen times a day if you use any lane. Most people smile or nod, but Janet never does, and her daughter stares straight ahead. She must be driving her in to her shift at the factory.

I wonder . . . Sally thinks.

When she stops her car a little way from the entrance to the gatehouse to Shipcott Manor, she isn't thinking consciously of what she's doing. A quick stretch of her legs with Baggage. How pretty it looks, with all the ox-eye daisies still frothing in the banks. It's warm, and she can feel herself sweating slightly . . . I could pop in on Di Tore, she tells herself. Make up some excuse.

She approaches the gates, lifting her hand to press the bell, then stops. Some creature is wailing in the gatehouse, a thin, high-pitched sound that makes the blood jump in her heart. It's a sound she has heard before, and the last she'd have expected: the cry of a baby, in pain or distress, calling for help.

28

Quentin Cultivates His Garden

Quentin has lurked around Trelorn, trying to see if he can catch Lottie at it with Beardy again, but to no avail. Obviously, they are keeping their affair secret, because it might cause a scandal. But even without the kiss he had witnessed, he'd know something was up. She smiles and laughs again, and wears red lipstick. Lottie never puts on much make-up, but she's one of those strong-featured women whose looks become striking as soon as she bothers.

How cruel I was, and stupid, he thinks; but mostly, he is consumed with hatred for Martin. To think of that bearded oaf with his wife – those fat fingers, the silly laugh – how can she stand him?

That racking, wrenching, twisting coil of agony and anger, the needle-like teeth of poisonous mortification, the sensation of being in the grip of a gigantic, malevolent snake whose heads cannot be cut off . . . this, presumably, is what Lottie too has felt. No wonder his wife had shrieked and sobbed. The only way to be rid of it is to stop caring, but how to cut her out of his heart? Being forced to live together again has also forced him to feel. Only it's too late. She hates him, and now the sale of their home is going through there will be no reason to stay together. He'll find some two-bedroomed flat in Zone 3 or further, one of those areas that the *Evening Standard* keeps telling him are 'up and coming', and that will be the end of everything because he'll be alone.

Lottie's remark has come back to haunt him:

We would at least have had each other.

He watches his mother caring for Hugh. She is astonishingly patient and gentle, though his father takes it as his due that she does everything from cutting his toenails to wiping the shit from his arse.

'I sometimes wonder whether she's doing it to make him feel guilty.'

'She loves him,' Anne said.

'He wasn't a kind man, why should he value kindness?' Quentin asked.

'I think we all value kindness, by the end.'

During the long hours when his mother rests and his father drifts in and out of consciousness, Quentin talks to Anne more than he has to anyone for several years. There are other nurses on the Marie Curie rota, but she's the one they see most often, walking up the path just when things are unbearable. Lean, bespectacled, her short blonde hair turning grey, she is the kind of woman that, normally, he would never have given a second glance at. Yet she is one of the most admirable people he has ever met.

'I worry most that he's in awful pain,' Naomi said.

'Nobody needs die in pain,' Anne answered. 'That's why we're here. Cancer gives people time to set their affairs in order, and come to terms with leaving this world.'

'You think there's another one?'

'I can only say what I've felt,' Anne said. 'When people die, something leaves the room that was there before. Where it goes, that's the question.'

'Into nothing, I've always thought.'

301

'Nothing becomes nothing. It's not the way the universe works.'

Quentin is suspicious of this. He has always, as a rational person, loathed religion. It isn't just priests putting on a special voice to talk to God in the same way some do to talk to children. Why do people feel the need to invent another world, when this one is so full of wonders? Maybe faith makes death less terrible, but it can't be made less sad for those left behind. He thinks again of the skull he'd dug up, then reburied, and all the vigorous life teeming around it, hastening its decay. Why is the mutilation, the desecration of a dead person's body so horrifying when the dead can no longer suffer? The instinct to treat another being's mortal remains with respect and tenderness is so deep that it extends to elephants and dogs. It's the only truth, yet it's the one we most like to avoid accepting.

Who, though, can live without delusion? Getting Hugh to accept that he is terminally ill has been the biggest battle. He has such a hunger for life that, despite feeling more and more tired, he demands to be told that he is getting better.

'I just want this to be over.'

'Yes, we all do,' said Quentin.

'I can't read, I can't eat. I can't drink.'

Having never had real pain himself, Quentin can only imagine just how much misery Hugh must be in.

'I can read to you, Fa, if you like.'

Quentin picked up *The Small House at Allington*, and continued where he had left off. He had never bothered with Victorian novels before; their moral certainties annoyed him. Yet seeing the comfort they gave Hugh, he thought there might be something to be said for Trollope, if only as another opiate. He'd have expected his father to want something more modish, but here was his father, whose own life was ebbing away, caring about wholly imaginary people of over a century ago, and finding that their joys and sorrows seemed as urgent as his own.

'So lovely,' Hugh murmured.

His father's face, once so distinctive, is softening and blurring, and his eyebrows and hair are almost gone. His skull looks like a walnut. It's frightening to see this. Every evening, when Quentin returns to his daughters, he looks at their perfection in astonishment and gratitude.

He remembers a conversation with Tore.

'I did so many bad things when I was young,' he said. 'I was given everything I thought I wanted by the time I was twenty, all those stupid things that money and fame can buy, and then I had to spend the next forty years trying to untangle the mess it caused.'

'Such as?'

Tore shrugged. 'I'm saving that for my biographer.'

Quentin couldn't conceal his disappointment, for even when he'd thought his landlord a tramp he had been intrigued by him. 'You've found one?'

'Maybe. You were asking about Ollie Randall, though.'

'Yes, I wonder if you know why he might have been murdered.'

'If I did, I'd go straight to the police.'

There was no doubting Tore's sincerity, and yet Quentin had interviewed enough people to have an instinct about when they were withholding something. He couldn't press: Tore was too shrewd to fall for any of the usual bromides. In a curious way, Quentin thought, he was so famous as to be beyond vanity. It was hard to tell whether he loved his ravishing wife and children, but it was clear that he really liked them. The manic energy of his stage persona was completely absent.

'I wish I hadn't let him live at Home Farm.'

'But how were you to know he'd meet such a terrible death there?'

'I didn't. It's being in the wrong place at the wrong time that gets people killed.'

Is it worse to be killed, or to die by inches like his own father?

'You're not alone,' Anne will say when Hugh wakes and yelps like an animal, caught in the trap of his own body. 'We're here.'

'What are you putting into me?' Hugh asks.

'Morphine, mostly,' the nurse answers.

'Any moment now I'll see a damsel with a dulcimer. Though I'd prefer gin.'

'Well, you can have that,' Anne said.

Hugh finds it increasingly hard to swallow, but Anne has a solution: frozen ice cubes of gin and tonic, which she passes over his lips. His whole face relaxes.

'Ah. I never thought I'd taste that again.'

When he had been at university, Hugh had announced he was coming up to see him. Quentin spent half of his meagre allowance buying a small bottle of Gordon's, only to have it mocked as an inferior brand; though he still drank it all.

'Bastard, bastard,' Quentin mutters to himself. He hates his father for a hundred reasons, yet he can't stop crying, furtively and awkwardly, at the horror of what is happening, at his mother's grief, at, unexpectedly, his own.

The next day he stops at the nearest big supermarket and buys a bottle of Hendricks.

'That's so thoughtful of you, darling. So kind. I know he'll appreciate it.'

No, he won't, Quentin thinks; he remains a cantankerous, stubborn, rude old sod, and he probably won't be able to taste the difference.

'When am I going to be well?'

Anne says, 'What do you think is happening to you, Hugh?'

Naomi, aghast, whispers, 'No. Don't say it.'

'I'm dying, aren't I?' he says.

Anne puts her arm round Naomi as if she were a grieving child as she cries, silently. Quentin, to his surprise, feels someone squeeze his fingers. He looks down. So this is what it means to wring your hands, he thinks, as though you could force grief out of your body like water. He is going to have to get through this alone.

'He needs hope,' his mother says, with something close to anger. 'He can fight this.'

'No, Ma. He needs truth,' Quentin says. 'We all need the fucking truth, for once.'

Anne says, 'We can't make you better, but you will feel better, I promise. We can give you stronger drugs now that you know what's happening to you. You can have the death you want, at home, with your family. However, you do need to sign a form. Hugh?'

His father opens one eye, irritably.

'Stop babbling, and give me the drugs.'

Later, Quentin and his mother agree that the bureaucracy of death is one of its oddest aspects. Without the form, Hugh's death will be far more painful and prolonged. Modern medicine means he is not allowed to die. If he begins to have a heart attack, they or the nurse will be obliged to call an ambulance, whose crew will then have to try to restart his father's heart while racing to Plymouth hospital, possibly breaking his ribs while doing so, even though a quick death is the best thing. It's the same if he gets pneumonia: without the form, his medics have to give him antibiotics.

This way, he can be given lethal doses of painkillers that will make him intermittently conscious but happy. Or, as he puts it, conscious and not unhappy.

'I should have been on morphine years ago,' he says.

'Yes, you should,' Quentin says. 'You're actually quite nice, on drugs.'

Hugh can hardly hold the pen as he signs his name. It occurs to Quentin that these are probably the last words his father will ever write. All those years of ink, and it has come down to this, giving permission to someone to kill him.

Outside the living room, Anne puts a hand on his arm. 'If

305

there are things you need to say to him, say them in the next day.'

'What's the point?'

'There's still time. When he's gone, there won't be.'

'The moment I saw through him, he wanted to crush me.'

'Maybe you can still forgive him. Parents don't always realise how deeply they hurt children.'

'I'd have thought, after a hundred years of psychoanalysis, they must have some inkling.'

'Children can hurt parents too, though.'

Anne now knows more about him than anyone else, including his own mother. It's a deep intimacy, and no less deep for being so sudden, for time has lost all meaning. Quentin has told Anne about how appalling Hugh had been as a father and husband, how he had never said a single word of love to any of them, how he had mortified them all with his affairs, how he had turned a blind eye to Quentin being bullied at school, and Anne listens. How many secrets doctors and nurses must keep, he thinks. Yet he knows that this is part of her job: to tend to the living as well as the dead.

'So there you are,' Quentin says. 'Not a pretty story.'

'Have you ever told your wife about this?' is the only question she asks.

'No. I don't think it would have done any good. There's no point in going over it now, on his deathbed.'

'Everyone can be helped,' says Anne. Quentin shrugs, and asks,

'What's it like when people die?'

'It's not as bad as you may think. I wouldn't say it's joyful, but it can be a good experience.'

Out in his mother's garden he finds some ease in turning over each clod, shaking out the loose soil, and dumping the mass of grass and buttercup into a wheelbarrow. To cultivate your garden was a moral act, if you believed in that crap. At least Naomi's weedy beds don't conceal a severed head. At some point soon he's going to dig the head up and bury it somewhere else, far away, where it can rot until doomsday.

'Interesting how the weeds always have fat white roots. If only the rest of life were colour-coded,' he remarks to Naomi.

'We had a lovely garden in Cape Town,' his mother says. She has been ordered outside by Anne, sheet-pale from staying indoors so much. 'If I regret anything about leaving, it's that. You wouldn't believe the flowers.'

Quentin gives an exasperated sigh.

'I don't believe in regret. It's a waste of energy.'

Naomi smiles. 'When you were a child, you'd march about saying, "I don't like that!" You never knew what you did want, only what you didn't.'

'Well, anger is a kind of energy.'

'Not always a good kind, though,' she says.

He stops, and puts his arms round his mother.

'How will you manage here, all on your own?' he asks, before starting to dig again. It's the only thing that seems to help his misery. 'You know, I'm here for you if you need it. You can't drive, and living here can't be easy.'

'Oh, I'll be fine. Plenty of people want a four-bedroom cottage, you know.'

The fork spears into Quentin's wellington boot, just missing his toes.

'You're going to sell up?'

'I've put my name down for the first of Lottie's new homes, in fact. I'll be moving in this autumn, if I get an offer.'

'Good God.' Much as he loathes The Hovel, he can't imagine his mother living anywhere else. 'Does Fa know?'

'Yes. I promised to stay here until the end.'

'I thought you were the one who insisted on living here.'

'No, Hugh was always a country boy. That's why he took the job at Knotshead. I grew up in a city, remember. I must say, I'm looking forward to having central heating.'

307

Quentin thinks of his parents, and their incomprehensible yet lasting union. How have they managed it? Di Tore, who informed him only yesterday that marriage is an outdated concept, especially now people are living such a long time, would be just as mystified, he thinks. A year ago, he would have said the same.

'My parents wouldn't agree. You know my father's dying?'

'Sorry. You never get over your parents' death, mate. Not that it's a pissing contest.'

Quentin has found an unlikely ally in Gore Tore. The friendliness that had grown when he thought Tore was a tramp has continued; Tore thinks it a great joke, like Quentin never having smoked a joint.

'I could never see the point of drugs,' Quentin said.

'Oh, drugs are great. Of course they are. They're just not worth what they do to you. You take them because you're curious, or you're bored, and then you're not curious or bored, you're only interested in drugs.'

'What got you off them?'

'Music.'

The ease with which they'd talked in the pub continues. Is he like this with everyone? Quentin is not so naive as to believe that he is Tore's new best friend. There's more than twenty years between them in age, and Tore can't lack for either entertainment or companionship.

Yet there is a kind of loneliness about him. Half his old friends, he's said, are dead. The other half are always touring.

'It's the only way. The music business is fucked by the Internet, just like your lot,' Tore said, with the grin that has no mirth in it. 'At least us dinosaurs still sell CDs. My fans haven't learnt how to stream music, or if they have they don't like it.'

Tore has a whole barn full of vinyl and CDs, and also, to Quentin's surprise, books. He reads a vast amount, some of it predictably crazy stuff but some of it serious.

'My father would never believe you've bought all his poetry.'

'I think I remember your dad,' Tore said. 'Gave my son a bollocking, when he was at school.'

'That sounds like my father, yes.'

'Right old sod.'

'Definitely him, then.'

Tore laughed. 'I've always had a soft spot for your mum, though.'

'So have I,' Quentin said.

'Maybe that's what you and I have most in common,' Tore remarked. 'Our dads were shits, and our mums were saints.'

Naomi remembers Tore, too.

'He was the oddest pupil at Knotshead. So bright, but he hated everything apart from music and writing songs. He was better going straight to the Royal Academy. Fa loathed him, but then he loathed a lot of people.'

'Why didn't you leave Fa?' Quentin asks. 'He's just so difficult.'

Naomi says, 'You know, in my generation you didn't divorce when things weren't perfect. Of course I was unhappy, for a time. However, it wasn't all the time, and there have been wonderful times as well. Only the two people concerned know what really goes on in a marriage. We both understood what we'd be losing – not just the love and shared memories, but all the friendships and experiences we had together.'

'Did you forgive him?'

'What mattered to me was you and your sister, and my work, and the life we made.'

'But he's never apologised.'

'I didn't feel he had to.'

Had his mother been duped as well as cheated? Is she a fool? He can't tell. If she feels rage, it's buried too deep beneath a naturally cheerful disposition of a kind that Lottie doesn't have.

I've ruined everything, he thinks; but I can still try not to become like my father.

29

The Wind in the Grass

Lottie is easier in her mind about leaving her mother, now that Xan is staying with Marta for a few weeks. It'll do both of them good. Even if she herself can't sleep there, London is his home as Devon can never be. She doesn't want him to live in a place where he will forever feel alien.

Still, she'll be back soon for her cousin's wedding to Sebastian. The party will be at Leighton House, which with its lavish Oriental décor seems entirely appropriate.

'Don't tell me there are going to be *two* Bridezillas?'

'No, of course not,' Justin answered, nettled. 'Just say you'll be there. You'll be my only blood relation.'

Lottie promised, though London is no longer a place she can tolerate. For Xan, of course, it is paradise regained. He's out and about again, no longer dependent on cycling (though he says he'll keep doing that as a student, to save money), and catching up with his mates.

'I wish I could spend the rest of the summer here,' he says.

'You can't, though. Oma will need her home back.'

But the main point is that he will be going to university. He will have to take out a student loan in order to obtain the education that she and Quentin once had for free; but he is once more on the right path – stimulated, encouraged, befriended, tested, and out of a place which isn't right for him.

Stella and Rosie won't have that kind of pressure, she suspects. Maybe her children will be disadvantaged as a result, or maybe they won't be. Driving back to Devon, Lottie thinks about the prep school which her daughters had been at previously, where the minimum spend for birthday presents was £30. She had been so wound up trying to make sure her children jumped through all the right hoops that she'd forgotten to ensure they enjoy childhood.

Martin has behaved with scrupulous propriety since his rejection. He isn't the kind of man who'd repeat an overture without encouragement, although strictly speaking it could count as sexual harassment. In practical terms, he'd be far better for her than her husband: her mother is right in thinking she should have married him, for Martin is kind, good, talented and honourable. They share a deep interest in their profession, even if they approach it differently, and she likes him. But even had she wished to, she'd known the instant he kissed her that he was wrong, on a purely animal level.

She can't return to her previous state, and she can't fool herself into thinking Quentin can ever be trusted. She has to become a new person in order to survive, someone who isn't afraid of being alone, perhaps for ever, and someone who is in control of her life.

There had been a time, right at the beginning, when she thought that she might be able to stand it. They could have an open marriage, as some people did, and eventually his libido would burn out with age and the family could be preserved. It worked for some people, by all accounts, and it's clearly what her husband would have preferred.

'You'll regret it if you divorce me,' he said, in the beginning. 'You'll die lonely if you divorce me.'

311

At that, she had come to her senses.

'Nothing is lonelier than a bad marriage,' Lottie answered. 'You don't seem to understand: I will never, ever be taken for granted, not by you or anyone.'

'So your pride means you'll destroy everything.'

'It's not my pride: and you're the destructive one.'

Lottie is back to churning the same arguments round and round, as if turning a liquid to a solid.

'He won't even take the cat to be spayed,' she mutters to herself. McSquirter reminds her of Quentin, so maybe it's not surprising. She's taken care of the females, naturally; it's been difficult enough finding homes for one litter of kittens, but the strict division of labour should mean that her husband sees to the tom.

The green of the trees makes her eyes dazzle. She can feel the way life is almost at the crest of its delight in its own existence, and although it must pass, nowhere seems lovelier than England in this time.

Or maybe my brain has rotted away, Lottie thinks. That's what Quentin would say. The swell of Dartmoor, with its bluebells stalking out of the turf, the rushing streams, the vast clouds, the deep lanes, the skylarks – all these are nothing special to him because he'd grown up with it.

Still, the summer has made it easier to get along, and as she is now earning twice what he does, he is notably more polite. Again and again, her thoughts return to money. She had never cared about it in the past, but it has come to mean a great deal. It's the weapon each holds over the other, and even if she, as the mother of two young children, is bound to get the bigger share, whatever she is awarded will not be enough.

There is some progress, however, in that they have come to an unspoken agreement in which Quentin cooks, which he is good at, and she washes up, which means it's done properly.

'I've always hated cooking,' she admits. 'It's nothing but drudgery to me.'

'Whereas I love it.'

There is a flat grassy area just outside the kitchen which, shadowed by the ash tree at noon, makes a perfect place to have meals. In the warm, dry evenings they grill sausages, chicken or fish over a rough barbecue of bricks, and get mildly drunk. They haven't holidayed together for years, but this feels like it. Stella and Rosie are in ecstasy, running around as dusk falls, pausing barely long enough for their suppers before zooming off again, shrieking like swifts as they dart through the garden. Often, they have new acquaintances over, including the Viners. Anne turns out to be not only the GP's wife but the nurse who had cared for Quentin's father, which Quentin at first finds slightly awkward.

'Anne is lovely. You know, she has five children?'

'How on earth do they manage that and work?'

'She gives each one a day of the week to him or herself, and the weekends to them all. But that's what they both wanted, and they make it work, especially now the eldest two can babysit. They're the kind of family that you'd never find in London now.'

'So? Civilisation is driven by people being in cities. Remember what Cecil Rhodes said, that if you're English, you have won first prize in the lottery of life? Well, it's even more true if you're a Londoner.'

'Yes. Thank heavens I'm out of it. I felt like a frog being boiled alive.'

They have both been round to Shipcott Manor, especially now the sale of the London house and the purchase of Home Farm have been agreed. Knowing that it's going to be her actual, permanent home instead of a rental has made her see all kinds of exciting possibilities for it.

'Look at the invisible man walking across the field, Mummy,' Rosie says.

'It's just the wind in the grass, darling.'

'Is it?'

Lottie opens her eyes, sees the long stalks parting and closing. 'Yes.'

She watches the grass swaying this way and that. It's an optical illusion, just that.

'It looks like the sea,' Stella remarks. 'Why don't we go to the seaside, Daddy?'

'I've never even seen the sea,' Rosie says.

Quentin and Lottie exchange glances, then glance away in mutual embarrassment. In happier times, such as their honeymoon, they had spent many days on the Amalfi coast.

'Let me look up the tide times.'

They are in luck, for the tide will be out in the late afternoon, when there'll be fewer people. Suddenly, they are all piling into the car with old towels and costumes.

'Won't it be freezing?'

'Not by now,' Quentin says. 'You two can hire wetsuits if you like.'

'I've never swum in the Atlantic,' Lottie says.

'Really? Well, you'll be in for a surprise then.'

They cross over the Tamar into Cornwall, and the landscape changes into flat, heathery fields which seem to stretch on and on, when not interrupted by giant white windmills whose blades turn smartly in the afternoon light. Then, when least expected, she can see a dip, and a patch that turns from denim to damask. A long straggle of beige bungalows fronted by hydrangeas, and then the thin tarmac plunges down past banks of wild flowers, and down again, past a caravan site and a couple of B&Bs. The road becomes stonier. At the very bottom, where boulders are heaped about like discarded toys, is the beach. There are gulls bouncing on currents of air, and rock pools, and the broad wavering watermark of streams which, having plunged over the cliffs, now meander to the sea.

The beach, a vast crescent of sand, is the most glorious imaginable, and beyond it the sea glitters. The smell of salt, the taste of it, is everywhere. The tide is right out, and her daughters rush ahead, bodyboards flying behind like sails, into the sequinned dazzle.

It's so different from the Mediterranean: a bubbling cold and effortless power which is wholly alive. The glassy heave soaks half her torso, then sends a suppressed roar. Lottie laughs, a little nervously, but the girls catch wave after wave, shrieking with delight as their bodyboards swoosh them towards the shore. She catches one too, with little difficulty.

'Oh, lovely, lovely!' she cries, shocked out of reticence by surprise.

They romp about in the waves together, laughing like lunatics. She wishes she could be like this more often; it's not her choice to be a martyr, as Quentin believes. Stella and Rosie are fearless, and the more they show how well they can swim, the more she relaxes.

Quentin can surf properly; she can see him longing to join the tribe that stands apart, waiting for the big swell which turns swimmers into gods standing on water. Yet he doesn't; he has chosen to prostrate himself on a humble bodyboard like theirs. She is surprised, and a little touched by this.

'Your turn, I'll keep an eye on them,' he calls.

Lottie nods and swims further out to where bigger waves are breaking.

It's rare to see him these days, for he's spending more and more time with his parents. It can't be long now. Lottie tries not to think about Hugh's death, chiefly because she doesn't want to think about her own mother not being there, but also because it's easier to see Quentin as a person without any redeeming qualities. The small acts of thoughtfulness and even kindness that he's been making of late are, she reminds herself, those of a practised deceiver. Maybe he'll be better as an ex-husband than as a husband: that's all she can hope for.

Waiting, she bounces, and with each bounce it's as if she is getting lighter. The fine sand puffs between her bare toes, and the sun has made a broad band of gold to follow. Out here, the turquoise and pale green have darkened to slabs of cobalt, cross-hatched by the wind. The water flexes beneath her board, making it thrum the length of her body, and then it catches, rises up in a long thrust which fizzes and boils on and on in a rush of momentum until, panting and laughing, with the taste of salt on her lips, and the beat and roar of her own blood in her ears, she is returned to shore.

It reminds her of something, but she can't think what.

30

The Silence of the Lambs

Sally dreads high summer. All the bustle of life, and then slaughter.

Up and down the billowing hills, the hedgerows ever bigger and shaggier. She sees the hawks quivering on the heated air, the trees bowed down by the weight of their own leaves, the evenings glowing until eleven at night. The ground chirrs with tiny green crickets, and the whirl of harvesters spins the meadows into bristling blonde blocks of new hay. When the moon rolls up the star-pricked sky, the fields are striped with silver.

Even when clouds shed thunderous water, turning roads into swift brown rivers, the rain is warm, and the heated earth releases its pent-up scents. Then the mists rise and bleach everything to the sepia tones of an old photograph, and the hills vanish in a veil of cloud. The weighing, the dipping, the dosing, the dagging and tagging are over, and the lambs are chunky adolescents. It is time.

Peter and Jip do it like carding wool, steadily and carefully separating the ewes from their young, rounding up the flock as

317

so often before and guiding the lambs through a series of pens. Stepping fearlessly onto the ramp of the hay-lined trailer, their felted wool bulking their bodies, the lambs seem almost to be enjoying each other's company. In they go, and now that the ewes can't see their lambs, their calls become more plaintive, their long bony faces dismayed. The calls become more and more noisy. Do the ewes remember what has happened before? Sally knows that animals have memories, and how could a living creature forget a loss like this? They can still smell each other, and the lambs' noses poke through the pens, their nostrils working.

'Mehh,' they say to the ewes, and the ewes answer,

'Meeehh.'

'Mheh.'

'Meh-meh.'

The trailer will be driven to Trelorn – and how lucky they are, that they don't have to be driven for hours up the motorway, increasingly stressed and thirsty like so many, and why don't opponents of fox-hunting protest about that? – and then guided to the place of concrete and steel. Here the lambs will be unloaded down a ramp and through more pens until, beneath a fluorescent light, each lamb eventually stands alone. It is a very clean place, hosed down and swept in accordance with strict hygiene rules, but of course the lamb can smell the blood, a scent all herbivores are exquisitely alert to. It won't walk forward, so the slaughter man will carry it into the room, kicking, and pin it to the concrete floor with a knee.

Even then, the lamb struggles, until the man retrieves a pair of electric prongs from a bucket. These are put on either side of its head, conveying an electric current which stuns it into collapse, so that, with its heart still beating and its legs twitching, it has its throat cut. It must be alive when this happens, because all meat must be halal so that Muslims will buy it, even if most Britons would rather it didn't have this additional bit of suffering. Blood sprays everywhere, dyeing the lamb's head and forelegs crimson, and its eyes glaze. A minute later, it is hoisted by its hind legs onto a hook, and its woolly hide is pulled off, like a jumper over a child's head. The red carcass dangling down is wholly anonymous, and ready. The belly is swiftly sliced and the hot entrails removed. Finally, the carcass is inspected, approved, stamped. Life has been rendered into meat. It is calm, efficient, relentless.

The first time Sally had seen slaughter, she felt sick and faint. It was shocking to think that the roast joints they enjoyed on Sundays had come from creatures she and her sisters had some-times bottle-fed. That they had devoted so much care and thought to an animal's welfare not for its own sake, but so that it would produce better food for human consumption. Later, she had come to accept it as part of the cycle of life and death. When she'd trained in London, she'd come across vegetarians who had no idea that the cheese they ate could only come from cows whose calves had been taken away and slaughtered; she'd despised them for their ignorance. Yet few people love their ani-mals as farmers do. They never name them, never look them in the eyes, and yet they have cared for them, and when the time comes to send them to be slaughtered, there are few that do it without sadness. This, too, was something townies could never understand.

'Jip, Jip, there will be new lambs in the spring,' Sally murmurs to the collie, who for once sticks close beside her, ears drooping, when they go out to inspect the remaining herd.

Peter is gone for at least a day and a night. The fields, after hours of frantic calling by the ewes, become increasingly silent. There are no lambs left. Sally uses the time to weed her vegeta-ble patch, go through her freezer and clean all the windows from the flecks of flies. Jip and Baggage get their fur trimmed with her electric shears, and frisk about like puppies once it's off. At five o'clock, Sally scatters grain for the new rescue chickens, has tea, bottles raspberries, folds laundry, matches socks and finds herself thinking, sometimes, how peaceful it is to be alone.

'You've earned a break,' her mum's voice says in her head. 'Enjoy it.'

Lying in the bath, her ears filled with warm water, she feels as weightless as a child in the womb.

'I will not be sad,' she says aloud. No woman is defined by motherhood; professionally, she is more valuable to her community by not having the responsibilities of children. If she longs for a child it's because she longs for a different kind of love.

She thinks about the daughter she will never see, and imagines her at, say, seven – the same age as Lottie's Rosie or thereabouts. She'd decided long ago that this child would have hair on the blonde side of hazel, like her own, and Peter's eyes, but the rest is hazy. She's haunted by this child, who is growing more and more dear to her as the chances of her ever being real diminish. She still has periods, but the hair on her upper lip has started to thicken, a sure sign she's perimenopausal.

When she surfaces, she gets a shock. The door, which she closed, is wide open. Has somebody come in when she was underwater?

'Hello?' she calls nervously. 'Who is it?'

Ever since the attack on the horse, she's felt unusually tense about being on her own. Mad, really, because Jip barks and barks at any intruder. In an old house like hers, plenty of doors refuse to shut properly, swinging open thanks to slight subsidence or slamming shut in a sudden breeze. Over hundreds of years, every timber warps; a building isn't only home to people but to mice, bats, insects and (unfortunately) rats. She knows every creak and squeak in the place, but nothing should have made the bathroom door open by itself.

Sally's arms are suddenly covered in goose pimples. If someone is in her house, she could hardly be more vulnerable, being naked and wet.

Very quietly, trying not to slosh, she sits up, grasping for a towel. She stands, and then, not looking down, puts her foot out of the bath.

There's a yelp, and Sally almost falls over in shock. Baggage has been lying on the bath mat, and is now several feet away, looking at her reproachfully. Every freckle of her speckled muzzle seems to be quivering with anxiety.

'Idiot dog!' Sally exclaims. 'What's the matter?'

Baggage thumps her tail. It's her supper time, she reminds Sally. She hadn't been able to see or smell her; order is restored. Smiling with relief, Sally gets out of the bath, wraps herself in a dressing gown and finds the big bag of kibble.

'All you think about is food and walks. Now, don't jump up! I have the hens to feed as well, and Bouncer. Even if I do love you most of all.'

Peter comes home eventually.

'Ah-rah-rah,' he roars, stumbling up the concrete path to the door, when his truck finally weaves up the track. 'Ah-rah!'

Drat, Sally thinks, I hope he doesn't break my pots again.

Mostly, the drink makes him less shy. Sometimes, he comes at her like a bear, snuffling and groping. He reeks of drink, and sweat, and not by one flicker of her eye does she show how this repels her. Still, it may be worth a try, even when thank goodness it's over quickly.

'At least our lambs have the best life,' he mutters. 'Better'n – better'n . . . '

Peter keeps the ewes for seven years, until their teeth are worn out so they can no longer graze, and then they, too, must go off to the abattoir to be turned into dog food.

''f I had a hunner . . . '

He topples off her and begins snoring. She knows what's on his mind. If he had a hundred thousand pounds, he could buy a beef herd. That's where the money is. At least, that's what farmers are saying this year. But the only real money in land is if it

321

gets planning permission for another housing development: in which case it rises a thousandfold.

'I know, appalling,' Lottie agreed when Sally mentioned an estate being built in a village closer to Okehampton.

'How can architects design such ugliness?'

'I can't believe any architect was involved. People love to blame us, but those boxes were probably just done by a developer using computer-aided design. They won't spend the money.'

Lottie has shown her some of the Trelorn plans on an iPad. None of these houses will cost over £199,000. They are so well insulated they won't need central heating, but still look like terraced cottages from a century ago, albeit ones with three bedrooms and two bathrooms cleverly fitted in.

'Are those roofs made of real slate?'

'No, synthetic.'

'It's actually *nice*,' Sally remarked in surprise.

'Oh, you can build anything now. That's what is so maddening about the awful buildings still being put up. Not enough developers think that ordinary people deserve attractive homes.'

Sally has never realised before how much thought and planning has to go into a building; it makes her wonder how her ancestors and Pete's had ever managed to build perfectly sound, attractive farmhouses which had lasted for several hundred years, just by using their eyes and hands and what could be scrabbled out of the ground.

'I wouldn't have thought someone as posh as Martin would have been interested.'

Lottie laughed.

'Of course! He cares about Trelorn, it's his town too. And now I do too. We've had a really good offer on our house in London.'

'You have?'

'Yes. You know the market there has gone crazy?'

Sally said dryly, 'We know every Londoner who owns a home is a multimillionaire.'

322

'But only on paper. It's meaningless unless you sell up and move out, and if you do you can never, ever come back ... My only worry is the winters, year after year.'

'You go abroad in January, if you can afford it.'

'Di Tore swears by Australia.'

'Well, she would do, being from there herself.'

'She is very beautiful, isn't she? I'm sure Quentin admires her deeply.'

Lottie's tone was light, but Sally knows what she's thinking, because all wives and girlfriends become twitchy around Di.

'Di won't even notice him, you know.'

'Is she really in love with a man twice her age?'

'I wouldn't presume to know,' Sally said, though she did have some ideas about Di's frequent trips abroad. Who could blame her if she had some private fun? Tore probably did, and as long as the boys didn't know it wouldn't harm them.

Peter's snores have reached almost ear-shattering levels. Sighing, Sally gets up. It's hopeless trying to sleep in the same bed when he's this drunk, no amount of kicking will make him stop.

She goes to the spare room, at the end of the passage. There's a nice double there, a brass bedstead, and secretly she's always preferred it. They've put up her nephews and nieces in this room when giving her sisters a break, and otherwise it's just used for old clothes.

Despite the warm summer, the bed feels quite chilly. She gets up and rummages in a chest of drawers. She never touches this stuff because half of it contains thick thermals of the kind they no longer use, and half contains papers. The drawer she opens is full of odds and ends, and she's about to close it when she sees a letter.

It's from a clinic in Plymouth. She'd gone to it herself, and she thinks, peering at it in the dim light, that it must be addressed to her, only it isn't. It's for Peter.

Dear Mr Verity,

Thank you for coming to see me last month. Further to your
tests, I regret to inform you that . . .

Sally reads on, unable to believe her eyes. The letter is full of
standard phrases, offering counselling, but what it tells her is
that she has been lied to by her husband for twelve years.

31

Nothing but Living

In the final days of their marriage, Quentin doesn't need to be asked to take out the rubbish, clean the bath, or do the laundry. He has actually become civilised, as well as civil. Too late, she thinks. Some other woman can profit from her nagging.

The halcyon weather continues, with every verge and field a garden. The high-altitude clouds drift from the south-west, like great ships passing to places elsewhere. It might be melancholy to think of, only elsewhere is where she and her children will live, for the foreseeable future.

The house sale is going through in London, and in a fortnight, Home Farm will be hers.

'We need to discuss what you're going to do next,' she told him, briskly.

'But can't things go on as they are?'

'No,' she said. 'They can't.' He looks so miserable that she feels sorry for him, and adds, 'I need to have things settled, you see.'

'Are you going to push the button?'

She doesn't answer. Of course she is. The moment the money comes into their joint account, she will be getting the quickest, cheapest divorce she can. No matter how sad he looks, or how miserable she feels, she can't risk backtracking. He'll only betray her again, and humiliate her again.

It's true that he doesn't seem to be going up to London. From this she surmises that his most recent affair is over, and he has his tail between his legs for as long as his father is dying – but as soon as he perks up, he'll be off again. She has his measure now. She can survive on her own; one day she might meet another man, but it's not as if she really needs one. There is sex, but the less people have of it the less they want, and because she can't sleep with people without love it seems unlikely she'll have another partner.

Lottie gets through two loads of laundry and settles down to pod peas, enjoying their sweet taste, the warm summer breeze and a Mozart symphony on the radio. It is a day meant for nothing but living.

There is no word from Quentin, who has been away since yesterday at his parents'. In the old days, when she waited for him to return, he would send her a text. OMW! What it meant was that he'd finished shagging whatever woman he was with at the time, and wanted her to prepare a meal. Well, that fool is gone.

She eats supper with the girls and puts them through their bath and bedtime, reading them the story of 'The Cat That Walked by Himself'. Her daughters love the story, delighted by the Cat's independence, cheek and cunning.

'He's so clever to trick the Woman, isn't he, Mummy?'

'Yes, he is. Though it's a good bargain they make, don't you think?'

'Are you sure we can't have a cat of our own?'

The kittens in the barn are growing up, and Rosie has repeatedly tried to smuggle one they call Smudge into their room, despite its mewling protests. She can't believe it doesn't love her with passionate devotion.

'Remember, Smudge will grow up to be like its dad,' Lottie told

326

them. The dreadful McSquirter is next on her list of problems to tackle at Home Farm.

The sun sets. A last bumblebee, heavy with pollen, buzzes its way out of a day lily, a blackbird flies shrieking out of a shrub and then even the trees stop rustling. Lottie kisses the girls goodnight, and sits out in the garden. Hugh must be dying at last.

Hadn't he said how he hated Hugh so much that he couldn't wait for the old man to die? She'd been shocked when she heard him say this, but his relationship with his father has always been deeply troubled. Nor could she blame her husband for feeling like this. Lottie has never liked her father-in-law, especially not after he'd told her that all architects were obsessed with penises.

'Really?' Lottie replied. 'So what do you make of the hospice I've been working on, which is one storey?'

'Probably for women,' he said.

The only good thing about him, as far as she could tell, was his kindness both to his granddaughters and her son. With children, he became a different person altogether.

'I hate him, I hate him,' Quentin would say after every visit.

'You don't have to rise to it,' Lottie said.

'He's such a bastard. He takes his failure out on me.'

'But that's his problem, not yours.'

'No, believe me, it's mine too.'

At last, she hears the sound of the car coming down the drive. It can only be him. She braces herself for whatever mood he's in, but there is no slamming of the door. Her husband gets out of his car, and bursts into tears.

She has hardly ever seen a man cry, least of all him – though he, of course, has seen her in tears often enough.

Without stopping to think, she runs over and puts her arms around him. He cries like a little boy, not a man, and all she can feel is pity.

'There, there. There, there,' she says, pulling him close and rubbing her hand against his back.

327

He bows his head on her shoulder, and the tears falling from his eyes soak through. They stand together, and around them, swallows flick into bats.

'I'm sorry, I'm sorry, I'm sorry,' he keeps saying.

'It's all right,' she says, hugging him tighter, not knowing or caring what he is apologising for.

'I'll be OK, just let me have a moment.'

'I know what it's like to lose a father.'

She remembers it, the ache of desolation, her seven-year-old self.

'I can't believe he's really gone. I kept thinking he would go on, no matter what, even if he drove us all mad,' Quentin says. 'It's stupid, but I did.'

Hugh had died just before dawn, but the dreary business of obtaining a death certificate from the doctor and calling the undertakers, choosing what clothes to bury Hugh in, and more, had taken all day, he says. They were like sleepwalkers, even as Anne shut down the machines, and left. It was so quiet without them. He had stayed as long as he could with his mother.

'I've just put her to bed. All she could do was sit and stare at her knees. I'll have to go back tomorrow, and the day after that.'

'I'll do all I can to help.'

'Thanks. I'm so sorry, Lottie.'

'You did the best you could.'

'No, I didn't mean that. I'm sorry about everything. I've been wanting to say it for such a long time.'

As they stand there they begin to kiss. At first it is the giving and receiving of comfort. They have passed through so many stages of anger, misery and mistrust that it is almost comical when it changes. Several times, she thinks – I should stop this, I could stop this – only she can't.

They become like sleepwalkers, and in fact most of the time Lottie has her eyes shut. She doesn't want to see, because to see is to think.

328

How long it lasts she has no idea. At one point she thinks how surprising it is that sex is, after all, so sexual. At another she thinks, Yes, I remember that. Mostly, she doesn't think. When she opens her eyes, the long summer evening has turned to dawn. Oh God, she thinks. What have I done?

Quentin slumbers on, a mound of masculine presence. He takes up so much room in the bed, he is hot and noisy and there is a lot of grey in his body hair. And yet, he is that wonderful thing: a man, and a man she can't help being addicted to. Everything she objects to is attractive. She has every right to be furious, but most of all she is furious with herself.

'This changes nothing,' she says, when he wakes.

'No. Though I can't help wanting it again.'

'No,' she says. 'Not a chance.'

He hesitates, then gets up, collects his clothes and leaves.

Half of her, the half that is rational, is appalled, and the other half is foolishly delighted. She sees every speck of silliness, meanness, dishonesty and vanity in his personality, and yet her stupid animal self still can't help wanting his.

They have to talk, eventually.

'I wish I were the person you once thought I was,' Quentin says.

'Yes, he was too good to be true.'

'I can't be that person. But trying to be him made me the best I could be.'

'For a while.'

'Yes, for a while.'

Lottie says, reluctantly, 'You changed me, too. I never had much confidence with men, before.'

'Yet you are such a strong woman.'

'Strength isn't the same as confidence.'

'I would give anything to undo what I did to you.'

'Would you?'

'Yes.'

Her face shows her scepticism.

'Maybe we can be friends,' she says.

'We aren't friends,' Quentin answers.

You can trust a friend, love a friend, value everything about them, yet it's not passion, and certainly not marriage. She knows that as well as he does. When people say of their spouse that they are each other's best friend, she always shudders, just as she does when parents say it of their children. Friendship is a wonderful thing, but it is voluntary, private and a matter of choice. No flesh and blood is involved. You can walk away from a friendship with hurt feelings but no punishment. Marriage might also be voluntary, and its conversations private, but it is also a public bond in which love and passion are intermixed with property and propriety. Lottie has been publicly humiliated as well as privately devastated.

'I don't want a divorce,' Quentin says, eventually.

Lottie almost cries. 'Stop it, Quentin. You can only make it worse.'

'My mother forgave my father, you know. I don't want to make his mistakes.'

'No, you've made enough of your own. I can't trust you. Without trust a marriage is nothing.'

He still doesn't understand, she thinks, and hardens her heart.

That one night with him has reminded her what it was to be desired, but she can't forget and so can't forgive.

Everyone has a face or series of faces they present to the world, more or less successfully, but lovers know the face of the essential self – that soft, naked being with all its flaws and virtues which, after childhood, is hardly ever shown to others. Constructing this outer self takes energy and effort, and so, too, does removing it. What Quentin has done to her was not only a comment on her physical charms; it was a criticism of that inner person, made at a time when she was already wounded.

'I slept with you out of pity,' Lottie says, coldly.

She knows this hurts him. Quentin's face closes; from then

on he is as reserved and polite as she is. The pain is something Lottie clenches to herself, unwilling to admit its existence.

Occasionally he does talk, but almost as if to himself.

'It's true what the nurse said. Something was in the room, and left it.'

Lottie wonders whether her husband is on the verge of a breakdown. He cries easily, but she refuses to try to comfort him again. It's not just a matter of rejecting him; if she puts her arms around him, they will end up in bed again, and then all her preparations for autonomy will have to begin again. The fact that she would like nothing better is an irrelevance.

Mostly, he's with Naomi or organising the funeral, calling the obituary editors of all the newspapers.

'Does it matter?'

'Oh yes. Fa was particularly attached to the *TLS* as what he called "the last bastion of serious literature, also invaluable for lining the cat tray". It drove him mad that I wouldn't publish poetry in the *Rambler*. He believed I refused to do so to spite him.'

'And were you?'

'Of course.'

Lottie looks at him, and shrugs. 'I'm not surprised he haunts you, then.'

When the obituaries come out, some that week and some later, they are surprisingly long and fulsome, describing Hugh Bredin as an outstanding nature poet, in the line of Wordsworth, Clare and Hardy. The prize he won in his youth is cited, and his poetry collection for children. His years as a teacher are alluded to; The *Telegraph* makes a sly mention of how his 'Byronic good looks were much admired by many at the progressive school, Knotshead', but passes over the scandals. Flattering comparisons are made between Bredin, Larkin and Hughes.

Hugh's passing is noted by Radio 4, the *TLS* and an increasing number of letters of condolence both from former pupils and other poets, including the current Poet Laureate. It has become clear that the modest ceremony planned for him won't do. A full Church of England service is assembled and Hugh will be buried in Trelorn rather than his local parish. Lottie has heard all this at second or third hand, but when she goes in to work she's aware that people look at her differently.

'He wasn't my favourite person,' she tells her mother during one of their weekly telephone calls. 'Seeing it all published like that, though, I'm quite sorry I didn't get to know him better.'

Marta says, 'That is always the tragedy of it. The old are so much more interesting than the young realise.'

'Xan did. He says Hugh was the best teacher he never had.'

'My grandson is an unusual young man.'

There is the funeral, which takes up a good deal more time than anticipated. Quentin and Naomi organise much of it, though Lottie cleans the cottage as best she can. She's fond of Naomi, who will always be her daughters' grandmother, and this at least can be her own contribution, for The Hovel, too, is going on the market. It's a higgledy-piggledy place, smelling so much of woodsmoke and old dog that it's hard to see its charm. Martin has told her to take the week off. She moves the sagging sofas back against the walls, clears tables and brings her own Dyson.

'My dear, it hasn't looked like this since we first moved in,' remarks Naomi two days later.

She seems much as she always does, though less tired. Lottie is surprised and touched to learn that her mother-in-law has put down a deposit off-plan on one of the first houses in the development at Trelorn. Quentin knew this but, typically, hadn't thought to tell her. His hostility to everything to do with the project would be depressing if it weren't so obviously caused by envy – or is it jealousy?

Does he believe she's sleeping with Martin? The idea is so absurd that she almost tells him she isn't. Some instinct, pride perhaps, warns her not to. Let him believe what he does, it will make their final parting easier.

There is to be a wake at the cottage after the funeral, and her girls have a happy afternoon baking brownies for the event. Quentin's son Ian joins them. He greets Lottie with a mixture of cheerfulness and sympathy. They've had very little to do with each other, but she can see that he is both very nice and good at what he does, in that unmistakable way of people who have found their path in life. Later, she comes into The Hovel's tiny kitchen and finds Quentin and Ian making canapés. On another occasion it might have struck her as comical to see two large, heterosexual men fussing over miniature sausage rolls.

'All they needed was to find something in common,' Naomi murmurs to Lottie. 'You know Quentin is about to become a grandfather?'

'No. That's going to put the finishing touch to his midlife crisis, isn't it?'

'He seems quite excited, actually.'

Xan has told her about Marta's astonishing revelation concerning his own father. He has every right to be angry; so does she. Why did her mother think she had the right to conceal such information all these years?

'Do you think it was racism?'

'One thing I'm sure of is that my mother hasn't got a racist bone in her body. I went to pieces when I found I was pregnant, and she was probably just being protective. Don't hate her for it.'

'I don't, but I . . . I don't quite know what to do. What if I find my father and he's awful?'

'You don't have to make any choices right now. It comforts me that he did try to get in touch.'

'Though he didn't try again. It's not enough to try just once.'

'But think how difficult it must have been, not knowing that I never got his message or his name. We were both hardly older than you are now. It's too easy to condemn others.'

The day of the funeral is fine, and the church in Trelorn is packed with people. They are mostly elderly, one or two quite famous. The smell of mothballs displaces that of bats.

'Much as poets hate each other, they stick together,' Quentin says, with a flash of his old self. 'Besides, they never turn down a free drink.'

Xan has chosen to wear his vintage Grateful Dead T-shirt. He sees her raise an eyebrow.

'Yeah, well, the skull beneath the skin, Mum.'

He plays the church piano, and the pieces – 'Jesu Joy of Man's Desiring', Gluck's 'Dance of the Blessed Spirits', Pachelbel's *Canon* – are beautifully rendered if, like the hymns Naomi has chosen, conventional.

Rosie tugs at her hand.

'Grandpa said he'd become compost, Mummy.'

Lottie squeezes her hand.

'Well, so he will.'

'But won't that be nasty?'

'No, darling. He'll become compost, and then flowers. You know how Grandpa loved flowers.'

Rosie's face clears.

The coffin Hugh's body lies in before the altar is not wood but wicker, a kind of pale oblong basket with a lid that Lottie recognises as having been used for some time in the living room of her in-laws' cottage as a coffee table. Its unexpected humility makes her eyes fill with tears, as does its smallness.

The vicar gives an admirable (and admirably short) speech about him, and then it's time for Quentin and Ian, as Naomi will not speak. Ian's speech is brisk, dry and sensible, talking about how he had come to know his English grandfather, and how much he had enjoyed getting to know him. Quentin's is much less expected.

'My father was many things – a husband, a father, a teacher,' he says. 'But most of all he was a poet. He spent his life writing poems, most of which he didn't consider good enough to keep let alone publish. Despite a couple of them being famous, he considered himself a failure.

'His life here was one deep source of solace, alongside my mother's love and support. This is one of his favourite poems, which he asked to be read aloud at his funeral.'

Quentin's voice wavered for a moment.

> THE loppèd tree in time may grow again,
> Most naked plants renew both fruit and flower;
> The sorest wight may find release of pain,
> The driest soil suck in some moist'ning shower;
> Times go by turns and chances change by course,
> From foul to fair, from better hap to worse.
>
> The sea of Fortune doth not ever flow,
> She draws her favours to the lowest ebb;
> Her tides hath equal times to come and go,
> Her loom doth weave the fine and coarsest web;
> No joy so great but runneth to an end,
> No hap so hard but may in fine amend.
>
> Not always fall of leaf nor ever spring,
> No endless night yet not eternal day;
> The saddest birds a season find to sing,
> The roughest storm a calm may soon allay:
> Thus with succeeding turns God tempereth all,
> That man may hope to rise, yet fear to fall.
>
> A chance may win that by mischance was lost;
> The net that holds no great, takes little fish;
> In some things all, in all things none are crossed,
> Few all they need, but none have all they wish;
> Unmeddled joys here to no man befall:
> Who least, hath some; who most, hath never all.

The service over, the hymns sung, they file out to more music, and the coffin is carried out to be lowered into the deep hole in the turf. One after another, they throw clods of earth onto it, smothering the flowers as the flowers smothered the coffin, and the coffin the body. It was over: so why does Lottie find herself repeating the words, *Who least hath some; who most, hath never all* – as if, improbably, they had been meant for herself?

32

Grief, or Relief?

There's a change of air, not so much a breeze as a chink in the atmosphere. He looks up, and glimpses his father's scowling face in the window.

'Piss off,' Quentin says, and a second later realises it's his own reflection.

All through the summer, he keeps seeing old men who look like Hugh. It's astounding how many of them there are. He'll be driving down a country lane, and a figure in a baggy tweed jacket and corduroys will be stomping along – not his father as he had been in the final year, but Hugh as he used to be, vigorous and fulminant – only the car is going too fast to stop, and when Quentin looks in the rear mirror to check, he has vanished into a mist of midges, or changed to a crooked tree. In busy crowds and shopping centres, he hurries impulsively after a man with Hugh's set of shoulders and old checked shirt; the shock when a stranger turns round is like a second bereavement.

If I could only speak to him one more time, Quentin thinks.

'Talk to him, even if you think he can't hear you,' Anne had urged while Hugh was dying, but resentment lay on Quentin's tongue like a stone.

'Fa, I want—' he began; then stopped. What did he want to say? That all was forgiven, when he couldn't forget? How could he?

'You weren't good for his confidence, you know,' Naomi said at one point.

'*His* confidence? Since when were children supposed to boost parents, instead of the other way about?' Quentin demanded.

'You did rub his nose in it, rather. Being in the swim of things.'

'Yet he was the one who chose to bury the family down here.'

'What kind of education do you think you'd have had otherwise?'

'But Knotshead was a *terrible* school!' Quentin said, appalled. 'Terrible. You can't really mean you thought you were giving us an advantage?'

'Yes, we were. It was a famous public school; it had its drawbacks, like many – but it also had some good teaching, and it offered us jobs and you an education. It was what we could afford. We tried to do the best we could for you.'

'Well, *you* did at least.'

'So did Fa, in his own way.'

Every hour he's shaken by emotions. Is this grief or relief? It's not as if he wants his father back alive. Hugh's talent was a deformity of personality for which the Bredin family had all suffered. Widowed, Naomi looks as if ten years have been smoothed from her face. She has her own friends, and now that Hugh has gone they appear, like timid woodland creatures, with food and flowers and friendliness. Naomi has always been loved. With one drink inside him, Hugh was charming; with the inevitable second his mood would turn and by the third he became a monster. It had been like living with a bomb that might go off at any moment. No wonder people kept away.

'Why do you stay with him?' Quentin had asked his mother, in his twenties. 'Why not leave?'

'He makes me laugh,' she said.

This always puzzled him the most. If she remained with his father because they had great sex, or she needed the money, or social status, or wanted to keep the family together, he could understand it – but to waste your life for *laughter*? Like many born with the gift of wit, Quentin is mystified by the emphasis the opposite sex place on humour, presumably as an antidote to disappointment. Sometimes, it's true, he has a flash of memory: his parents sitting together with tears of mirth running down their cheeks. What was the joke that was so funny it had been worth all the insults and ignominies his father had heaped on them all? His sister, younger and more vulnerable, had been so wounded she had fled to the other side of the world, disowning all of them. How could jokes be worth so much?

Yet often he himself has thought that he must tell Lottie about some ridiculous thing that has happened to him – only to remember that of course, he can't. That easy communication had been severed the moment she knew he had been unfaithful. To laugh with somebody is to be with them, contra mundum, and since that day he, not the world, has been the enemy. He can eat with her, live with her, even sleep with her, but the shaft of sunlight in which the happily married spend their lives no longer shines on them.

He has, it seems, fallen back in love with his wife. The fact of this dismays him. Is he really someone who can only want what he can't have?

Quentin gazes out of the window. How little this landscape makes him feel, and how transient. *The lopped tree in time will spring again* . . . The hedgerows here are hundreds of years old, thick woven walls of living leaves: hazel, ash, holly, hawthorn, beech, field maple, service, blackthorn and elder, the forgotten foot soldiers of England's fields. Once laid by skilful coppicing they are now cut back to bristling branches through which the wind whines in winter. Yet there are elms here which have escaped the ravages of the rest of the country, shooting up long after the breed is believed extinct. Only they will never grow into the trees they were supposed to have been.

Maybe I will have to accept the Shed of Doom, he thinks. If it's in London.

His daughters are playing in the garden. Rosie calls out in her queenly manner,

'Daddy, I'm a unicorn, and my name is Horny.'

He suppresses a smile.

'You might want to call yourself something else,' he suggests.

'Like what?'

'Like, um, Moonshine?'

Stella neighs agreement, stamping her foot, and both girls gallop off. He watches, wondering how much of this he will miss.

Again, he hears Lottie saying in that meeting in the kitchen almost a year ago: *We could at least have had each other*; and his own response, *One must be thankful for small mercies*. What a pig I was, he thinks.

She's back from London with Xan once again, having gone up to see her cousin Justin's wedding. They hadn't invited him, needless to say. It had been an enormous party, and by Lottie's account, both glamorous and enjoyable.

'I suppose it's only gays who can afford to get married these days, because they don't have children,' he remarked.

'I hate to break this to you, but quite a few do have kids, too. They're just like anyone else.'

All his life people have been decrying marriage as 'just a piece of paper', but it isn't the paper, it's the words on it, those terrible and beautiful promises to bind you to another person, they are as much spell as promise. His love for Lottie now seems to him to have never gone away but to have sunk into a kind of subterranean river, lost to sense and buried beneath guilt, only to erupt again like a fountain forced through a fissure.

Yet Quentin needs his capacity to hate, for it's almost the only thing that still gives him any energy. The service and singing, the former friends and colleagues coming to pay their last respects, the platitudes overlying the desolation of what will come to them all.

He will never see his father again, never speak to him, hear him, hold him or hate him. Nothing is normal, and at times he glimpses the moment when Hugh lofted him high above a crowd onto his broad shoulders, or raced beside his frenetic attempts to balance on a bicycle, or picked him up from the last train as a student instead of leaving him to hitchhike home in the dark. The man who shouted, swaggered, bullied and denied has receded; and the man who had strewn books his way, who had fed his intelligence, and who could quote Churchill's wartime speeches, remained. Hugh had taught Quentin to strike a fire, build a den, fly a kite, track a deer, avoid self-pity, throw a punch and always know where the sun set and rose. In this version, his father was a good man. He thinks of how Hugh's breathing had stopped, then started, then stopped, over and over for hours, until there was no breath left at all.

It's such a relief, and yet – he will never not miss him.

'I'm sorry I can't help you more,' he says to his mother.

'Don't worry. I know things are hard.' Naomi looks weary again. 'Are you still divorcing?'

'That's what she wants.'

'It'll be difficult for her to work full-time without you, of course.'

'I suppose there's Janet. She helps Di Tore with the boys, doesn't she?'

Naomi makes no answer. He knows she dislikes Janet, as his girls do.

He can hear Janet, or rather the Dyson, downstairs. He's determined not to listen to these cavils, especially given the filth in his parents' house – caused in part by Naomi's refusal to ever have servants, as she calls them.

341

The washing machine lets out a banshee wail as it goes into its spin cycle, then stops abruptly. He finishes his piece, and tries to email it. This is always the tricky part, because the broadband signal, like the mobile one, seems to come and go. Impatiently, he watches the symbol rotate at the top of the screen like a miniature Wheel of Fortune, to no avail. The signal, or whatever it is, won't load.

'Fuck.'

He goes downstairs, and finds that, as expected, the modem is in the wrong place. This small curved box is the one thing connecting him to civilisation, and it's never supposed to be touched.

'Janet? Janet! Have you moved this?'

'Oh, yes I did.'

'I've told you before, you *must* not touch it. If you move it, I can't send emails, and if I can't send emails I don't earn any money, and if I don't earn any money, I can't pay you.'

'All right, all right, you're as bad as my Ex, he was always complaining about it, it's bloody British Telecom—'

'If you move it again when I'm on a deadline, you're fired.'

Sweating with stress, Quentin tries again, and a minute later his piece flies off into cyberspace. In London, he'd never stopped to think about it, but here he can see any email in the form of a green bar that either grows from left to right or freezes, like a *Star Wars* light sabre. Go on, go on, he wills it silently, his stress stretching out and out. He imagines his email battling through all the millions of other texts coursing through the wires at the telephone exchange, perhaps with a light sabre. It's all utterly mysterious to him, the process by which he is able to earn a living out in the middle of nowhere. His children's generation take this technology for granted, but he's old enough to remember when copy had to be typed on a typewriter, and brought into the office, or else dictated. In those days, you actually knew what your colleagues and commissioning editors looked like, instead of talking to a disembodied voice, or merely receiving a text.

There's a ping, indicating his column has been received. Quentin sags. Then he revives. He goes through this misery several times a week, but as soon as his piece goes off, he's free.

'Let's go to the beach,' he calls to the girls. 'The tide is out.'

Trips to the seaside have become a regular treat. They can't afford a proper holiday abroad, but the nearby beaches are, he has to admit, far cleaner than those of the Mediterranean, less touristy – and the ice creams are better.

'Is Mummy coming?'

'I don't know. She might be able to get away early.'

'Shall I wake Xan up?'

'Let him sleep, Stella. He can come with us another time.'

It's one of those evenings which coincide again with low tide, and Lottie follows from work in her own car. Ever since they had slept together, he's been hoping that things might be improving, that she might be thawing towards him. He can't tell. It's like seeing her in a wetsuit, she's somehow both visible and impervious.

Once again, they ride the waves that are always different and always the same. The wide crescent of pale gold beach is almost empty, and the lifeguards have packed up their flags. Once again, they fling themselves face-first onto the salt water. He has the trick of it, born of his own boyhood on these same beaches, and being able to play with his daughters is a compensation for not being free to surf properly, in lonely glory. Sometimes he catches gentle, playful waves with one daughter, sometimes with both, and sometimes with Lottie, all of them caught up in the same twisted skein. Sometimes he doesn't catch waves at all, the imperious surge for the shore losing impetus and slumping flat just when it should grow. Yet sometimes, unexpectedly, what looks small and unpromising will magically heave and swell into a great, muscular steed, its neck maned with foam, which gallops gloriously on and on, its body bucking beneath his board until its last exhalation on the sand. These are the best of all.

Such a wave is carrying him along when he sees an old man standing on the shore. The sun catches his white hair and beard, and in that instant, Quentin staggers through the surf and tries to run, because here is his father, his way of walking, the same pale fawn trousers and old blue shirt.

'Wait! Wait!'

He throws his bodyboard down on the sand, racing to catch up with Hugh. He's much further away than he realised, and then not.

'Wait!'

Hugh turns, and it's not Hugh, not his father, but some other man, much younger and still strong enough to walk along the sands.

'Can I help you?'

'I – I'm so sorry. I thought you were somebody else.'

The man nods and smiles. Perhaps this kind of thing happens to him often. Quentin walks back to Lottie and the girls, picking up his brightly coloured bodyboard. He feels an idiot.

Lottie is silhouetted against the sun, her hair slicked back. Apart from the gentle swell of her stomach you would never think she'd had three children.

'Did you know him?'

'No. I just thought I did.'

'The waves are perfect.'

'There's hardly any current, you know. I'll keep an eye on them if you want to surf.'

She nods, and paddles further out.

He doesn't want to think of such matters, turning instead to their daughters. Stella is shooting out, her legs and arms elongating her into a miniature of the young woman she'll become, and even Rosie is changing from the happy rotundity of infancy. Every week they seem to grow lovelier and more interesting.

'Daddy, Daddy, watch me do a somersault in the water.'

Rosie turns bottoms up, like a duckling, and emerges to get a slap in the face from a wave. She sinks at once, flailing in a trail of frantic bubbles, and he rushes up to haul her, gasping, into the air, colliding with Lottie.

'Is she all right?'

'Daddy, Daddy,' Rosie wails, but her arms and legs clamp around her mother.

You're as bad as my Ex, he hears Janet's voice say.

Quentin turns, is slapped by another wave, and there is another ghost of his father walking out of the dazzle. Salt water streams from his nostrils, his head sings, and then the figure says to him,

'Xan.'

33

The Only Thing

Ever since he returned from London, Xan has been itching to
leave. The plan is that he, Bron and Chen are going inter-railing
round Europe at the start of September. When he searches online
for hostels, he can hardly contain his impatience.

Family life is more dysfunctional than ever. Lottie is always
at work, and when she is at home she's fully preoccupied with
catching up on chores and the girls. Xan loves his little sisters but
sometimes it's hard not to resent them. After all, he's the one who
has been away, and he'd have thought that before he leaves for uni
she might just *try* and pay him a bit of proper attention. It's going
to be his last year as a teenager, a strange thought. He wonders
whether they'll even remember his birthday is coming up.

Meanwhile, Quentin keeps cornering Xan, saying things like,
'The only thing that matters in life, the *only* thing, is love.'

He's like someone who has discovered religion or psycho-
therapy, and in fact Xan wonders whether some deep-level shit
isn't going off in his stepfather's head. Annoying though the old
Quentin had been, the new one is just as bad, embarrassing himself and everyone else.

'Dud seems pretty cut up.'

'I think Quentin's only just realised that he loved his father,' Lottie answers.

Xan hopes she isn't setting herself up for another disappointment. Once a selfish dick, always a selfish dick, and he doesn't trust his stepfather just because he's lost his own father and is sad about it.

Lottie sometimes says how sweet he'd been as a child, and it always annoys him. Why doesn't she value the new Xan? He can't go back to the past versions of himself, only forwards into the future, like the creature living inside the nautilus shell needing bigger and bigger rooms. It's both thrilling and frightening to feel this, and also sad because he will be leaving his family. The only person who understands it is Marta.

However, his grandmother isn't going to be there for him either. Her fall has made her decide to do two extraordinary things: to sell her house, and to move to Italy.

'I have always loved that country, and my friend Ruth is going there also. We will be two wicked old ladies together.'

'You aren't wicked, Grandma, you just like stirring people up.'

'Exactly! What is wickedness but that?'

Marta's house in Hampstead has sold for so much money ('Six million, even though it is not in mint condition!') that she is going to buy a serviced flat in an Edwardian block around the corner as well as a house in Tuscany. From the pictures, it's not nearly as pretty as Church Row, but it has a lift, three bedrooms and a living room big enough for a grand piano.

'You see, I am upside-downing as well. Eventually, your Mutti will inherit all. But if I give Lottie anything now, your step-papa will get half of that. So, to protect her, I give nothing.' Marta paused. 'I hope your own house sale in London is now happening?'

'Yes.'

Xan is surprised by his own lack of feeling. The London house had loomed so large in his imagination as the one place where they'd been a proper family, that he'd expected its loss to be devastating. But those memories have lost potency. He'd gone back just once, while looking after Marta. It was OK, but it was the place where a lot of things had gone badly wrong. Houses really are just shells, he thought, and the spirit that had made this one feel so uniquely theirs has moved on.

Marta sniffed.

'They need to sort out their lives.'

This, Xan reflects, is perfectly true. Returning from a night shift, he has encountered Quentin coming out of his mother's room, having obviously passed the night there. Xan stiffened, stared, and made a sound like a dog growling. Quentin smiled weakly and put up his hands.

'Look . . . It's complicated.'

'If you hurt her again, I'll bash your fucking face in.'

He was bigger and stronger than his stepfather, now, and they both knew it. She acts as if she doesn't need a protector, but the truth is that any man behaves differently towards a woman if she has another man in her life to back her up.

'This isn't about what you want, it's for Lottie to decide,' Quentin said.

Xan didn't want to upset his mother and sisters, so he went to bed where, as usual, he slept like a log. The next day, however, the others are not around (Quentin having taken the girls off surfing again), and he has tea with Lottie in the dappled shade of the great ash. He wants to warn her that she is almost certainly making a mistake. What makes him hesitate is that she looks better than he's seen her for ages. He hopes it's not Quentin who has brought this about.

'We'll be getting our furniture delivered next week. Just think, proper beds and sofas!'

'Are you serious about staying here, Mum?'

'Yes.'

Xan says, 'But the country is empty and lonely and dark.'

'Those are all natural things. I'm not afraid of them. Of course I miss my friends there – though Hemani and her husband are coming down soon. You know Daniel's a professor now? Just think, you might even be taught by him! But I don't need to *live* there. I know it's what you want, Xan, because it's what you need, but when you are older, London is different. You think you're being stimulated but it takes things from you. Maybe it is middle age, but I need peace.'

'What about the winter?'

'Thrilling.'

'You're mad. What about *us*?'

'You will be here in the holidays if you want to be. The girls are happy. It's only Quentin who wants to return.'

'And will he?'

Lottie shrugs. 'I'm not asking him anything.'

'Will you?'

Lottie is silent for a moment, then says,

'You know, when I was a child, you couldn't own a credit card or hire a TV if you were a woman. A decade before you were born, rape in marriage was legal. Most girls I was at school with were not expected to go to university, let alone have careers. A hundred years ago, my father's grandmother was put in prison for asking for the vote. But I can earn enough to keep us. I love what I do and do what I love. I don't need him.'

'Let us know what you decide, will you? Just because the girls don't talk about it doesn't mean they've stopped worrying.'

Still, what does he know about relationships? When he came back from London, he'd texted Katya. He'd assumed that things could pick up again where they left off – after all, Trelorn is hardly heaving with young people. Yet when he looked round the factory floor at Humbles, Katya wasn't there. He asked Maddy if she knew where she was.

'Gone off, hasn't she?' said Maddy.

'Where?'

'You mean, Who? That big bloke, Arek. He's got a wife and child in Poland, too.'

'Oh.'

'Pretty girls like that don't stick around, Xan.'

'But she's *Catholic*.'

'Since when did that stop people? Anyway, she's set up a Polish bakery in Trelorn, and she'll make a go of it, there are enough of them here.'

For the rest of the shift, Xan hardly noticed anything else. It's not as if he'd been in love with Katya, but it is a shock, like missing a step that you thought was there. Girls, they're all crazy, that's something he and his friends have all agreed on for years, but without Katya, the endless flow of pies and the squeaking shriek of the conveyor belt grates even more on his nerves. It has not been difficult to get back into the rota, but when his shift finishes he decides to tell the agency that he doesn't want any more.

The next day, cycling through the late afternoon sunlight to the factory, he thinks how strange it is that he will have seen a whole year through in this place. It's driven him half-mad with tedium and despair, and yet it has also propelled him into a different future. Had I stayed in London, he thinks, I probably wouldn't have been bored enough to be desperate enough to do something. Though in summer, he has to admit, it is pretty. The one big copper beech halfway along, the square Norman tower of the village church, the field where sheep graze under a solar farm, the long stone walls topped by trees and the gated entrance to Shipcott Manor, the curve of the road plunging down into a wooded valley, and birdsong – he suspects that he might miss these.

He won't miss the factory.

'I just want to say goodbye, Maddy. I'm stopping here after today.'

'Lucky you,' she says.

'Lots of new faces,' he says. Rod is doing his usual touching-up routine, and nobody stops him. Maddy follows his gaze.

'Sooner or later, one of the immigrants is going to have a fight with him.'

'It's machines that will do for us all, not immigrants.'

'You think?'

'Soon as the recession ends, they'll go for automation.'

Xan looks at her haggard face, and asks,

'Isn't there something else you could do, Maddy?'

Maddy says, 'If I could get a regular job, with proper hours and pay and everything, course I would. But where's the likelihood of that?'

'I know. It sucks.'

'I can fit my shifts around my husband and the kids,' she says, her expression hardening. 'It's really not so bad. It's clean and dry in a factory, which is more than can be said for most of the work round here.'

Xan thinks how his own family has felt in the past year. Poverty for them has meant no luxuries, not the terror of being actually homeless and actually hungry. The gulf between his life and Maddy's has always been there.

'Is it really not possible to find a better job?'

'The good jobs, they always go to people with connections,' she says. 'Her mum—' she jerks her head towards Dawn. 'We'd all like to hear how she landed on her feet. There are people who'd kill for that job with the Tores, and a cottage too.'

'Maybe Janet will leave.'

'Even if she did, I'd probably not get it. I can clean and cook, but I've no qualifications.'

Dawn shuffles by with her trolley, leaning into it like an old woman. She looks odder than ever, her flesh a kind of waxy yellow and her hair invisible under its cap. It's hard to tell whether she stares at him out of general vacancy or hostility or something else.

'Hi, Dawn.'

There's a long pause. He can see her mouth the words, 'You went away.'

'I've been staying with my gran in London. She broke her leg. Have you been on holiday?'

'No.'

It's impossible to have a conversation with her, even without the jiggling shriek of the conveyor belt.

'Do you still play the piano?'

She gives him her sleepwalker's stare, and turns away. What's *wrong* with her? Xan wonders, as the shift bell rings. When he's changed out of the overalls and boots (his heart singing at the knowledge that this is the last time he'll have to wear them) he fishes his mobile out and messages Bron. He probably won't be up yet, but with medics, you never knew.

Any news about the bloods?

The line on his mobile takes for ever to stretch across the top of the screen, but eventually pings off. It's a small mystery, but one that nags at him.

He looks around at the big white room, with its flat neon now supplemented by the rising sun seeping through the corrugated plastic skylights. It's depressing to think that all this will continue, hour after hour and day after day, long after he's gone, the ingredients arriving, being turned into processed food, being boxed up and transported, all through the labour of people who are invisible and voiceless, who though often sick or even mad must somehow ensure the highest standards of hygiene for the lowest legal wage. He doesn't think he'll ever eat another pie again, though the truth is, he'll probably forget.

Deep in his pocket his mobile quivers. When he takes a toilet break and checks, it's from Bron.

Hypothyroidism.

Typical of Bron. What does it mean? Xan tries to look it up on Google, but no matter how he tries to get a signal again, the

352

factory is sunk in a dead spot. Still, it must mean that Dawn is ill, as suspected. He must tell her, and her mother. If they know what she's sick with, she can be cured.

At the end of his last shift Xan catches her eye, smiles and jerks his head towards the exit to indicate that he wants to talk to her. She nods, slowly. Without the blue hairnet he can see how thin and lank her hair is. If he can just tell her what Bron has found from her blood sample, then he will have discharged any responsibility. It's impossible, though: by the time he's out, she has been collected by her mother.

'Dawn!' he calls, waving after Janet's grey, dirt-speckled car as it turns out of the factory gates.

'Got your eye on that, have you?'

Xan turns, and sees Rod. He's grinning in a way that, even without his words, would have told him that his old persecutor is spoiling for a fight. A retort rises to his lips, but he turns away to unlock his bicycle.

'What do you want with her?'

'I wanted to tell her something.'

'Don't bother. She's a lazy slag, our Dawnie.'

'She's ill,' Xan says. It's an effort not to show Rod how much he detests him. 'She needs help.'

Rod grabs the handlebars of the bike, and thrusts his face forwards into Xan's. Most of the factory workers are hurrying home, or getting into their cars, but some stop to watch.

'What the fuck do you know, smartarse?'

'I know enough to be calling the police, if you don't let go,' Xan says, evenly.

'Piss off, monkey. Keep your nose out of other people's business.'

Xan wrenches the handlebars out of Rod's grip, and shoots off, pedalling and breathing hard. A few minutes later he finds his arms are shaking. He's never got into a fight but has no doubt that he has come as close as he hopes he'll ever be to either hitting or getting hit. It isn't only the racism, and the stupidity.

Something comes off Rod that is as poisonous as the mephitic breath.

He slows and again tries googling hypothyroidism on his phone. The single most maddening thing about country life is its lack of connectivity – the mobile signals that waver and shrink, the Internet that has everyone on a laptop watching pages and images that freeze or shatter into fragments. The twenty-first century, just out of reach.

He cycles back along the narrow twisting lanes. The sun is rising above the mists, and the long grasses are bent over, each head heavy with a single droplet. All along the road he can see flashes of falling dew, and spiderwebs bright as mirrors. The sky with its vast, radiant clouds expands, illimitably. He pumps his pedals, enjoying the glimpses of secrets over hedges: a doe and her fawn poised on their delicate feet, grazing; a hare lolloping across a meadow where new grass has grown through shorn stubble; a hawk, circumflexed over its prey. The warming air is rich with honeysuckle, hay, mud.

At Home Farm, he falls into bed, and when he wakes, Quentin and his sisters are leaving for the beach.

'Come along, if you like,' Quentin says.

'I'd start snoring on my bodyboard,' he says. 'See you later.'

Alone in the house, he potters around, thinking about making himself some supper – or is it breakfast? The afternoon is one of those late-summer days so saturated with sunlight that it seems to drip from the trees like honey. Xan half-regrets not going surfing too; but then he hears the noise of a car outside. Wondering whether his family are already back, he looks out and sees Janet. It must be her day to come and clean.

'Oh, hi,' he says awkwardly.

She nods at him, then starts up the Dyson. He gets on with his meal, then remembers to look up what the word Bron sent him meant. It makes sense, all of it – the listlessness, the hoarse voice, the loss of hair and worst of all, intelligence. There are old

354

photographs of sufferers, who are the original cretins, stunted, bloated and without expression. It can be congenital, so that a child is born with it, or appear later on. Either way, it must be countered by a lifetime of medication.

'Janet?'

'Yes?'

She switches off the machine. In the silence, he looks her full in the face and feels again the sense of disquiet. There's something in her expression, a hardness. He pushes down his instinctive dislike, ashamed of it as a form of snobbery. His mother has done the same, he knows: they all bend over backwards to be nice to her because of their middle-class guilt.

'Tea?'

'No, thank you.'

'There's something I need to tell you.'

Stumblingly, he explains what he has discovered, and the symptoms he's noticed. The only thing he doesn't say, for reasons he doesn't quite know, is that Dawn herself had asked him to look at her blood.

'She's ill, you see. It could be really serious if it goes untreated. But it can all be easily reversed with some pills called levothyroxine.'

'I see.' She doesn't seem alarmed or upset by the news, but goes on wiping surfaces. 'Did you work this out by yourself? Are you going to be a doctor?'

'No. I just noticed . . . It was chance I looked into it,' he says.

'Very clever of you, I must say.' She doesn't sound altogether happy about it. 'Well, you can be sure I'll do something about it.'

'I'm sure it could be sorted out, but you've got to get Dawn to a doctor, Janet.'

'Oh yes, a doctor. We aren't with one at the moment.'

'But I'm sure there are good GPs here,' says Xan. 'What about Dr Viner in Trelorn? He's been looking after my stepfather's parents.'

'I'll make sure Dawnie's safe, don't you worry.'

Reassured, Xan sits at the table. He feels very tired again. At least I can sleep through the night from now on instead of doing my shift, he thinks. And then I'll be abroad with my friends.

Janet has gone off to continue her work, but in a few minutes she returns.

'That cat has got into the cellar somehow, and the door is stuck. I can hear it calling, and the door's too heavy for me to force. Can you help? I know your mum doesn't like it being in the house, seeing as you're allergic.'

'Sure,' Xan says.

He shambles off, followed by Janet, and hears McSquirter yowling for release.

'Give it a big shove, it's stuck,' she says. 'Must have swollen in the damp.'

He puts his shoulder to the door, prepared for resistance, but it yields at once, so that he staggers in and crashes to the ground, painfully.

'Ow!'

For a moment, the pain blots out everything, but when he turns round, the door is closed. Xan picks himself off the floor, and rattles the knob.

'Janet? Janet, the door has closed, and I can't open it.'

There's no answer.

He is locked in a small room with a cat.

34

Sour and Sweet

For a farmer, and a farmer's wife, there is no such thing as a summer holiday, any more than there is a weekend. Perhaps it's just as well, given what Sally has to work out.

The letter she had seen goes round and round in her head. Why had Peter lied? They were supposed to share everything, why hadn't he trusted her with this? On Sunday afternoon, when he'd expected their usual fumbling tumble, she'd pleaded a headache.

'Sorry, m'dear,' he said, turned over, and fell asleep.

Did he really think it would make her happy to continue like this? If he'd told her the truth twelve years ago, they'd have had no problem. But then, how often did men tell the truth?

This week she's been fielding a new mum who, apart from the usual trouble, has discovered her partner's porn addiction on the house computer.

'I just feel so terrible, Sally. I never knew he went in for that kind of thing.'

'Were children involved?'

'No, but it was *gross*. How can anyone look at that stuff? Does it mean he's dangerous?'

'You'd be surprised by how many couples have this issue,' Sally told her. She doesn't add that it disgusts her, too. Men, she thinks. Everything that's wrong in the world is their fault.

'And now he knows, he wants to try the things he's seen when we do it,' the mum said, bursting into tears. 'He thinks that's normal. How can he expect me to doll myself up, when I've had no sleep for a month and stitches halfway up my fanny?'

Sally answered, 'Just remember, you've had nine months of changes to your body to prepare you for being a mother, and he hasn't. Maybe you could see it as his way of waiting until things get back to normal.'

'Do they, ever?'

'Oh yes,' Sally lies soothingly.

From what she's seen, women never get their old lives back again. What they have to accept is the start of a new one, in which they must always put someone else first. Only why is it always the women who have to do that?

'He doesn't understand what hard work it is, being there every second.'

'You'll be fine now the mastitis has gone.'

She doesn't tell her mums that their libidos are depressed for as long as they breast-feed, because the emphasis has to be on giving the baby the best start in life. Few women want to have more than two, even if they can afford it, unless they're like her sister Anne. The toll is too great. Yet it's one she'd pay willingly, herself.

'It's such a terrible time to have a baby. I don't know how we'll afford it.'

'There's never a good time for a baby. But you will find it all worthwhile. How are you feeling, in yourself? Do you think you might have a touch of the baby blues?'

It's hard to concentrate when she has her own problems. I

must tell my sisters, Sally tells herself, only it's too personal and painful. It exhausts her, giving to other people. Kindness is seen as a weak, watery thing – much like mother's milk, which shocks people by not being yellow and creamy like a cow's. If you are poor, or disappointed or depressed, as everyone is at some point in their lives, then being kind to someone else takes a lot out of you, and most of the time people don't even realise it. But quite often she wants to go home and cry her eyes out. She's still in mourning for her mum, and in mourning, really, for the marriage she thought she had but didn't.

It isn't Peter's fault he's infertile: she should have guessed that, with his chaotic upbringing, he wouldn't get inoculated against mumps as a child. What is wrong is his not telling her the truth, and allowing her to hope ... Maybe he dreads a repetition of his own childhood, and of turning into his father, or maybe he doesn't understand how love, unlike anything else, is not a finite thing to be rationed but grows and expands to embrace each new person. But she should have had a say in it, too.

She can see the women jiggle their buggies, absent-mindedly, as one begins to wail. Are any of them the mother of the baby near Shipcott Manor? She doubts it. Twice, she's stopped outside the gatehouse, and twice heard the same sobbing, trembling cry.

Could it be that Janet is looking after a friend's child? Possible, though unlikely: Janet doesn't seem to have made any friends since moving here, unless you count Rod. There's the Tores' old gardener, but he doesn't have any children or grandchildren that Sally knows. Altogether, the gatehouse reminds her of Hansel and Gretel in the story.

Sally thinks, I might just pay a visit to that gatehouse. It's on my way, and I can always say I'm collecting for something if there's anyone there.

On the back seat, Baggage settles down with a sigh. Sally tells herself she's calm, but mashes the gear change turning up the hill. When she draws up under the estate walls, with an irritable squeak of brakes, she is sweating with anxiety. Behind her, Baggage whines softly.

'Now you keep quiet, do you hear? I'll be back soon.'

Sally walks up to the gates. The granite posts on either side are topped with a kind of curved point, like helmets. The gates between them are all thorns and roses, cast in curling black iron. The lodge cottage has battlements, and tall chimneys decorated with twisting plaster ornaments that are supposed to make them look Tudor, and the narrow windows have points at the top, like staring eyes. It's painted a gingery biscuit colour. The whole thing is absurd, yet oddly sinister. Strange to think of Tore as a boy, over sixty years ago, living here with his mother. She's seen a photograph of him, startlingly handsome with the dark hair, narrow eyes and high cheekbones of a Romany, back in the days when music came on vinyl, and you saved for a year to buy a record-player. Her mum told her that he'd go to school wearing wellington boots because these were the only shoes he had. And now he owns the whole estate.

At first glance, the gates look shut; only the snib hasn't caught. It feels like fate not to have to ring the keypad. Sally pushes gently, then slips through the gap and walks briskly to the door. It's painted the traditional bright, soft blue; there are red-and-white checked gingham curtains in the windows, and a pot filled with red geraniums. It looks clean, tidy, innocuous, respectable. She finds herself thinking, *What am I doing here?*

Nobody answers when she knocks.

'Hello?' she calls softly. 'Is anyone in?'

There's no reply. High up in the heavy boughs, the wood pigeons repeat their lulling call. Almost, almost, she turns back, and then something (she will never be sure what) makes her walk forwards.

With a backwards glance at Baggage, who is poking her long anxious nose through the window, Sally goes round the side of the gatehouse. A high hedge lurches across it, and suddenly

360

this is not at all like the homely, well-kept exterior facing onto the drive, but a narrow path, pitted and pocked and stinking of cat-piss. Brambles claw at her, and a spindly, red-tipped fuchsia sprawls out from below, like a creature fleeing for the light. Sally knows how to stand still, patiently unhooking the thorns from her hair, and clutches her bag. She pushes forwards, determined.

At the back, the woods press against the house, and the long grass is rank, and waist-high. Once, presumably, it had been tended: there is the edge of a terracotta rope tile bordering the path, and the thin grassy mound of a vegetable patch where some kind of cabbage has bolted into a long etiolated neck with a tiny head on top. Sally is used to the neglect of farmyards, but the thicket of thorns and hogweed before her is the work of many years. An old table pokes through like a rotten tooth. She steps onto the porch and looks into the green gloom of the back.

Even before her eyes adjust, she can smell something is wrong. It's a smell both human and inhuman, sour and sweet, and it is so pungent that if Baggage were here she would be whining.

There is a small rectangular mound on the porch floor. As her eyes adjust, she can see it is a dog's cage, heaped over with rags that hang down in stained tatters. The stench is definitely coming from there. Gingerly, Sally breaks off a stick and shifts the rags aside, dreading a sudden explosion of barks and snarls. There is no movement, however. She kneels, and looks in.

Curled on more rags is a baby, dressed only in a nappy and T-shirt. The child's eyes are shut, but as a little light and air reaches it, it whimpers. Horrified, Sally sees its mouth open to cry, only no sound comes out. It's the size of a six-month-old, but it has all its milk teeth, the stomach swollen and the limbs thin to the point of emaciation. It's lying in a pool of excrement. She gasps, her gorge rising, before she gets out her mobile.

There is no signal, but her phone has a camera. Switching it to silent, she takes photograph after photograph, her fingers trembling. Every detail must be recorded, from every angle. The porch, the cage, the inside of the cage, the child. There is an empty bottle with a grubby teat which has contained either water or formula. She must feed it; it's clearly dehydrated and hungry. She must take it out of its overflowing nappy. She must take it out, and away from this terrible place.

She opens the cage, and gently lifts the child out, placing it on one of the cloths on the porch. It stirs. The face is so streaked with filth that it looks almost feral, but a few curls cling to the forehead. Sally takes a wet wipe from the emergency pack in her bag, and gently cleans the face, murmuring,

'Hello. What are you doing here? There you are, that's better.'

Its nose, cheeks, chin appear like pearls in grime, and then, without uttering a sound, the child opens its eyes. They are enormous, pale blue, and crusted with dried tears. Sally gazes into them, and a rage boils up in her, so scalding that if the person responsible for this cruelty were to walk in, she would punch them. But there is nobody in the house.

If she reports this, as she must, she knows what will happen. The child will be taken into care, and there will be a huge scandal, with prosecutions and people pontificating about parenting, and a concealed birth, and in the middle of it all the child will get lost, passed from foster care to the adoption service, when here she is aching with every fibre for a child. She has found it, when nobody else thought to look.

'Go on, take it,' says her mum's voice.

'Oh, shut up!' Sally says to it.

Her heart seems to squeeze into a single arrow of pain and longing. She knows what she ought to do: find a signal and call the emergency services. Nothing ought to be touched or changed. She should not even have cleaned the baby's face. She should not touch its nappy, and she should not give it anything to feed or comfort it, unless it is at the point of death.

The baby is, however, out. It's as scrawny as a rabbit, but never takes its eyes off her. They follow her movements, good, that means not blind at least. Can it hear? No time to test for that yet, and the ears might well be blocked with the filth of days or even weeks. How can a child, in Britain, in the twenty-first century, look like this? Yet it can, and this is what she has been trained all her life to find, and face. Whatever wickedness this is, she must deal with it. She must find the cool, calm place in her that has made her a good nurse, and hold on to that.

There is something deeper than her training, however, and if she does not allow some release of anger and concern, she might faint or burst into tears. She can't leave this child in its filth and stench. She has to do something, even if it means disobeying the proper procedure.

'You are loved, you are loved,' she keeps murmuring. 'Oh you poor child.'

Again the mouth opens, as if screaming soundlessly. Sally makes a decision. She takes off the filthy nappy, and puts it into a plastic bag, together with the wet wipes that got off the worst, and then puts the baby down again for examination. Nothing broken, as far as she can tell, and no bruises. It's a little girl. Her fine hair swirls around her head like tiny whirlpools of copper. Her arms move, minimally, and the tiny hands clench and unclench. Sally touches the baby's cheek in a caress. For the first time, the child gives a sigh.

'You poor little lamb,' she says. 'Who did this to you? Whose child are you?'

The head fits into the curve of her hand as if it was always meant to be there, and the small body tucks into the crook of her arm. For a moment, Sally stands there, and it is as if she is standing in sunlight for the first time in her life. The child opens her mouth and the faint pitiful cry comes out again. There's a bottle of ready-made formula milk in her bag for emergencies; she gets it out and puts it between the child's lips. Without hesitation, the mouth closes over the teat. In a minute, the bottle is emptied. The baby gives a deep belch, and closes her eyes. Sally feels her own body drenched in a sudden, boiling sweat, like a wave of fever.

'I won't leave you. I can't.'

Wrapping the child in her long cotton scarf, and picking up the plastic bag of rubbish, Sally goes back through the passage, out through the side door, and towards her car.

35

The Iron Hook

To say Xan can't breathe is not true, or not yet. His throat is constricting and his lungs are turning to stone, but there's still a trickle of air rasping through. He gasps, and gropes for the inhaler that is supposed to be in his pocket. It isn't there. He stopped bringing it everywhere months ago.

He's bewildered. Why is he here with a cat? He shakes the door. It won't budge, and putting his shoulder to it does no good because it opens inwards. Why won't it open? Where is Janet? He can hear the sound of the Dyson again, far away, and thumps on the door.

'Janet! Janet! Let me out!'

No answer. She has done it deliberately. Why? He looks at the ceiling, the big iron hook stuck in it like an upside-down question mark. No matter. What is more urgent is that he gets out.

Xan's last severe asthma attack happened several years ago, occasioned by going to a party at the house of someone who forgot to tell him that his family kept a cat, because Xan himself forgot to ask. Many people, even now, don't understand how serious it is, even when they know about the anaphylactic shock

365

that can stop your heart with a wasp sting. Allergic asthma takes longer but is no less deadly; without antihistamine or his inhaler, he'd been carried off within minutes to A&E, and put on a nebuliser. That time, however, he'd been in London.

Here, in the middle of nowhere, it will probably take hours for anyone to find him, let alone bring help. The thought makes it even harder to breathe than the snot pouring down the back of his throat. At all costs, he mustn't panic, as this constricts breathing further. All these months of being normal and healthy, even in winter, and now this. Asthma crawls through his lungs, swelling and squeezing. It does not as yet have total control of his body, but it will. According to memory, he has at best twenty minutes left. He needs his inhaler, the blue one that squirts a dose of salbutamol deep into his lungs, opening up the thread-like airways. Instead, he has a cat, a creature as deadly to him as a cobra.

He's pushed the cat onto the floor, but it is still twining hopefully around his ankles. Poor creature, it's killing him through no fault of its own. He is allergic whether it's alive or dead because of the dander on its fur. McSquirter is, unfortunately, one of the worst for someone with Xan's condition. Large, fluffy, and inclined to moult on a warm day, it is in full possession of the feline perversity that makes them avoid the enthusiast and pursue the rejecting. It dances up, trilling insistently, then rolls over to reveal an expanse of pale apricot stomach, determined to win him over.

'Shit,' he mutters. 'This is not good.'

His eyes are itching and streaming, and both eyes and nose are swelling up. It's a misery that no amount of blowing or rubbing will do anything to help. Far more urgent are his wheezing, whistling lungs. Already he is stooping, buckling, like a young man being transformed into an old one.

He is squinting to see, but the door is definitely locked. The tiny window which allows some daylight into the room doesn't open, and is made of security glass. He tries wrapping his T-shirt round his fist and punching it, but all that happens is that his fist gets bruised. The floor is concrete. The ceiling is barred by beams, floorboards and hardboard.

I can't get out, I can't get out.

He thinks of Lottie and Marta, and how desperately upset they will be if he dies; he thinks of his little sisters, he even thinks of Quentin. When will they return from the beach? If only he knew that, he might feel less panicked, but they are bound to be gone for at least three hours. By then, it will be too late. He has to save himself.

'Come on, think,' he tells himself. He has rejoiced in his body recently, but it's his brain whirring in its skull with all the things he knows, and can do that might save him. He can't let that be lost. Breathe, breathe. The action every living thing performs unthinkingly until it dies is becoming an effort.

No amount of banging, kicking or turning the door handle affects his predicament. The hinges are long, and made of iron; the door itself is solid. He can't break it, not without a tool.

Xan looks around, wiping his streaming eyes. A quarter of the room is taken up with the stone bath, carved out of a single piece of granite, like a kind of sarcophagus. The stone is flecked with tiny red specks, like blood. He remembers Quentin telling them what it was used for, and shudders to think of the pigs hanging upside-down with their throats cut, and the way it would have been filled with salt to cure the pork for winter. Is drowning in your own blood worse than drowning in your own snot?

The rest of the room has been used as what his family call a sin-bin – a place to put things they can't throw away but don't tend to use. It's a perfect place for a prison, or a tomb. Apart from old wellington boots, all he can see is a plastic bucket with a ragged mop in it. Hopefully, he tries unscrewing the mop-head from its pole, but the plastic splinters as soon as he jabs it at the

367

window. The cat, frightened, retreats to a dark corner, where it watches him, warily. He can see its hairs floating like thistle-down through the air in a shaft of light. To be killed by such tiny things . . . his efforts have caused his lungs to constrict even more. He's gasping, now.

If he could just find a crack to the outside, and breathe through that, his allergy might be reduced. He staggers over to the door. It's a tight fit around the frame, but there's a keyhole. He kneels, and puts his eye to it. The key has gone, surprise, but he can at least suck a trickle of clear air through it.

'Help,' he gasps; then, gathering more breath, 'Help!'

There is no reply. In the country, Quentin had told them, nobody can hear you scream. It's true. He tries to remember the tricks he's been taught: Stand upright to allow your lungs to expand. If that's impossible, hunch over on the ground, face down with knees beneath, to get a tiny bit more air from deep within. Never lie on your back. Breathe through your nose, not your mouth. Breathe out, because breathing in happens auto-matically. He can hear his airways whining like an aeroplane trying to climb too fast.

Xan sits down on the edge of the granite bath and tries to straighten up. Outside, life simmers and seethes in a summer sun so strong that its syrup stains the little room into a semblance of warmth. It's cold, inside. At least, he hopes it is cold. Xan holds up his hand to the light to check. His fingertips are not blue, yet . . . The pain of his lungs and back and face is almost driving him crazy, he wants to rub his eyes until they fall out of his head like weeping jellies. His nostrils are stuffed with salt glue, his sinuses have a skewer through them, his lungs are continually constricting. He'd cry, if he had enough breath.

For as long as he's alive, the inflammation to his mucous mem-branes will continue; and then it will stop. His sinuses will no longer react, his nostrils, eyes and face will go down and he will look perfectly normal again. It will seem as if he had an attack

368

while alone – for asthma is a mysterious affliction which can take its victims suddenly.

It really is the perfect crime.

McSquirter comes and sits by his feet, purring loudly. It wants to be his friend, not his murderer. It's a beautiful animal, like Orlando the Marmalade Cat, gooseberry-green eyes and all, only not to him. Death by cat, how ridiculous it sounds. But why has Janet done this? Why does she hate him so much? It can only be because he'd told her about Dawn's illness – and now he comes to think about it, she hadn't been surprised.

Janet knew what was wrong with her daughter, because what she wanted was for Dawn to become more and more stupid. Why? He can't imagine, but thanks to Devon's glacial broadband speeds, he has seen enough about hypothyroidism to know that it's something all babies are tested for immediately. To be at all normal, Dawn must have been on thyroxine from birth. Only then could her brain have grown normally, so that she had been, until a year ago, bright and beautiful, instead of the weak, slow, stupid girl she is now.

The most horrible realisation is that for Dawn to change as she had done must mean that her medication has been withheld, deliberately, for months and months. It would have been a gradual process. Wouldn't a GP have noticed? Possibly not, if the practice was overburdened.

Why would a mother have stopped medicating her daughter? Presumably, she cared about her. If anything, she seemed overprotective, driving her to the factory and back. Dawn isn't starving, quite the reverse, she has clothes and a roof over her head. Yet a parent might do all that and still hate their child. Xan has seen enough fights between his peers and their parents to know that this is possible, and he can remember the struggle for control on the one hand and independence on the other. Even he had rebelled against the constant nagging. Lottie had almost had a heart attack when she found out he was smoking

369

weed. She wept and begged him to stop because of his asthma, and when he took no notice, cancelled his allowance.

'I hate you,' he had told her, in a passion of resentment; and for a short time he'd seen her face reflect this. However, she'd backed off. But some people he knew had quarrelled so badly with their parents, or vice versa, that the breach had been irreparable. He'd heard boys in his school say that they wished their parents were dead; it was entirely possible that a parent might feel the same way.

Or maybe Janet had just wanted to make Dawn less stroppy. Didn't most mothers of teenagers wish for more docility? A child could be as aggravating as his little sisters, but full-scale rebellion of the sort he's heard about, especially from girls, is a whole other story. Maybe Dawn had been full of all that girl-power stuff they all got into as teenagers, and Janet just wanted her living doll back. He remembers how she'd brushed and plaited her daughter's long blonde hair, how creepy that seemed. She must have either denied Dawn the thyroxine, or substituted it with something else. One pill looks much like another, and the change would be so slow that the girl had probably not noticed until it was too late. She would have become more tired, more depressed, more exhausted. Perhaps Janet gave her just a tiny bit of the real medication so she could do her factory job. The cunning required to do this makes him shudder.

He tries unscrewing a nail on the handle of the locked door with his thumb-nail. It snaps in a white flare of pain.

Tears pour down his face. I will die here, he thinks. His heart feels as if it's going to burst, and he can't even find the breath to sob.

Suddenly, there's a burst of music. He wonders whether he's hallucinating, then realises that somebody is playing the piano next door. The long, sinuous ripples of melody unfurl, rising and falling up the scale, repeating and reinforcing each other with propulsive energy, like a great and marvellous plant spiralling

towards the sun. 'Jesu, Joy of Man's Desiring' . . . The long inter-
locking melodies sing to him, so gentle yet so unshakeable in
their goodness that they could go on for ever. As he listens, his
heartbeat slows and his breathing steadies.

He thumps the door feebly.

'Dawn!'

The music stops. There's silence, then a hoarse voice says,
'Hello?'

Xan leans against the door, exhausted. His voice comes out in
gasps. 'Help!'

'Who is it?' She shuffles to the back hall.

He tries to sound authoritative.

'Xan. Call – 999.'

Each word comes out on a gasp. He can picture her moon-face
looking blank. They are both sick, and he only has her to help
him fight her crazy mother. Then another thought strikes him.
He puts his mouth as close as he can to the keyhole.

'Mobile?'

'She won't give me one.'

Of course Janet wouldn't give her a mobile. Why would she,
since she has kept her daughter as a virtual prisoner? Whom
would she have to ring, anyway?

But Quentin has a landline.

'Try—' he's going to say stepfather, but it takes too much
breath – 'upstairs. 999. Ambulance. Asthma.'

It's like talking to a child, but he can hear her climbing the
steps. Has she understood? If she can remember how to use a
telephone, if she can recognise a telephone, she might get help.
It's a small chance, but better than none. She probably doesn't
even know the postcode here, but they can trace a landline, can't
they?

Xan slumps on the floor. The trickle of cat-free air is not
enough. His head has grown boiling hot with effort. What he
needs is something to prise off the hinges, smash the window or

371

widen the keyhole. A lever. There must be something. His gaze wanders to the ceiling, and the big iron hook sticking out of the beam as if inviting him, over the granite bath. If I could get that out, I'd have a lever, he thinks. It's bound to be fixed deep though, or it would never have taken the weight of a pig.

Painfully, he reaches up, and tugs. Nothing. He gives it a twist, more in despair than hope. Perhaps the beam is starting to rot, but unexpectedly the hook rotates. He can hear Marta's voice saying, Practise, practise, your strength must be in your back and your wrists.

Sweat pours down his sides and back. Even reaching up is agony, but the iron screw turns. Its thread has not rusted. Flakes of old wood come off. He uses one hand, then the other. His weakness would be shocking if it were not for the ache in his lungs.

The hook releases itself, and suddenly he's holding it. He shuffles back to the door, and puts the hook into the jamb. Give me a lever long enough, and I shall move the world, Archimedes said, and he leans on the arm of the hook so that its curve goes into the wood, and pushes. Come on, come on, come on ... It sinks in, splintering, but not enough.

He pauses, and listens. Is that Dawn on the other side?

'Hello?'

Some instinct of caution makes him not say her name, and the next moment he's glad because Janet says,

'It's no use. You won't get it open without the key.'

'Why?' Xan gasps. He hasn't the breath to say it all – but she grasps his question.

Janet answers, 'To protect her.'

'*Protect?*'

'From herself.'

Xan says nothing. A spell of dizziness has overtaken him, so intense he thinks he must faint.

Janet's voice continues, 'And from her father, my shitty Ex. He couldn't be bothered to marry me, but he loved *her*. He thought he could take my Dawn away from me. Only I stopped him.'

'How?'

Xan's head is steadier. He works at the handle. What he'll do if he gets out and is confronted by her, he has no idea. All he can think of is air.

'I thought you must have worked it out, seeing as you're supposed to be so clever. He was going to ruin our lives all over again.'

'What?' Xan asks. He has no idea what this lunatic is on about.

'Don't you know what happened here? I bet your ma and stepfather do. The bastard who lived here before was my Dawnie's dad.'

Xan prises the handle off the door at last. It pops its screws, and the plate and handle come off, falling to the floor with a clatter. He almost loses consciousness again but the shaft is loose. He slides it out. With a bigger hole to breathe through, he might be able to break the lock itself. A nasty thought strikes him: all she has to do is squirt some household spray through the hole, or block it with a cloth, and he won't have any hope left.

'So?'

She can't resist telling him. Xan can hear the hate hissing in her voice like steam from a kettle.

'He used me, didn't he, and then when I had his kid it was all change. He'd do anything for Dawn, just not the woman who'd given her life.'

'Difficult.'

Janet gives a short laugh.

'You can't imagine how. There he was, the successful musician, and there I was on benefits. I wouldn't put him on the birth certificate, just in case, and he wouldn't give me money. Dawn and me, we came down here to make a new life, but he followed us. I didn't find out for ages. Thought he'd been clever. Shaved his head, grew a beard, got a job as a music teacher just so he could see my daughter. I never even knew he was there!'

But Dawn's father doesn't sound like a bastard at all. He sounds to Xan like someone who cared a lot for her. More than his own father had done, at least. It all sounds so petty. If only I had my inhaler, Xan thinks. He dreams of its acrid tang on his tongue.

'Why hurt Dawn?'

'Oh, I haven't harmed her half as much as she's harmed herself. She was the sweetest, prettiest little girl you ever saw, but she turned into a monster. She called me a bitch and a bully – me, who gave her everything – and that I was a pathetic drudge she couldn't wait to leave behind. And as if that wasn't all, she and my Rod . . . She did it deliberately, to hurt me, little cunt.' Janet pauses.

'What about *him?*'

'Oh, he couldn't help himself. But she was fifteen; she should've known better, the slut. She knew what she was doing, and then when it went wrong, she ran to her dad to cry and complain.'

Xan listens, appalled. So Janet had been jealous of her daughter twice over, Xan thinks. But what had her father done? Where is he now?

'He was all for blaming me, said Rod would go to prison for doing what he'd done. He was going to tell the police, only he came to see me first, and that was his mistake – don't think I don't know what you're doing to that door. You won't get out, and if you do, don't think I'll let you live, either.'

Xan resumes his sucking at the air through the keyhole. His hands are increasingly cold and useless. He whispers,

'Why not – help her?'

'I was the wicked witch, wasn't I? She went to her fucking father, and told him all kinds of lies. But then he always did believe her, just because she was so pretty.'

'Not – now,' Xan says.

374

'No, I took that away from her.' Janet's voice is gloating. 'I made sure of that. She never thought to thank me for making sure she took her pills every day. I used to have to crush them up, just a quarter of a pill in a teaspoon when she was a baby, and I never forgot, not once. So it was me that made sure she grew up pretty and clever, and me that took it away from her, to teach her a lesson.'

'Stop this.'

Suddenly, he's aware that the hole is obstructed. He looks through it, and there is Janet's green eye, looking at him from the other side. The intensity and hardness of her gaze makes him shiver. How could he and his family have lived with this person coming in and out of their home for almost a year, and not noticed she is raving?

Stella and Rosie had, he thinks. They called her Maleficent, and had had their fears dismissed as childish. But maybe they hadn't been blinded by all the adult dramas swirling round his mother, stepfather and himself. To them, Janet had been little more notable than a piece of domestic machinery. They'd taken her on trust as someone reliable and responsible, had been embarrassed because she is English like them, rather than foreign, and never thought that she was a person too, with her own history and issues.

'You've no idea what trouble your kind causes,' she says, and moves away. For a moment, Xan hopes she's given up, and redoubles his efforts to break the lock, kicking at the door, wrenching the hook into the wood, but then he hears her switch on the vacuum cleaner. Its nozzle obstructs the hole he's made, and the cat hairs swirl as the suction draws out the air from his prison.

Immediately, he's streaming again, gasping and banging on the door, weakly. He can feel his nose and feet and fingers go numb, and he falls into blankness, the roar of the machine turning into the roar of his dying heart.

375

36

Some Chance

Lottie can't think why Quentin has rushed off without a word of explanation. Has she said or done something to upset him? (She reminds herself that she is owed a lifetime of offence where he is concerned.) One moment they had been together in a long buoyant glide, and the next he shot out of the sea and was running towards the car park. She stares after him with a familiar sensation of hurt, and suspicion.

Could it be a forgotten newspaper deadline? It's unlikely. Maybe he left a pot boiling . . . The board attached to her wrist tugs like a tired child. There is an obvious answer: another woman. There will always be another woman, and if there isn't, she will always suspect there is. This is why she cannot allow herself to care about him, ever. She turns back, and is stopped by a cold wave.

'Fuck!'

The taste of salt water is misery, yet she must swallow it or distress her daughters. If only I could let my rage out, she thinks. If only I could *use* it, somehow.

The wind hisses through the dry grasses, all but two of the

other surfers have left. Lottie wades out to her daughters. It's getting cold. The wetsuit, with its property of enabling the water inside it to be heated by her own heart's blood, is no longer enough, especially not when shivering from sorrow.

'Time to go home, darlings. The tide is coming in.'

'One last wave!' says Rosie. Stella, though her lips are almost purple, adds her own plea. She can't bear to disappoint them, not when they've had such a happy day.

'Just one, then we must hurry home.'

Following in their lacy wake, Lottie is overcome by melancholy. They will not remain childish much longer. If only one could hold on to them at this stage, she thinks; while they are so beautiful, and love you, and are happy. Xan had once been like this, and she misses that child more than she can say; though when she sees the V shape of his torso, his legs, and the muscles sliding under his arms, she is also happy. He has become a beautiful young man, strong and healthy and clever and good. She loves them all so much. She is, despite everything, lucky. This is the thing to remember.

'It's the bestest feeling isn't it Mummy?'

'Mmm.'

'Can't we stay a bit longer?'

'No, look, the waves are coming all the way up the beach.'

Only a few days ago they had come without consulting the tide times first, and the contrast had been unnerving. The miles of pale, placid sand were sunk beneath ferocious pummelling brine. All the familiar rocks were invisible except when the muscular water peeled back to show them bristling with black shells. The violence shocked Lottie, but Quentin laughed, no more fearful than a gull.

'This is real sea!'

He was trying his best to charm, and she wishes he would stop. People who have fallen out of love don't fall back in again, it's not a tide. Or is it? She wishes it were possible to excise every emotion for him. As long as she hates, she loves, though she loves her children more.

Why doesn't Quentin feel this?

'But I do – I adore them,' he said when she accused him of caring as little for his daughters as he had for his abandoned son.

Adoration is not the daily bread of love, however. Lottie could never have rushed off as he did, confident that someone else would be there to pick up the pieces, because without her there *is* nobody else . . . She had thought that marriage would make him grow up. Then, when he remained just as impulsive, she thought, yes, but fatherhood will sort that out. Then, when it didn't, she thought, but age will certainly bring him to maturity.

No matter what has happened, he remains unreliable in everything but his unreliability. Why had she not understood what that would lead to? For there are men, many men, who are wonderful fathers: she's seen them, holding their children with tenderness and pride, or simply plodding along, faintly embarrassing and yet putting others first, patient and loyal and always there. The unsung heroes of family life, sticking at jobs that probably bored and humiliated them just to do their duty by the wife and kids. Why had she not married one of *them*?

Back up the sands now disappearing beneath the flat frills of advancing surf, stopping to scoop up towels and flip-flops, the colourful polystyrene boards banging heavily on her back as they catch the evening breeze. Under the waterfall, rinsing hair and skin with sweet cold water that clatters unceasingly from the edge of the cliff onto the beach.

'Come on,' she says. 'We need to get back.'

In single file, they wobble across the shingle to the concrete steps. Behind them, the setting sun has stippled the sea bright bronze; ahead, the high banks sway with the fullness of summer. It won't always be like this, but it's what she wants.

'You do realise that you'll never be able to come back? You will

378

be locked out of the London market, permanently, and I'll never see the girls.'

Lottie said, 'Quentin, *this is what you chose.*'

He put his head between his hands. 'What can I say or do? All men are stupid sometimes.'

'I wasn't married to all men,' Lottie said. 'I was married to you.'

'You know, someone told me that he wished he'd stuck a knife in his heart before he divorced, because he's no happier.'

'So, the grass is no greener? Wonderful! That makes it all better.'

It was the same old argument, but this time he said,

'You're right. I'm even prepared to live in this place rather than the city I love in order to stay with you. I hate the country-side, it's full of death and it smells of shit, but even that doesn't matter. You won't forgive me because you can't. You want me to be perfect, because you're so nearly perfect yourself. But nobody can be that.'

She shrugged. 'We've stayed together because of the money, and now it's over.'

'No, it wasn't only the money, Lottie. Couples who really hate each other can't spend another second in the same house. They can't stop quarrelling.'

'Isn't this a quarrel?'

'No, it's—' he stopped, sighed. 'It's an argument. Married people have arguments. If you love each other, it doesn't matter. We agree to disagree.'

'That does not include agreeing to disagree about fidelity, and you knew it.'

'There's nothing I can do to show you that I'm not a monster, is there?'

Look forward not back, that is Marta's advice. She won't be flying off in a chariot drawn by serpents, she won't be preventing him from seeing his daughters; she will just move on.

'Can we have an ice cream?'

'There's ice cream at home.'

'I'm thirsty.'

'There's water in the car.'

'But it'll be all warm and yucky.'

'Sorry.'

A sense of urgency grips her. She needs to get home, right now.

They scramble into their clothes in the empty car park, then drive back past the usual expanse of bungalows, and over the moors.

'Mummy, can we have pancakes for tea?'

'Yes, darling.'

'Daddy showed us how to make them.'

'Did he? That's nice.'

Lottie drives as fast as she can. They will not be exiled from London. Marta has said that, as she herself will only be flitting back occasionally ('Ryanair to Perugia, my darling, so convenient even if fat people complain about them'), they can borrow her new flat whenever they need, adding,

'As long as you never lend the keys to Quentin.'

'No, that won't be happening.'

Going down the long lane to Home Farm, she thinks again how strange it is to feel so at home here. Rationally, she knows that nature is indifferent to her existence; only to her it feels intimately involved in her life. The huge ash tree by the house, whose silhouette and long black-clawed buds once frightened her, has become an eccentric king fronded with rippling plumes; the buzzard breaking from its boughs to sail over the valley is a benign familiar; the ferns all along the deep lanes seem to wave in friendly greeting. Quentin is wrong. The countryside is full of life, and it smells of green.

The slope of the drive means she always turns off the engine for the last two hundred metres, saving fuel and sliding down noiselessly, with the grasses gently scratching the undercarriage.

When she stops, the cooling engine ticks like a clock. She's surprised to see Janet's car there, beside Quentin's. It's late for her to be working.

Luckily, the girls have fallen asleep on the back seat. Maybe I can get supper going before they wake up, Lottie thinks. Or maybe I can catch Quentin at it. She leaves them there, pushing her door gently shut.

She goes into the boot-room, and through to the kitchen to start making some supper. Fat flies are battering themselves against the windows. Predictably Quentin has prepared nothing; he is so selfish it should not surprise. She opens the fridge, and begins to root around for an onion. Someone looms up from the other side. Lottie jumps.

'Oh! Hello Dawn.'

She's sorry for the girl, but annoyed at finding her in the house. In her deepest self she knows it's prejudice, and she is ashamed of herself for reacting like this. Dawn, so lacking in animation, so fat and odd, is just not welcome. Janet has no business bringing her along when she's here to work.

'Is everything all right?'

Dawn shakes her head, and puts her finger to her lips.

'Poorly,' says Dawn, in her croaky little voice, like an old woman.

'What?'

She follows Dawn, who trundles through the boot-room and the playroom beneath her own bedroom that the girls have littered with toys; then, just inside the living room, stops.

Puzzled, Lottie stops too, and hears a noise by the stairwell. She can't see who is making it, or how, and for a moment she thinks some large animal might be trapped there, a dog perhaps, or a badger. Then she thinks that she has caught Quentin in flagrante, for the grunting and panting could well be those of sex.

Only when she actually sees her husband does she realise that he's fighting, and that the person fighting back is Janet. Has he

381

gone completely mad? She's about to shout at him, when the figures shift, and everything changes.

Janet is holding something which she recognises as one of Quentin's special knives. It has a curved black handle and a shiny curved steel blade. Lottie knows how perfectly it is balanced, how from tip to shaft it is sharp enough to slice through flesh and bone with hardly any effort. Janet is using it to try and stab her husband.

Quentin's face is so white he looks like his own death mask. Janet's face too has a strange cast. Her dark eyes glitter, and she wears a grin like that on a dog. Lottie knows, instantly and instinctively, that she is mad. The hair on her neck prickles with intense fear. Until now she has always pitied the insane; now she understands why the sane have always shrunk from them.

All this takes seconds to see and understand.

'Stop,' Quentin says.

All Lottie can think of is getting away, only her body, as if under enchantment, has stiffened into icy immobility. If she could, she would run, and drive far, far away with her sleeping daughters. Quentin is a man, bigger and stronger than she, and he can be left to cope with this, or not. Hasn't she wished herself a widow? Only there is Xan, and with this thought the horror dawns. Where is he?

'I'll kill you,' Janet pants. 'I'll kill you all.'

The knife in her hand is like a rip in the air.

'Leave him,' Quentin says: not Quentin as he has been, despicable, dishonest, unfaithful, selfish, but the person who is not running away.

Before she had children, Lottie had been fearless. Fast cars, bungee jumps, rock-climbing were a challenge; but from then on, every bad thing that could happen to them ran in the back of her mind (and sometimes the front) every day, on a loop. Once, in the early stages of their courtship, she had asked Quentin what he'd do if attacked, and he'd always answered, 'Run.' Yet he has stayed, for her son.

'Oh God,' Lottie says.

Her husband warns her off with a rapid, furtive movement.

'I'm calling the police,' she says, in a trembling voice, only there's no signal on her mobile. The bars that show reception have shrunk to nothing, as if they, too, are afraid. She lies, 'They're coming right now. Just leave.'

They all know it's hopeless.

Quentin is tiring. Something dark and sticky is everywhere, like paint but not like paint. Why is there such a mess? The walls she painted white are all smeared and spattered and smudged. Then she understands: Quentin has been stabbed. His chest is bleeding, and his shoulder. There is a slash across his forearm.

Rage fills Lottie, so enormous it blots out fear. She shouts,

'Janet!'

Janet makes no answer. Her short bulk makes her much more frightening, not less. Quentin, being tall, is at a disadvantage. He's not used to violence, and even chopping logs hasn't made him as strong as someone who has done physical labour for many years. Yet surely the two of them can overpower her. Lottie grabs a cushion from the sofa with the wild idea of using it to stop the blade, and is about to dart forwards when Quentin, his eyes never leaving Janet's face says,

'Help Xan.'

'Where is he?'

'Sin-bin,' Quentin says.

Janet cackles. 'Sin-bin,' she repeats. 'Oh yes, with a cat.'

'You put a *cat* in there with him?'

Lottie comes out of the fog of incredulity that any of this could be happening and is about to fling herself forwards but then Quentin staggers back, and hits his head on the low door frame. He collapses onto his knees. Lottie shrieks in horror.

'Oh God, oh no.'

In the background, Dawn says, in a hopeless voice,

'Mummy, Mummy, Mummy, stop. Please.'

Lottie hates violence, she can't watch it in films without flinching, but in those few seconds she knows that she is perfectly able to kill, too. Her trembling stops and a cold rage blazes in her veins, as if her blood had been replaced by something else. The poker by the wood-burner is too short. Something like a lance or a spear, something to hold the assailant beyond arm's length, and there it is, the ugly floor lamp, with its long steel pipes and a metal disc like a small shield at the end of it. It's in her hands, the heavy base acting as a perfect counterweight, and then Lottie advances, knocking the knife away.

She says, 'Leave, bitch.'

Janet gasps, and in that moment she is all the other women who have had some part in harming Lottie's marriage and home. She hadn't wanted to blame them, and yet the truth was, she hated them. The steel disc catches her opponent's head below the jaw, and Lottie has Janet pinned to the wall, both of them panting. She knows that with a little more pressure on the neck she could kill Janet, and Janet knows this too.

'Drop it.'

Even so, Janet lifts the knife, but she can't reach past the length of the improvised lance, and the knife falls. Still Lottie won't release her. She stands locked in her rage, breathing hard. Janet slumps to the floor, and Lottie raises the lamp to smash it down.

Quentin crawls over, clutching his shoulder.

'Don't, Lottie.'

He picks up the knife and throws it well away from them all. It lands in the living room, and then, still sitting, he gropes around the floor with his one free hand.

She almost shrieks, 'Help Xan!'

'I'm trying. Key, key. Ah, found it,' Quentin says, kneeling on top of Janet and feeling in the pocket of her apron. He staggers up, and turns the key. 'Xan, it's open.'

There is no answer from inside, and Lottie's panic rises. Quentin pushes against an unseen obstacle.

'Xan, can you hear me? Xan?'

Lottie lunges for the door. She kicks it again and again. It's clear that Xan must be behind it, blocking the opening; but the crack widens. She can get her hand in through the gap.

'Ambulance,' Dawn says. 'I called it. Ambulance.'

'You poor child,' Quentin says. He's sitting on Janet's chest. Lottie runs up the short flight of steps to her son's room, finds his inhaler, almost falls back down and, snaking her hand round the door, gropes for her son's face. The touch of his still features almost makes her break down, but he's breathing, although his wheezing isn't audible. He needs to be hospitalised, but if she can get some of the inhaler into him, the magic Salbutamol . . . His lips are slack, and his teeth closed.

If he's conscious, he gives no sign. Any dose may help, if it can just get inside him. She thrusts the mouthpiece between his lips.

'Breathe,' she says, and pushes the cylinder down. '*Breathe.*'

An Inescapable Web

Halfway to her car, Sally comes out of her dream. This is not a fairy tale, where babies are found under a bush or dropped by an eagle, and she should know that better than anyone. She can hear her mum's voice saying loud and clear: It's not good enough, and the child isn't yours.

'Oh,' she says.

She looks down at the bundle swaddled in her scarf, at the tiny hands curled like two buds by her cheeks. Someone has given birth to this little girl, probably in pain and fear, and somebody had tried to care for her. Although she has been treated almost like an animal, there had been a nappy, even if it was overflowing, and a bottle in the cage, even if it was empty. There had been rags to pad the bottom, and to screen the child from the sun. It wasn't much, but it was something.

Also, the baby is, as far as she can tell without knowing her age, not actually starving, even if her muscles are underdeveloped. Her vest is grubby and ill-fitting, but she has seen worse. Although no child should ever be left unattended, it's possible the cage had been to protect her. But from what – or who?

'Hush, now,' she says, as the baby sets up a weak, fretful cry.

Sally has always thought of herself as a good person, which means not only trying to become better but choosing not to be bad – which is a very different, if not unrelated, matter. How could she possibly imagine she might pass off a baby that isn't her own? It's not as if babies are lambs. Peter would be appalled, her sisters, her colleagues, everyone would be shocked at such an act. She herself will go to prison or, at the very least, lose her job if found out. In the moments when she'd picked the baby up and carried her to the gates an entire life story had spun through her head, in which she took all her savings out, and the passport she has never used, and bought a plane ticket from Exeter Airport to one of the many places she's always wanted to visit. She would find some remote place, and bring up this child with love and tenderness, and nobody would be any the wiser.

For a moment, Sally is unable to move. It's not a question of courage. She's faced down demented mothers (and fathers), set off down strange tracks in thick fog, helped her husband find lost sheep on Dartmoor and waded through mountains of grief, anger and stress every day. She has been hurt, humiliated, appalled, attacked by dogs, berated and despised. If saving this baby meant more of the same, she is better equipped than most to do so.

Coroo-coroo, say the pigeons in the tall trees. Why not? What would be the harm?

It isn't virtue that stops her, it's the regulations. Everybody in modern Europe lives for better or worse in an inescapable web of Health and Safety. An unregistered child will not have access to health care, education, a passport and an identity. You cannot exist below the radar of the State these days, not if you want any kind of future, not if you are a loving and responsible parent. If she took this child, she would be far, far worse than Lily Hart with her unvaccinated kids.

Besides, how does she know where this baby even comes from?

The child might have already been kidnapped from somebody, she might be the subject of a desperate search somewhere else in the country or even abroad. Far more likely, however, that she is the product of a concealed pregnancy and birth, either by Janet or by Dawn. It could be Janet – she might be young enough – but it's far more likely to be the daughter.

Sally thinks of the little she knows about the teenager, and how drastically she has changed over the past year. She hadn't always been fat, and clearly, it wasn't only fat. Of course something has gone dreadfully wrong: it seems clear now. Why had nobody raised the alarm? There is one obvious answer: Dawn is seventeen, the age between official childhood and adulthood, when all kinds of unhappy teenagers disappear into the cracks, unable to access specific kinds of care, yet not fully independent. At such an age, you needed a parent or a responsible adult to fight for you in all kinds of ways. The girl has been living with her mother, to all appearances a responsible single parent with a respectable job and home, but in virtual isolation. She'd gone to the village school, and then to the Secondary in Trelorn, but she had made no friends.

'Standoffish,' was the general opinion, alongside 'Stuck-up and snooty.'

Dawn's academic abilities had not won her any allies: if anything, the opposite. She'd never gone clubbing or done any of the things normal kids do. Even singing in the choir hadn't helped. Dawn had a beautiful soprano voice, but it only served to isolate her further.

Also, the two women are not local. They may live and work and even be educated here but are not part of the community. Even if they wanted to be so, it would have taken decades for them to become fully accepted. Without relations and without friends, Dawn was never going to be noticed in the way that even Lottie's son would be. That is the good thing about life here, and the bad.

A small breeze blows on her face, a gust of cool air breathing from the trees. Still she stands and thinks. This has to be Dawn's baby: people would have noticed a pregnancy in Janet, though she isn't popular. It would have been a source of scandal, especially given her job with the Tores and her affair with Rod Ball. Dawn, though ... why hadn't she gone to the doctor? Had she been afraid or ashamed? And who is the father?

Ah, Sally thinks. That's the question. It wouldn't be the first time that a woman has a boyfriend who is really after her daughter. If Rod had abused Dawn, and Janet loved him more than her own child, then it made more sense. Either way, this infant must and will end up under child protection, with many agencies involved in sorting out the mess.

All this will come later, but for now Sally thinks how terrible it must have been to have gone through it alone, without pre- and antenatal care, without anaesthetic, and almost certainly without support. What horrors have gone on, unseen and unsuspected, beneath the roof of this gingerbread cottage? If the baby is indeed Dawn's, what pressure must have been put on her to give up school and any kind of independent life or future? The image of Janet and her daughter comes into her memory: always so close, always together. How much of that was the closeness of love, and how much the relationship between gaoler and prisoner?

Even so, why hadn't Dawn simply asked for help? She might not be able to drive or even ride a bike, but she could have walked to the village and found Dr Viner or his wife. Or maybe she was too afraid.

The baby sighs and makes a small, birdlike cry.

'You need help, don't you,' Sally murmurs. Tears pour down her face, and she rubs them off with her shoulder. She needs help herself, really. Pete doesn't understand this desperate need she has for a child, or what is worse, maybe he *does* – and this is why he'd concealed his infertility and allowed her to go on hoping.

Her anger at his deception, his presumption, is partly what has driven her to the brink of this madness.

'Oh, what to do, what to do?' she mutters.

To grow up in care is not something anyone in social services would wish for their own child. A baby like this stands a good chance of being adopted, but it's always a choice between two or more sorrows. Every moment that passes will make Sally's decision more difficult. She yearns for this child as she has never done for any of the thousands of babies that she has helped into and through the world. She is entrancing, with her delicate features and curling copper hair. But she is not Sally's.

Baggage is looking at her through the gate with anxious eyes and a frown on her long face. When the springer sees Sally, she barks, imperiously. It's a tone Sally has rarely heard, and it reminds her that she has a responsibility to Baggage, too.

'Just a moment, dear one,' she says.

Peter isn't the one whom Baggage comes racing to see, plumy tail whirling, or rolls over for in a shameless display of neediness and affection. Peter isn't the one whom Baggage approaches to thrust her head onto her knees, to sit and gaze beseechingly for a walk, or who jumps onto a sofa for the pleasure of snoozing by her side. If I carry on another step, she thinks, I'll never see my dog, my darling dog, again.

The betrayal of trust hurts her as much as if he'd gone with another woman. Clearly, Peter hadn't known before he married her, and she would have noticed if he'd caught mumps after. He must have had the disease at some time during his short, neglected childhood, perhaps after his mother died. It must have been devastating to find out; no wonder he's been so insistent they could be happy without children.

'But that wasn't a choice for him to make on his own,' she says aloud.

The memories are a rip tide. All those years of trying for a baby, at first thrilled and confident, then less and less thrilled and less confident, until the joy seeped away. Pete hated any intrusion on his privacy, but eventually, after much persuasion, they had both been to see the fertility clinic and had tests.

Sally winces at the memory. Just getting Pete to provide two sperm samples had been a struggle. It was an affront to his pride, and also his sense of decency. He'd been given a dirty magazine, and told to go to the toilet.

'I kept wondering what trouble those poor girls had got themselves into to be making such an exhibition of themselves,' he mumbled.

Typical of her husband to worry about that.

It had never occurred to her to ask to see the doctor's letter to Peter. She'd accepted it when he told her that everything was fine: not a direct lie, but an implied one. For her, the tests had been much more complex and invasive, needless to say, but worth going through the agonising cramps caused by having her tubes blown just to be told she, too, was fine. Of course she was: she has been able to conceive all along.

'I'd sooner trust a vet than a doctor,' he said. 'Load of old cobblers.'

She bought multiple packs of pregnancy test kits, because each month she would go through the ritual of peeing onto its stick every day for ten days, praying for the blue line of success to show in its window. Each time she did it, she would pray: to God, to Nature, to whatever might control conception. There were stories about women who had periods when pregnant, and false negatives, and she could not understand why she was so persistently unlucky. She'd heard of couples who were allergic to each other, or who had undertaken pagan rituals.

When she went back to the GP again, five years later, one of old Dr Drew's successors had suggested that maybe they try other options while they were young enough, like IVF. He must have been bound by patient confidentiality, unable to tell her that no amount of hoping and waiting would do the trick, but why couldn't her own husband be honest? Now, in her heart, she knows he'd probably never have felt comfortable with such a decision. Artificial insemination is for sheep, but not his wife. Even if he hated his own dad, he'd want a child to be his and hers alone. Pete can't understand how families have changed. The rock-like qualities he has have made him stick to farming in the teeth of the foot-and-mouth crisis, fly strike, blizzards and droughts. It's a sacred duty, a debt he pays with no sense of the land belonging to him, but he hasn't thought about her, and what she needs.

As she stands there in the late afternoon sun, the baby lying so sweetly heavy in her arms, Sally makes up her mind. She might not get this baby, no matter how she loves her, but Peter can't deny her one any longer. He has lied to her, and she is going to lie right back.

Her mobile has, at last, picked up the wavering signal that flickers along the Tamar Valley. She presses a number.

'Hello?' Sally says. 'Hello. I want to report a concealed birth.'

There has been nothing like this in living memory round here, but then she thinks of her mother's story. It has been nagging away at her for months. What had happened to Dr Drew's daughter's baby? Adopted, her mother told her: beautiful little baby like that was never going to lack a home. That was over forty years ago, but she wonders who the adoptive parents had been, and where. And then, like a key turning in a lock, something else clicks in her mind.

'An unreported birth, yes, of a baby of about ten months. It's a priority case.'

It's the hardest thing she's ever had to do, but the poor child must go back into the cage, if not into her filthy nappy, though she will keep that. The cream she rubbed onto her poor raw legs will have helped take away some of the chafing, but she's still a terrible sight. Going back down the passage into the porch and opening up the cage again is like returning a prisoner to gaol.

She cuddles the baby as much as she dares, hoping that the love will somehow soak through. Under her breath, she sings,

Sally go round the sun.
Sally go round the moon.
Sally go round the chimney tops
Every afternoon . . .

Then she kisses the little girl and walks to the road and strokes her dog's soft fur, crying. For a few minutes she had felt like a mother, and now she isn't any more.

By the time the police and other services arrive, her tears have gone. She's calm and composed, explaining that she had happened to stop by the manor gates to make a call, and heard the baby crying. The sight of the child in the cage, the contrast between the exterior of the gatehouse and the filth and abandonment inside, and Sally's own status as a health visitor are enough to forestall other questions. The baby is photographed, weighed, measured and taken away to a temporary foster home.

'Where is the present tenant?' a policeman asks.

Of course, Sally doesn't know, and neither does Di Tore when she turns up with her sons soon after.

With Di's arrival, the scene takes on another aspect. She is as appalled as any of them, but she immediately calls her lawyer and press agent. Di understands, as they do not, that someone will leak this story to the media. The Tores will shortly be under siege.

'I had no idea! No, you can't take my statement until I've taken legal advice, honestly!'

They retreat to the manor house. Sally is seen as a friendly face in the chaos, and it's a better place to give her own statement once the lawyer does arrive. Besides, her mind is still churning over what she'd realised.

'I can't believe such a dreadful thing has happened on my own doorstep.'

Sally asks the question that everyone around has been dying to ask for the past seven years:

'How did Janet come to get her job with you?'

'Oh – someone recommended her. Gordon knew someone who knew someone, I think. She seemed fine. Good cleaner, good plain cook.'

'We never liked her, Mum,' Dexter says.

'I know, I know. Oh my darlings, I should have listened!'

'There's no answer,' Sally can hear a policeman saying, after trying Janet's mobile and leaving a message.

'Does anyone have a number for the daughter?'

No, it turned out. There was no number for the daughter. Nobody could remember ever seeing Dawn with a mobile. Which should have been another red flag, Sally thinks to herself, guiltily.

What has Dawn gone through? The more she thinks about it, the more traumatic it must be.

'I'm horrified to think I let her babysit my own sons,' Di says to Sally. 'We trusted Janet. Why didn't she ask us for help? Is she some kind of religious nut?'

She has already called her husband, and he is coming home as soon as possible.

'I knew he shouldn't have got rid of his helicopter,' she mutters to herself.

'I'm sure nobody will blame you for employing her,' Sally says soothingly.

'Won't they? It'll be all over Twitter, and Gore hates that kind of thing.'

Sally wondered how it was possible, for a man who had lived so much of his life in the public eye, for this to be the case; though really, Tore is not nearly as much of a public figure as you might think.

*

394

Di doesn't want to be left alone, so Sally, at her request, stays on. She's bone-tired, but until the business of the baby has been sorted there's not much she can do officially, and Peter can get his own tea. She's sent him a text; right now, she's more concerned about feeding Baggage.

'I've tried calling Lottie, but there's no answer from her phone. Maybe she can take Tiger and Dexter for the night,' Di says fretfully. 'God, why does this kind of thing keep happening to us here?'

There is the sound of tyres on gravel, and two powerful Mitsubishis with dark windows sweep up outside. Tore, Sally thinks, and it is. He's brought his lawyer, and a PA, and as soon as he arrives the household seems to snap into focus. The lawyer has prepared a statement for them both to approve. Apparently there is a crowd of reporters and photographers waiting for them at the end of the drive, and the police have already intercepted one who climbed over the wall to try and sneak some pictures with a long lens.

'There's some new story about Janet, sweetie,' Tore says. 'I heard it on the police radio when we were coming.'

Di looks blank.

Tore sighs. 'Janet's gone nuts. She's tried to kill your friend Lottie's son, and her husband. With a knife.'

Di went sheet-white.

'Why did you let this woman into our lives? Why did you?'

'Because I was asked. I couldn't say no.'

Sally says, 'Were you being blackmailed?'

'Yes,' Tore answers. 'In a way, you could say that I was.'

38

The Ash Tree

Afterwards, she thinks of stories in which people (usually young women) are woken by a kiss. One moment her son was dying, the next he is able to breathe.

The inhaler has worked its magic. There is no other word for it, even though it takes several puffs before Xan can draw enough of the drug into his lungs. Then, it's like dying in reverse: on the other side of the door, he uncurls from his foetal position. A few minutes later, he shifts away from the door. A gap opens. McSquirter is first out of the room, wearing an expression of outrage and a tail like a bottle-brush. Then Lottie squeezes through, and with a big effort, hauls Xan to one side so that the door can be opened wide. She can't drag him out altogether, however, and Quentin doesn't dare leave Janet: that has to wait until the emergency services arrive, with a great clatter of sirens and blue lights.

They each tell their story, and the blood still seeping through Quentin's makeshift dressings would be convincing enough were not Janet so clearly disturbed. After a brief struggle, the police caution her, restrain her and drive her away, together with the knife, the lamp, Quentin's T-shirt and numerous photographs.

Quentin refuses to come to the hospital. His wounds, though they look nasty, are less bad than feared.

'You never know with knives,' says one paramedic, after checking carefully, stitching and dressing the most visible cuts.

'I'll be fine. What matters is our son.'

The ambulance carries a nebuliser, and oxygen; once Xan gets a shot of antihistamines his breathing calms.

'You're going to be right as rain, my lovely,' says one of the paramedics. The warm burr of their voices is as comforting as any blanket. 'We'll take you in to Exeter Hospital just to keep an eye on you tonight.'

'Thanks. But you need to take Dawn, too.'

The paramedics look at the yellow skin, the puffy face, the vacant gaze, and see what all but Xan had missed.

'Yes, I think you might need looking at too.'

'I can't – I can't leave—'

'Who can't you leave? Your mum? I think the police want to have a few words with her first,' says a paramedic.

'I can't leave my baby,' Dawn says.

'What baby?' Xan and Lottie ask. But at this point, the police radio crackles. There's an exchange, and then one of the policewomen comes over and says,

'Are you Dawn Pigeon? We need you to answer some questions.'

'Not until she's been to hospital,' said the paramedic. 'She's ill, can't you see? Don't worry, love, your baby will be looked after.'

'How are you, sir?'

'Bloody sore,' Quentin says. Lottie looks at him, and sees with alarm that his eye, overlooked in the emergency, has swollen to a slit, and is an alarming shade of black and purple.

'Oh dear.'

'It hurts much more than any of the stabbings.'

'Yes, it would. Anything that's close to your brain does.'

'Am I going to lose my sight?' he asks, trying not to whimper. 'I keep seeing black shapes floating across my vision.'

'No, I don't think so,' said the paramedic, after shining a torch into it and doing what seemed like very rudimentary tests. 'It's a black eye, not a detached retina. It'll pass. You can always come to A&E if you want.'

'No,' Quentin says. 'Our daughters are in the car. I can't leave them, and I can't leave my wife alone in this house.'

Lottie looks at him with surprise, and gratitude.

'Will the police be coming back?'

'Yes, I should think so. They'll need to take a statement tomorrow.'

'Good. There's something else I want them to see.'

Quentin doesn't mention the head. It has stayed in the compost bin long enough; another few days won't matter. He wonders whether he should mention having discovered it months ago, but thinks it's probably best not. He can always disturb the ground again, and make it seem very recent, just to avoid tedious remonstrations and possible legal complications.

'Thanks,' Lottie says, quietly.

So Xan and Dawn leave together, and although Lottie offers to come with him she is now more anxious about Quentin, and of course their daughters. Somehow, Stella and Rosie have managed to stay asleep in the car, ignorant of all the noise and disturbance around them – and for this, Lottie will forever be grateful.

For a long time after the police and ambulance left, they stand there, and the immense silence of the landscape closes over them like water flowing into a breach. In silence, they hold each other.

'Are you OK?'

'Yes. Are you? Your poor eye . . . '

'I think we need a drink,' says Quentin.

'I think we should get the girls out of the car and into bed. They mustn't see all this – the blood.'

'No.'

Quentin lifts Stella, groaning slightly, and Lottie takes Rosie, silently blessing the profound sleep of childhood. They are carried up into their beds and tucked under their duvets without stirring.

'Look at them, two Sleeping Beauties,' says Quentin.

Lottie shudders. 'Don't. I'll never be able to read that story without thinking of Dawn.'

They have no appetite, but force themselves to eat and drink. He makes scrambled eggs and toast, and they drink a little wine. It's an effort even to raise their glasses.

'I'd like to wash the stairwell,' Lottie says after a while. The walls are spattered with brownish blood and grey streaks of fingerprint powder.

'Later. They won't notice, or if they do they'll think it's paint.'

'We can paint it. Yes.'

There is no question that they will share a bed this time, though they both fall instantly asleep. Quentin is woken after a few hours by the pain of his eye, which means he can't lie on one side; but he can lie on the same side as Lottie. *My wife*, he thinks. Their bodies curve into each other, and he sleeps again, at peace. When he wakes the next morning, she's up and dressed.

'I need to fetch Xan,' she says. 'You'll look after the girls, won't you?'

'Of course.'

'What's wrong with your eye, Daddy?'

'I walked into a door,' he says, smiling at the bitter old joke.

'Was the door Mummy?'

'No. And we've given Janet the sack. She turned out to be – not a good person.'

'I'm glad,' Stella remarks.

It all seems so crazy, like a dream, but perhaps violence always does. For a few minutes, his life had become a bad film. Now it's more or less back to normal.

They are pestered by newspapers, but it's different for a journalist. Quentin is able to write his own account of it all and more importantly, an interview with Tore. For this, he negotiates such a high fee that he begins to think that it might really be worth asking whether the rock star would consider him writing an authorised biography.

There are, of course, things he leaves out of his account to the police.

'I saw Fa, you know,' he tells his mother when she comes to see him. 'After he died. I saw him on the beach, and he told me to see Xan. I know it sounds mad.'

Naomi shrugs.

'He did say he'd come back and haunt you. Though so far, he's left me in peace.'

'I'll be as bonkers as you are if I stay here,' Quentin says. 'Believe my car is protected by witchcraft, the lot.'

'Would that be such a bad thing?'

'Yes. I have a hard enough time as it is.'

'My dear, this isn't about you,' Naomi says.

'Without selfishness, I'll have a life of misery and boredom.'

'Really? Have you ever tried it?'

'No, but—'

'Quent, you have to listen to me.' She sounds as gentle as if she were waking him up on a school day, and as stern. 'Lottie is the best wife you could possibly have.'

'Yes, I know – I know. I don't need telling.'

'You *do* need telling. You still think this is about you – about what makes you happy. It isn't.'

'But you put up with Fa,' he says.

'You can't go on blaming your parents for your faults, you know. You're at the very last moment in which you can change.'

'Even if I can change, she'll never believe it.'

'She might if you ask.'

Sally has become something of a local heroine. Dawn's concealed pregnancy has also been in the news, mostly because of

400

her proximity to Gore Tore, but her graver issues have not been made public. It is thought unlikely she will be prosecuted.

'She must have had extraordinary determination to survive as she did, let alone look after her child and make that call to the Emergency Services,' Josh Viner said, privately. 'Hypothyroidism is very nasty if it isn't treated. That tiny gland in the neck regulates everything. How fast your heart beats and how well your brain works, how many calories you burn, even whether you feel happy or depressed. Medically speaking, she was hardly functioning. Her mother was giving her about a half of what she needed, but as she became larger she'd have needed a higher dose.'

'It seems such an extreme thing to do,' Anne said. 'To deprive your child of medication she needed from birth.'

'It is. But just think how many parents medicate their children for ADHD – well, you can see the temptation.'

'But what mother would do that?'

'Even without her extreme jealousy of her daughter, and her relationship with Dawn's abuser, I suspect that for Janet, Dawn was always a kind of doll: someone to use and manipulate. Only the doll became a young woman, talented enough to draw attention to herself. She was loved by her father, Oliver Randall. He would do anything to be with his daughter, but was powerless because Janet wouldn't register him as Dawn's father. Without his name on the birth certificate, he had no recourse. He thought, like many men, that he could somehow walk away from the relationship but still see his child. So Janet had her first revenge.

'Dawn had the correct dose pretty much from birth, as long as she was in London. That's why she seemed normal, because the brain does most of its growing in the first two years of life. But Janet never registered herself or Dawn with any GP here. She bought thyroxine over the Internet – it's not expensive – and she must always have kept it in mind as a way of controlling her child.'

401

Anne shivered. 'What a monster! I dread to think what Janet would have done to her, or the baby, in the end.'

'I don't think she would have survived the winter,' Sally said. 'Dawn did what she could. She knew enough to breastfeed her daughter, but being more and more ill herself . . . and then there was Rod. I've no doubt he raped her. God knows what he'd have done to his child.'

Dawn's baby has gone into care, which is either the worst thing that could happen, or the best. Sally can only hope that, if adopted, she goes to parents who want her as much as she herself had done. In starving her daughter of thyroxine, it's possible that Janet also starved her granddaughter of the chance to develop normally.

One particular satisfaction is that Rod Ball will be prosecuted for rape, and sex with an under-age girl. Dawn has been quite clear that it had begun when she was fifteen, and the more her intelligence returns the more horrifying her ordeal is understood to be.

'I told my dad about him,' Dawn said to the police. 'Mum didn't know he'd followed us to Devon. It was a big shock for her to find out she hadn't left him behind. He turned up at the lodge and accused Mum of not looking after me, and said he was going to take me away. It was what we'd both wanted. To be together. But Mum killed him.'

'You knew that?'

'Yes. She told me. Really pleased with herself. She said she'd knocked him out, and cut off his head. I went there later, and saw – I saw him. I couldn't bury his poor body, so I just buried his head. And I let Bluebell out.'

'Why didn't you tell anyone?'

'I was afraid she'd do the same to me.'

With each day that passes, Dawn looks brighter and better. The change isn't instant – Sally's brother-in-law says it's like going 'from dial-up to broadband' – but it's distinct. Her face loses its puffiness, and her speech is no longer halting. She's staying with Sally's sister Tess, though Gore Tore has offered her a home in Shipcott Manor. She has told Tess that she feels safer with her.

'I didn't feel very different, when I was hypo,' she's told Xan. 'Just so tired, and cold, and I thought that was because I was pregnant.'

'Will you go back to school?' he asked.

'I don't know. I might. But what I'd really like is to study music in London. If I'm well enough.'

'Do you want to give the baby up?'

'I don't have to decide yet, and even if I do I might not get to keep her. I tried so hard to keep her alive, but I can't feel—'

It was, and is, a hideous mess which will take weeks and months, maybe years, to sort out. Janet is in custody, though whether she will go to trial is another matter. Her mind has gone.

'I've heard she thinks she's going to be married to Rod,' Tess tells Sally.

'Why *do* women get so obsessed by marriage, still?'

'I don't know. Security? Prestige? But neither of those apply in his case, you'd think. He's a small-time crook, as well as a rapist and child-abuser. Maybe it's the lure of feeling chosen, by someone. Even if it's the wrong person.'

'You'd think, wouldn't you, women might have more sense,' Sally says. 'Instead of being fools for love.'

'I was the biggest fool of all, marrying a man who hit me.'

'But how were you to know? Anne lucked out with her husband, but how does anyone who gets married know what the other person is really like? How can they, when so few of us even know ourselves?'

However, there are more private matters on Sally's mind.

She spent many hours considering whether to tell Peter that she knows about the secret he has kept from her, and how tempted she had been to steal another woman's baby. Should she confront him? He had been such a coward, not telling her.

She knows why he didn't. He was afraid of losing her, even though she isn't going anywhere. How can she? She's too old, and too settled where she is. Yet her disappointment is corrosive. As a couple, they should have faced infertility together and decided together; this way, he had held all the knowledge, keeping her in ignorance and sorrow. Her marriage is not, in short, what she had thought.

But what would be the good of exposing this? She knows him too well to expect any good would emerge. He'd only become angry and defensive, and their relationship, happy in so many other respects, would be ruined. She doesn't want to leave her life and home, and she doesn't want him humiliated and despairing. Even in her disillusion, she loves him, and knows he loves her: it's just that his love lacks the crucial ingredient of imaginative sympathy. If Sally had to put her finger on the single worst characteristic of everyone who has ever inflicted harm on others, it's the inability to comprehend that other people feel pain, humiliation and loss just as intensely as you do yourself.

In the circumstances, her only option is to try for a baby without his knowledge. He might be shocked, but she knows that once he's presented with a fait accompli, he'll accept it. His lack of imagination is what will make it easier. Looking online for a human sperm donor is not as simple as it is for a sheep. It isn't just the expense: when Sally thinks about what kind of man would willingly donate, she hesitates. Obviously, some might do it out of pure altruism, but undoubtedly many must go into it for the money, which in itself suggested something not quite right. There's also the issue of what you might get from a stranger. Although some sites promised genetic screening for certain diseases, they did not screen for things like mental health or the kind of family the donor came from, did they? She has seen too many children not to suspect that nature has as much influence on personality as nurture, and whoever she might wish to father her child – assuming she's still fertile – should, ideally, be someone she might have loved.

There is only one person she can trust with this secret, and that's her sister Anne; Anne to whom she had introduced Josh Viner, all those years ago, after Sally's affair with his brother Tom. Josh is a lovely man without a bad bone in his body, and has given Anne five handsome children. Sally would have happily married him herself, had she had the luck. But whether he would agree to become a secret sperm donor is another matter. Thinking it over, she very much doubts it. However she framed it, it would be an immoral act, and one that, as a doctor, he'd probably refuse.

'What am I to do?' Sally asks; and Anne says,

'Well, it's obvious.'

The mechanics of it involve an ovulation kit, a diaphragm and a syringe. Anne's husband will never know why his wife happened to turn enthusiastically to him in bed one particular morning, or why almost immediately afterwards, she announced she must dash over to Sally. They are both nurses, pragmatic and practical, and though neither had done this before it's straightforward. Baggage was the only witness, and seeing her dog's loving face with its white hourglass reassures her. Of course Sally does feel bad about deceiving Josh; but it's not, after all, adultery.

'You know you have less than a five per cent chance of conception, being over forty?'

'Yes, I know. I'll take my chances with that.'

'It's bound not to work first time,' Anne says; but it does. Three weeks later, Sally's periods stop and the test kit shows that she is pregnant. She keeps her jubilation secret, and will do so until she's sixteen weeks. The following May, if all goes well, she will have her heart's desire, and neither Josh nor Peter will be any the wiser.

'I know, I feel bad about deceiving Josh, bless him. But in the end, it's we who really want babies, not them,' Anne says. 'The human race would die out if men had any choice.'

Will Peter ever suspect? Probably not, and if he does, how will he ever be able to confront her without revealing his own lie?

The child Sally bears will look like his or her cousins, given that both sisters have married tall men with curly brown hair. The rest – well, heredity is always a game of Russian roulette, and people see in a child what they expect to see. Josh's child may have different talents, and ideas about a future that does not involve farming; but that doesn't matter. All that does is that Sally, at forty-one, will become a mother.

'Don't ever tell,' Anne says.

'I won't. He kept his secret, and I'll keep mine.'

'Every married couple needs a secret or two,' Anne says.

Sally wonders what her sister's is, but knows better than to ask.

The Bredins, now they can afford to divorce, are in a strange state. They discuss it in an endless iteration, much as they once used to quarrel.

'Why didn't we see she was off her rocker?'

'Because it's not what you expect.'

Lottie shudders.

'Violence is so improbable.'

'But it's also real. Almost everyone encounters it at least once,' Quentin points out. 'Think how often Xan got mugged when he was young.'

'Don't remind me.'

'We believe violence to be something extraordinary and exceptional, whereas the opposite is true for most people, in most of the world.'

'Any minute now you'll tell me this is the justification for the male sex.'

Xan had gone off for a fortnight to Croatia with Bron and Dylan, and returned with a tattoo and a bead necklace. As university approaches, his excitement is such that his hair looks as if it's been electrocuted. Lottie has bought him all the basics he will need, from a new laptop (also his birthday present) to a wooden doorstop.

'Just so you don't get locked out in Halls,' Quentin said.

Xan rolled his eyes.

'Stop helicoptering, Dud.'

'I wish you wouldn't call him that,' Lottie said; but Quentin answered,

'It's OK. I'm not your dad.'

Xan said, 'I'm going to meet my real father, you know.'

'*What*? How did you find him?'

'The Internet.'

There was a small pause.

'Does your father live in England?' Quentin asked.

'Yes, in London. He's a molecular physicist at Imperial, how cool is that?'

'How did you trace him?'

'I found some kids on Facebook with the same surname, and they look a bit like me. They're Nigerian. So I messaged them, and they turn out to be my half-brothers and -sisters. They sound really nice. I'm going to meet them before Freshers' Week.'

'Good,' said Lottie; 'and when you do—?'

'Yes?'

'Tell him I'm glad.'

Quentin wonders whether Lottie, too, will want to meet Xan's father. He has no idea what the situation is with Martin. Lottie continues to go to work, but whether her boss is more than that to her is something he can't bring himself to ask. He does all the shopping, he takes over the cleaning, he even lures McSquirter into a cage, and takes him to the vet.

'Sorry old chum,' he tells the yowling ginger fury, who manages to get in a good few scratches nonetheless. 'Your tomcatting days are over.'

He had done so well out of his account of the drama on Tore's doorstep that he is, once again, in demand. Even if it's short-lived, the attempt on his life has reminded people of his existence. But there was one thing he had withheld.

A few days after this, Quentin rings the Tores to ask for a private meeting.

'I know what the real connection between you and Randall was,' he says, without preamble.

The Tores exchange glances.

'Oliver Randall was your son.'

Tore claps.

'How did you find out?'

'You do have a reputation,' Quentin says, with what he feels is flattering tact. 'Also, Randall had your eyes and chin.'

'Yeah,' Tore says. 'He did. His mum said that, too. I never saw him.'

'Your own son.'

'Look, I'll never not feel bad about what that girl did to herself, but I never promised her anything. She had this fixation. You get such a lot of that, you know, in the business, and you don't think about what it can lead to. Just that they're there, when you're bored and lonely. Know the feeling?'

'Yes. It has led to catastrophe for me, too.'

'I didn't know she was local, I thought she was just another groupie. I was drunk, I was high, there was nothing different from a thousand others . . . I was a bastard, but so was everyone. Correction: so *is* everyone, given the chance.'

'It must have been terrible,' Quentin says, with irony.

Gore waits a beat, his dark eyes gleaming; then cracks up.

'No, man, it was great! For a while. Everything you ever dream of happening when you get rich and famous is great, for a while. But then you realise, you're pissing away the only thing that matters.

'Ollie found me when he turned eighteen; he didn't under-stand why he was so musical when neither of his parents had the slightest interest in it. When he got into the Royal Academy, they told him he was adopted, and he discovered he was my son.' Tore pauses, and looks up. 'He was the only one of my kids who had any talent.'

'Dexter's musical,' says Di, affronted. 'He's always making up tunes.'

'Sure, he's a great little guy,' Tore responds, indulgently. 'But Ollie had it, the gift and the application, both. I thought that he would take the path I didn't, and become a classical musician. I said that if there was ever anything I could do to help . . . And I meant it. But unlike most people, he didn't want anything out of me.

'He never told anyone that he was my son. I thought it might help him, but he was proud. The life of a musician is always hand-to-mouth unless you're very, very lucky, but he was a good session player and a better composer, so he began to make his way. You remember what it was like in the boom, when the money got going? Yeah, well, a bit of it even came into the arts.'

'Only, he met Janet,' Quentin prompts.

'Yes. I never met her when she was young, but from what Ollie told me they had nothing in common, apart from the child. It only lasted a few days. She got pregnant, wanted him to marry her, and he wouldn't.'

'But Janet didn't know he was your son?'

'No. If she had, it would have been far worse. She didn't even know he was the one who got her the job here.'

'How did that come about, really?'

The dazzling smile vanishes.

'I thought I was doing a good deed. He was desperate to be near his kid, and Janet wouldn't give him access. He paid her maintenance whenever he could – in cash, of course – but she hated him with the fire of a thousand suns. Otherwise, she was doing some agency cleaning when she could get cover. He hated it. However much he disliked Janet, he adored his daughter. It was such bad karma. But his worst problem was, he couldn't afford to go on living in London.'

Like so many of us, Quentin thinks. He asks the other question he wanted answered.

'So when did you discover you were a grandfather?'

Tore grimaces.

'Not for a while. Thing is, Ollie told me about the situation, and finally asked me for help. I was in. We were moving down here, and I thought, why not let him live in one of the empty properties on the estate? He went to live in Home Farm, and he got back on his feet again teaching. That part was easy. But there was something else he asked for.'

'Janet?'

'Yeah.'

'You asked her to come here?'

'My PA found out where she was working, in a hotel, and told her she had a client who was looking for a live-in housekeeper in a country house. We brought her down here, told her she'd get her own home and a good salary. She didn't know she'd be working for me at first. I didn't feel too happy about it, but on the other hand, we knew we needed someone to clean and help with the boys.'

'She was a good cleaner, I'll give her that,' Di says. 'And her cooking wasn't bad. We got caterers in when we had people over.'

'I liked the idea of helping my granddaughter and doing her mother a good turn, without her knowing. After all, I'd grown up in the gatehouse with my own mum, just the same.'

Quentin looks at him, and sees neither the tramp nor the rock star but somebody naïve, idealistic, and rich. He likes Tore, while wondering how many lives this combination has ruined.

'Did you get to know Dawn?'

'No. I'd see her, from time to time, but I didn't get to know her.'

'Why not?'

'Well—' Tore is embarrassed, then admits, 'I wasn't sure I was ready for the world to know about Dawn. And then, when she got fat—'

Not by one flicker does Quentin show how much this shocked him. He remembers what he'd said once to Lottie, about morality not applying to the rich.

'It's been awful being without a cleaner, I'm exhausted,' says Di. 'Look at my nails.'

'Babe, I've told you, just call my PA. She can sort everything.'

'No need. This local woman, Maddy, she's called me to ask if she can be given a chance. I checked her out. She's been working in the food factory, but Sally knows her.'

'Ah, Sally the spy.'

'Sally found Dawn's baby, remember? Your *great*-granddaughter, sweetie.' Gore groans. 'Better get used to it, there'll be more on the way. Anyway, this Maddy is honest, hard-working, and she's got a disabled husband who used to be in the Army. Ideal for keeping paparazzi at bay, though he's mostly going to shoot grey squirrels, if you want him on the payroll too.'

Tore perks up.

'Definitely. Those bastards are always killing my new trees.'

'They don't want to live in the gatehouse, because they've got three kids, but she's signed the confidentiality agreement.'

Gore gazes at Di with admiration. 'What would I do without you?'

Di smiles serenely.

'Sweetie, I don't know what you *would* do, but whether you could is another thing.'

She leaves the room. Both men follow her retreating bottom with their eyes, but over Quentin's there floats a black shape, either very large or infinitesimally small. He wonders if it's a hallucination, or a warning.

Gore says to Quentin, 'You know, I've been thinking about my legacy.'

'For, um—?'

'My autobiography. Or rather' – he waves a hand – 'my biography. Your agent's been calling my agent, suggesting you write it, and as you're not a total cunt, I think we could do it.'

'You do?'

'Yes.' Gore gives him a look in which shrewdness is mixed with mischief. 'Otherwise, it'll go to somebody I don't trust.'

Quentin is moved. What would that be worth? Half a million? Quarter of a million?

'Think about it.'

'I am thinking. Thank you. It'd be a great – that is, I'd really like to accept only first I must – you see, I need to—'

He hears himself floundering and sees Gore's expression darken.

'What's the problem?'

'I think what I'm trying to say is that I need to consult my wife.'

When Quentin gets back, he sees two young rabbits making purposefully for his vegetable patch. He's too tired to frighten them away, and besides, what's the point? They'll only return. The feeling that the wildlife all around is merely tolerating human presence is always strong: no matter what he does, nature will win in the end.

Lottie is in the garden, watching the two buzzards wheel over the valley, calling to each other. He stops. She's wearing a blue dress, cotton or linen, with a full skirt, like a figure out of an old painting. Her skin and hair seem to glow in the afternoon sunlight.

'Were you right?'

'Yes.'

'I expect Dawn will end up living with him and Di.'

412

'He's asked me to write his biography. Tore, I mean.'

'And will you?'

'I know nothing about rock music, but it'd be interesting. He's interesting, even if he's a shit.'

They sit outside, under the shade of the old ash tree. He thinks of all the myths about the ash: how it was believed to hold up the sky, but have its roots in the Underworld, continually gnawed yet continually renewed. Its thick trunk is corded with bark, as if it is straining. Its feathered branches are already falling off, leaving the inky nibs of before. It's so bright and warm that the season might almost be mistaken for another; despite the field maples beginning to turn orange and red, many roses and primroses have produced a second flush of blossom. There is a fresher feel to the air, as if the year were quickening rather than dying.

'I was thinking,' Quentin says, 'that I might collect the girls from school every day, until they're old enough to go by themselves.'

Lottie is silent. She knows what he's really asking.

'Quentin, I've thought a lot about this situation, and the future.'

She can see a ghastliness creep over his features.

'Which is?'

'I still want a divorce.'

He says,

'I was afraid you'd say that. I won't fight it, as long as I can still see the girls.'

'I have to divorce you, because it's the only thing that works for me. I need legal independence from you.'

'I see.'

'But you could stay, on one condition.'

'What's that?'

'You give all the money you made on the house to the children – to Xan, and Ian too.'

'Everything, then.'

'Yes. They're going to need it. They'll need tuition fees for uni, and a deposit for a home of their own, one day. Ian is about to become a father himself. You have the option to divorce, and get some money with which to start a new life. But if you stay with me, as my partner, you have nothing. If you stray, I will find out, because now I know what you're capable of, and then you will have less than nothing.'

Quentin says in a dry tone, which has a tinge of amusement to it,

'I'm surprised at you, Lottie.'

'Think of it as a post-nuptial agreement.'

'Money is a sordid thing to base a relationship on.'

'Actually, it's very traditional. I gave you love, and you didn't value it. Now you say you do. Well, prove it. Prove it by giving away all your money. Or you can go back to your old life. You'd lose the children, because most divorced fathers who move away do, and you'll probably be miserable – though of course you might not be. I'm not the only woman in the world, any more than you're the only man.'

'And what if you're the one to stray? You could find someone else yourself.'

'Yes, I could. That's a risk you'll have to take.'

Quentin cries,

'But I love you, Lottie. All I want is for you to forgive me.'

He reaches out and touches her arm. She flinches, but doesn't withdraw.

'Some people are lucky enough to get it right first time, and go on living happily ever after, but we aren't those people, are we? I wish we were, but we aren't. I don't think any marriage, any real marriage, is like that in fact. It's work, and it's sacrifice. It's not about romance. It's not about being young and beautiful. It's not about power. But it is about being brave, and honest and true, and the best people we can make ourselves for each other.

'You were prepared to die for my child, and that's the reason why you might be worth a second chance. But I am never going to be deceived by you again.'

She can see a kind of struggle going on in him, and turns away so that he won't see the tears in her eyes.

Eventually he bursts out, pleading,

'But what if I can't help myself?'

'You can. If you want to enough.'

They sit there, in the shifting, flickering light, looking at the long green grasses that, growing up beneath the stiff dry hay, bend and sway.

What redemption can there be? Yet to believe that no change is possible is impossible too, for life is change; and change, life. They can only wait, not quite together and not quite apart, and hope.

Acknowledgements

The very first thing I should say is that my husband is not Quentin (any more than I am any other character in my novels). It should be otiose to say this, but women are too often believed by some to be incapable of imagination, or creation. Writing fiction is often a risk not only for authors but for their families, and neither my beloved Rob nor Leonora and William in any way resemble the Bredins. I would like to thank Rob and Leonora for being my first readers of a novel that took seven years to write; and to thank my excellent fellow authors Kate Saunders, Jane Thynne, Elizabeth Buchan, Danuta Kean and Alex Preston for generously offering their time and encouragement during its many revisions. I appreciate it all more than I can say.

I have too many friends of both sexes who have been, or are going through, the agonies of divorce. I would like to thank them for trusting me with their emotions, their stories and their dignity. Being lucky in love myself does not stop me from feeling anger and sadness at the hideous things people who once loved each other can do when it goes wrong. I remain profoundly grateful to my parents for not only remaining married all my life, but for showing me how disharmony is an essential part of the best music. My father died in my mother's arms, and this book is dedicated to my mother, whose wisdom, courage, love and sense of humour are qualities I appreciate more with every year.

This novel is set in Devon, a county and countryside I have loved ever since I first came to it as a child to stay with my godparents Euan and Su Bowater in their farmhouse near Dartmoor. I would particularly like to thank Dave and Lynne Hatwell (otherwise known as Bookhound and the Dovegreyreader) for much hospitality. In Cornwall, Charlotte Mitchell and Alice Boyd generously lent me their scholarship concerning local names and topography.

I have helped with lambing (though not dagging) in the past; it's something anyone interested in animals and husbandry can do if not squeamish. However, I'd like to thank Martin and Nicky Bridgeman and Dan Genders and Louise Canham-Rayner for telling me things about sheep that I wouldn't have known otherwise, and also I recommend James Rebanks's book, *A Shepherd's Life*, to anyone who hasn't read it.

My thanks go to my loyal, patient and tireless editor Richard Beswick, to Susan de Soissons and to the team at Little, Brown, to my eagle-eyed copy-editor Steve Cox and to Nithya Rae and Steve Gove.

Also to Ant Harwood, who has been all that I would wish for as an agent, and his assistant James MacDonald Lockhart.

What a reader knows about a character is only ever the tip of the iceberg. Many years ago, I asked the *Observer*'s architecture correspondent, Rowan Moore, about the psychology of architects. Chris Dyson, Emily Patrick, Isabel Perry, Barry Marmot and Tatiana von Preussen all added their insights into this fascinating and often maligned profession.

I would also like to thank all the health visitors, including Lynne Hatwell, who have talked to me about their job over the years, and remain relieved that the very first one did not take my infant daughter's demands for whisky seriously. All mistakes are my own.

The Humble Pie factory in Devon is of course imaginary, as is the town of Trelorn, and Shipcott village, even though the Tamar River and the beautiful West Devon landscape are both real.

Last but not least, I would like to thank the cancer charity Marie Curie, and the nurse Meg Scobie, for telling me about the charity's extraordinary work with the dying. They are in truth a light in the darkness.

Readers of previous novels may recognise characters here who have grown up or aged. The Harts and their daughter Lily first appeared in *A Private Place*, when Lily is a baby, as does Gore Tore. Josh Viner comes from *A Vicious Circle*, as do Ivo Sponge, the Slouch Club and the *Chronicle*. Polly Noble and Hemani are principal characters in *Love in Idleness*, Quentin and Lottie come from *Hearts and Minds*, and Marta will reappear in a future novel. Some novelists, from Balzac to Alison Lurie, can't bear to let go of their invented world, and I am unabashed to be one of them; those who want to hunt down what happened to Grace's little son Billy from *A Vicious Circle* (and to Ian and Katie, also from *Hearts and Minds*) might like a Quick Reads novella also published this year, *The Other Side of You*.

Only one detail is true: we really did sit next to a farmer's wife in the cinema at Okehampton and she really was more concerned about Gabriel Oak's horse than the lovers in the recent film of *Far from the Madding Crowd*.

About the Author

Amanda Craig is a well-known journalist and broad-caster. She is the author of *A Vicious Circle*, *In a Dark Wood* and *Hearts and Minds*. You can visit her website at www.amandacraig.com.